BARLOW'S ORACLE

BY

MAC CUSITER

BARLOW'S ORACLE

Cover Design: Mac Cusiter
Model © Dolgachov | Depositphotos 23773900
Background Haywiremedia | Depositphotos
Back Cover Design: Mac Cusiter
Computer Images © Vladimircaribb | Depositphotos

Gurumbi Publishing
ISBN: 978-0-9941582-6-0

Printed in the United States of America

*To Jane, who has suffered
the horrors of
child abuse*

*The author would also like to thank his beloved wife Val
for all her help and encouragement*

BARLOW'S ORACLE

To knock over an idol
You have to get off your knees

CHAPTER 1

The camera rose slowly towards the small lighted window on the second floor of the mansion, probably a bathroom. James stared mournfully at the monitor screen, almost without hope. He had made another stupid mistake. The woman was probably stretching out on some luxurious bed in her rented Gold Coast apartment, writing new code on her laptop after spending the day sunning herself on the beach. After all, that's what she had been doing in the video she had sent him only a few hours ago. Sunbaking, laughing, without a care in the world, so different from their last encounter. How he wished he could unsay those words. Why would she send him anything? An insane suspicion that was all, soon dismissed were it not for the absence of a tiny detail, a relic from their childhood, the memory still fresh and vivid. How could he forget? He had got into so much trouble. But they had been friends then.

He began to doubt his sanity. They were wasting their time.

The camera was creeping slowly above the windowsill. The top of a shower screen came into view. Now he could see the taps, the towel rail, the top of the bath. His breath caught in a horrified gasp. The bath was occupied, not by some naked figure bathing but with Cherry's body, her face deathly white, her eyes closed, her skirt, and the entire bottom of the bath awash with blood. One arm was draped over the edge as if she had been carelessly thrown there, the other, covered in blood, was lying by her side. Her body was utterly still, no flicker in the eyelids, no movement of her limbs. Dead.

The woman he loved was dead.

James suddenly felt paralysed, his mind numb, unable to speak, his whole life imploding before his eyes. He had been right, and bitter irony, he was just too damn late.

CHAPTER 2

Arthur Barlow lifted his eyes from the image of the naked girl erotically displaying her wares all over the monitor screen. The rest of the youth group were gathered in a holy huddle around Paul Denton, the new Youth Minister at St. Stephens Anglican church Terrigal, their expressions ranging from interest to terminal boredom. The laminated sign above the door said "WOG Kids" which he had learned stood for "Word of God Kids", and not, like anyone else would have thought, a derogatory description of the children of Italian immigrants. At the back of the assembly, Sally O'Brien and her boyfriend were holding a Bible in one hand and softly stroking each other's legs with the other, foreplay to the main event on the moonlit beach later on that evening. The leader smiled at their apparent rapt attentiveness.

They smiled back for a completely different reason.

Young Arthur was all of sixteen years old, but the naivety usually associated with the age had long ago evaporated into full if cynical knowledge in which the beach, the internet and his own home had been impersonal but effective teachers.

He had been coming to this Friday night group without fail for a full twelve months now, never missing a single evening. Not that he entertained any interest whatsoever in Christianity. On the contrary, his experience had served only to deepen his private cynicism.
It was partly the food.

Paul always handed out a generous supply of pizza at the beginning before the childish games began. It was the best meal Arthur enjoyed all week.

The main attraction was the computer.

It was a really good one, bequeathed by the wife of a parishioner who had died suddenly, in the hope it would shorten his time in purgatory, somewhat confusing reformed with catholic belief. Nobody had been able to get it working except Arthur, who formed the opinion, whilst deleting a great many files, that the deceased would be in purgatory for a very long time. In the short space of a month he had made himself indispensable to the Church Office, updating the church website, podcasting the Rector's long weekly monologues, backing up files, and generally keeping the machine in perfect working order.

Little did they know that pressing 'Control' plus 'F7' and 'Shift' keys at the same time now booted the machine into a totally different operating system where Arthur ruled supreme and alone every Friday night. He occasionally joined in the games, but never the talk, telling Paul he would listen carefully as he did his weekly computer maintenance. Indeed, the first few minutes were dedicated to this very task. Then he would press 'Control', 'F7' and 'Shift' together and trundle off into more pleasurable pursuits.

Now Paul was winding up with the usual impassioned plea for converts. Sally O'Brien was heading into ecstasy as her boyfriend stroked under her toes with a feather he had found on the floor. The rest of the group were preparing to exit the hall and be picked up by family or friends. It was church policy no one walked home by themselves.

Arthur closed the website with some reluctance, making a note of where to visit next week, rebooted the machine into Windows and shut down. Damn, he had to go to the toilet. The pizza hadn't agreed with his stomach, either that or he had eaten far too much of it. He returned to find the hall completely empty, save for Angela, Paul's attractive young wife. She was picking up the food scraps and other rubbish the thoughtful Christian kids had left all over the floor. She smiled at him.

"Hi Arthur. Paul's out the front supervising the transport. See you next week."

"Sure, I'll be there." He smiled back and headed for the door. He liked Ange, she was pretty. He had often fantasised how she would look lying naked on a beach towel in the moonlight.

Paul stood alone on the street, watching the last of the WOG Kids being bundled into cars. The last car left. Arthur made an unsuccessful attempt to meld into the shadows.

"Where's your ride, Arthur?" Paul turned towards him. "Want me to make a phone call?"

"No, we don't have a phone at home. It's okay. I'll just walk. It's not far," Arthur said, silently cursing his bowels which had precipitated the situation he had so far managed to avoid.

Paul frowned. "I can't let you do that, Arthur."

"It's okay, I tell you. I'll be all right," Arthur assured him. "I walk around at night all the time. Nothing happens up here. It's Terrigal, Central Coast, a nice, friendly neighbourhood."

"It's still church policy," Paul said very seriously. "I'll drive you home. Where do you live?"

"Around. Listen, Paul. Ange looks really tired tonight. I think she needs some help with the chairs. You should take her home and put her to bed. I'll wait here while you check."

Arthur arranged his face into an expression of wide-eyed concern. The Reverend Paul mulled over the possibilities.

"All right, I'll go and see if she needs help. Stay here while I do, will you?"

Paul disappeared back into the building and Arthur disappeared into the night. He flipped himself over the low hedge which ran in front of the homes bordering the church, dived down the owner's driveway, and emerged over their back fence on the street behind. Now to take a leisurely stroll across to the beach to see if there was anything worth watching on the sand.

CHAPTER 3

The beach had been disappointingly empty, and Arthur had eventually returned to number twelve Beach Boulevard where he was currently domiciled. He tried the front door – locked – then walked round the side of the house and scrambled in a window. Jeanette, onto whose bed he fell, woke up with a shriek and a string of foul four letter words.

"Sorry, just trying to get in. Front door's locked." Arthur slid off the bed without a single glance at the naked woman sitting bolt upright in it, her doona around her waist and her dignity a long way below that.

"Get out of my bedroom you pathetic little ... or I'll ..." With another tirade of foul expletives the girl threw herself back onto the pillow, and drew the doona up around her ears.

Arthur headed out the door, shutting it quietly behind him. So Jeanette must have failed to score and come back early, much the pity. Still, anything was better than sleeping in some garage or other when you had your own bed to lie on. He half entertained the idea of going out the back door and repeating his entrance after she had gone back to sleep, just to see if she could improve on the language. *Better not*, he thought. Jeanette could be viciously creative in revenge as several of his older friends could testify.

He awoke early the next morning, threw on a pair of shorts and headed for the kitchen to see if someone had left any food hanging around. A quick inspection yielded a glass of milk, a piece of tasty cheese and a half filled jar of peanuts. Not bad, his reward for getting there first. None of the other occupants of number twelve had emerged from their bedrooms, either because they were lazy, hung over, or because they had found something better to do in bed, certainly not because it was Saturday. The weekend was no different from any other day when you belonged to the privileged class who had elected never to work and allow every other Australian to feed them. The only important day was every second Thursday when they went down to Gosford to collect their dole money, something you had to do in person these days. George and Henry would make sure everyone coughed up their share of the communal rent, and extracted the usual fifty percent of what remained for the common purse. Such were the rules, and there weren't many of them. Most people agreed, but occasionally some of the newer members objected. They only objected once. After that they were as docile as lambs or on a train back to Sydney, sometimes feeling very sore and sorry for themselves. George and Henry, who had been bouncers at several Sydney clubs before they became enlightened with this new and glorious lifestyle, were very adept at reminding the commune members of their fiscal responsibility.

Arthur stuffed another handful of peanuts into his mouth and headed back to his room. On the floor he found a T-shirt which was more or less presentable and put it on. He slipped his feet into a pair of thongs which had seen better days, and donned a pair of expensive sunglasses he had relieved from their owner on the beach. He ran a comb through his hair, threw a swimming costume in his sports bag together with his wallet which contained all of six dollars fifty, and climbed out the window.

Leaving his sports bag on the path, he detached the nozzle from the garden hose and turned it on ever so slightly. Creeping round the house a short distance, he gently fed the dribbling hose through Jeanette's bedroom window until he felt sure it was resting on her bed. Listening carefully for any sounds that would indicate that the girl was waking up, he kept the hose in place until he was satisfied that the bed would be suitably soaked. Carefully withdrawing the hose, he crept back towards the tap, turned it off, and replaced the nozzle.

Bedwetting at eighteen, how deplorable. He would ring Suzie when he got to the public phone down the street and ask her to check if Jeanette had come home, because he was worried someone had bashed her. No way to hide the soaking bedclothes after that. Then he would concoct a press release which said scientists had discovered a new strain of HIV whose early symptoms were loss of bladder control at night, and shove it on Henry's Facebook page. That should ensure Jeanette, who slept around for fun and profit more than any other girl he knew, would remain properly corked until she got herself tested at the HIV clinic in Gosford.

You had to swallow quite a lot of dignity to go to the HIV clinic in Gosford. Do her good. Don't mess with Arthur Barlow.

Arthur made the phone call and caught the bus to his place of weekend employment, 'Martin's Custom Computers' in Gosford's main street. He came in to find the owner, Martin McFarlane, at the back of the store staring gloomily at a monitor screen full of error messages.

Arthur cast his careful eyes over the monitor and the machine attached to it. "Good morning Mr. McFarlane," he said in a cheery voice.

"What's good about it?" McFarlane ran his hands over his face. "I've had this flamin' machine on the bench for two solid days. Can't work out what the blazes is wrong with it. Supposed to be lightning fast, latest everything, but it doesn't work. Or it works sometimes. Then we get all this load of rubbish." He waved his hand towards the screen. "The bloke who bought the system is coming in this morning to pick it up. He's going to hit the roof."

Arthur stuck his head in the side of the high power gaming case containing the machine's entrails, checked the screen again and smiled. "Want me to fix it?"

"If you can fix it before he comes into the store there's twenty dollars extra in your pay."

"Only twenty? How about forty?" Arthur smiled innocently.

"Forty then. You better not be bullshitting me."

Arthur pressed his finger on the power button long enough to shut the machine down, went over to the shelves and retrieved a new solid state drive. McFarlane snorted at him. "The thing's already got an SSD. Can't you use your eyes?"

Arthur, undeterred, began to remove the solid state drive he was accused of not seeing and replacing it with the one he had brought from the store. When all was done he powered up the machine and watched with some satisfaction as it booted perfectly. McFarlane stared at the monitor in disbelief for a while, dug into his pocket and handed Arthur two twenty dollar notes.

"So tell me," he grumbled, "how is it a kid like you can fix the flaming machine in minutes when an old computer engineer like me can't fix it in two days?"

"It's the disk controller built into the solid state drive," Arthur explained, pocketing the money. "You're using the Z68 on-board chipset and running the solid state drive as a cache, aren't you? Well, that chipset won't work with that model of drive controller. I simply changed the make of solid state drive. Thanks for the dough. Any other stuff you want me to build this morning?"

"How come you're so damn smart?" Why didn't I know that?"

"I read a lot," Arthur said, rebooting the machine and bringing the bios setup on screen. "There was a note about it somewhere. We can overclock the processor now, make it really sing. Like me to have a go?"

"Sure, go ahead," McFarlane sighed, throwing the unwanted packaging material into the rubbish bin. "I'll go back to the counter. See if I can sell some Ethernet cable or a pair of Bluetooth headphones. Should be able to manage that." He pointed to the back of the storeroom. "There's a couple of builds I was going to start but never got round to it because of that machine. You can do them if you want to. Shouldn't take you more than fifteen minutes."

He ambled back into the shop. *The kid's a genius*, he thought to himself. *He already knows more about computers than I do, and he's only sixteen. What will he be like when he's got through university?*

Had he known Arthur's mind he would have realised the thought of his going to university was just as abhorrent as the thought of him finishing school, and he was carefully planning to avoid both. On the other hand, he wasn't going to go on the dole like the other commune kids. No, he had other plans, and McFarlane was going to help him achieve them, whether he wanted to or not.

The weekend passed incredibly fast. A total of six high power computer builds were handed over to very satisfied customers. The news item about HIV was delivered to Henry's Facebook page and thence to the whole community. Jeanette was walking around with a worried expression, and the guys were avoiding her like the plague. Some of them seemed worried too. Mission accomplished. Martin had given him a fifty dollar bonus, and all in all he felt pretty pleased with himself. Monday would be school again, but that was finishing for good at the end of the year.

✻ ✻ ✻

Period one at Terrigal High was English, and ten minutes into it the headmaster's secretary came to the door and said the school Counsellor wanted to see Arthur Barlow immediately. Arthur stood up, incredibly relieved to be spared from any more terminally boring English. He shuffled subserviently behind her until he came to the Counsellor's office, and knocked politely. A voice from the other side bade him enter. Waiting for him behind a modest desk was the rather pretty young woman who had recently replaced Gabrielle "Motor Mouth" Hastings after she had suffered a nervous breakdown.

Arthur saw it as his solemn responsibility to initiate the same process in the latest incumbent. "You wanted to see me, Miss?" he asked politely.

Roslyn Tanner cast her young eyes over the child in front of her. A handsome lad, yet there was something defiant about the set of his chin, the stance of his legs, his hands in his pockets. He was looking at her the same way a pet shop owner would stare at a kitten who had just peed on their favourite jumper. She had been in this job for a whole six months and had so far enjoyed it, yet suddenly an irrational foreboding seemed to stir the tranquil waters of her soul. "Yes. Arthur Barlow, isn't it?" she said pleasantly. "Please sit down."

Arthur sat down, his expression unchanged. Ms. Tanner shuffled some papers on her desk, pulled out a folder and extracted two sheets. "Arthur, this is a copy of your school report. You topped your year in mathematics with a perfect score and failed everything else."

"Yes, Miss. I intended to." Arthur's eyes sized up his prey.

"We sent this home to your parents by confidential post. We offered them a counselling session so we could improve your attitude to study. Apparently this is their reply." She pushed the other sheet towards Arthur. On it was written, in large black letters:

> 'Our son is a complete pain in the arse. Boot him out or flog him until he does as he's told. Don't come bellyaching to us'.

Ms. Tanner waited until Arthur had read the missive, then replaced the paper in the folder. "Did this note really come from your parents, Arthur?"

"No Miss. I wrote it. Just trying to imagine what they'd want to say." Same defiance in the eyes.

A slight frown furrowed Ms. Tanner's smooth brow. "Did your parents ever see your school report?"

"Not unless they have extra-terrestrial powers."

"What on earth do you mean?" Ms. Tanner enquired, oblivious to the pun.

"Because I haven't the faintest idea who or where they are."

Ms. Tanner stared at Arthur as though she hadn't heard properly.

"Pardon? You're adopted? But you must have parents, foster parents?"

"Nah," Arthur laughed. "I'm a Commune kid. Some chick got nailed, had me, gave me to one of the cows, disappeared. Sometimes they go, sometimes they stay. We like them to stay, brings in single mother benefits. More dough all round."

Ms. Tanner' face wrinkled into a deeper frown, for in truth Arthur's answer had left her feeling somewhat discombobulated. She tried to form a mental picture of Arthur's family, failed, and sought further clarification. "Cows?"

"Girls with full jugs. Some girls just love feeding and taking care of babies, so they get a lot to look after. Breeders and feeders. Place wouldn't work without them."

There was another long pause. Ms. Tanner was wishing very much she had handed Arthur Barlow's case over to her fellow counsellor, George Campbell. "What... what happens to the babies after they've been... weaned?"

"The Commune takes care of them," Arthur replied casually. "Passes them around, that sort of thing. Most get used to it. Some of them go funny, but that's where people like you come in. There's a lot of Commune kids in the school."

"You mean – here? Why don't I know about this?" Ms. Tanner's eyebrows followed her frown up her forehead.

"Because you're new, naïve or stupid, take your pick," Arthur answered evenly.

Ms. Tanner's eyes blazed for a second, then they glazed over. She drew a long breath, pursed her lips tight and said nothing.

Arthur decided a good dose of reality would facilitate his goal no end. "It works like this," he said. "There's a lot of people up here who've decided they'd rather sit around and let other people like you feed them. They get the dole. It's not a fortune, but when you get two hundred or so people collecting and pooling their money it adds up to a lot, especially with all the kids attracting single mother benefits."

He pointed to the map on the wall behind Ms. Tanner.

"Most of the houses down Beach Boulevard and Campion Way are rented by the Commune. Great lifestyle if you like that sort of thing. Lie on the beach all day, smoke dope and have sex all night, do bloody nothing. Local shopkeepers don't mind, they get most of their business from the Commune. Cannabis sales bring money into the district, and the Commune girls are easy. Everybody benefits – except people like you, I guess, shelling out your tax money and counselling the kids who go funny."

Ms. Tanner sat back in her chair and briefly shut her eyes. Instead of a sunny, sleepy beachside town she'd landed in the middle of Hippie-Ville. She gave a soft groan. "Kids who go funny?"

"Well Benny Murchison, for example," Arthur replied. "Comes to see you, doesn't he? He's the one who goes round strangling cats because they wake him up at night and he can't get back to sleep, but his real problem is his sister. She wants him dead. Surprised you haven't worked that out with your professional expertise."

Ms. Tanner began to play with a pencil on her desk.

Arthur smiled encouragingly. "It was at the Commune Christmas party last year. A lot of dope and grog went down, you know how it is. He knocked up his own sister, easy mistake to make when you're stoned, and she had a girl. Now he's got some sort of paranoia because Anne says she's going to have him whacked when she's saved enough dough. The cows are taking care of the girl anyway, 'cause Anne's still in year twelve and doesn't want to walk round the school with big, leaky jugs. Stuff like that. I'm sure you can sort out his screwed up little psyche. Have a go at Anne while you're at it. She's about as sane as an emu on acid."

The pencil snapped in Ms. Tanner's hand.
"The authorities... the Department of Social Services, they must be appalled. Surely..." Her voice trailed off unsteadily.

"I'm sure they don't know," Arthur smiled, "and before you think about telling them, remember the Commune is big business on every front up here. Everybody's happy. The last social reformer was found in a lobster pot after a month or so. Fish ate most of her face off."

"Mercy!" Ms. Tanner's horrified face turned a shade of pale. This was a combination of Hippie-Ville and hell. Before lunch she would be filling in an application for transfer.

Arthur grinned at her in a friendly sort of way. "Don't worry Miss, I'm not like them. I want to work for my money, so I'm leaving the Commune at the end of the year, and I won't be coming back to school either. Waste of time."

"You haven't finished your HSC. You're only in year eleven … "

"Sarah Miles was a Commune kid, left school when she was fourteen. Nobody minded in the least."

"W… Why?" Ms. Tanner knew she was going to regret asking.

"She got nailed by one of your fellow counsellors," Arthur explained patiently. "You haven't taken up with George Campbell, have you? Now Miss, is there anything else I can help you with?"

Ms. Tanner felt her forehead with one hand and waved the other in Arthur's direction. George had offered to take her out to dinner that night and she had accepted.

"No," she said, "I think that about covers it," and put her head down on the desk.

Arthur took this as his cue to leave. On the whole he felt the interview had gone very well. The fate of the social worker was purely an invention of his own, but it had produced the desired effect. He mightn't know much about English, but he had a pretty good understanding of human nature.

✼ ✼ ✼

True to his promise, Arthur left school and the Commune a week before the Christmas holidays had started and went to work – and live - at Martin's Computer store. McFarlane had been rather surprised that a young lad would endure the hardship of sleeping on a blow-up mattress and going to the community centre every time he wanted to take a shower, but then he had no comprehension of the burning desire which lay behind everything Arthur did. Computer hardware and programming languages attracted him with a passion which overwhelmed all else. They offered him total control, in contrast to many things in his childhood years that had rendered him powerless and afraid. Perhaps it was this that made him so different from other young men of his age, especially those from the Commune. They were already heavily into sex and certain chemical substances, but neither of these had any attraction for Arthur at all. His unwelcome education had taught him that weed slowly sent you insane and sex was a tool of exploitation and abuse. On the other hand, his passion for computer programming led only and always to intense satisfaction.

Over the next four years his initial knowledge and ability, which were far from insignificant, grew to quite extraordinary proportions, something McFarlane was quick to appreciate. Indeed, the kid was a genius the like of whom he had never seen before. Builds of astonishing speed and complexity were beginning to attract high-end customers with very specific needs. The latest machine consisted of no less than eight Xenon processors on four cluster connected motherboards, running Arthur's own multitasking optimisation kernel. It had been bought by New Wave Reality, a Sydney company specialising in high end animation for the film industry. They were happy to pay one hundred and twenty thousand dollars to own it. Money was rolling in. The only problem was McFarlane himself, who realised he was impossibly far out of his depth. If young Barlow ever decided to leave he would be finished in a week.

The time had come to retire.

"I'm out of here in a month or so," he announced at their morning tea break. "I'm going to sell the business. You needn't worry, the next owner is sure to employ you. He'd be insane if he didn't."

"I'm not worried at all." Arthur stuffed the remains of a large blueberry muffin into his face. "Because the next owner is going to be me."

"What?" McFarlane put down his mug of tea suddenly. "How can a kid like you afford a hundred grand? I won't sell for a cent less."

"Not your worry," Arthur said through a mouthful of muffin. "Besides you're probably going to take a lot more than a cent less. In fact, I think you'd take fifty grand, because all I have to do is pull out and you're stuffed."

McFarlane grimaced. The kid was too damn smart. "You must have some well-healed friends," he muttered under his breath.

Arthur swallowed the muffin before speaking. "I do," he grinned, "and after I've had a chat with them they won't be able to lay their money down fast enough."

CHAPTER 4

C herry Graham sat in the darkened room, slowly shredding the page she had torn out of the Bible her mother had given her. Pieces of paper lay scattered about her feet along with the occasional crumb left over from some plate as it had been passed around amongst the guests. For the last four hours she had been hugged, cried over, and offered enough food to make her sick. Her ears had rung with thousands of words assuring her of God's ever present help, the certain hope of the resurrection, the joy which came through life's hard trials, the comfort of His loving presence when she felt alone.

Then they had left, all of them, happy in the knowledge that this broken hearted little girl would be cared for with all the love and warmth their words had promised.

Only Mrs. Benson, the church secretary who had organised the food for the wake, was a little troubled as she walked out of the room, empty save for its ten year old occupant sitting silent on the lounge, a Bible in her hand. *Her faith must be so strong,* she thought to herself. No doubt those who were to care for the girl would be back soon.

The twilight of evening had deepened into night. The light of the streetlamp shining through the window into the unlit lounge room cast bizarre shadows on the silent child, her dark tearless eyes, her busy little fingers, the circle of shredded paper around her feet growing larger.

MAC CUSITER

✳ ✳ ✳

"I don't want you to go away," she had pleaded with her mother just five days ago. "Something might happen to you and Daddy. Please let me come with you."

"It's only for three days, my darling," her mother had assured her, stroking her daughter's soft hair on the pillow. "You know you love being at Amanda's house. God will take good care of us. We have this wonderful Psalm – one hundred and twenty one. Shall I read some of it to you?"

"Please Mummy." The child turned round, filling her eyes with her mother's lovely face.

Her mother took the Bible from its usual place on the bedside table and read. "The Lord watches over you— the Lord is your shade at your right hand; the sun will not harm you by day, nor the moon by night. The Lord will keep you from all harm - He will watch over your life; the Lord will watch over your coming and going both now and forevermore."

Caroline closed the Bible, bent down and kissed her beloved little girl on the cheek. "Father in Heaven," she prayed softly, "take care of this little one we love. Help her to trust you, help her to know you love her. Take the fear out of her heart and give her a good night's sleep."

✳ ✳ ✳

Cherry had searched for that Psalm, number one hundred and twenty one. It was the first page she had torn out. Her mother's words had echoed so clearly in her mind as she began, yet with each shredding they started to fragment and blur as if she was tearing them apart as well as the paper. By the time the cover of the Bible lay empty on the floor, they had vanished completely. Every lovely memory of her parents, each so exquisitely precious and unbearably painful, had begun to blur as well. The pain which threatened to paralyse and leave her screaming in terrified anguish, blurred and softened along with them. Perhaps her mind had entered survival mode, and begun to seal off the memories which threatened its continuing existence. By now her hands were red and sore, but she didn't feel it, only a nameless burning in her heart, a numbness which prevented her from remembering.

She was tired, so tired.

The shards of the world she once knew lay scattered at her feet, a world of happiness, love, hope and God. None of these remained, only the nightmare, not yet completely transformed into reality.

The police had come to her school, taken her out of class, told her of the terrible accident. Just a short joy flight over the Gold Coast, only thirty minutes long, but the plane had plummeted into the earth after ten of them. Amanda's parents had taken her home and cried all over her. She hadn't shed a tear. All the rest was a blur, the funeral people, the lawyer, the endless phone calls, until she had sounded like a recording.

"Yes Mum and Dad are dead..."

The funeral, the wake, and now the blessed silence of solitude. Her aunt and uncle, her only surviving relatives, had not even bothered to show their ugly faces, no doubt because they couldn't have cared less, the one small mercy in a merciless world.

At least she was at home, surrounded by familiar things, and little by little she would organise herself into her new life. She still had her computer, her laptop, her books to comfort her. She often lost herself in them for hours until someone called her to do chores or to dinner. Well, now she would decide when to eat, when to stop learning. She gave a small shudder.

She was tired, so tired.

Would she go to bed? No, the thought of passing her parent's bedroom was not to be entertained tonight. She drew a rug from the linen cupboard, lay down on the lounge and threw it over herself. In the early hours of the morning she fell asleep.

The morning light shining through the uncurtained window woke her up. Slowly, uncomfortably, she stretched out, threw off the rug and went to the toilet in the laundry, still not willing to go down the hall past her parent's room. In the back of her mind she could pretend they were still asleep, but she knew if she passed that doorway she could not prevent herself from opening it and rediscovering the truth she already knew. It was Friday, time to go to school. Would she go to school? Now she was the one to decide. Yes she would, not because she loved school so much, but because she was afraid to remain at home. A short rummage in the laundry basket produced a slightly crumpled school uniform which she put on without her usual morning shower.

A plateful of cereal and some milk sufficed for breakfast. She quickly buttered two slices of bread, spread them with honey, and placed them in her lunchbox. Now she was off to catch the bus which would take her to Miranda Primary School on the other side of town.

The bus came and she got on, moving down the aisle past sixty pairs of eyes who stared at her, and sixty mouths suddenly struck dumb. Indeed the whole bus had grown quieter as she had sat down. Occasionally she would see one or two of her classmates turn round and stare silently at her. The only spare seat was next to a boy in year six, who never took his eyes off the magazine he was reading upside down. Apparently losing your parents in a plane crash was equivalent to losing them from some fatal contagious disease, now carried by their offspring, because that's the way everyone was reacting. Cherry pulled a book entitled 'Unix for Beginners' out of her bag and disappeared into it.

The same reaction persisted all through the day, the furtive, guilty stares as if even looking at the victim risked catching the disease. Her classroom teacher took a few minutes to tell her how sorry she was – again – and the school counsellor called her out of class in period three to ask if she was all right. Would she be staying at the school or moving, and what were the names of her guardians? Cherry had said she had no idea right now, and the counsellor said that was okay, she could understand.

Understand? Nobody can understand, Cherry thought to herself.

She decided to walk home instead of catching a bus full of staring eyes, and besides, she needed to get some cash out to buy food for dinner. Arriving at the shopping mall she inserted her mother's key card into the terminal, typed in her pin number and withdrew one hundred dollars, asking for an account balance at the same time. Eight thousand two hundred and fifty dollars thirty five cents, sufficient for the time being unless her computer broke down and needed costly repairs.

Cherry Graham was a ten year old orphan with a difference. Where most other children of her age would be saving money to buy new clothes and shoes, Cherry thought only of computers. Perhaps she had inherited her talent from her parents, both brilliant programmers, if there is a gene which encodes such ability. Perhaps they had unwittingly passed on their own passion for the subject.

Her father had given her a desktop PC on her eighth birthday, and she had been using her own laptop since she was three. At first she had just played games, but at a very early age she had begun to astonish her parents with some of the things she could do. The PC upgrade had come as her ninth birthday present. The processor had been replaced with the latest Intel quad core, the floppy disk drive with a DVD writer, the hard drives with faster ones of ten times the capacity. Cherry had assembled them all herself, and it had worked first time. So had the Linux operating system she had opted for instead of the usual Windows.

Now those skills were her lifeline. If push came to shove she could always get a job in a local computer store – if she lied about her age, that is. For the present there was enough money to buy food and the occasional item of clothing. No doubt there would be other expenses, but she would deal with these when they came.

For the next six months Cherry Graham lived alone. Amanda's parents were among the very few adults who knew of this appalling state of affairs.

At first they had tried gentle persuasion.

"Amanda would love it so much if you came to live here, darling."

This was followed by expressions of adult concern with just a hint of legal repercussions.

"We are very worried. Cherry, and if the Department of Social Services ever learn what is happening, they may have to act."

Nothing made any difference. Cherry refused to live anywhere else. What more could they do?

"We have to report it," Shirley argued as she sat on the lounge with her husband Alan one evening after Amanda had gone to bed.

"What good would it do?" Alan gave a long sigh, and turned off the television which was murmuring in the background. "If we do they'll pull the child out of there, and I'm not sure if she would survive. She acts pretty brave, and she is in one way, but I think there's more to it than that. She's in familiar surroundings. I think she needs them more than we might like to give her credit for."

"All the same," his wife returned, a worried note in her voice, "if anything were to happen to her, you know, she opens the door to a stranger and he rapes the girl, we wouldn't forgive ourselves. Neither would the Department of Social Services when they found out we had known and said nothing."

"I think Cherry is very fragile as it is," Alan shook his head. "She's not the average girl, Shirley. She has an incredibly analytical mind, but it comes at a cost. I think if she was ripped out of her world and placed in foster care it would destroy her." He reached for the beer on the low table in front of the television. "I don't want that on my conscience either. Besides, if she disappeared, our Amanda would go berserk, especially if she found out we had anything to do with it."

"I'm not happy doing nothing, Alan. I think we should contact DSS. At least I insist we write a note to the school. They have to know. Perhaps they can get one of their counsellors to talk to Cherry, tell her about the dangers of living alone. I'm sure they'll contact DSS themselves if needs be. I wish the girl would agree to stay here. Amanda would be so happy. I thought they were really close friends."

"They are." Alan finished his beer, put the glass back slowly on the table. "That's just the point. They are really good friends. Why doesn't she want to come here when she's fond of our daughter? Because she can't bear leaving her home. Somehow I think her parents are still alive while she lives there. I guess she'll come back to reality one day, but if we were to rush the process... I'm not sure we wouldn't have a breakdown on our hands – or someone would."

The discussion continued for some time, but in the end they agreed to write a note to the principal and have Amanda deliver it the very next day. They hadn't reckoned with their daughter, however.

The next morning Shirley handed Amanda the letter, and asked her to take it straight to the principal before school. Amanda agreed with large honest eyes and a nod of her head. She had overheard her parents talking about Cherry the previous evening, and wondered if the note had anything to do with her best friend. Ducking back into her room, the girl snatched a fresh envelope from her desk and headed out the door. The bus came, Amanda checked Cherry wasn't on it, took a seat near the back, extracted the letter from her bag and ripped it open. If she liked the contents she would replace the envelope with the new one. After spending most of the journey reading the letter, Amanda decided she didn't like the contents at all, and delivered the letter to a rubbish bin inside the school grounds after she had shredded it into little pieces. No one was taking Cherry away, and that was that.

If Cherry had been able to read the thoughts of Amanda's father she would have agreed with every word. While she remained in her home her parents could be both dead and alive. Formally dead, imaginatively on a long holiday, formally buried, imaginatively sleeping late every morning. She knew her imagination would eventually bow to her reason, but not yet, not while she could escape into her machine, writing routines in C++ which ran under her Linux operating system, learning, learning, learning. Each new program represented a new challenge which filled her mind so totally the rest of the world retreated to a safe distance. Some days she didn't go to school at all. Her meals became somewhat erratic. Spider webs all but covered every window, and the grass in the back lawn had turned into a jungle.

At first there had been lots of phone calls from the church her parents had attended. They hadn't seen her around for a while. Did she want any help? No she didn't. Did she have enough food? Yes, she did, thank you. When was she coming back to church? Never, she had told them. God had allowed her parents to be killed and she hated Him, or words to that effect. This comment had almost always been met with silence. Certainly nobody repeated their previous assurances about the comfort of the resurrection and the warmth of God's love. Thank goodness. She answered the more serious questions with lies. Was she living by herself? Oh, no, her grandma was there taking care of her. Was her grandma a Christian? Heavens no. Slowly the phone calls became less and less, and eventually they petered out altogether.

One Friday morning there was a knock at the door. Cherry was practically ready for school and feeling very tired, because she had spent most of the previous night writing a little routine in C++. It stripped the headers out of email packets and shoved them in a database. Now she knew a lot more about who was sending her mail, which was very useful. The knock came again. Cherry went down the hall and half opened the door. There was a man in a grey uniform outside with the name of some electricity company emblazoned across it in yellow.

"Yes?" Cherry held onto the door tightly, ready to slam it shut. "I'm late for school. What do you want?"

"I need to talk to your Mum." The man explained politely but firmly.

"She's not in. Gone to work, so has Dad."

"Where can I get in contact with them? They apparently don't read letters."

"They're very busy," Cherry said, fighting to keep her voice level. "What do you want to talk to them about? I can pass on a message."

"I'm here to disconnect the electricity," the man continued with some reluctance. "Your Mum and Dad haven't paid their account for six months. We've sent them warnings but we get no reply." He stared at the young girl's face. Something was wrong. Her eyes were fearful, suspicious. What was going on? "Don't you worry," he continued, forcing his face into a smile, "it's not your problem. I'm sure there's been some mistake. Your parents will sort it out when they come home."

Cherry shut the door in his face, collected her schoolbag and went out the back, down the path and over the back fence into the lane behind, not wanting to meet the man again.

She returned home from school that afternoon tired and thirsty. A cup of hot chocolate would be nice, then back to her favourite pastime. Throwing her schoolbag down in the hall she went into the kitchen and switched on the jug.

Nothing.

The lights wouldn't come on either. She tore down the hall into her bedroom and pressed the power on button on her computer. Dead. Cherry gave a howl of rage, balled her little fists and thumped them again and again on her desk in anger until they hurt. No light, no shower, and worst of all no computer. How was a girl to live? Cherry trotted out into the garage, shouldered the long power lead her father used with the electric edger, and headed off to the neighbours.

Fiona and Max Trevallen were the sort of neighbours who kept to themselves and expected others to do the same. Not a speck of dust lingered anywhere in their house, nor a stray leaf on the lawn. They were so totally private nobody in the street would have known they existed, were it not for Fiona's unfortunate habit of bellowing raucously out the back door to summon their cat Sheena from her latest escapade to have her evening meal. Sheena would arrive to find her food heated to just the right temperature and served on an imported porcelain bowl. Their two daughters, Georgia and Tamsin had left this sterile, obsessive environment long ago for freedom in some distant land.

The Trevallens knew the parents of the little girl next door had died, and to their shame had never so much as sent her a sympathy card. As far as they were concerned she must have gone to live somewhere else, because the place was becoming a shambles. One day soon they would write a letter of complaint to the local council.

Fiona answered the doorbell that afternoon understandably surprised to find the child herself standing there with a long power lead slung over her shoulder. "I thought you'd gone to live somewhere else," she snapped with a grimace. "What do you want, Charlie?"

"It's Cherry, not Charlie." Cherry concentrated to maintain the lost-little-angel expression on her face. "The power in my house has gone off. I wonder if I could plug this cable into the power point in your shed so I can see my way around at night?"

The thought of an ugly power cable extending from their tidy shed through the jungle next door sent a shiver of revulsion into Fiona's immaculate soul. Besides, children should not be playing with power cables. There might be an accident, and horror of horrors, someone might sue them. The feelings in her soul found expression on her face.

"You can't be serious," she objected. "Wait until your carers come home and get them to check the power box on the side of your own house – that's if you can find it amongst all the rubbish."

"The power box isn't the problem," Cherry said, concentrating even harder.

"Of course it's the problem," Fiona snorted. "Haven't you been taught not to contradict an adult? Where's your manners? Pity your parents didn't teach you some before they died."

The lost angel expression vanished. Fire kindled in Cherry's eyes, but she kept her voice calm. Her comfort over the next twenty four hours relied on that power lead. "I'm sorry, but I've checked the breakers," she said. "If I don't have any power I won't even be able to see my way around when it gets dark. I get frightened in the dark."

Fiona had had quite enough. Why didn't the persistent little minx go away?

"The power point in the shed is faulty," she lied smoothly. "I'm not responsible for what goes on in your home, and you should tell whoever is I'll have words with them tomorrow about your rudeness and their incompetence. Go away."

She slammed the door right in Cherry's face.

Cherry went slowly back to her home, her mind seething with revenge. The PC was out of service, but her laptop still had a good hour or so before the battery died. Opening up the lid, she carried the machine into the spare room which was nearest to the Trevallens, detected their wireless router easily, and in less than five minutes had hacked into it. The default password on most routers was 'admin' and in common with most people , Ms. Trevallen hadn't bothered to change it . The lady's own computer showed up on the network because she was using it to watch an episode of her favourite TV show. Excellent. Now what was her password? What was she always going on about? Her pet cat, Sheena. Try that, no, without the capital, no, how about sheenatrevallen? Got it. Now to set the properties of every hard drive to 'share'. Good.

She opened the 'my documents' folder, browsed around it briefly, then deleted everything. The 'my music' and 'my videos' met the same fate. Now to empty the trash. What else? Ah, the data drive. She formatted it. Now the last stroke. She logged back into the Trevallen's wireless router and made some subtle changes to its operating parameters, ones which would stop it working completely and be difficult to detect. Listening carefully she hit return. At first there was nothing, then Fiona's voice came drifting into the open window. The words weren't all that distinct, even with the rising volume, but the message they carried was crystal clear.

Cherry closed her laptop with a smile.

"Don't mess with me, you old cow," she said quietly to herself and went into the kitchen to make a sandwich for tea before it got dark.

The neighbours on the other side were away on holidays, so she would have to go without power tonight. There wasn't much food in the fridge to spoil, and she had a good torch. Dragging a stool over to the pantry she took several large candles from the top shelf, set them on the dining room table and lit them. Good. Enough light to read by. She went to her bedroom, extracted her C++ manual and a notebook from the bookcase, and returned to the kitchen with a portable drive and her laptop. There had been a little problem in her latest routine, and she was determined to find it.

The laptop died an hour later, much to Cherry's disgust. Time for bed, but she was a trifle chilly. Filling a large saucepan with water from the sink, she carried it over to the gas stove and began to heat it. Now to fill the bath and keep adding saucepans of boiling water until it was at just the right temperature.

❋ ❋ ❋

Mrs Trevallen never associated the destruction of her computer with young Cherry Graham, after all she was only an ignorant, insolent child. But yesterday's short encounter and the deplorable condition of the house next door, finally prompted Fiona to do what she had promised to do, and complain. Without a computer she couldn't email the council, so she wrote them a letter, telling them in no uncertain terms how she had suffered from the disgraceful behaviour of her next-door neighbours. Their home was in a deplorable condition, their child unruly and ill-disciplined by her carers. Mrs. Travellen had no idea who 'they' were, because they never so much as showed their face outside, or made any attempt to clean up their yard. Every morning there would be another unacceptable carpet of leaves strewn all over her immaculate lawn, and every morning she had to rake them up and throw them over the fence. She would have given them a piece of her mind herself if only she had been able to see them.

❋ ❋ ❋

The letter duly arrived on the desk of the appropriate council bureaucrat. Under any other circumstances Tony Cavendish would have put it where it belonged, right in the circular filing cabinet at his feet, but there was something which attracted his attention, and it had nothing to do with the condition of the Graham's yard. The letter mentioned carers. Who owned the property now? After a brief search he discovered the home was still owned by Caroline and Peter Graham, who still paid their rates by automated monthly payments from their account seven months after they were deceased. He rang the bank for clarification.

Alexander Scanlett, the manager of the local branch, said he would look into it. He brought up Caroline and Peter Graham's joint account and discovered there had been continuing activity on it every couple of days. Not large amounts except the last, over a thousand dollars. Apparently someone was using their key card, and using it most successfully. The bank had been negligent. In a matter of seconds he had frozen all the Graham's financial assets. Next he alerted the police.

❋ ❋ ❋

Sergeants Nancy Donahue and Stephie Powers had been assigned to the investigation because they were women. After a couple of hours work the Fraud squad were almost sure they knew who the culprit was, and care was called for. Stationed discretely outside the ATM machine in Miranda Shopping Mall, they waited for the felon to arrive at her usual time after school was out. Sure enough, Cherry Graham appeared on the other side of the parking lot, came over to the machine, slung her schoolbag onto the ground and inserted her card. The screen responded with a request to contact her bank. The card had been disallowed. She tried again, same result.

"Are you having some sort of trouble, young lady?" Stephie said gently.

Cherry turned round to find the two police officers standing next to her. "My card won't work," she protested. "The machine says it's been disallowed. What does that mean? If I can't get money I can't eat."

Nancy took the card from her hand. "Are you Caroline Graham?"

"No," Cherry said, defensive for the first time, "Caroline Graham was my Mum."

"Was?"

"She died about seven months ago, so did my dad."

"Don't you know you shouldn't be using her card like it was your own?" Stephie said carefully, beginning to appreciate some of the situation.

"No," Cherry objected. "It's my money. I'm the only surviving relative except for Aunt Fay and her husband who never even bothered to come to the funeral. Mum and Dad hated them," she added with a note of complete certainty.

Stephie knelt down beside the child who was becoming upset. "Where are you living now, darling?" she asked gently.

"At home, of course. Where would I be living?" Cherry said indignantly.

"At home by yourself?" The worried look on Stephie's face deepened considerably.

"Yes. I manage. I didn't pay the electricity bill last week and the stupid company cut off the power. It's all fixed now, but I had to pay extra to get it back on."

"Why didn't you pay the account?"

"I... I didn't like opening Mum and Dad's mail." The child looked steadfastly at the ground. "I had to rummage through them all, piles and piles of letters before I found the bill from the stupid company. It cost me over a thousand dollars." She paused, stared intently into Sergeant Stephie's face. "Can you get my key card working, because if it doesn't I'll starve."

Most times Stephie Powers enjoyed her job. This wasn't one of them. The child was so defenceless. What had happened to the care network which was supposed to surround children? She nodded towards Nancy who was brushing her eyes with the back of her hand. "I think we should take her home, don't you?" Then turning towards the child, "but perhaps you would like something to eat first, until all this key card business is fixed up."

"Yes, thank you." Cherry smiled for the first time. "I didn't get time to make any lunch this morning. I'm starving."

Stephie handed the child her key card back and the three headed off towards the café in the mall. Over the next half hour they watched

Cherry consume a plate of barbecued chicken and vegetables, a sundae and a large glass of milk, chatting to her casually as they collected the whole picture.

When the child had finally finished Nancy took the plunge. "Cherry, your parents would have wanted you to stay with someone, and they would have made all the arrangements so you would be taken care of. Stephie and I are not sure why this hasn't happened. We need to go to your place and find something called a Will, a piece of paper where your parents must have set all these things out. Would you like us to help you find it?"

"What happens if we can't find it?" Cherry asked, her eyes brimming with fear.

"Well, we should try at home first, then we will talk to the people your Mum and Dad worked for to see if we can find their solicitors. We'll check to see if they've left the Will in a safe deposit box at the bank. Let's not worry about anything else yet. Would you like us to help?"

The child nodded slowly, turned away, struggling to regain her composure. "I... I don't like touching their things. Every time I do I get... I get..."

She burst into tears, the first time she had ever done so publicly since the terrible news. Stephie took her into her arms, doing her best not to cry herself, while Nancy sat at the table, her face covered with her hands.

They went out of the café into the police car and drove Cherry home. Nancy made a cup of tea in the kitchen while Stephie and Cherry began the search. Two hours later they came back to the kitchen and sat down. The elusive Will had not materialised, and they had searched everywhere, even her parent's bedroom. Actually Stephie had searched there, because Cherry said she couldn't bear to do it.

Stephie sat down on the settee and drew the child to her side. "Sweetheart, you can't stay here tonight. You have no money and no food. You've told me your neighbour is a horrible person. I can't leave you here, in fact I'm not allowed to."

"But this is my home!" Mum and Dad live... lived... lived... " She burst into tears again.

It took a long while and a lot of gentle persuasion before Cherry would consent to allow Sergeant Nancy to ring Amanda's parents and ask them to take care of her for the next few days while all her affairs were sorted out. Stephie found a suitcase in the linen cupboard, and helped Cherry to pack her clothes. The suitcase was hardly one third full.

"Don't you want to pack some of these pretty dresses?" Stephie asked, running her hands through the collection in the wardrobe.

"No," Cherry shook her head. "I won't have room for my books and my computer if I fill the case with all that rubbish."

"Your books? Computer?"

"Here, like this." Cherry handed Stephie her latest book on programming in C++ along with her workbook containing her latest efforts.

The young policewoman stared disbelieving at the collection in her hands. It was quite a while before she found her voice again. "You write programs in C++? Where did you learn to do this?"

"I read books, and there's a boy who helps me when I get stuck."

"At your school?" The amazement remained on Stephie's face.

"Of course not. His name's Arthur Barlow. He answered a question on my blog. He was pretty rude at first. He told me I was programming like a pathetic ten year old, but when I told him I was a ten year old he was different. He's very clever."

"I think the same applies to you," Stephie answered. She mentally added 'incredibly gifted' to her picture of the brave young girl. Gifted? The child was bordering on incandescent. Before she went into the police force Stephie had studied computer science, and knew enough to recognise the complexity of the work in her hands.

Without another word she helped Cherry pile everything into the suitcase. Soon it was loaded into the police car along with an extra pile of books, her desktop computer, monitor and keyboard. Cherry locked the house, got into the car, and they headed off towards Amanda's place.

An intensive search conducted over the next three weeks failed to find the much sought after Will. With a very heavy heart Stephie picked up the office phone and called the Department of Social Services to report a neglected child.

CHAPTER 5

F ay Babbage was just about to leave her home in Cabramatta for work when the phone rang. She paused, undecided. Should she answer it and risk being late? Her boss, manager of the Three Monkeys Nightclub, could be a demon towards his employees if he was in a bad mood. As his Personal Assistant she had been privy to several of these occasions and never wanted to be the object of another.

On the other hand, perhaps he was the one ringing her on some urgent matter. There had been some trouble with the latest girl she had employed. Apparently one of the nightclub's clients had been dissatisfied with her performance. *After all the training I gave her, stupid little bitch*, Fay thought to herself. She put down the briefcase she was carrying and headed down the hall to answer the ringing instrument. Emblazoned on the case was the nightclub logo, three monkeys, one with its hands over its eyes, another covering its ears, and a third its mouth, a well-known depiction of the proverb 'see no evil, hear no evil, speak no evil'.

It would have been hard to find a less appropriate logo to represent the activities of the nightclub, infamous for the prostitution and drug abuse which occurred within its walls and the surrounding area. The local Anglican minister on the street opposite had complained several times about the stoned couples who for some reason had decided to have sex on his front lawn, probably because it was the only piece of grass around. He was always picking used syringes out of his garden. His children were often woken up at night from the screams and occasional gunshot which echoed across the car park behind the Three Monkeys, as some other poor human being came to the end of their mortal existence.

Fay picked up the phone. It wasn't her boss.

"Ms. Babbage?" An unfamiliar voice said, "this is Neil Harrison from the Department of Social Services. I'm ringing you concerning your niece, a Miss Cherry Graham."

Curse the blasted instrument, Fay thought. Why did I have to be such a fool and pick it up? "Yes, what do you want?" She snapped angrily. "I'm just about to go out. I don't have anything to do with that side of the family."

"We believe you to be the child's only surviving relative. You were aware her parents had died?"

"I'd heard a rumour."

"We were ringing to ask if you and your husband would be willing to take care of the child, seeing as there would appear to be no one else," Harrison continued.

"See here," Fay complained, hovering her hand over the hook, "we aren't wealthy people. We don't have the resources to care for a young girl. Her parents never left us a cent, so—"

"I'm sorry to contradict you," Neil Harrison replied with some misgivings, "your sister and her husband never made a Will. I believe the matter is now in the hand of a state government appointed lawyer. The estate is likely to be equally divided between yourself and the child, to be held in trust until she comes of age. In the meantime, whoever is her guardian will be entitled to draw from the estate for the purposes of her welfare and education."

Fay sat down on the chair near the phone table. This was a different matter. The Graham's home at Miranda was worth a pretty penny, and if there was a life insurance payout as well, the total could run into a couple of million dollars. Why have half when you can have the lot? She thought to herself. She glanced at her watch. Getting to work on time had suddenly become less important. "What would I have to do?" She said, adding a generous dose of sugar to her usual acerbic voice.

So it was that two months after that fateful phone call, Cherry opened the front door of Amanda's house anticipating the arrival of her Mum, and found Fay Babbage and some other man she had never seen standing there instead. Before she had a chance to slam the door on their faces, the woman had pushed her way in and embraced her with a smothering hug.

"Darling Cherry," she gushed, kissing her on the cheek time after time, "how wonderful to see you, sweetheart. The police told us where you were staying or we would have been searching high and low. Now, darling, let me introduce Sam."

At this point the stranger came forward and repeated the hugging process, rubbing his hands all over her back while he did it. "Hi Cherry," he said. "You poor little girl. We would have come sooner, but there were things to sort out first."

Cherry pushed herself away from his smothering embrace and fixed her aunt with a withering stare. "Who's this? And don't 'darling Cherry' me. You didn't even come to the funeral, not a card, not a phone call. Don't try to—"

I'm so sorry," Fay lied with the liquidity of long practice. "We couldn't come, darling. Sam and I were overseas. He has business connections in the USA. We've only just come home—"

"Who's Sam?" Cherry demanded, cutting her off. She didn't believe it for a second. "Why is he here? Where's uncle Chris?"

"Uncle Chris decided he didn't want to live with me anymore," Fay said stiffly. "Sam is my partner now. You'll like him. He loves little girls."

At that very instant Alan and Amanda joined the gathering in the hall. "Why are you here?" he demanded angrily.

"Why are we here?" Fay beamed. "To take Cherry back to live with us of course."

For a second or two you could have heard a pin drop, then all hell broke loose. Amanda screamed first, grabbing Cherry by the arm and dragging her away from her aunt. "She's staying with us. She's not going anywhere," she screamed.

"There has to be some mistake," Alan stammered in a shocked voice, "Shirley and I have applied to adopt her."

Cherry stood silent, her mind going round and round in circles. Her world was beginning to crack apart. She clung to Amanda, staring fearfully at her hated aunt.

"I'm afraid there's no mistake," Sam grinned. He fished some crumpled document out of his pocket. "It's all there, sewn up and legal like." He turned towards Cherry. "You see your folks never bothered to make a Will, sweetheart, and as a result your Aunt Fay gets half their property, you get the other half. The Department of Social Services awarded us custody, and the rest of the money from your parent's estate will be used for your education and so on."

"For goodness sake, not now." Fay gave her partner a withering stare. Cherry's mouth had dropped open in horror. Not only was her aunt threatening to take her away, her parent's money was going to her foul aunt and the man with the wandering hands.

"No!" She screamed. "Dad and Mum would never have wanted that. You know they wouldn't. Why don't you go away and leave me alone?"

An ugly smile spread over her aunt's face. Her eyes bored into Cherry in triumph. "That's the way it is," she snapped. "Get used to it. Your mother always got the best of everything. Now it's my turn, yours too. We can afford it. Your parents were very well off. That home will fetch a good price on the market."

"You're not selling my home!" Cherry lunged towards her aunt, her fists balled. Sam stepped in the way and lifted the struggling child off the floor, one arm around her waist, the other up between her legs. He was very strong, and for the first time Cherry formed the impression he enjoyed the way she was struggling against him. She suddenly became very still. Uncle Sam put her down, caressed her head.

"That's better," he said soothingly. "No need to get upset. We've got your bedroom all prepared and pretty. Your aunt has been wanting to take care of you for a long time."

Cherry turned pleading eyes towards Alan. "They can't do this, can they? Please say no."

Alan came forward and took the document from Sam's hand, read it carefully and gave it back. At length he spoke.

"We're going to challenge this in court. Why not give Cherry a couple of days to get used to the idea before you take her away? She's settled in here, and no matter what you think she's been very fragile since the deaths of her parents. Amanda gets on incredibly well with her. They're close friends."

"She'll make others," aunt Fay sneered. "You've read the paper. We're taking her, now. Cherry get your things. There's a van in the street, so you can put the lot in there." She turned to Alan. "Try to stop us and I get the police."

It was a terrible ultimatum. Alan was seething with rage, Cherry clung to Amanda, crying her eyes out. Sam's face said he couldn't care less, and Fay wore an expression of complete triumph. Over the next hour all the things Cherry had brought to Amanda's were bundled into the van without her consent or assistance. Finally Cherry was physically prised apart from Amanda and Alan and bundled in as well.

All the way to Cabramatta, Cherry sat in the back of the van silent and in shock. Now her world had totally disintegrated. Her heart seemed to stop beating, and she felt so cold. Neither her odious aunt or her newly acquired uncle said a word to her, or to one another for that matter. After an hour's drive they turned off Cabramatta Road and down a street flanked on either side with large blocks of cheap, dirty units. The van stopped outside one of these.

"Welcome to your new home, darling," aunt Fay leered, turning round to the sad little bundle in the back. "This is where you live until you grow up to be a big girl. We're your parents now, and you'd better bloody well get used to it."

The final descent into hell had begun.

CHAPTER 6

Arthur Barlow put down his beer and watched the two men on the other side of the table with an expression of practiced incredulity. "Are you out of your minds?" He asked. "Here I am, offering you the prospect of good money as well as a way out of the mess you're currently in up to your necks - and you're hesitating. Don't you realise you're on to a good thing? No, you don't, do you? Too much weed before lunch."

Henry stared out the rather dirty window at the sea creeping its way in slow stages up the beach. His head was aching like it always did when Arthur bombarded it with his crazy schemes. So complicated, why did life have to be so complicated? George, who sat on the settee next to him smoking a joint, said nothing. Perhaps he was drifting off to sleep.

"Explain it to me again," Henry grumbled, "and use shorter words so I don't lose the thread."

Arthur smiled at him. *Idiot*, he thought, but an Idiot who had to be humoured, at least for now. "Of course Henry," he said agreeably, picking up his beer from the table.

"You and George are going to lend me eighty thousand dollars. I know you've got that in the Commune's housekeeping account, because that's where you put the dough from the dope sales. I agree to pay you back one hundred thousand dollars within ten years or you'll come and whack me. When my company has been duly and legally gazetted, I use it to launder your money from the sales of cannabis so they look legit. Full statement of transactions available on request. I'll keep a proper tally of expenses and profits, not like the way it is now. The growers are ripping you off. Besides, if anyone were to poke their nose into your affairs, you'd spend quite a few years in the Long Bay jail, uncomfortable beds, unfriendly company. What's more they make you work, and you know you're allergic to work, Henry."

Henry's tiny eyes narrowed, a sign he was concentrating for a change. He glanced towards George in a pleading sort of way, either for an opinion or another joint.

"I think we can trust Arthur," George said, smiling. "Besides, the crop growers are expanding their activities, and we need new ways of handling profits. Don't want anyone mucking around with the Commune, do we? Okay, Arthur, you've got your dough. Now, what would you like to do for the rest of the day? There's a few girls down at number fifteen who would enjoy your company."

"Yeah," Arthur laughed, a cynical smile crossing his face, "and while I'm in bed with Marianne, Jodie and Francine are taking pictures with that little camera you've got hidden. So useful for future blackmail. I'm quite disappointed. Thought you knew me better than that, George."

The expression on George's face clearly indicated he was disappointed too.

"Only thinking of your enjoyment," George grunted. "You should come back more often, Arthur, find a nice girl."

"Here?" Arthur exclaimed. "Remember I grew up here. Loving mother, caring sisters, always warming my little heart. Your definition of a nice girl is one who does it for free, George. Now I have to go."
"By the way," he added, "I'm moving down to Eastwood in a couple of years, where the action is. More clients, bigger machines." He grinned, "and really nice girls. Won't bore you with details."

Arthur drained the last of his beer, stood up and went out of the room. Now that he had the cash he would finalise his offer to buy McFarlane's business for fifty thousand. He would keep it running until he had regained the capital outlay, then close down and reopen in Sydney as Barlow Maximum Speed. He had big plans, and the Central Coast wasn't the place to initiate them. In the meantime he would keep his word to Henry and George and set their business on a secure footing. Nothing on any computer, everything on the Cloud, set up in a way which made access by prying eyes totally impossible. Little bits of information would be spread all over the world, each protected by a formidably long password. He would write a little routine which would make accessing the data a seamless process. Perhaps he could use some of the cannabis capital to generate extra income on the stock market. No need to tell the others about that, of course.

✳ ✳ ✳

McFarlane grudgingly took Barlow's offer for his business and retired to his holiday cottage in Ettalong along with his latest squeeze, grateful to be out of the game. At least he was grateful to be out of Barlow's game, which gave him a constant headache. Geniuses were strange people, he reflected. Polite on the outside, they had minds like a steel trap, always one step ahead of you. He had really had enough.

Over the next two years the business made a huge profit. Barlow bought the adjacent shop and knocked down the wall between them. His reputation was growing. Well-heeled clients made the long journey to the Central Coast from every capital city in Australia. The majority of these were high end gamers, but a significant and growing proportion were from digital animation companies, who found that their images would render on Barlow's machines in half the time it took using the conventional machines in their studios. It wasn't just the number of processors, it was the optimised multitasking operating kernel, written by Barlow himself – Barlix, he called it. In his spare time Arthur was working hard to expand his kernel into a fully-fledged operating system, which bypassed many of the time-wasting security routines embedded in other conventional ones. If he could work directly with those who wrote the animation software, he would be able to make a machine which would really fly. Yes, this was the direction in which to head. The gamers were all private individuals with limited bank accounts. The film industry was not shackled with such small budget restrictions. Writing code was certainly his first love, but making money, lots and lots of money, came in a very close second.

CHAPTER 7

Cherry moved through the next twelve months like a pre-programmed robot, mechanically eating her food, taking care of her toilet and going to her new primary school not far away from her new home. The children were unfriendly. Any kid from the Shire where she had lived was automatically regarded as an undesirable alien here in the West. They made no effort at all to help her with anything, and neither did her teachers, who seemed oblivious to the young child's patently obvious sorrow.

Her aunt, while depriving Cherry of any shred of motherly care, was happy to spend any amount of her parent's money on the miserable little girl, seeing as it cost her nothing to do it. She bought her nice clothes – which Cherry wouldn't wear, and furnished her bedroom with everything a materialistic child could want. Cherry couldn't have cared less. Anything she wished for in the way of hardware or software or books was hers for the asking. Cherry would spend an increasing number of hours lost in her machines, her one and only method of escaping the alien world around her. She blocked out every thought of her past life, of Amanda, of her home.

It was just as well in one way, because Fay had arranged a company to auction off everything saleable inside her parent's house and take the rest to the rubbish tip. One month afterwards the home had been sold for a good price. She dreaded the day her niece would ask for some piece of childhood memorabilia, but she never did.

Despite her self-imposed isolation, Cherry became aware of other abnormalities associated with her new home. Tacked onto the side of the house at the end of the drive was a large garage which was always kept locked. Sam had threatened her with violence if she ever went near the place, which only served to heighten Cherry's natural curiosity. She had woken late one night to the sound of soft voices floating through her window. Slipping out of bed, she peeked surreptitiously through a slit in the curtain. Sam and a couple of other men were carrying boxes down the drive towards the garage and returning empty handed. After that she had made several furtive attempts to wrench open the garage door when Sam and Fay had gone out, but it was too well fastened.

One day an expensive wireless printer arrived, and Aunt Fay asked Cherry to help her connect it to their network. It was the only prolonged conversation they had ever had.

"I can't get it working," she complained. "I've done everything it said in the brochure, but the damn thing still doesn't go."

"Let me do it," Cherry said, mostly because she wanted to use the printer herself.

Her aunt lifted the printer to its new home on the corner of the dresser in the kitchen, and Cherry sat down in front of her aunt's desktop.

"Was there a disk included in the box?" Cherry asked innocently.

"Never you damn well mind what was included in the box," Fay retorted. "Can you fix it or not?"

"I'll have to get some drivers from the internet," Cherry said, already regretting her helpfulness. The printer box was all broken up around the edges anyway, and perhaps the disk fell out."

"Perhaps," Fay sniffed. "Can you get it working?"

"Of course I can."

Fay watched fascinated as the child downloaded the latest printer drivers from the internet, then ran the application. She accessed the network router and assigned a fixed IP address to the printer in the routing table, and set the new printer to default. A short time later at test page rolled off the machine in the next room.

"What would you like me to print out?" Cherry smiled with satisfaction. "Might as well check if it's working properly."

"Some of my emails," Fay replied appreciatively. "Such a nuisance to have to wait until I'm at work and do it there. Can you show me?"

"No problem." Cherry opened the email application. "What's your email username and password, or do you want to type them in yourself?"

"I'd better do it." She leant over Cherry and typed 'jodiesexangel1659' password: 'gloriousafterglow'. Cherry, memorising every keystroke, wondered why her aunt would use such ridiculous character strings.

Several emails downloaded. Fay pointed to one. "Can you open and print that? You're a clever girl. Did Caroline teach you computers?"

The mention of her mother's name wiped the smile off Cherry's face, but she answered civilly enough. "She did a bit, and Dad. I've learnt heaps and heaps since then. Now, its printing, can you hear it? Want to go and see if it's OK?"

"No, I'll read it later. Thank you, Cherry." She gave the girl a genuine smile. "How about we go down the shops and get an ice cream? You like ice cream."

Cherry did like ice cream, but there was a problem in the latest routine she was writing she wanted to solve. She hesitated, uncertain of what to do. Her aunt had said something nice for a change, and such things were to be encouraged. She turned her head up and smiled in return. "I'd like that," she said.

If her relationship with her aunt was showing tiny signs of improvement, her relationship with her pseudo uncle was steadily heading in the opposite direction. It had nothing whatsoever do to with the way he spoke to her. Apart from the garage incident, he always called her 'darling' or 'sweetheart' and never raised his voice.

It was the way he touched her.

He was always giving her long hugs, and while everyone else had hugged her round the shoulders, Uncle Sam always managed to get one of his hands around her backside. Several times she had physically pushed it off, only to have it return. Sometimes when she was sitting on the lounge watching TV he would sit beside her and stroke her legs, running his fingers lightly up the inside. Cherry had locked her legs together.

"I don't like you doing that," she had complained time and time again. Sam had stopped, smiled, and stroked somewhere else.

Eventually Cherry summoned up her courage and spoke to her aunt about it. "I know he wants to show affection," she complained, "but I don't like it, and he doesn't stop when I ask him to."

"You're worrying about nothing," Fay snapped. "Just relax and enjoy it."

This was a most unsatisfactory reply. Cherry went back into her room and began to think about the whole business long and hard. She logged onto a government website on child abuse, and read it carefully. It confirmed her darkest suspicions.

Her uncle was fondling her, preening her for sex.

She shuddered with revulsion. What had she done to deserve this? Was it really her fault? She couldn't help being a pretty little girl. Surely beauty wasn't a bad thing? She ran her hand up and down her legs as if to wipe out the memory of his touch. Had she encouraged him in any way? No, she was always telling him to stop. Perhaps her very protests encouraged him somehow. Suddenly another thought struck her. Aunt Fay had dismissed her fears as ridiculous. Surely she could see what was happening... Then the truth Cherry had been so frightened to face exploded into ugly reality. Her aunt cared less than nothing about her. The only reason her presence in the house was tolerated was so that Fay could keep spending her money, not from any desire to help or heal or love. The distrust and hatred, so slightly ebbing of late, was renewed with a vengeance. For a long time she tossed up one alternative and then another.

Trapped, she was trapped.

No, she mustn't think like that or else she would soon be paralysed with fear and incapable of taking any action at all. In an hour or so her aunt would call her for dinner, then she would have a shower, get into one of her pretty nightdresses and endure another session with Sam as he came to say 'goodnight' with his wandering hands. Nothing else had happened yet, but now Cherry was completely certain it was only a matter of time.

But what to do?

Who would believe a thing she said? Her aunt would side with her perverted partner. She could trust no one. At first she thought of running away, but realised the futility of such an act. The police would bring her back, and then it would be so much worse. Publicly branded as a liar, her credibility shot to pieces, Sam would have a free hand. She shuddered at the metaphor. He eyes roamed around the room for a weapon. Dangerous. If she attempted to hurt her uncle he would probably carry out the act with violence. Apparently this had happened to other girls and they had died as a result. No, something else, but what?

Her eyes fell on her laptop, sitting closed beside her bed. Suddenly she had an idea. Rummaging in her desk drawer she found a thirty two Gigabyte SD memory card, and inserted it into the slot in the side. That would give her the storage she needed. The small lights which signalled the laptop's activity were hard wired into the motherboard, so she painted them out with a mixture of nail varnish and black marking pen ink. Now to write a small routine which turned on the video recorder as soon as she brushed the touch pad, and kept the screen dark. Her fingers trembled slightly as she programmed. She had to get it right, make it work. *Concentrate, Cherry, concentrate or join the ranks of abused children*, she thought to herself.

It took three attempts, but eventually the routine was working. The laptop looked for all the world as if it was dead, but when Cherry touched the pad in front of the keyboard, the camera on top of the screen began recording. Touching the pad again stopped it. When she hit 'Control', 'Alt', 'Delete' the laptop screen would burst back into life. She opened the movie player and checked the recording, a picture of herself sitting white-faced in front of the machine. Good. Now to plug the computer into the power to make sure the batteries were fully charged, and place it on her bedside table in view of the door. Anything Sam did to her would be faithfully recorded on the memory card. All she had to do was touch the pad. As an extra precaution she opened her makeup cabinet, extracted a pair of straight nail scissors, and took them back to her bed, stowing them underneath the pillow within easy reach.

Over the next three nights Cherry recorded Sam's every unwelcome visit, along with her vociferous complaints. The last night Sam had slapped her face hard and walked out of the room. Violence had entered his nightly routine. Cherry stayed awake most of that night, her hand never far from her laptop. In the early hours of the morning she fell asleep exhausted, a few hours before the alarm clock woke her up.

She went to school feeling like a zombie, attended her English class where the roll was called, then snuck off to the storeroom at the back of the gym and went to sleep on top of a pile of exercise mats. No one seemed to notice. Everyone had gone home when she woke, climbed out the window at the back of the storeroom and went home. Somehow she knew this would be the night. She already had video evidence of Sam's behaviour, but it wasn't enough to put the man behind bars. How much more would be needed? She shuddered at the thought.

She went to bed early that night. Deliberately leaving her bed lamp on, she took the scissors and placed them carefully under her pillow, determined not to go to sleep at all if needs be. Half an hour later Sam opened the door in his dressing gown.

❈ ❈ ❈

Robin Naylor, chief commissioner of police and his wife Ruth were returning from a function at Fairfield Diggers' Club, where he had been asked to speak. The sight of a barefoot child in a blood spattered nightdress, holding a laptop in one hand and waving desperately with the other, would have made any motorist stop, and the Naylors were no exception. Robin slewed the car into the kerb, flicking on his hazard lights at the same time. Without waiting for an invitation, the strange child wrenched open the back door and vaulted onto the back seat, slamming the door after her.

"Drive. Drive!" she screamed. "Take me to the nearest police station." There was more than a touch of hysteria in her voice. Ruth Naylor, a shaken expression on her face, turned round and stared at the girl.

"My dear," she said as kindly as she could, "whatever is the matter?"

"My uncle tried to rape me," she said in between great gulping breaths. "My aunt wanted him to. I hate them!" she hissed.

The way she spoke made her accusation completely believable. Ruth turned round to her husband, shocked to the core. Robin squeezed her knee as if to say, "we don't really know what's going on here yet."

He spoke to the child. "I think we should take you home and sort this out."

"No, No!" Cherry cried out in panic. "Try, and I'll jump out of the car!" She paused, breathing rapidly. "All right, I'm a dangerous psycho who's just stabbed her little brother to death. See? I've got blood all—"

The child stared down at her blood-spattered nightdress, gave a funny hiccupping sound, and passed out. Ruth, waiting for the rest of the sentence, turned round to see what had happened.

"Robin, stop!" she cried out in alarm. "She's unconscious. Let me get in the back. I really think we should do as she asks."

Robin stopped the car for the second time. Ruth got in the back, clipped her seatbelt into place, and dragged the child upright against her shoulder. Robin pulled away from the curb heading for Liverpool police station. The child, after making a groaning sound, opened her eyes and nearly jumped out the opposite door.

"Don't touch me!" she screamed, her eyes wide and terrified.

"We're taking you to Liverpool police station, my dear," Ruth said, almost as shocked as the child seemed to be. "Please, I'm not going to hurt you. How did you get the blood on your nightdress? Are you injured anywhere? Have you been sexually assaulted?"

"He tried, but I stabbed him," she said defiantly, then clamped her mouth shut.

In a short time Robin pulled into the police station. He went round to the back of the car, opened the door and held out his hand to the girl. "We're at Liverpool police station, and I'm escorting you inside," he said firmly.

It wasn't a suggestion. Cherry grabbed her laptop, allowed the man to take her arm, and went obediently with him into the building. There were two officers on duty, a man by the name of Sergeant Davies, and another Sergeant from the Fraud Squad, Stephie Powers, who had been working in the area. She looked up from her desk at the commissioner of police, his arm holding a blood-spattered Cherry Graham in a nightdress, and wondered briefly if she was hallucinating. She stood up, confusion all over her face. Now the child had seen her, and wrenching herself free from the commissioner's clutches, raced towards her. Putting her laptop down, she flung her arms around Stephie, sobbing her heart out, her little body shaking, her breath coming in great gulps. Stephie hugged the child, kneeling down beside her.

"Cherry, what's happened?" She asked gently. "Come on, darling, you're safe now. Come on, that's the girl."

Sergeant Davies stared first at the Commissioner, then at Stephie holding the child, and wondered what was coming next. He made an attempt at politeness. This wasn't just his boss, this was his boss's boss. The water was well and truly out of his depth, and getting deeper by the second.

"Commissioner... Mrs. Naylor. I didn't know you were coming... I..." His voice tapered off into silence.

Robin Naylor stared at the sobbing child, then at his wife who was terribly upset. He squeezed her arm. "It appears Sergeant Powers knows this child," he said half to himself. "Well, that's the hand of the Lord if ever I saw it."

He waited until the sobbing had calmed down to the occasional gulp, then made his way over towards the pair. "Sergeant Powers, I take it you have met this child. Who is she?"

Stephie stood up, half embarrassed to find herself addressing the Commissioner, half boiling mad. She put her arm protectively around the girl who was still clinging to her. "Commissioner, this is Cherry Graham. Both her parents died in an air crash. When we found her, she'd been living alone for months and months in her empty home. Eventually she was placed in the care of her only surviving relative, a Ms. Babbage and her partner, a Mr. Blackman, who live at Cabramatta. I don't know what's happened since, but I would stake my career that she's not to blame."

"I'll take your word for it," Robin replied, nodding his head, then more gently to the child, "Ms. Graham, can you tell us what happened? Would you like a warm drink? I'm sure we can find her something, can't we, Davies?"

Davies said he most certainly could.

Cherry turned around in Stephie's arms and stared at the Commissioner. "Are you a policeman?" she asked. "Why does everybody seem to know you?"

"I'm the commissioner of police, Cherry," Robin said gently. "You know one of my staff, Sergeant Powers. Perhaps you would be kind enough to sit down and tell us just what this is all about?"

Without saying another word Cherry reached for her laptop, opened it, and pressed a few keys. The latest video appeared. Four pairs of horrified eyes stared at the atrocity being enacted on a child. When the video had ended she showed them another. She closed the laptop and went to stand near Stephie who had tears in her eyes. Stephie closed her arms around her. Robin's face was like thunder, his wife's white with shock.

Sergeant Davies reached for the phone. "The bastard," he said, breaking the silence. "Shall I organise a squad to pick him up?"

At that instant the instrument rang. Davies snatched it up, spoke for some minutes and replaced the instrument in its cradle.

"That was a couple of our boys from Liverpool hospital," he said with a grimace. "It seems they've just interviewed a Sam Blackman and Fay Babbage. Stabbing wound, he's okay, going home. They were very worried about their darling niece who suffers from paranoia and tells whopping lies. Shall I call them back and have him picked up?"

"No," Robin said grimly. "We'll leave it until the morning. I think you'll find there's a file on Blackman. I'd like to get a DNA on that blood, might help with a couple of other outstanding criminal matters. I don't want to go into details in the present company. Sergeant Powers, could you please find Cherry something else to wear? I'd like her nightdress down at forensic as soon as possible. Davies, could you drive it there? Good. Thank you."

Stephie went out of the room and came back with a large T-shirt and a blanket. "It's all I've got," she said. "We could wrap the blanket round her legs, and she could wear the T-shirt. It's too big for her, but it would keep her warm."

Cherry took the clothes from her hand. "Thank you," she said. "Can I go somewhere to change?"

"I'll help you," Stephie said, and the two went out of the room.

Davies scribbled some notes down on a pad. "What do we do with Ms. Graham? She could stay here in the cells. We could get a blow up bed for her and she'd—"

"She's coming home with me."

All eyes turned to Ruth Naylor. There was an expression on her face which silenced all argument. "The child comes home with us. Poor little girl. She's suffered so much, what with the death of her parents and now this. I couldn't live with myself if we didn't do something to help her. That's okay, isn't it, Robin?"

Robin knew that look. One thing was certain, the child was going home with his wife. "Of course, my dear," he nodded. "Good idea. She can wear some of James' clothes. I'll have to tell DSS, of course. They have to know what's happened and where the child is. Tomorrow. I have to organise some things here now." He turned to Stephie who had just come back into the room with her blanket-clad charge.
"Sergeant Powers, could I ask a favour? I have to stay here for a while working on the Blackman case. Would you be kind enough to take my wife and Cherry Graham home? Thank you."

In less than an hour Cherry Graham, feeling warm and safe, was carried in Stephie's arms right through the Naylor's front door and tucked into bed. She was asleep before Ruth had turned out the light.

CHAPTER 8

Two years and six months later Arthur Barlow sold his shopfront in Gosford to a Sydney restaurateur for two hundred and eighty thousand dollars. He paid back his loan to the Commune and headed to Sydney to continue his dream. He leased a large factory floor in Talavera Road Marsfield, not far from Macquarie University, and furnished it exactly to his liking. He divided a portion off the back as his own private quarters, a bathroom and bedroom – after all, why bother living somewhere else. Next to these was a large workshop, equipped with the latest gear, fed with filtered, dry air. An antistatic floor, benches with special lighting, each with its own array of assembly tools, completed the arrangement. A door on the other side of the workshop led to the secure storeroom containing computer hardware of various sorts. Everything required to construct and service powerful machines was provided. Through a secure door at the front of the workshop lay a large reception area, luxuriously furnished with soft, quality carpet. Examples of Barlow's machines were set on glass topped tables. Large pictures of others and their satisfied customers were framed on the walls.

In the centre of the reception area was an ultra-modern desk, especially designed so prospective clients could admire the stunningly attractive woman sitting behind it as they conducted business in front.

Annette Robertson came through the door of Barlow Maximum Speed nearly certain she was wasting her valuable time. A man was sitting behind the most elegant all-glass desk she had ever seen.

"Ms. Robertson?" The young man rose to his feet. "My name is Arthur Barlow. Glad you could make it."

He looked her up and down the way men always looked her up and down. She was used to it. Most of them weren't slow to tell her they liked what they saw. She wondered if Arthur Barlow would do the same.

"There's a conference room through the doorway," Arthur said smiling, but without the expected compliment, "and the chairs are more comfortable. Shall we go in there?"

It was Annette's turn to look Arthur up and down, and she could feel herself blushing while she did it. There was something about him which attracted her, though she couldn't explain why. He was quite handsome, and in some mysterious way he seemed to fit her mental picture of a man she would like to spend time with, a lot of time with. She was being ridiculous, she scolded herself, and followed Arthur into the conference room. Sitting down on the opposite side of the table, she opened her briefcase and tried not to stare at him.

"There's my C.V., she said, drawing a sheaf of papers from her briefcase and thrusting them across the table towards him. "What made you call me? I work for a firm of accountants, and I don't even like them. I'm sure they didn't recommend me."

"Why don't you like them?" Arthur asked politely.

"I'm bored silly. The rest of the staff are all men, and I get sick of the way they gawk at me," she answered, well aware that this was probably the worst way to begin an interview with a man who was staring at her.

"How are your parents getting on?" Arthur asked unexpectedly.

"My parents?" Annette exclaimed, totally taken aback. "What business is it of yours how my parents are getting on?"

"Just wondered," Arthur said evenly, ignoring the furious stare smouldering in his direction. "What are their names again?"

"I beg your pardon?" Annette wasn't sure whether to walk out right then and there or throw her briefcase at Barlow first.

"The names of your parents. I wondered what they were."

"I'm adopted, is that what you want to know? The names of my real parents? I don't know and I couldn't care less." Annette's eyes blazed like fire.

"Thank you. Did you have more than one set of foster parents?"

"What sort of interview is this?" Annette fumed. "I'm out of here!"

"Don't you like people asking about your family life?" Arthur asked gently.

"Can't you tell? Get yourself another P.A." Annette jerked herself away from the table and stood up, blazingly angry.

"I was about to offer you the job," Arthur said evenly.

"What?" Annette snapped. "Give me one reason why I'd want to work for you."

"Your starting salary would be five hundred and twenty thousand dollars."

Annette sat down. Arthur counted ten seconds of silence.

"What do I have to do to earn that?" Annette growled. "Warm your bed as well as run your business?" She pressed her hands over her scarlet face. "I'm sorry, I don't know what came over me. I had no right to—"

"No bed warming or special favours will ever be required," Arthur reassured her.

"I want you to manage my accounts and be my personal assistant, take care of the general day to day running of the place so I can get on with what I love to do." He smiled, "I've had the desk in the front office built just for you, so I really do hope you get to sit behind it."

"It's made of glass," Annette said, because right then she was so flabbergasted she couldn't think of anything else to say. "Why would you make that for me?"

"Because you are an exceptionally beautiful woman," Arthur said with a reassuring smile. "I predict a steady increase in customers from the moment you sit behind it. Now, shall we start the paperwork? Perhaps the salary is too small?"

"No!" Annette exclaimed, unconsciously fanning her burning face with her fingers. "The salary is unbelievable." She paused, frowning. "You're not trying anything on, are you? You really mean it? Why would you pay me so much? That's more than ten times my current salary. You haven't even seen my C.V. I might make a complete mess of your business."

"I don't think so, and I'm a very astute judge of character. Is that settled? You'll take the job?"

For weeks afterwards Annette could give herself no adequate reason for why she had instantly agreed. It wasn't the money, which was amazing, it was the man himself. There was some sort of physical thing at work, something, which contrary to every grain of common sense, told her that Arthur was a someone she would like to work for, even enjoy getting to know.

The process had been unconventional, but Arthur had made the right choice. In the weeks to follow Annette proved to be as clever as she was beautiful.

Business picked up immediately, and soon a dozen or so staff were busy in the workshop doing the hack work on the builds. Barlow was merciless if they made the slightest mistake or ventured to try and improve on his predetermined design.

Several staff left very suddenly, only to be replaced with others until those remaining understood the boundaries of their employment.

Do what you're told, do it well and don't ask questions.

Barlow worked practically round the clock, disappearing late at night into his private quarters when he wanted to sleep, and rising early in the morning to get on with the job. He was fulfilling his dream, and he enjoyed every moment of it. Annette made sure he was always carefully fed, selecting his favourite menu from caterers in the nearby district. She made sure their service was excellent, and ruthlessly dispensed with them if it wasn't. The way to a man's favour was through his stomach, and Barlow was no exception.

Annette's already fabulous salary increased at regular intervals as proof of her insight.

Besides keeping an eagle eye on everything happening around him, Barlow was engaged in another project, the details of which he kept totally to himself. The other technicians could see from a distance what was going on, but that was all. They could hardly miss it. In an especially cordoned-off section of the workshop, Barlow was building a machine. It was huge, a quantum leap larger than anything else they were constructing. The machine case was man high, still mostly empty, and in the bottom lay the mother of all power supplies. Little by little motherboards were added in rows, each containing spaces for two processors.

Not only was Barlow building the machine, he was working on the operating system required to run it. This new system was totally incompatible with any other, peeled down to highly optimised code which ran at blistering speed, code which would only interface with a handful of specialised applications. What these were was a mystery to everyone except a select few. This outlet for his genius occupied most of his mind, and he would dispense with less important matters in as short a time as possible without compromising his thoroughness. Nobody got the better of Arthur Barlow, as those who tried discovered to their detriment.

That is not to say he was without friends, if friends is the correct term for fellow computer geeks. Paul Yang and Viktor Greshnev, both employed by New Wave Reality, a leading CGI Animation company, would often meet with him and discuss some of the problems they were having.

They alone were allowed within the cordoned off area.

The three would spend hours discussing something in the conference room, and Annette was regularly summoned to provide superb quality sustenance.

Viktor and Paul had come to know Arthur when their company had bought one of his early machines from his Central Coast shop several years ago. It had performed magnificently, but the requirements of their industry were changing. The demands of higher rendering speeds, better software, and better interface methods, were escalating at an exponential rate. Their goal, in common with most advanced Computer Graphic Imaging companies, was to make an animated feature film with photorealistic human CGI figures. That day was still in the future, and the more they learned about the difficulties in rendering lifelike human skin and features, the further into the future that day had receded.

Human beings know how to recognise their own species. A photorealistic CGI version of a human being had to mimic the real thing in the tiniest detail. That included the distortion of skin pores, the bulges in the face when the eyes moved, the small changes in skin shape when muscles tightened and relaxed.

Ironically, the closer the CGI practitioners approached photorealistic human figures, the more disturbingly off-putting the images became. It was as though a chasm had opened up between the image they had created and the one which worked. The 'Uncanny Valley' was the name those in the industry gave it. New Wave Reality were aiming to be the first CGI company to reach the other side. Viktor with his mate Paul were absolutely certain Arthur Barlow was the key to that goal.

Arthur, on the other hand, was in it for the money.

CHAPTER 9

James Naylor woke to the ringing of his alarm. He stretched, threw off his doona and staggered out of bed. All of twelve years old, the only child of Robin and Ruth, he was a good looking young lad, lean, athletic, blessed with a developing wisdom and the same Christian faith possessed by both his parents. He yawned, stared sleepily at the alarm clock, and made his way towards the bathroom. Another boring day at school, enduring Ms Bateman yakking on for ages about maths he could already do, then forty minutes of English he didn't want to. Life seemed so flat and repetitive at times. It was still Wednesday, two more days to go before the weekend when he could play soccer with his team then go riding with his Dad in the afternoon.

Last weekend they had ridden twelve kilometres, right down to Bobbin Head on the river in the Ku-ring-gai Chase National Park. Coasting downhill all the way had been very nice, and peddling back uphill had been very tiring.

He completed his toilet and headed to the kitchen for breakfast. Boring cereal, chosen carefully by his mother for its healthy nutrition and certainly not its taste. He came through the door, glanced at the breakfast table and stopped suddenly. A girl was sitting in his usual place at the table, finishing off a bowl of boring cereal, but she wasn't boring at all. She was wearing his clothes for starters. Her long hair was tied back in a ponytail. Her blue eyes were concentrating on her food, shovelling it in as though she hadn't had a decent meal for a long time. There was a certain wariness about the way she ate, like a gazelle at a waterhole, mindful of nearby predators. James' boyish heart was instantly fascinated. Who was she? Why was she here?

He cleared his throat. The girl nearly jumped off her chair. She stared wildly at him, then at the spilt cereal on the table.

"Sorry," James apologised. "Didn't mean to startle you. I'm James."

"I'm bloody annoyed," the girl snapped.

She went over to the sink, retrieved a cloth, and wiped up the mess on the table. Returning the cloth to the sink, she sat down to resume her interrupted meal.

"That's a funny name." James began to laugh quietly. He tried to stop because the stranger obviously wasn't enjoying the joke, but the grin on his face had a certain infectious quality.

The girl watching him gave a tiny smile as if she couldn't help herself. "Cherry. You frightened me," she said at length.

"Sorry. What are you doing here?"

"Eating breakfast, what do you think I'm doing?"

"I mean…"

"I know what you mean. I'm not your problem."

"Suppose I want you to be."

James was never quite sure why he said it. He had always associated with boys of his own age, never girls, yet there was something about this girl which intrigued him. Whatever it was, it was the antithesis of boredom. He fixed Cherry with eyes full of boyhood sincerity.

"Go to school," she ordered. "I can fix my own problems."

"Suppose I'd rather help you than go to school. What would I have to do?" James' eyes never left her face.

For the first time Cherry stared closely at the boy. She liked the look of him, and there was a certain sincerity, a genuine desire to help, an anticipation of excitement in his eyes which she found attractive. *Forget it*, she thought. He was stupid, that's why he didn't like school.

"You think I'm stupid, don't you?" James protested. "I tell you I want to help and you just think I'm stupid."

He had read her thoughts. *He's not so stupid after all*, she thought. *I guess I could do worse.* "I have to get my stuff out of hell," she said. "Sure you want to help?"

Being an attentive boy in church, James had a pretty fair idea what hell was all about, and the thought of getting anything out of it ran contrary to his theological understanding but not to his anticipation of adventure.

"Sure," he said, "how do we do it?"

"You got any money?" Cherry slid off her chair. "We'll need two train tickets. Finish your breakfast and make as though you're going to school. I'll slip out and meet you down the road a bit. Don't know my way around here. Have you got a spare pair of shoes? These slippers will get wrecked if I keep them on."

"They're in my room," James said. "Door's open, down the hall on the right. I'll have my breakfast now."

James spooned a generous amount of cereal into his bowl and added milk to match. Somehow it tasted great this morning.

Ruth came into the room to check progress. "Morning, darling," she laughed, giving James a hug. "Where's Cherry?"

"Gone to get some shoes out of my room," James answered. "Why is she here, Mum? Do you know her from somewhere?"

"I only met her last night." There was a sorrowful expression on his mother's face which James didn't miss. "She needed a place to stay, James, really needed one. A lot of bad things have happened to her, and, well, Dad and I felt we could help."

James nodded his head. It made sense, the startled gazelle thing. Fascinating. He shovelled cereal into his mouth as though he was running late for a train.

"You're enjoying your cereal, this morning, James," Ruth said surprised. "I didn't think you liked it very much."

"It's fine, Mum. Don't want to be late," James said through the latest mouthful.

In all of ten minutes he was heading out the door, his Mum's kiss on his cheek and his schoolbag on his back. Glancing up and down the street, he saw Cherry's arm stretch out from some shrubbery a couple of houses down then disappear. He made off in that direction. When he drew level with her, the arm reached out again and pulled him inside a Camellia bush.

"Steady on," he complained. "What'd you expect me to do? Squeeze through there?"

"No, come over here, where no one can see us." Cherry let go the arm. "Come on," she said impatiently. "You're getting cold feet, aren't you?"

"No," James protested. "I just don't like being dragged through Camellias, that's all. Now, what do we do?"

"We go by train to my aunt's place in Cabramatta," Cherry explained. "She'll have gone to work, probably, but Sam might still be home. If he is he'll try to get me. That's where you come in."

She produced a large kitchen knife from under her shirt.

"When he comes to do me I'll scream. You race in and ram this knife through his back while he's on the floor. Do it really hard until it comes out the other side, then do it again."

She demonstrated the ramming action, gripping the handle with both hands and slashing viciously downwards, narrowly missing her thigh. James stared at her in disbelief. What was she? Nutcase? Child assassin?

"You're scary," he said, firmly gripping the knife handle and trying to pull it gently out of her hand. "How about we just get him out of the house first?" He suggested. "Then you wouldn't get done and I wouldn't have to kill anyone. Sound like a good idea?"

Cherry wrinkled her forehead. Sweet reason began to break through the fierce hatred she felt for Blackman. The boy's proposal made some sense. Finally she relinquished the knife. James stuck it in the ground under the bush.

"All right," She grunted. "How do we do that?"

"I've got a mobile phone." James dug into his pocket and produced it. "I ring your house, tell this Sam character you were shoplifting for clothes in Wollongong and I got you away from the cops. Now you want to go home because you're starving and cold. It'll take him an hour at least to drive down there."

"Why would I want to go back and be done over every night?" She retorted.

"Because... because you've got nowhere else to go? Because... I don't know. You think of a better idea, one which doesn't involve rape and murder."

Cherry thought. "Give me the phone," she said, after a pause. "I can carry on a lot better. I like the Wollongong bit. I'll tell him unless he arrives with food and takes me to Amanda's – she's my old friend - I'll walk into the nearest police station and give them my nightie with his blood all over it."

"And that will help?" James asked, frowning. "He's hardly likely to believe that you'd hand stuff over to the police which would get you into trouble yourself."

"I gave my nightie to your Dad last night," Cherry answered. "He wanted to do some analysis on it. I think my loving Uncle Sam has been doing other awful things as well. Anyway, I bet that'll get him moving. Stop arguing and hand me the phone."

Cherry rang the number several times with no response. She rang it again when they were on the train. It took quite a long while to go from Turramurra where the Naylors lived to Cabramatta, which was quite okay with James. Cherry spent most of the journey telling him about her life. By the time they reached their destination he was glad he had decided to help her, and Cherry was glad too. She had told a boy – a stranger – all about her horrible life, and all he had done was hold her hand and sit silent beside her. Cherry had appreciated his silence as much as his willingness to stay.

They eventually came to the unit where it had all happened one long night before. Just to make sure, Cherry rang the number again, ready to dive back down the drive of the block next door if anyone answered. No one did. The battery in James' phone died, preventing further calls. Together they approached the front door. Cherry lifted the large fuchsia pot on the porch where the spare key was hidden. Before she could open the door, she heard Madge Beaumont bellowing from the window of her unit which was directly above theirs.

"That you, Cherry darl?" Madge's raucous voice floated down. "Glad you're okay. Where were you last night? You missed all the action this morning, thank heavens."

Cherry turned round and looked up. "What happened, Mrs. Beaumont?"

Madge stuck her head further out the window. "Well, I'm just gettin' meself a tea to wake up with, and I sees all these cop cars parkin' down the street a bit, not that I poke my nose into anybody's business, you understand."

"Of course, Mrs. Beaumont," Cherry agreed politely. "Please go on." Two pairs of eyes stared up at the woman.

"Well, three of them coppers comes over to your front door, and another three go round the back. Your aunt opens the door, they barge in and there's a lot of shoutin' and stuff goin' down. Next thing I hear some awful language comin' from round the back, and there's Sam Blackman being frogmarched along between two coppers. He's got a gash on his head, and so's the other copper. He's strugglin' like mad, and suddenly he gets the better of 'em. Knocks 'em both over. He makes a bolt for it, but them other coppers come peltin' out of the 'ouse and jumps him before he's got to the road. They put the cuffs on 'im and bundle 'im into a police car. He's swearing fit to make a sailor blush. Glad you weren't there to hear it."

"What happened to my Aunt?" The smile on Cherry's face said it all. The thought of Sam being knocked around by the police was the nicest one she'd had all morning.

"Your aunt comes out and talks to the cops. Very loud she is, complainin' they 'aint done nothin' wrong. They bundle her into a car too, but she comes back in a taxi an hour or so later and goes to work normal like. Guess that's where she is now. You're gonna be late for school, darl. Who's your little friend?"

"He's a boy from my school," Cherry lied quickly before James could add anything. "He's going to help me transport my artwork to class. It's very large. Come on, Frank, we're going to be late unless we get started." She pointed to the wheelie bins lined up in front of the unit. "Empty the yellow and the green ones out on the lawn. Hurry up."

Mrs. Beaumont pulled her head inside the window. James tipped the yellow bin upside down. Recyclable waste spilled all over the concrete. Grass clippings spilled out from the other one. He wheeled both in through the front door.

"Quick, inside the bedroom." Cherry pointed to a door and grabbed hold of the yellow wheelie bin.

James grabbed the other and followed her. He stared at the bloodstained sheets on the bed. "What happened in here?" He asked nervously.

"I stabbed Sam," Cherry answered, a note of triumph in her voice, "then I kicked him hard in the you-know-what's. Stop asking stupid questions. Open the lid of that bin. Now help me to shove all my clothes in. Have to have a soft place to put my desktop."

Clothes went in until the wheelie bin was three quarters full, then Cherry carefully carried her desktop PC over and settled it down on top of them.

"More clothes, then we put my monitor on top and pack it with underwear. Soft. Don't want it scratched. I'd better do that. Shouldn't be showing you all my private stuff. Go and shove all those books in the bottom of the other bin. Careful. Shove some more clothes down first. I don't want the books to get wet or dirty."

"What about all these clothes? They're pretty fancy." James pulled an armful out of the wardrobe.

"Couldn't care less," Cherry retorted. "Shove them in. Now the books, all of them. Then some more clothes, then shoes, then cover them with these rags."

"They're good nightdresses—"

"They're RAGS, okay?"

"With these rags. What then?"

"All the computer hardware from those draws over there. Come on, move."

The task was completed in less than half an hour. The bins had become very heavy. James wheeled them both out the door and into the lounge room.

"We're ready to go," he said anxiously, half expecting someone unfriendly to walk through the front door at any time.

"No we're not," Cherry contradicted. "Come into the kitchen."

Cherry ran back up the hall and dragged him into the kitchen by the arm. On the kitchen bench was a jar containing permanent marker pens. She snatched one out and handed it to James, taking another herself.

"We're going to write a message for my loving aunt," she hissed. "On the kitchen bench first."

Taking her marker in her hand she wrote in huge letters "I HATE YOU."

"Now," she ordered, turning to James, "you write it. You write it everywhere I tell you. I want my aunt to keep discovering it for months and months and months. I want her to remember. I want her to BURN." She shouted the last word.

James stood there with his mouth open. "It's none of my business," he protested, "but writing that won't make it any better for you or for her. Why don't we just go?"

"Write it!" Cherry screamed at him with such ferocity he thought she was going to hit him across the face. "Write it. That cookbook on the shelf. Pull it out. Pull it out!" she yelled. "Page fifty two, her favourite curry recipe, write it on that."

The next hour was spent writing those three words in every place Cherry dictated. They moved from the kitchen into her aunt's bedroom, from the bedroom into the bathroom, then the lounge room. Most books on the shelves, and several magazines in the rack got the treatment until their markers had all but run out.

James, who was feeling increasingly uncomfortable, tried once again to bring the girl to reason. "Come on, Cherry," he implored. "We've written it enough. What happens if your aunt comes home early? We're stuffed. I'd hate to arrive back home in a police car. Dad would kill me."

"One more thing." Cherry headed back into the kitchen. "Up there in the top cupboard over the bench is her special dinner service. I want to break every plate."

"Forget it," James protested loudly. "You can't get up there. She must have used some steps. Forget it."

"No!" Cherry shouted.

Cherry dragged a kitchen stool over towards the bench and lifted it on top. Jumping onto the bench like a girl possessed, she climbed onto the stool, leant over, and opened the top cupboard.

"Told you I could. Now go and push the bins right up to the front door. We'll be leaving in a minute."

James was relieved to hear it. He wiped his marker pen on his handkerchief to remove tell-tale fingerprints, threw it in the kitchen tidy, and headed down the hall to shift the bins out of the lounge room where they had left them. He was just about to pull them towards the front door when there was a scream from the kitchen, followed by a smashing sound.

He raced back along the hallway to see what had happened.

On one side of the kitchen bench lay the overturned stool, and on the other lay Cherry. She had fallen on top of a drinking glass which had shattered. A large shard was protruding from her shoulder. James arrived just in time to see her slip off the bench and land on the floor, dazed and bruised. She struggled to sit up, noticed the shard, and pulled it out of her arm.

Suddenly there was blood everywhere.

Cherry took one look at the bright red stream gushing down her arm, and passed out with a soft groaning noise. James stared at the mess. Here he was, two wheelie bins of stolen goods next to the door, and an unconscious girl bleeding to death on the kitchen floor. He remembered wishing for some excitement in his life. Well, he'd had enough in one day to last him quite a while, thank you.

James was a capable and sensible lad for his young age. First stop the bleeding, he thought. He pulled a tea towel from the rail and pressed it against the wound in Cherry's arm. The blood kept flowing, making an ever increasing red stain. He abandoned the tea towel and searched around until he found a cupboard marked 'medicines'. Inside was a box of adhesive plasters. Racing back to Cherry, he pinched the sides of the wound together and held them that way with a plaster. It took three to stop the bleeding. He rummaged around until he had found a larger adhesive pad, squirted some antiseptic on it from a tube, and stuck it over the wound and the plasters. Now to clean her up a bit. He took the tea towel, rinsed it in the sink and set to work. Cherry had still not recovered consciousness. Things were becoming serious. Sitting down on the floor, he pulled the girl upright and let her sag against his shoulder. He thought of slapping her face, or shaking her. Just then she gave a little moan and snuggled her head into his neck. Another moan and she threw up all over him.

James jumped to his feet in protest. "For goodness sake. Did you have to?"

"Sorry." Cherry laid her head back against the bench cupboard and shut her eyes. "It's the sight of blood, it does something to my head." She felt her shoulder, averting her eyes. "Has it stopped bleeding?"

"Yes it has," James said urgently. "Are you ready to go now?" He took off his school shirt and threw it into the sink, turning on the tap hard. The rest of the vomit had landed on the floor. Well, it could stay there. He squeezed his shirt out with his hands and put it on. "Ready?"

"Please give me a minute," Cherry begged. "Help me up. I feel shaky." She stretched out her arm, and James pulled her slowly to her feet, only to have her drop her head on his shoulder and wrap her arms around him. "Please don't move for a bit. It's all spinning. Can you put your arms around me? That's better."

For the first time in his young life, James was holding a girl in his arms, a girl who needed him. Something deep inside him was slowly waking up, though he was hardly aware of it. All he knew is he wanted her to stay there, and hoped sometime in the future she would let him hold her again. A good five minutes passed before the girl pushed herself gently away.

"I'm all right now," she said softly. "Let's get out of here." She glanced back carefully at the mess of blood and vomit on the floor. "It sort of blends together, doesn't it? Leave it. I want my aunt to see it like that."

They went down the hall, grabbed hold of the wheelie bins, and dragged them out the front door. Cherry replaced the key under the pot, and they began walking slowly back to the train station. It took quite a bit of effort just to wheel the heavy bins up the hill, and even more to get them up the platform steps and onto the train. All through the journey other passengers stared at them in an unfriendly manner, which James thought completely understandable. Two kids carrying two wheelie bins full of goodness knows what, one with traces of vomit all over his shirt, the other with a large pad on her arm through which blood was visible. It was three in the afternoon when they finally returned to the Naylor's house in Eastern Road Turramurra.

"Let's go round the back," James suggested quietly, "then we can park these in the shed for a bit until I find the right time to—"

Striding out to meet them, his face like thunder, was Robin Naylor.

"Where have you two been?" He shouted. "What gives you the right to absent yourself from school, without permission from your mother or me?"

James had never heard such anger in his father's voice before. More was to follow.

"What's in those bins?" he roared. "James, what have you done?"

"We went to Cherry's place to get her things, Dad," James stammered.

"She never wants to go back there. There was an accident and she cut her shoulder. I stuck some stuff over it. I'm sorry. It was all my idea. Cherry tried to stop me. I'm really sorry. I did a dumb thing."

"Know why I'm home James?" His father thundered. "I've got half the police in this district searching for you both. So you went to Cherry's home? I've had Blackman arrested for multiple instances of child sex abuse and receiving stolen goods. He's got a garage full of them, and lots of nasty friends. They could easily have come back to the house to grab goods which might incriminate them. These men don't rape little girls, they kill them. You put this young woman and yourself in deadly danger. How does that make you feel?"

James hung his head, tears were very close. He had never thought ...

All of a sudden Cherry blurted out. "Mr. Naylor, James is lying to protect me. It was all my idea. I did my girl thing on him and made him come. If it wasn't for him I'd still be there bleeding all over the floor. I think he saved my life. If you want to blame someone, blame me. I'm a mess. I cause trouble wherever I go." Silent tears were flowing down her face, and watching them James felt pain in his own heart.

"Dad, she didn't do a thing to me," James protested nervously. "I wanted an adventure and I wanted to help. I did the wrong thing. I should have asked. I'm really sorry, Dad. I stuffed up."

It was some time before Robin Naylor replied. His eyes moved from one child to the other, his son, his head hung down, tears peeping around his eyes, and the girl, tears flowing down her cheeks. It struck him with some force that each child had been willing to take the blame for the other, although he had no doubt each of them were equally responsible. A bond had formed between them, and in such a short time. Perhaps even they were not aware of it. Thank God they were safe, oh yes, thank God.

He gave a long sigh. "Son, I forgive you, but because you have done a dangerous thing and bypassed your parents, I have to punish you. For the next three weeks you will not be going to soccer on Saturday mornings. I know this will mean you'll miss out on the Cup Final. Instead you'll do extra homework. Cherry will do it with you. Now come inside and say sorry to your mother. She's been out of her mind with worry since the school rang."

"Yes, Dad." There was nothing else to say. Both children followed Robin as he went back towards the house.

Saying sorry to his mother was far worse. Ruth Naylor burst into tears at the sight of her son, ran over and wrapped her arms around him. He said "sorry Mum" over and over again, but he wasn't sure she even heard him.

Cherry stood afar off watching, her heart beating furiously. Here was a woman who loved her son, like... like... Tears flooded down her face. How she craved to be loved, and there was nobody. There never would be.

Ruth looked up. She saw Cherry standing there alone, and whether it was the working of the Spirit of God in her heart, or simply a mother's wise intuition, she suddenly knew exactly what was passing through the mind of the young girl. Relinquishing her son, she came slowly towards the child, knelt at a short distance, and opened her arms. For a full five seconds nothing happened. Cherry stared at the woman in disbelief, then she launched. Ruth thought she was going over backwards. Cherry clung to her like the last tree trunk in a tidal wave. At first she was silent, then she began to howl, not cry, a terrible sound coming from the mouth of one so young. Robin watched from the doorway, his face deep with worry, as little by little Ruth calmed her down. It took a long time. Not a word had been spoken by either of them, yet a bond of love had begun to form, a bond which would endure the pain of separation, and one day become the lifeline of grace which would change Cherry's life forever.

CHAPTER 10

Max Velban drew the white napkin from his lap, wiped the last traces of raspberry mousse from his mouth, and surveyed his prospective patrons with a wary eye. The significant remains of uneaten food returning to the kitchen, told him that meal had failed to achieve the standard of excellence required to lubricate them out of their cash. He felt like drowning the chef in his own inedible gravy, or forcing him to consume all the uneaten portions at gunpoint. The wine, which he had chosen for its particularly high alcohol content, had been confused with some other variety which a child could have drunk until they threw up without the slightest risk of becoming inebriated. All in all a disaster in the making.

This was the first fund raising dinner the Australian Society for Artificial Intelligence had hosted. They weren't bankrupt, but the cost of research over the last six months had exceeded the society's income for that period, and so drastic steps had to be taken. He had argued strongly against the very method he was currently engaged in. The general public were fickle. Perhaps they assumed the task of making a computer so user friendly a child could play with it, was child's play itself. All the hard work and long hours put in by dedicated programmers, psychologists and mathematicians was completely invisible – and meaningless - to the end user.

On the other hand, he mused, we've hoisted ourselves on our own petard. We've managed to make modern computers so seemingly cooperative and intelligent, the general public assumed the machines could design themselves without any assistance whatsoever. Recent movies had no doubt played a role in this unreasonable delusion, and ironically made a lot more money in the process than the computer programmers ever did.

He dragged himself to his feet, walked deliberately towards the microphone some distance away on a slightly raised dais, and turned it on. A deafening screech of feedback gained the attention of the dissatisfied diners in the worst possible manner. He glared at the waiter who hastened to remedy the problem, while the guests covered their ears and vociferously filled the room with complaint. The squealing stopped. The guests unplugged their ears and swivelled round in their chairs, whether to listen to him or hurl the remains of their desert was not immediately apparent.

"Ladies and gentlemen," he began, clearing his throat and poised to duck flying objects, "welcome to this special benefit evening. Allow me to introduce myself, Professor Max Velban, society president. This evening, apart from a brief introduction, I would invite you to ask questions from the floor. I will do my best to answer them." He smiled warmly at the sadly sober audience. "You may think Artificial Intelligence is all about creating machines which think like people, but a great part of our work has to do with sponsoring efforts to make computers easier to use."

He paused. There was utterly no response.

"You will admit there have been massive advances in this direction over the past ten years," he continued. "Think about the things we take for granted today, phones which respond to the human voice, games which can read body position, cameras which can recognise human faces."

He paused again. Still no reaction from the audience.

"There are devices for the disabled which can respond to hand movements and enable them to communicate with others," he said, moving his hands around in front of him.

"These machines could be regarded as intelligent in the tasks they perform. One day a machine may be able to replicate every aspect of human intelligence, so much so it will be hard to tell the difference. Sir, you have a question?"

A gentleman sitting on one of the tables closest to the dais had raised his hand. "Leonard Ballard, CEO of Breakwater Systems. Why are we trying to make machines as intelligent as human beings? Most human beings I've met are just plain stupid."

A titter of laughter ran through the diners.

Ballard frowned heavily. "An aeronautical engineer doesn't try to make planes fly like galahs so exactly they can fool other galahs. Why aren't we trying to make a machine which can outperform human intelligence? In which case, why do they have to be like human beings at all?"

"A good point," Velban replied, smiling at the speaker. "It's a question of our current technology. At present we're unable to make a machine which is even capable of human intelligence, let alone strive for something which surpasses it."

"How would you know if a computer has human intelligence in the first place?" Another guest, on a table a little further back had raised their hand.

"Well," Velban replied, warming to his subject, "there's a famous test called the Turing test. Suppose you're sitting in front of two monitors, one connected to a human being, the other to a computer. You can type any question you wish on a keyboard in front of you. If you can't tell which is the computer and which is the human being by the way they answer you, the computer is effectively intelligent."

"Does that mean a computer can become self-conscious? Surely not."

A woman at another table, power dressed in a cream leather suit had spoken. Max smiled at her. The discussion was warming up, and he had hardly said a word.

"That's a much more difficult concept, ma'am," he replied. "Self-consciousness may or may not be an essential element of intelligence at all. For example, in nineteen ninety seven a computer called Deep Blue beat the current world chess champion Garry Kasparov."

Velban lifted the microphone which was slowly sinking down towards the floor and tightened the knob around its stem. "Using the Turing test and restricting the questions to chess, we could say the computer was intelligent. It's quite another matter to argue whether Deep Blue was aware of the significance of the chess moves it was making, or indeed whether it understood anything other than the programmed instructions it was executing during the game."

"But doesn't that mean we will never be able to make a machine which is self-aware like a human being?" The same woman was standing on her feet, an almost empty wine glass in her hand. Max began to revise his opinion of the vintage.

"Not at all," he replied, smiling. "Reason is really nothing but reckoning, so self-awareness presumably derives from complex calculations."

He paused to let that statement sink in. It was clear from the expression on the woman's face it hadn't got past her ears. "After all," he continued regardless, "what is the human brain in any case? Simply a fantastic computational neural network, capable of enormous processing power, even more remarkable since it accomplishes this feat with only chemical reactions of great complexity and speed."

He paused again, took out his handkerchief and wiped his brow. "Since around nineteen ninety six computer system memory has increased by a factor of ten every four years. If that trend continues at its present rate, we will have reached the memory capacity of the human brain by the year two thousand and twenty nine."

The woman laughed, took a last drink from her glass. "The same year Skynet became self-aware in the Terminator movies." She giggled. "Aren't you worried something like that could occur? Machines become intelligent like us and start acting like us, telling lies, taking over, killing us like we kill one another. That'd be scary, hey?" She sat down a little unsteadily.

Before Max could reply another gentleman raised his hand. Velban nodded in his direction, unwilling to enlarge on the woman's last remark. Pessimism never opened pockets.

"Professor Velban, wouldn't a so-called intelligent robot always be programmed to maximise the effectiveness of its actions? Wouldn't that guarantee it would always try to please? Be selfless? It could hardly achieve its programmed goals if it was unfriendly. I suppose you could even interpret such selfless cooperation as love."

The previous woman turned towards the speaker. "Is that what you call it? You inject a girl with something so she does everything you want, maximises her new program goals, and you call that love? I'd call it sexual slavery. I know your type, always—"

"I think there are good grounds for optimism," Max interposed hastily, "and I would certainly hope any future robot design would ensure antisocial behaviour was impossible. I would remind you, ladies and gentlemen, we are nowhere near the point of constructing these sorts of machines, and unless societies which promote such research – like this one - receive sufficient financial support, that day may never arrive. I'll take one further question."

He scanned the room for a benign face. "The gentleman towards the back has had his hand up for a long time. Sir, you wished to say?"

The man rose to his feet. "Doesn't all this talk about machines becoming as intelligent as human beings presuppose human beings are simply machines of some kind? We have minds, not computers."

Once again there was a murmur of approval from the diners. The woman who had last spoken raised her glass in mock toast. The speaker continued. "*Brains* cause minds, silicon based processors do not. We're trying to compare apples with bananas. They may both be fruit, but they are fundamentally different."

"Surely you're not suggesting we've got a soul or something?" Another woman interjected. She was dressed in a particularly low cut black evening dress. She pushed her dining companion's restraining hand away from her arm with an angry gesture. "What do you mean by brains cause minds but computer processors can't?"

The gentleman towards the back answered in a carefully levelled tone. "I mean there's more to the human mind than a biochemically based neural network. Human beings are more than machines. We have a spirit which somehow enables us to make judgements, not just decisions. I can't see emotions such as love and delight, fear and even hatred reduced to a set of mathematical equations. There's something about a human brain which makes it unique, and any attempt to turn it into some giant computer diminishes it irreparably in my view."

"For goodness sake," the woman retorted, "just because we don't know the equations which result in something we call love or whatever, doesn't mean they don't exist. They're probably all related to our built-in evolutionary need to breed."

The expression on her companion's face made it clear to everyone that any thought of attempted breeding was the last thing on his mind. The gentleman towards the back continued.

"So, in your view we are simply machines, is that it? Products of an evolutionary process driven solely by pure chance? Then how can you object when a stronger machine overcomes a weaker, when a woman is raped, a child is assaulted, one man kills another? I know it's fashionable to bleat survival of the fittest, but when push comes to shove nobody is very happy with the world it produces."

The woman in the revealing black dress sprang up from her chair. Her companion grabbed her arm and pulled her back into it. She turned round and swiped him across the face. A hubbub of voices was beginning to rise from the diners. Max could see he had better do something before the entire room polarised into contributors and those who would love to see ASAI go bankrupt. It was always the same, allow metaphysics into the equation and the next minute you're up to your neck in moral dilemmas. No, nip it in the bud, make both sides happy. He cleared his throat.

"I willingly admit there is much about the human brain we do not understand. I'm not denying the existence of the soul or spirit or whatever you want to call it, please don't get me wrong. Perhaps we could put it this way. When we give birth to another human being, or construct a machine of sufficient intelligence, we are simply providing mansions in which a spirit or soul can live."

He paused again, smiling appreciatively at his audience. "However unless we are able to acquire sufficient funds, those working on the forefront of this field will be denied the financial encouragement to pursue their research."

Back on track, Max thought to himself. He had stimulated interest. Now was the time to convince them how personally indispensable they were, how valuable each contribution would be, no matter how small. Larger contributions would, of course, enable Australia to remain in the forefront of the game. He hoped his audience were well-healed as well as patriotic. With a tiny wink and a huge smile towards the woman in the black dress, he began his well-rehearsed spiel. When he had finished he would saunter casually over to her table and engage her in consoling conversation. Might even end up with her name and phone number.

The evening, despite its culinary shortcomings, was a modest success. In the taxi on the way home Max made some quick calculations and figured, less the catering costs, and the promises of cash which would never actually materialise, he had managed to accumulate a grand total of fifty four thousand, one hundred and thirty dollars, a name and a phone number. Not bad for one evening's work.

CHAPTER 11

In accordance with his father's punishment, James Naylor spent the next three Saturdays doing his homework with Cherry instead of going to soccer training. He missed out on the Cup Final, but his team won anyway, and sad to say James had become so preoccupied with the girl he wouldn't have cared if they'd lost. The punishment had somehow become a blessing. His initial fascination was changing into affection and boyish delight, even though his ego was regularly flattened by her prowess in mathematics and computing.

He had to do an assignment on whales. Cherry wrote a routine which searched the internet on the subject, downloaded relevant recent data from educational institutions and compiled it into one long essay, even putting his name on the top. Thirty pages rolled off the printer.

"Now we can play Scrabble," she said. "Come on, you don't have to read it. No one else will."

James swallowed another chunk of his pride and went to fetch the Scrabble board. So she was clever, well, he could admire that, and he still won at Scrabble at least half the time.

Little by little Cherry began to change in her own right. At first she would spend long hours by herself in the spare bedroom, which she had turned into a chaos of programming manuals, bits of hardware, notes, and exercise books mixed up with items of clothing. Creativity thrived in chaos, or Cherry's creativity did. Ruth would occasionally suggest a tidy up, and the girl would respond obediently, but in a day or so the chaos would return. Little by little the hours spent in digital solitude gave way to time spent with people, mostly James, then Ruth, then mostly Ruth.

After a couple of weeks she began attending Turramurra Primary School. She kept to herself at lunchtime, but would let James walk home with her provided nobody was watching. When they reached their front gate she would run into the house and find Ruth. The two would go into the kitchen and drink Cocoa while James went into his room to do his homework. He would come out an hour later and find them still talking to one another, sometimes right up until tea time when Cherry would help get things ready for dinner. James had the wisdom to recognise these times were very important to the girl and made no complaint, although he missed having her around to talk to. At first she hardly spoke during the evening meal, especially to Robin whom she always seemed a little afraid of. This had been improving of late, and just the other evening she had told a funny story and laughed at her own joke.

Cherry had forbidden anyone except Ruth to go into her room at bedtime, but she would knock on James' bedroom door and say 'goodnight' from the doorway. Such an occasion had precipitated their first and only argument. Before he went to sleep James would read his Bible. He was using a little booklet which set down a passage every day. Cherry opened the door before he had finished.

"What are you reading?" She said, coming over to the bed to see.

"My Bible. Want me to read it to you?" James lowered the Bible onto his bed.

"Are you kidding? No."

"Have you ever read it?" James noticed fire kindle in Cherry's eyes.

"Yes," Cherry said angrily.

"I had one of my own. Do you know what I did with it? I shredded it into tiny little pieces, all over the floor. I left them there for days so I could trample all over them, then I vacuumed them up and burnt them in the incinerator."

James stared at the girl, protectively covering his Bible with bedclothes at the same time.

"Are you nuts? Why?"

He was sorry he said it.

Cherry exploded into a screaming monologue. "Because it's a load of rubbish, nonsense. You read that, you'll poison your mind. I hate it, hate it, hate it! There's no God, and if there is He hates me, so I hate Him."

She stood there clenching her fists, her eyes blazing with wrath. James had the sense to realise he had triggered something horrible in her past, but how it could be associated with God's Word completely baffled him.

"You're wrong," he said, trying to keep the defensive tone out of his voice. "It's all about following Jesus, you know—"

"If you want us to be friends," Cherry snapped viciously, "you'll never talk about it again. You think I don't mean it?"

The expression on her face left no room for doubt. James answered quietly.

"I don't understand you. Can't you see it was God who rescued you, brought you into our family? Can't—"

Cherry swore, and turning on her heel strode out of the room slamming the door behind her. It was days before she would speak another word to him.

The weeks went by, and apart from this unfortunate incident the two children lived amicably with one another. Any stranger to the Naylor home might have guessed they were brother and sister. For the first time in her life since her parents died, Cherry was beginning to feel she had a family. Little by little her damaged spirit was beginning to heal, and with it the natural warmth and joy which should fill a young girl's heart occasionally shone through the clouds, giving hope that one day the sun would come out to stay.

Then one terrible evening the gavel fell. After dinner, Robin asked everyone to come into the lounge room, because he had something to say. There was an expression on his face which dispelled any thought the news could be good. Ruth sat next to Cherry, her face heavy with the same expression, James in another chair opposite, his heart gripped by a foreboding for which he had no name. His father spoke.

Robin cleared his throat. "Three weeks ago Ruth and I applied to adopt Cherry."

He saw the child's eyes light up with joy and winced.

"Yesterday we heard our application had been rejected by DSS. They believe we're too old, and when I asked if we could be her foster parents instead, we were told the same criterion would apply. In short, there is no way Cherry can remain with our family."

The light faded from Cherry's face. She sat on the lounge as if turned to stone, her face visibly white, her eyes staring in shock. Ruth was crying silently. Robin went on.

"I'm afraid there's more. It appears DSS have chosen a foster family for Cherry, one in which they feel she will be able to grow up and recover from what has happened in the past. I asked them if we could take on the roles of uncle, aunt and cousin, but they have strongly advised against it and refused to give me any information as to where Cherry would be living. They believe it would be detrimental to the process of her settling in to her new permanent home. They have forbidden us to contact her in any way at all."

He gave a long, sad sigh. "I've tried everything I know to change this decision, to no avail." He turned his sorrowful eyes toward the girl. "They're going to come on Friday and take you to your new home. Cherry, I'm so sorry. I did my best to keep you. We all love you, we want you to stay. I... tried, I really tried."

Ruth put her arm round the girl. There was no response. Cherry sat rigid in shock, her eyes seeming to grey over, bereft of tears. For a long time she just sat there, saying nothing, then without a word of explanation left and went into her room, closing the door softly behind her. Eventually Ruth stood and came down the hall to Cherry's room, knocked on the door. There was no response. She hesitated then went in. Cherry was sitting at her desk, her computer springing into life.

"Cherry, darling, I'm so, so sorry. I…" Ruth was in tears.

"I'm all right," Cherry answered mechanically. "I've got work to do."

The child never even turned her head, and the tone of her voice left Ruth in no doubt further words would avail nothing. She left the room and returned several hours later to say 'goodnight', but Cherry was already in bed and the light out. She shut the door quietly, worried and very upset.

It was without doubt the worst week the Naylor family had ever experienced. Cherry walked around the house like a zombie, all the light and joy drained permanently out of her eyes. She spoke in monosyllables and hardly ate a thing. Every time Ruth saw her she wanted to cry, and often had to go out of the room for a short while to regain her composure. Her mood oscillated from grief to fury. If she ever got her hands on the incompetent little gatekeeper responsible this horrendously destructive decision she would throttle the life out of them.

James walked around with a broken heart, his pain beyond the expression available to a young boy. Several times he had flung his arms around Cherry as a physical expression of the feelings in his heart. She had never once responded, standing rigid and silent within his embrace until he felt so awkward he had released her and gone away even more despondent.

The terrible day came. All Cherry's things had been packed into crates lined up at the front door. James came into her empty room and found her standing in the middle of the floor staring at nothing. Every part of him wanted to hold her in his arms, yet he knew she had passed beyond all such affection. Nonetheless, he would not let her go without saying the words which burned like fire in his heart.

"I don't care where they take you," he stammered. "I'm going to find you. I'm going to search everywhere and—"

"Don't." Cherry came to life for a second. She turned towards James, her eyes bright, her lips set in a thin line. "Don't. When I leave this house I'm going to forget you. All of you. A week in my new place and I won't even remember your name. Do yourself a favour and forget me."

"No," James protested. "I'll never forget you. Why do you want to forget me? Haven't we—"

"Get out of my way," Cherry shouted into his face. She pushed past him roughly, and disappeared through the doorway. A van drew up outside the house, a woman alighted and came towards the front door, rang the bell. Cherry answered it.

"Hello," the DSS lady greeted her, smiling broadly. "Are you Cherry Graham? Well, I've come to take you to your lovely new home. You're such a lucky girl. Are those things all yours?"

Cherry glared at her in silence, picked up the nearest crate and began to carry it out to the van. The DSS lady stared after her. *What a strange child,* she thought, *incapable of normal social interaction, autistic to some degree maybe.* She would add that to her notes when she got back to the office.

It didn't take long to load the van. Cherry went back inside to go to the bathroom prior to the journey. She passed Ruth in the lounge room, attended to her toilet and returned. Ruth stood in the hallway. The expression on her face made Cherry stop in her tracks.

"Cherry," Ruth said softly, struggling to keep her voice steady, "if you ever manage to find your way back, I'll be here to love you."

The girl paused for a second in silence, then without a word walked out the front door and into the van, without even turning to say 'goodbye' to Robin and James who were standing next to the path. The van drove away. Cherry was gone. James and Robin turned back into the house.

"I'll find you," James muttered through his angry tears. "One day I'll find you, and I'll bring you back. I swear I will." He pressed his lips hard together, ran into his room and slammed the door. Burying his face in the pillow he sobbed his heart out for a long, long time.

CHAPTER 12

The journey to her new home was a long one, all the way from Turramurra to Bringelly in the countryside south of Sydney. The house was massive, set on what must have been many acres of rolling pastureland. A windmill turned slowly next to a large water tank on top of a tower, and horses grazed on the grass beyond the house. Cattle were lying down in the shade of some trees in a paddock to the left, and sheep pulled at the lush grass in another to the right. The van drove up the long drive bordered on either side by flowering shrubs, and came to rest on a wide pebbled area outside the front door. Two adults were standing there to meet them. Cherry stepped out of the back and crunched on the pebbles towards them.

The man came forward with his hand outstretched. "Cherry, welcome to Mulbring Hill," he said warmly. "My name is Martin Frobisher. You may call me Martin." He turned slightly towards the woman behind him. "This is my wife Helen."

Helen stretched out her hand as well. "Welcome, Cherry. We hope you will be very happy here with us."

Cherry shook her hand mechanically, and gave a smile which never reached her eyes.

She followed Helen and Martin into the house, enjoyed a long drink of lemonade, then helped to carry all her things from the van into her new bedroom. It was much larger than before. Long French windows with plantation shutters opened out onto the fields. The DSS lady vanished without another word. Helen helped Cherry put her clothes away, and had a little chat about the rules of the house. There weren't many of them, and they all seemed very reasonable.

"You're very quiet, dear," she said cheerfully. "DSS told us you've had quite a difficult time. If there's anything I can help you with, you will talk to me about it, won't you?"

"Yes," Cherry answered woodenly, searching for a power point to plug her desktop into. "Do you have wireless internet available here?"

"I don't think so." Helen frowned. "The house is wired with cable which sounds like the name of some animal, I can't remember what. There's a point behind the curtain near the floor over there. We're on the National Broadband. Very useful, or at least Martin thinks so." She saw Cherry's eyes light up. "You know much about computers, dear?"

"Yes. It's called CAT five cable. I can see the wall plug now. Thank you. Do you mind if I connect into it? You don't? Thank you."

Helen left the room, more than a little concerned. Cherry set up her machine and browsed around her new digital environment with obvious satisfaction. Yes, this was a nice place to stay, and the Frobishers seemed kind people, but she would never let them catch a glimpse of her heart. Sitting quietly on her bed, she reflected on the lessons her eleven years had taught her. God, if He existed, was a sadistic fiend, ripping every good thing out of her life, waiting only until she had come to love it before he snatched it away.

He had snatched away her innocence, too.

Instead of learning about sex in its proper place and time, beautified and protected within the boundaries of a loving relationship, it had been shoved prematurely into her face mixed with violence, depravity and threat, a self-centred pleasure only to be enjoyed at the expense of decency. Well, now she knew. Could innocence ever be restored? No, it had gone forever. Perhaps there was something about her which attracted such perversion. What could it be? How did they know she was like that?

Then and there she made herself a solemn promise. She would dedicate her life to destroying them, the men who sacrificed the innocence of children on the altar of their despicable lust. She would be merciless. She stared out the French window at the solitary horse standing in the paddock.

Yes, she thought, *and I will always be alone.*

❋ ❋ ❋

For the next seven years Cherry lived with the Frobishers and various other foster children who came and went. They were kind people, and no doubt would have come to love their long standing foster child, had the girl allowed it. Cherry refused any affection and gave none. Always polite, responsible and distant, she was content to remain within her own world, and placed little demand on anyone else's. She attended Innaburra High School in the Southern Highlands, and in year twelve topped the school in Mathematics and Physics. She came third in Chemistry, and managed an excellent pass in English only because she was clever, not because she did any study for the subject she hated.

On the weekends she would work in a computer store in Macarthur Square at Campbelltown. By the time she finished school she had earned enough money to move to student accommodation not far from Sydney University, where she elected to study Mathematics and Computer Science.

In the space of those seven years the little girl had grown into a very beautiful young woman, much sought after by the young men in her later high school years. Not one of them managed to take her for coffee, let alone a date. Among the wider on-line community of computer geeks it was another story. Cherry Charlie – as she called herself – was greatly respected and well known. Even Arthur Barlow, who continued to help her through some of her more challenging problems, had given her the occasional compliment, something unheard of. On receipt of such praise

Cherry had danced around the room for joy. Arthur was her mentor, the one she respected, but even then she had no desire to meet him in the flesh.

❄ ❄ ❄

In the third year of her degree, Cherry received a letter from the lawyer entrusted with the endowment from her parents. 'Would Ms. Graham please come and see Mr. John Lockhart, Suite seven, one hundred and eighty six Macquarie Street Sydney'.

Ms. Graham walked up two flights of stairs, and knocked on the polished wooden door bearing Lockhart's name in black-edged gilt letters. She was ushered into a plush office decorated with old style furniture. Behind a large mahogany desk sat a middle aged gentleman, who rose to his feet and shook her hand in a patronising sort of way.

"Ms. Graham, thank you for coming," he intoned. "Please sit down. I'm acting as administrator of the trust which the court established from your parents' estate. According to the terms of that trust, the balance less the cost of your education and care reverted to you in your twenty first year."

"So I heard," Cherry replied, frowning. "How much? My parents wanted me to have it all, as my foul aunt knew."

Mr. Lockhart shifted slightly in his chair. He smiled at the young woman sitting on the other side of his desk with the practiced leer of a lawyer who regularly dispensed bad news and always managed to benefit from it. "Well, that's just it, Ms. Graham," he said smoothly, "it would appear the capital has been totally depleted by your educational expenses."

Fire kindled in Cherry's eyes. "Explain."

"The court established a trust account on your behalf which your aunt could access to pay for your educational expenses—"

"My aunt never paid a cent towards my educational expenses," Cherry snapped, "unless you count buying me nightgowns so I could learn what it was like to be raped."

Mr. Lockhart paused. This was not a response he had anticipated. He straightened some papers on his desk and regained his legal composure. "That may be the case," he gave her another legal smile, "but I'm afraid the account is completely devoid of funds. The last withdrawal, the sum of twenty three thousand dollars fifty two cents, was made less than a year ago. I take it this did not go towards your education or wellbeing?"

"Why did you allow it?" Cherry demanded. "My aunt has embezzled my estate and you damn well know it. Where is she?" There was a look of pure murder in her eyes.

"Err... I'm afraid we don't know." Lockhart stammered, watching Cherry's face with some concern for his immediate safety.

"What?" Cherry exploded. Thrusting her chair out backwards, she stood up and leant over towards Mr. Lockhart in a most unfriendly manner, her hands splayed out on his desk, her arms straight.

"Is this what you've brought me here to tell me?" She shouted. "My aunt has embezzled a million or so dollars out of my estate, the estate you were in charge of, and you don't even know where she is?"

"Ms. Graham," Lockhart replied sharply, struggling to regain his air of legal superiority. "This office has no jurisdiction to maintain records on your aunt's whereabouts." He straightened a pen on his desk. "You could attempt recovery through the courts, and I would be happy to act on your behalf, but I'm afraid it would cost you quite a large sum." His patronising smile returned. "In the end there is no guarantee of a good outcome. My costs could well amount to more than the sum you recover. I can assure you there is no legal redress against this office, and you would be unwise to attempt such an action in any court."

John Lockhart felt himself relaxing, as much as a lawyer can relax when a young woman with fire in her eyes was nearly standing over him. The law was always on his side, he made sure of that.

He might have known the law, but he didn't know Cherry Graham.

"Is that computer over there connected to the internet, or is it just for show?" Cherry barked, pointing over Lockhart's shoulder.

"I beg your pardon?" Lockhart asked, pushing backwards to get further away from the arm. "That machine is for my personal use only. Of course it's – hey, what are you doing?"

"Get out of my way." Cherry barged round the desk towards the machine. John Lockhart made an attempt to stop her and found himself pushed aside with such force he almost fell backwards out of his own chair. The woman was out of control. He reached for the phone to call security.

"Don't." Cherry's arm shot out and grabbed the instrument. "Shut up and sit down while someone else does your job, and stop behaving like the fool you are."

Ignoring the stream of threatening legalese spouting from the mouth of one John Lockhart, Cherry sat herself down in front of the machine and brought up internet webmail.

"What are you doing?" The stream of legalese succumbed momentarily to curiosity.

"I'm seeing if my aunt kept her email account. She was stupid with computers, so she might have."

In the rectangle headed "username" she typed 'jodiesexangel1659' password 'gloriousafterglow'. In a second or two the screen was filled with a list of files from her aunt's inbox. Cherry scanned down the list.

"You've got a printer attached to this? Make sure it's got a lot of paper. Go on, move," she commanded.

Mr. Lockhart moved towards the printer as though someone had hypnotised him. Sheets of paper began to spill out into the tray. Cherry opened every folder on her aunt's email account and printed a great many emails, making sure she marked all those she had opened from her inbox as 'unread' so her aunt wouldn't be alerted to her presence.

Jumping up from the chair, she took the pile of paper from Lockhart's hand and began to sift through it, placing the emails into different piles on his large mahogany desk until it was covered. Next she went back to the computer and began to do things Lockhart had never seen before. More paper spewed out of the printer. Cherry took several of these sheets, came back to the desk and picked up the phone.

Lockhart made a final bid for mastery. "That's my private phone," he protested lamely. "Please put it down. Who are you calling?"

"The police," Cherry snapped at him.

"I beg your pardon?" The last vestige of legal superiority drained from Lockhart's face. A young woman he had tried to belittle with legalese had taken over his office, his computer, his life. What a tour de force. He had never seen the like. He picked up the fallen chair and sat down on it.

"Why do we need the police?"

"Because my wonderful Aunt has been engaged in procuring young girls for prostitution, laundering money, oh, and embezzlement. By the way, that's her address." She flung a piece of paper towards Lockhart's face. "Fat lot of good you are. Couldn't find a dingo in a chicken coup." She dialled a number on the phone. "Hello, call connect? Give me the police fraud squad, yes, officer Stephie Powers if she's still there."

Officer Stephie Powers was still there, only now it was Detective Inspector Stephie Powers. She greeted Cherry's voice with a shriek of delight. A long conversation followed. Cherry put the phone down at last, sat on the desk and began to collate the paperwork.

"Have you got some folders I can shove these in? Yes you do, over on the shelf. We wait here for the police to arrive." Cherry took the proffered folders from Lockhart's outstretched hand. "Now I'd like a nice cup of coffee, flat white, one sugar," she grinned at Lockhart's incredulous expression. "How about you have one yourself?"

John Lockhart hastened to comply with her wishes. The law had succumbed totally to woman power.

* * *

As a result of that morning, Fay Babbage, alias Claudia Chambers, went to jail for seven years. The court awarded Ms. Graham the sum of one million, eight hundred and fifty thousand dollars from the Babbage estate, the compensation being the estimated price of the Graham's original family home and effects. The Babbage estate was far larger than this sum, and the police were interested to find out why.

During the trial and the court hearings, Cherry and Stephie spent many hours together, enjoying their renewed friendship. In keeping with her original goal, and on advice from Stephie, Cherry decided she would apply to join the Federal Police division of Cybercrime when she finished her honours degree.

CHAPTER 13

Arthur Barlow came to consciousness at exactly seven fifteen a.m. as he always did, without the use of an alarm clock. He stretched, went over to his ensuite bathroom and completed his toilet is all of ten minutes. Back in his bedroom, he put on a business shirt and suit instead of his usual T-shirt and jeans. Today was special. He had important visitors, ones who would hopefully make a handsome contribution to his personal life goal of becoming a multi-millionaire before his thirtieth birthday. He slicked down his hair in front of the mirror, slipped his feet into a pair of very expensive shoes, and strolled out into the workshop, glancing towards the empty space which had remained cordoned off for so many months. He had enjoyed working on that machine. Even more, he had enjoyed selling it for three hundred and eighty thousand dollars. He quickened his pace into reception where Annette was bustling around preparing for the special company her boss was expecting.

"Good Morning, Annette. I like the new outfit." Arthur smiled appreciatively in her direction.

"You do?" Annette pirouetted a full turn so Arthur could enjoy the garment from every angle. "Bought it at a tiny boutique in Paddington," she added. "What do you think?"

Arthur's immediate thought was the size of the boutique suited the size of the designer clothing they purveyed. If the woman had come to work in her underwear it wouldn't have exposed much more.

"You've got a superb body, Annette," he laughed. "I know our clients appreciate it. Nice of you to share it so generously with us all."

"I'll take that as a compliment." Annette ran her hands down her sides and thrust her chest out. "There, do you think your special visitors will be impressed?"

"More than you know."

"Do you really like it, Arthur?" She turned hungry eyes towards him.

"I do," Arthur said seriously. "You've got a body to die for, Annette."

"Can I ask you a personal question, Arthur?"

"Sure." He glanced at his watch. "Fifteen minutes before they get here."

"I know you like looking at girls. I've seen their pictures on your monitor wearing even less than me. Don't you ever want to hold the real thing? There's more you can do with a girl than just look at her."

"You'd be surprised what you can do in front of a picture, Annette."

"You'd be stoked with what you can do with the real thing. Are you shy or something?" She averted her eyes downwards. "I'd be happy to help you, if you are."

"Shy?" Arthur laughed, not unkindly. "No. I was brought up in a commune, Annette, and let me tell you, what I don't know about girls can be written on a postage stamp. It's taught me they always come with unpleasant strings attached. Better I stick to the pictures."

"I feel sorry for you, Arthur, living your life without love," Annette replied sadly. "Aren't you ever lonely?"

"Heck no." Arthur gave her a genuine smile. "You're wrong about me living without love. My life's filled with it. I love building machines, and I'm deeply in love with my bank account."

"It can't keep you warm at night," Annette retorted with a sniff.

"But a thermostatically controlled water bed, with silk sheets and a goose feather doona can." He pointed towards the front door. "They're coming early. Sit down at your desk, Annette. Stretch out your lovely legs towards them. I'll be in the conference room setting up. Give us half an hour then lean over them with coffee. Get them purring for me."

A minute later his two friends, Paul Yang and Viktor Greshnev, together with the General Manager of New Wave Reality and a couple of his lackeys, walked in the door. Arthur motioned them to sit down.

"Thank you for coming gentlemen," Arthur smiled cordially from his seat at the end of the conference table. "I take it the machine you bought has met with satisfaction?"

"Satisfaction?" Viktor laughed. "It's fantastic. You know how we were running behind time on the animation job for Fox Studios. We thought it would take at least six months to render all the images. Well, it took three weeks. They're impressed—"

"Thank you Viktor," the General Manager interrupted. "We are impressed, Arthur. So are Fox Studios. In fact it's because they're so impressed we've been offered another project, quite a feather in our cap if we can pull it off, and we'll have a lot of egg on our faces if we can't."

"I'm all ears," Arthur said attentively. "You realise Viktor and Paul have been collaborating with me on the machine."

"On its design," Paul corrected, "but not on the multitasking kernel which runs the monster. Two hundred and fifty six logical processors, sixteen motherboards running dual Xenon eight core CPU's, all connected by wideband fibre channel. But it's that Barlix kernel which makes the whole thing run like the clappers."

"I totally believe you Paul," the G.M. replied, nodding appreciatively towards the two geeks. "Without Arthur's genius we would be in quite a bit of trouble instead of hitting the top of the pile." He turned round to the gentleman on his right. "This is Tony McMillan our project manager. We have a little proposition to put to you, Arthur, but first I'm afraid you will have to sign a document of confidentiality which George" – he turned towards another lackey – "will hand out to you. In fact, all my staff have been given such a document."

George sprang to perform his only function in the meeting, besides keeping his chair warm.

Arthur glanced at the piece of paper in front of him and signed his name at the bottom. "So, what happens now? I take it you want me to design another machine?"

There was a significant pause.

In the end Viktor broke the silence. "This is very exciting and very, very confidential. Arthur, we think we've done it – managed to cross the Uncanny Valley and produce photorealistic CGI images of human beings." He opened his laptop and touched a few keys. "I'll send this wirelessly to the conference room screen." The high resolution projector above their heads sprang into life. "Now it's only ten seconds long, but I think you'll agree we've nailed it." He pushed 'play'.

A young woman appeared on the screen, sitting down, her hands in her lap. "Welcome to New Wave Reality," she said," the world's leading animation company, and the first to open the doorway into the new age of photorealism in human CGI." The short clip came to an end.

Arthur stared at the screen. "You're going to tell me that was a CGI rendered image and not a real woman sitting on a chair?"

"That was a CGI image." Paul was so excited he was jigging up and down. "It took us a full year to work out how to do it. That image is indistinguishable from a human being. Good-bye Uncanny Valley. We're on the other side."

"We showed this clip to Fox," the General Manager beamed, the same excitement modulating his voice. "It blew them away. It seems they've been working on a project involving CGI images of real actors as well as those same actors themselves. Until now they only contemplated using the CGI images for distant shots, where facial features wouldn't be all that noticeable. That clip has made them rethink. They want us to redo the scenes with close up action shots." He banged the table with the palm of his hand. "If we can pull this off, we're heading for glory. Every major film producer will be beating a path to our door."

"If," Paul cautioned, turning towards Arthur. "That ten second clip took your machine two weeks to render, and it was really only her face we had to worry about. The rest of her is covered with clothes, easy as pie to reproduce, and besides, her face and head are really the only bits which move very much. To render a whole body involved in the sort of action Fox are talking about would take forever – years."

"Just how fast do you want this new machine to go?" Arthur stared at the image on the screen as if he couldn't draw his eyes away.

"An awful lot faster." Viktor glanced uncomfortably towards Arthur. "I've told our G.M. it's impossible within our budget. Supercomputers have tens of thousands of processors, occupy enormous spaces and cost billions. We don't have that sort of capital."

"I'd like to see how you did it," Arthur said, still staring at the screen as if he hadn't been listening. "Can you show me?"

"Created the photorealistic image? Of course," the G.M replied. "Just work out the details with the boys. Yeah, I know it can't be done, that's why we're here. You specialise in stuff which can't be done."

"It's certainly a challenge," Arthur agreed, still mesmerised by the image on the screen. "I may have a few ideas, but there's no guarantee they'll work this time." He paused, scanning the eager faces around the conference table. "I won't even start the project without seed capital. If it goes wrong, you've lost your dough."

There was another pause. The lackeys seemed uncomfortable, the G.M. thoughtful, Victor and Paul excited. The pause lengthened.

Finally the G.M. spoke softly. "How much, Arthur?"

"Two million dollars. If it works you've bought a machine. If it doesn't I'll take it to the rubbish tip for free."

More silence. The lackeys appeared even more uncomfortable.

"You've got your dough." The G.M. grimaced towards Arthur. "If you stuff around with my money, you never get to build the industry another machine. Sure you want to try?"

Arthur lay back in his chair and folded his arms behind his head. "Sure you want to risk your dough in the first place? I'll want Viktor and Paul to work closely on the software angles. You can forget the stuff you're using. We'll get the source codes and recompile for Barlix, strip out some of the nonsense, change the user interface. In fact, I want them working with me exclusively for six months to a year. Okay?"

"They're yours." The G.M grimaced again. "If you haven't struck oil by then you can pay me back their salaries. Deal?"

"Deal."

Just then Annette came in to take coffee orders, a welcome distraction if ever it was called for.

✳ ✳ ✳

Three days later Arthur was escorted by security into a special section of New Wave Reality studios. Viktor and Paul were already there. He stared at a huge spherical arrangement which resembled a Buckminster geodesic dome, with hundreds of bright point source lights mounted all over its surface, and hundreds of small cameras mounted in between them.

"This is it," Viktor exclaimed, running towards him. Each of those light sources is polarised. We get our actor to stand in the centre of the sphere under totally even illumination on all sides. There's one thousand and twenty four high definition cameras mounted on nodes all around them, collecting pictures at the rate of fifty a second."

Paul continued the explanation. "The actor goes through a whole range of facial expressions first. We photograph them from every angle. The polarisation is set so we get the reflection off their skin. Every other frame we change the angle of polarisation ninety degrees so we get the image of their skin pores themselves without the surface reflection. After we've collected all that data we get them to move their limbs around. You can appreciate how massive the file sizes have become by this time."

"I can imagine." Arthur was silently impressed. The setup must have cost millions. "What happens over there?" He pointed to what resembled a small glass diving board suspended a metre above the floor.

"That's where we laser scan the actor to get their 3D shape," Viktor explained, pointing to the machine mounted lasers nearby. "They stand naked on that platform, and we move the lasers around them. We use the output to make a high definition wireframe of their body. We clean it up, then we correlate the expressions and movements with those from the sphere. When we're done, we stretch the skin covering over the wireframe, add skin reflection, animation vectors, and we have our basic CGI actor, ready for animation."

"It must take ages," Arthur mused, almost to himself. "Won't your real life actors object to being scanned naked in full HD? I thought there were clauses in their contracts which prohibited that sort of thing."

"Oh they don't mind being scanned in the altogether," Paul laughed, "as long as not one frame of anything forbidden gets into the media. If it does they own our souls, together with New Wave Reality, our homes, our wives and kids. The G.M. said he'd buy a gun and shoot us first. Mercy killing, he called it."

"I can see why you need a faster machine." Arthur said slowly. "If you wanted to animate your CGI model in real time, what computing speed are we thinking of?"

"Around eight petaflops would be really good," Viktor said with a shallow laugh. "Quite a challenge for Arthur this time."

"What's a petaflop?" The G.M. had just walked onto the floor.

"A thousand million million floating point mathematical operations per second," Arthur explained. "The fastest machine in the world is only capable of four times the speed you're suggesting. You're not asking much, are you? I suppose you don't want it to cover an acre or so and consume megawatts of power."

"No space. Is it possible, or are we wasting our time and yours?" The G.M. hadn't missed the worried expression on Arthur's face.

"It's probably not possible," Arthur said slowly, his frown deepening, "but perhaps there are ways around the problem. Those supercomputers run versions of Linux, and their multitasking kernel is pretty straightforward. As well as that, they strap the individual motherboards together using fibre channel or InfiniBand high speed serial data connections. These limit the speed and the multitasking. Besides, your software relies on standard machine calls, routines available on anything from the common PC upwards. We need to rethink all of that. An unconventional machine, running unconventional software, and we're in with a shot. Try to use a monster for the job and we're stuffed before we start."

The G.M. seemed even more worried. He shook his head, turned, sat down on a chair.

"This setup you see here cost us around five million," he muttered. "We've already stuck our neck out. I guess sticking it out a bit more can't hurt." He took out a handkerchief and wiped his forehead. "If you really think it can't be done at this stage of computer technology, for goodness sake tell us. We can sell a lot of this stuff back to suppliers."

Arthur disappeared into his own thought. *A long shot, yes, but what if…
What if he could pull it off?* The insane idea which had been lurking in his
mind ever since he had seen that photorealistic CGI image, rose again
and began to solidify. What if? History would change, at least for a while,
and he would stand to make millions, literally millions… He slowly
returned to the world around him.

"I think it's worth a shot," he said at length. "I'll need my fellow geeks to
rally round. And about the two million. I'd like to be able to draw down
on that starting next week."

The G.M. nodded wearily, wiped his forehead again and walked out of
the room. Viktor and Paul gathered round Arthur, their eyes bright with
anticipation.

"You've got an idea, haven't you?" Viktor said eagerly.

"Some new architecture, a new operating core, something like that?"
Paul echoed the enthusiasm.

"Something like that," Arthur smiled. "You boys are going to have the
mother of all headaches by the end of the week."

He walked over to a large table at the other end of the studio, pulled a
sheet of paper out of the printer, and began to draw. "Suppose we scrap
the idea of linking multiple motherboards together with high speed
serial data lines. The best we can do is a dual processor motherboard in
any case. Any more processors and the blasted things run slower. No, we
use no more than, say sixty four or one hundred and twenty eight dual
processor motherboards, and we don't link them serially at all. We get
them all to share a massive central core of multi-port system memory."

"How much system memory?" Paul was leaning over Arthur's diagram,
his elbows on the table.

"About two hundred and fifty six terabytes," he answered quietly.

The two stupefied geeks stared at him as if he had lost his mind.

"Th... that's impossible," Paul muttered after a long silence. "Maximum system RAM is thirty two gigabytes per processor. You're actually thinking of building a machine with eight thousand times that system memory?"

"No," Arthur smiled quietly to himself, "I'm going to build two."

CHAPTER 14

D etective Sergeant James Naylor slid his keyboard aside under the untidy chaos of paper which covered his desk, lay back in his chair and rubbed his eyes with the back of his hand. Still no progress, and he was rapidly approaching the end of the road. He reached out for the mug of coffee permanently occupying its designated spot, and stared unhappily at the discolouration in the bottom.

He sighed, stood up and made his way wearily through the silent office to the machine in the common room at the back, only to find it cold and lifeless. Some of his colleagues suffered from ecological paranoia. He switched it on and flopped back into one of the comfortable lounge chairs scattered around the room.

Curse Arthur Barlow. The directive from the Fraud Squad had been quite specific. The man was suspected of laundering drug money. Nail him, and do it quickly, signed Inspector Stephie Powers. And he'd tried, chalking up more unpaid overtime every long evening alone in the office, when all his other sensible mates had gone home. The man seemed as clean as a preacher's sheets, but he knew Inspector Powers wouldn't be satisfied with that answer.

On the nearby table his mate Jack had left a small picture of his daughter, a beautiful twelve year old. James stared at it, memories flooding his mind. Cherry had been beautiful, too. She had come into his life like a little tornado and turned it upside down, wrenched his boyish heart for the first and only time, then vanished cruelly into thin air.

"I don't care where they take you, I'm going to find you." He heard himself say the words again.

He remembered the pain in his heart, remembered how he had searched every crowd for her face, until his parents had despaired of taking him anywhere. At the beach he'd scan the bathers rather than swim. At the football he'd be more interested in the spectators than the game. On the bus, on the train, wherever he went, faces, faces, faces, but that one face, the one burned into his heart, never materialised.

"You're Commissioner," he had often pleaded with his father. "Find her."

"James, you know I can't do that, especially because I'm Commissioner. How would it be if I overturned a DSS recommendation?" His father had told him every time.

"Dad, she needs us, I know she does." He remembered his own indignant words, repeated on each occasion. He also remembered his father's constant reply.

"You must think of Cherry, James. She has to move on in her life, become comfortable with her new family. Jesus wants us to put other people first, not ourselves. You know that. There are other lovely girls in the world waiting to get to know you. I'm sure she's moved on. She'd be very unhappy if she knew you hadn't."

There was truth in his father's words, but they had done little to heal the ache in his heart, an ache he knew his own mother shared, although she never spoke openly about it.

He smiled to himself as the memories flashed past. It had been such a hard time, yet it was through searching for Cherry he had discovered his gift for recognising faces, for remembering tiny details with photographic precision. It was a useful skill, especially since he had chosen to follow his father's profession after his science-law degree. But his new found gift had not yielded the result he had sought so ardently. Neither had the hundreds of hours he had spent on the internet, searching through all the C. Grahams living in Australia. There were thousands of them. Still a teenager, he had made a list of the most likely candidates and begun to ring their numbers, until his father had got wind of what he was doing, and given him another unpleasant lecture about leaving her alone. It was hopeless. It had always been hopeless. She had probably changed her name, or decided to live overseas.

Hopeless.

Yet deep in his heart one small seed of hope remained, and tonight, alone and tired, it had suddenly germinated into full blown desire. Where was she now? She had told him to forget her, and he truly wished he had been able to.

He began to reprove himself severely.

How immature, he thought. How stupid to allow a childhood memory to become so much a part of one's life. She was probably married by now, with children who loved her and a man who adored her, fulfilled in every way. He shuddered at the thought, willing her to be single, willing her to be waiting for him.

He glanced at the coffee machine, its winking red light telling him it was ready to make another contribution. He rinsed out his mug and pressed the button, waited until it was full of dark liquid, and returned to his desk.

Inspector Powers had given him a couple of bank statements from Barlow Maximum Speed, a company limited by guarantee. At first sight they seemed impeccably correct except for the sums themselves. Barlow was making incredibly expensive computers, and his customers paid a lot of money for them. Every sale had checked out so far. There was only one customer left to check, some sort of resort on the Central Coast, headquarters at Terrigal. They regularly bought expensive machines and paid a lot of money to have them serviced. Why would they need them? Barlow apparently spent a lot of time enjoying their best facilities, because he spent almost as much money there as he received.

James searched the internet for Blue Haven Health Resort, and came up with a website. Start here, he thought. The front page opened with a picture of crystal blue water lapping against shining white sands. The page offered a guest login. He clicked on the box, typed his name as Fred Nurk, occupation Grocer. He hit return. At first nothing happened, then the screen went blank. Finally a single sentence appeared in large white letters. James stared at them in sheer disbelief.

WHEN THE POLICE TELL LIES WHO CAN YOU TRUST?

He groaned, shut down the machine and went home.

✳ ✳ ✳

He arrived back at work the next day to find the office in a state of panic. Phones were ringing constantly, his colleagues and the support staff were staring at their monitors and helplessly banging their keyboards.

Frank Bauman, his boss, emerged from the common room with a mug in his hand, his face pure murder. He made a bee line for James. "What did you do last night?" He bellowed. "Were you still working on the Barlow case?"

"Yeah," James said. "I got onto a Resort web page and they played silly business. What's going on?"

"Every bloody email account is frozen," Bauman groaned. "Thousands of fake emails sent from every member of the Force in Victoria to every officer in this division. The server went down an hour ago. You can't even log on now. Just before you arrived, our phones started ringing. Calls from everywhere, interstate, overseas, all with the same damn message."

"What message?" James could feel the blood rising in his face.

"Ten seconds of the Hallelujah chorus. Some bastard is making fools of us." He thumped his mug down on the nearest desk.

"We're being flooded, targeted, whatever you call it. I'll bet you a quid to a cent Barlow's behind it. Hold on." He snatched his mobile phone out of his pocket and held it up to his ear. "Bauman here. You can see what's happening? Yeah, one of our guys. I'll send him over personally within the hour. Boiled or fried? You choose, fine with me either way."

He put the phone in his pocket and grinned at James. "You're in for a treat. Federal division of Cybercrime have sent for you. They can see what's going on here. I think they're going to hang you by your fingernails. Seeing as we're off the air, they want you in person to tell them what you did to precipitate this brouhaha." He grinned. "You're going to meet CC."

"Who's CC?" James had a sinking feeling he didn't want to know. The grin on Frank Bauman's face had widened, a sure sign Detective Sergeant James Naylor was heading for something unpleasant.

"Cybercrime's top hacker. She's feral. Works twenty four-seven. Has a blow up bed next to her desk. Goes for crims like a dingo on acid. Almost feel sorry for them. Had more convictions than rest of the division put together. She's taken down some very nasty people and their organisations. Hates cops who stuff up."

"So I'm the sacrificial lamb to be fried by some vicious old crow for the satisfaction of the troops?" James scowled, dropping his briefcase to the floor, and his usual optimism along with it.

"Old crow?" Bauman threw back his head and laughed loudly. "I'll tell you one thing, Sergeant Naylor, she's not old."

"What does CC stand for?" James asked unhappily.

"Cunning Cow, I don't know. Heard her called worse." He took his mobile phone out of his pocket again, still grinning. "Better start heading across town." He walked a short distance and turned. "If you're not back tomorrow I'll come and collect your hide from wherever they've hung it out to dry." He turned and strode back to his office, an occasional laugh still audible over the cacophony all around.

Mac Cusiter

✴ ✴ ✴

Cybercrime headquarters was located in a modern high rise office complex at North Sydney. James caught the lift to the third floor, a feeling of dread slowly rising with his altitude. The lift opened. Across the corridor were two large glass doors with the words 'Federal Division of Cybercrime' etched onto their smooth surface. He pressed the button under the sign which said 'Visitors', and waited. Eventually a sour faced young woman walked towards the doors, waved a card in front of the reader, opened one of them and beckoned him inside.

"Err.. James Naylor from Central Station Detectives." James withered under the unremitting scowl. "I take it I'm expected?"

"You're in heaps of trouble," the scowling woman snapped at him. "CC's had the devil of a job stopping the attack. This way."

The sinking feeling grew worse. He followed his unfriendly guide down a long corridor. The door at the end had two large white enamelled 'C's close together near the centre, and a small brass plate below with the words "Go away I'm busy" in black gothic letters.

"Knock and go in," his guide commanded with the smile of an executioner. "Don't wait until she hears you. Sometimes she doesn't." The woman beat a hasty withdrawal down the corridor.

James knocked. No response. He opened the door and went in. The room beyond was large and filled with chaos. Several sturdy tables were strewn high with books, manuals, and reams of paper. Two huge monitor screens ablaze with code, stuck out above the mess. No doubt there were keyboards as well, but they were buried under the flood of paperwork. On two sides bookshelves rose to the ceiling in a similar state, the books – mostly programming manuals – serving to keep the hordes of loose leaf folders from plummeting to the floor. In one corner of the room lay a blow up mattress, three quarters hidden by the untidy pile of bedding on top of it.

At the table nearest the door sat a woman with her back to him, facing another pair of huge monitor screens. So this was the much to be feared 'CC'. She was certainly young. Her long brown hair swished over her shoulders as she typed furiously on the keyboard. Suddenly she gave a grunt of satisfaction and turned round to face her victim.

James' eyes practically fell out of his head. He stared dumbfounded, his mouth half open, all thought of his original mission wiped completely from his mind. It was quite a while before he could speak at all.

"Cherry!"

James stared at her, his mind updating the image of the child with that of the beautiful woman who had replaced her. He felt his heart hammering in his chest. She was staring at him in silence. Perhaps she was doing the same thing. He spoke again, a little louder, a little clearer.

"Cherry."

"James." She hesitated, then as if some switch had been thrown inside her, stood up, came towards him and threw her arms around his shoulders. Only for a second, then she went back to the table.

James found his voice again. "CC? What happened to Cherry Graham?"

"Cherry Charlie. My cyber name. Had it for ages. Don't use real names round here."

"I... I searched everywhere for you," James stammered, still barely in control of his voice.

"Later." Cherry cut him off. "I've managed to stop the flooding. A distributed denial of service, clever, many pronged. Your server went down with an amplified Network Time Protocol attack, but there was much more to it. What stupid thing did you do to provoke this?"

James' mind was having great difficulty dealing which such mundane matters whilst standing near the woman he had sought for so long. He wished the rest of the room would disappear and leave her very close to him. She raised her eyebrows, expectant of a reply.

"I was investigating a crook by the name of Barlow."

James tried valiantly to concentrate on the reason he was there. "He's been laundering money through his company. There was a huge amount coming in and going out to some sort of resort on the Central Coast. I accessed their web site and logged in as a guest."

"With a fake ID?" He'd been on the receiving end of that expression before. Cherry turned round and began typing on her keyboard again.

"How was I to know it wasn't genuine?" James replied defensively. "I logged in as Fred Nurk, a Grocer by profession, and the whole screen went blank. Then up comes a message saying when the police tell lies who can you trust? or words to that effect."

"Obviously the web site checks the authenticity of guest logins by accessing their servers." She swivelled her chair around to face him, her eyebrows raised. "What makes you think Arthur's a criminal?"

"Arthur? You know this guy?" James asked, astonished.

"He's been my C++ mentor since I was ten years old." She turned round again and brought up the internet. "What was the name of the place?

"Blue Haven Health Resort. Barlow must enjoy the facility himself. He pays them a small fortune. Perhaps they offer special services for special guests."

Cherry whipped round for a second and gave him a disgusted scowl. She turned back and brought up the website. James could see her reading through the HTML script, making a note here and there. For the next ten minutes she was totally occupied with stuff James could only guess at.

At length she swivelled her chair round to face him. "The trace has gone. Script was clean, what I can read of it. My guess is it gets cleaned once your login has activated an alert. You're right about something fishy going on, and someone pretty clever is helping them. Could be Arthur, but why he would want to do it beats me. He's a genius, builds incredibly fast machines. It's his life."

She paused, stood up and went over to where a cold mug of tea stood balanced on a pile of paper. "If it is Arthur, and I really think you're barking up the wrong tree, you'll never get him."

"What do you mean, we'll never get him?" James found himself moving towards her like a nail to a magnet.

"You'll never get him because he's heaps more brilliant than me, and if I can't get him, you can't get him." She picked up the mug and drank the remainder of its contents in one gulp. "The hit was a warning, in any case. They could have destroyed you, but they played a game instead. The Hallelujah chorus, wasn't it?" She gave a cynical laugh. "So appropriate. Do you know where all this was apparently sourced from?"

"Some big corporate server which we couldn't access without making fools of ourselves?" James suggested.

"No," she sniffed. "A small computer belonging to St. Stephen's Anglican church Terrigal. Minister probably gave them access, thought it was a repairman. Christians are so gullible and stupid."

"I'm one of them, just thought I'd remind you."

"Yeah, well, if the shoe fits." She was smiling at him. "James, I know there are things to say. I don't want to say them here. If you want to talk, take me to dinner."

James' heart leapt. "Are you married? Attached to someone?"

"No. Later, I said." She paused. "Are you?"

"Not even a girlfriend," James said emphatically. "Tonight, Giovanni's, near Circular Quay, seven o'clock? If I can't get a table I'll ring you. Can I have your mobile number?"

"What a tired old pickup line. Think I'm stupid?" Her voice was cross, but her eyes were smiling. "Okay, give me your phone." Cherry took his phone and typed her number into it.

James left her office on cloud twenty. The unfriendly woman who had escorted him down the corridor was sitting at her desk in sight of the entrance. She scowled as he passed.

"Must have given you the third degree," she simpered. "No doubt you deserved it." She gave him a patronising smile. "Next time be more careful or you'll be seeing her again. I'm sure you'd just love that."

"I certainly would," James replied, returning her patronising smile with extra. "In fact I'll be seeing her again tonight when I take her out to dinner."

The stunned disbelief on her face as he walked out the door was icing on the cake. He pulled out his mobile phone and made the booking at Giovanni's.

CHAPTER 15

The lights of the city rippled on the dark waters of Sydney harbour, the glowing arch of its famous bridge spanning from one dark shore to the other, bright in the colourful cheerfulness of Luna Park. On the far right the white sails of Sydney Opera House dominated the esplanade at Bennelong Point. Their table was near the window, a huge pane of glass extending from floor to ceiling. James wore his one and only black suit, the beautiful woman on the other side of the table her only evening dress in blue satin, supplemented by a thin white woollen cardigan thrown over her shoulders. The reflected lights from the water rippled in her deep brown eyes, her thoughts impossible to read. James stared at her, filling his eyes with her beauty, drinking in the sweet fragrance of her perfume which wafted around him, the feelings he knew as a child slowly morphing into their adult forms.

"You're so beautiful, Cherry." He reached out and touched her hand. She drew it back.

"Thank you, James. You've grown up very nicely yourself." She turned and stared out of the window into the darkness.

"It's been so long, Cherry," James said with feeling. "Why didn't you write to me? You've always known where we lived. You just disappeared. I searched everywhere—"

"I told you to forget me, didn't I?" She turned towards him suddenly, her eyes sharp, defensive. "I forgot about you as soon as I got into the car. I said I would. Why didn't you do as I told you?" She turned her head away again.

James sat silent, taken aback by her words. "Yet somehow you remembered my name," he said at last, smiling at her in the hope she would return the gesture.

Cherry continued to stare out into the dark waters. A tiny tear budded in her left eye, the only one James could see.

"You'll never understand, James," she said at last. "You've always had a family to love you, I've had nobody. Everything I came to love was ripped out of my life, by fate or God or whatever, just when I thought I could depend on it. Add the other horrible things, and that's my past. Remembering rips my heart to pieces, so I choose not to. I choose to move on, because if I didn't I'd curl up and die."

She turned towards him, her eyes burning with fire. Suddenly she grabbed his arm, squeezing it uncomfortably hard. "Instead I chose to fight them, the vultures who prey on the old and vulnerable, those who eat the lives of children and defile them. I'm damaged, James, but I've turned the damage into a weapon. That's my life. If you care about me at all you'll let me live it."

She let go his arm, wrapped her own around herself as if she was suddenly cold. "Sometimes the dark tentacles of the past reach out and find me. I go to pieces. Please don't make it worse."

It was a long time before James spoke. He sat there stunned by Cherry's words, trying to think of a way to reach her, sooth away some of the heartache, open her eyes to the man sitting beside her who very much wanted to heal the pain in her heart. "You don't have to live without love, Cherry," he said gently. "Life is lonely and sad without it."

"My whole life is filled with love, James." She grabbed his arm again, her eyes shining.

"I love destroying my enemies. I love it when the prosecution, using my evidence, wipes the floor with their greasy defence lawyers. I love it when the judge incarcerates them for ten or twenty years." She squeezed harder.

"They never change. I remember their names. When they're released I'll destroy them again. I want them to know a woman did it, smashed their lives like they devour the lives of others. I want my face to haunt their memory. I want them to *burn*."

"You're really hurting my arm," James protested quietly.

Cherry relinquished the arm and hid her hands under the table. "Sorry, now you know," she muttered, turning away from him. Minutes passed in silence. Finally she turned back. "There was a friendship we shared once, when we were children. But children grow up, James. The river flowing between us has widened. You're a Christian, I'm a God hating atheist – oxymoron I suppose. I think it would be better if you never saw me again. I don't want you to get hurt."

"Suppose I'd rather get hurt than not see you again." He massaged his arm where Cherry had left her handprint.

"Then you're a fool." Cherry spat the words into his face.

James stared at the tears brimming in her eyes, their message somehow conflicting with her words. "Then I'm a fool." He paused, trying to think of something else to say. "Mum says she'd like to see you very much. Can you—"

"No." Cherry covered her face with her hands, and when she lowered them, her cheeks were wet and shining. "Tell her... I haven't found it... yet."

"You haven't found what yet?"

"Just tell her. She'll know what it means." She brushed her face again with her hands. "If you ever tell anyone, I mean anyone, you saw me cry, I'll never speak to you again as long as I live."

She turned away towards the window. "I'd like a nice cup of coffee and a tawny port. Give me a moment, I'm trying to pull myself together."

James beckoned the waiter and placed the order. In a strange way Cherry's last words had comforted him. He imagined few people had succeeded in making her cry, proof her heart wasn't as dead and cold as she thought it was. Perhaps a certain James Naylor might still matter to her, even though she had done her best to remove his memory from her life. He waited patiently for her to turn round. The coffee and port came first.

"I've an idea," he said drawing the deep red liquid into his lips. "We were partners in crime once, how about we become partners in crime again."

Cherry turned round, raised her long dark eyebrows and picked up the small port glass.

James continued. "I'll ask Frank Bauman if there's a possibility some of our boys can assist you in your efforts to bring nasty people to justice. Must be something we can do. I'll have a word or two with dad about it. He might warm to the idea. Nothing like influence when you need it."

"I'd like that," she smiled. "I get sick of working through Sylvia all the time, she's such a wet blanket." She slapped his arm in the wrong place. James jumped slightly. "And you had to tell her about our date, didn't you? I never thought I'd hear the end of it. Quite ruined her day."

"I'm really glad," James laughed, picking up his coffee. "She tried to ruin mine."

The short remainder of the evening went well. James avoided any reference to the past, any mention of his own feelings, and any mention of his family. Within these unspoken constraints conversation flourished, each enjoying the renewal of their childhood friendship, although Cherry would never have admitted to it.

Finally Cherry said she had to go, busy day tomorrow. James said 'goodbye' and walked back to his car in the Opera House parking station deep in thought. The old Cherry was still there, he was certain, deeply buried in the new one, but alive, waiting only for someone or something to set her free. He would visit his parents tomorrow night. There would be a full and frank exchange of information in both directions.

❋ ❋ ❋

James rang his mother the next morning and received an instant invitation to dinner. After the meal he began the information exchange by passing on Cherry's words.

"What does it mean?" He asked, watching his mother nod her understanding.

"It means we keep praying for her." His mother stood to clear away the dishes. "Don't make the mistake of thinking you can change her, James, because only Jesus can do that."

James ignored the comment and turned towards his father. "You knew where she was all the time, and you never said anything. You know how I felt about her. Why, Dad?"

His father slowly pushed his chair away from the table and frowned. "I thought you could work that out." He wiped his mouth with a napkin. "In fact Cherry told you herself she wanted nothing to do with you. If Frank Bauman had checked with me as he should have done, you would never have gone to see her in the first place."

"You deliberately kept her from me." James leant forward angrily. "I thought it was my life."

"I thought it was God's life." Robin sighed heavily. "James, you mean a great deal to me. I found out Cherry was working in Cyber, and knowing how much you wanted to find her, I made some discrete enquires. I was told she was brilliant in her job, feral, I believe was the word, and hated anything to do with religion. Those who knew her, described her as incapable of sustaining a relationship with another human being for more than five minutes. All good reasons for not telling you where she was, I felt."
He reached out and gripped James' hand.

"I don't want you to get hurt son. There are heaps of delightful young women who are followers of the Way. Why don't you make yourself a little more available?"

"Perhaps I don't want to." James picked up his glass of water and drank the remains slowly. There was obviously no point in pursuing the discussion. His father had decided Cherry was no good for him, and, damn it, he was probably right. He wished his own heart was susceptible to such clear reason, but it wasn't. He put down his glass.

"Dad, on another related matter, I suggested to Cherry some of the boys in our department might be able to help her. She's been incredibly successful, but sometimes the culprits have slipped through the net right at the last moment through lack of manpower. I was wondering—"

Robin heaved himself to his feet. "I've already had a lot of political pressure placed on me to provide her with assistance of some sort. Cherry Charlie as she calls herself, is the political flavour of the month. I was thinking of setting up a special unit. James, do you really want to be part of this? I don't see any way it's going to work out well for you."

"Yes, Dad, I do."

Robin sighed heavily. "Very well. As you say, it's your life. I guess God's more than capable of working with it. I'll talk to Frank Bauman about it, after I've skinned him for sending you to Cyber without my permission."

James gripped his father's hand. "Thanks," he said, and went to help his mother in the kitchen.

CHAPTER 16

The proposed interdepartmental cooperation actually took a full month to materialise, mostly because, no matter how willing the troops, department heads just don't like cooperating. Frank had been against it from the start. Cybercrime should do their own recruiting. 'What makes them think we have spare men on the ground, we're under resourced as it is,' and so on. After a lot of haggling on all sides, three detectives from Central were provisionally assigned to assist the Federal Division of Cybercrime in apprehending felons, James, Harry Trench and Tony Dawson. Tactical Operations was born.

Their first operation took place a full two months later. In theory, James was the leader of the group. In practice, Cherry recognised no authority save her own.

The house was dark save for lights in a couple of rooms downstairs. Tony, who did mountain climbing for fun, had previously shinned up the power pole in the street and clipped a small box onto the telephone line which picked up the ADSL signal travelling down the copper wire. Cherry was outside in a white van with the name of some television repair company on the side. The box transmitted the signal to the van along with any ordinary telephone traffic. She was busily hacking into the carrier signal and would communicate with the boys via radio when she felt like it. Harry was hiding in the front yard behind some shrubbery near the fence. The dog next door had insisted on revealing his location by scraping the fence behind him and barking its head off. Eventually Tony had come over and given it a tasty treat of steak laced with sedative which he had thoughtfully added to the supplies in the van in case local animals proved to be a problem. He moved off towards the rear of the house to check for activity there.

Harry plucked a thorn out of his backside and pressed the small insert in his ear. "How long does it take you to hack into his computer? We're not exactly sitting in comfy lounge chairs out here."

"Patience," Cherry gave a chuckle. "I've synched the ADSL carrier. Okay, now I'm piggybacking their phone and computer. Nothing of interest yet. Stay put. Where's Tony?"

Two clicks told everyone that wherever Tony was he had unfriendly company close by.

James, who had taken residence in a large pine tree, was peering through the lighted window at a desktop computer and an empty room. "No one visible yet," he reported. "Where are they? Must be round the back somewhere near Tony."

"Click, click."

"They're coming into the room," James alerted the team a short time later. "One's armed, gun in holster. Cherry, when all hell breaks loose, stay in the van."

"Yes, captain my captain," Chery giggled disrespectfully. "I've got traffic. Recording now." A pause, "deal's been finalised. Got you, and the IP address of the buyer! You're going down too." Excitement modulated her voice. "Got your account and password, sucker. Boys, the buyer's coming round to pick up the goods. We have to get these swine before he arrives."

"Do we go?" Harry asked tersely. James began scrambling down the tree.

"He's signing off," Cherry continued. "Got their domain name. This is huge. What are you waiting for?" she yelled. "Get them."

Harry began to cross the front lawn. "James," he said quietly, "go the side window?"

James touched his comms device "You go the window, I'm going up to the front door and ring the bell."

"Ballsy," Harry panted, almost at the window. "I'll get in and come up the hall behind them. Keep them busy. Got that, Tony?"

"Click, Click." Tony signalled.

Harry disappeared through a window in the side of the house. James reached the front door. He rang the bell. From somewhere down the hall a man's voice swore. Footsteps approached the door, it began to open.

All hell broke loose.

James heard Harry yell from down the corridor. The man behind the door tried to slam it shut, but James' boot was in the way. Another yell. James shouldered the door into the man's face. He staggered backwards then pelted down the corridor for all he was worth. James gave chase. Gunfire echoed from the back door.

Harry appeared from the lounge room, a nasty gash on his head. "Don't ask," he yelled. "Out the back. Quick."

Both men belted down the corridor, into the kitchen and out the back door. Tony was slowly staggering to his feet, another man was lying face down on the ground.

"Round the side," Tony yelled, clutching his chest. "Blighter's getting away."

James and Harry raced towards the path which led round the side of the house. Suddenly they heard a man yell, followed instantly by a metallic clang, then Cherry's voice. "Enjoy that?"

"Cherry!" James pelted round the side of the house like a Scud missile. The second man had measured his length on the path. Cherry was standing near the corner of the house holding a steel garbage can lid in her hand and wearing a smile on her face.

"Well, don't just stand there, cuff him," she ordered, turning the unconscious figure over with her foot, none too gently. "Oops, sorry about his face. I whanged him pretty hard with the lid."

James knelt down beside the man, his handcuffs on the ready. There was blood seeping out of his mouth together with the odd tooth, his bleeding nose bent nearly at right angles. James rolled the man over, brought his arms around his back and cuffed his wrists together.

He stood up and faced Cherry. "What part of 'stay in the van' don't you understand?"

"What part of 'get them' don't *you* understand?" Cherry retorted cheekily. "This is the king pin. You nearly let him get away." She heard a noise and glanced down the path. "What happened to you, Tony?"

"The other bastard shot me twice in the chest before I got him," Tony panted. "Thank goodness for kevlar. He's still alive. Time to call backup and paramedics. Man, I feel like I've been gored by a bull."

"Don't forget the buyer will be here soon," Cherry reminded them, dropping the lid on the path. "James, come with me. We've got to get the merchandise out before he arrives. Can you boys handle these two?"

Harry glanced at Tony. James was their leader, but there was no doubt as to who was running the show. He smiled at Cherry. "Sure CC. Just don't get caught in there."

"You coming, James?" Cherry called impatiently, bounding along the path towards the back door. Once inside she found a light switch, turned it on. "Quickly," she shouted, "we have to get them out."

"What are we searching for?" James asked.

"A door with a lock of any kind. You start here, I'll go upstairs."

Cherry flew up the stairs. Lights came on in every room. James walked round the side of the staircase. There, under the stairs was the usual cupboard, only this one was locked with a bolt. He drew the bolt aside and opened the door. There was a light switch on the lintel. He turned it on and gasped in horror. On the other side of the cupboard, clinging to one another in terror were two young, olive-skinned girls. They shrank away from James, whimpering and shaking with fright. At first James was so shocked he couldn't speak.

"Cherry, Cherry!" He yelled. "I've found them." He heard the woman's footsteps drumming down the stairs. She saw the children, rushed into the cupboard and threw her arms protectively around them. They began to cry.

"It's all right," she coaxed, "we're not going to hurt you. We've come to take you to a safe place." She kept on repeating the same message until one of the children nodded her head. They allowed Cherry to take them by the hand and lead them out the back door and into the van. James was stunned. For the first time he began to feel some of the fire which drove Cherry's remorseless crusade. He followed them out to the van.

"I'll stay with them," Cherry said, turning to James. "They're terrified. Poor little things. Can't be more than ten years old. Sick bastards. Make sure the buyer doesn't get away. Shoot him in the head. I've got enough to take down their entire organisation, the filthy swine." There was a burning fire in her eyes. James was glad she didn't have a gun.

"Where did they come from?" He said, pointing to the two frightened children, still clinging silently to one another.

"Malaysian child prostitution racket," Cherry growled. "Parents come to this country, sell their kids, make enough money to set themselves up. I'd like to export them back to a firing squad. Some parents shouldn't be given a licence to breed." She turned back to the children, and in a much softer voice, "it's all right. You're safe. I'm going to close the van door now. You must be very quiet. Can you do that?"

One little girl nodded. Cherry shut the van door. Just in time, the headlights of an approaching vehicle were coming down the street.

James vaulted into the bushes. Harry, who had just emerged from the back, ran into the house. Tony stood point over the groaning men at the back door, his gun in his hand. The car drove into the driveway, right up close to the house. Two men got out. One opened the boot ready to receive its young cargo, the other went up to the front door, knocked three times, then another three. The door opened and Harry jumped out holding a gun. Simultaneously James came up behind the other man. He thought about ramming the gun into his spine, remembered the faces of the two children, and whacked him over the head with it instead. Some of Cherry's fire had taken hold. The other man, seeing his partner collapse to the ground, made no attempt at resistance. He came meekly towards James at gunpoint. James handcuffed him, his face grim with disgust.

Five minutes later Frank Bauman arrived with reinforcements and an ambulance. Cherry emerged from the van holding a child by each hand.

Frank nodded approvingly towards her. "I can see this was a worthwhile operation," he said, slowly shaking his head. "Well done, all of you." He turned around and nodded at the three men. "I had some misgivings at first, but I think they may have been misplaced. In future you'll go with a couple more men. You took a risk. Both these coves were armed. James, the one you got is a really nasty piece of work. Glad you hit him when you did. So three of you take down four armed men. Not bad."

"Well actually Cherry got one of them," Tony explained, a little apologetically. "He would have got away otherwise. She rearranged his face with a garbage tin lid. Very efficient. His own mother wouldn't recognise him now."

Frank turned towards Cherry and the children, respect of a different nature kindling in his eyes. "A girl of many talents, I see. Well done, Ms. Charlie. We should get those children down to Central so we can identify them. Do they speak English?"

"One of them does at least. Probably both. Then I'm taking them home." There was a note in her voice which silenced argument. "I'll work from there for a day or so until you've sorted out some place to take them. Their parents will be in jail before the end of the week, along with a lot of other people. I've got the whole network in the bag." She grinned at the men. "Thank you, boys. I like this arrangement. Let's do it again."

❄ ❄ ❄

They did it again, and again. In the space of twelve months Tactical Operations had established a well-deserved reputation for getting their man.

Within this work environment James and Cherry functioned as an efficient team. Outside its task-orientated walls things did not go so smoothly. They dated on a number of occasions, always at James's instigation. Cherry never refused to go out with him, but he soon learnt there were strictly enforced borders within which he had to remain, or else endure her distain and cruelly cutting tongue. Any mention of his feelings for her would precipitate the frozen treatment. Any attempt at physical intimacy, even holding her hand, would result in stony silence which could endure for the remainder of the evening. As the number of these disastrous events escalated, James became increasingly mystified as to why she agreed to go out with him at all. It was almost as though she enjoyed punishing him for his devotion to her. If only she would return a kind word, an encouraging gesture, but she never did. To make matters worse, she showed more friendly affection towards Tony and Harry than she ever did towards him.

Any other man on the receiving end of such discouragement would have been quick to take his cue and move on, but for some reason her rejection had precisely the opposite effect on the heart of one James Naylor. He looked forward to every field operation simply because she was there. Here he could take care of her, prevent her from thoughtlessly endangering her life, something she was all too prone to doing. In his heart he cherished the totally irrational hope that she would one day see how much he loved her and run into his arms.

Perhaps she might have, but then Sylph came and the world changed.

CHAPTER 17

The large yellow signs outside Barlow Maximum Speed telling the world the company was no longer constructing machines for the general public, had faded somewhat over the previous ten months. Their message seemed to belie the enormous amount of activity associated with the place. Trucks arrived daily carrying specialised equipment. Couriers arrived by the hour with sealed packages.

Annette had never been busier.

The designer outfit from the tiny boutique and its like had long given way to more practical and less provocative T-shirts and jeans. There were no new clients to impress. Although Arthur was always unmoved by her tasteful nakedness, Viktor and Paul were not endowed with such inexplicably frustrating restraint. Each day began at seven thirty and ended after six in the evening. Annette, caught up in the general atmosphere of excitement and anticipation hadn't minded in the least. The boys depended on her and the boys were grateful.

Arthur had increased her pay to extraordinary lengths and praised her thoroughness. In the workshop, two enormous machines were slowly growing. Next to them was a massive uninterruptible power supply, a nitrogen gas dryer and cooler, and a whole rack of highly specialised test gear and logic analysers. Paul superintended the task of designing the motherboards, and involved a large part of the geek community in the process, as well as some highly paid engineers from overseas. Viktor was in charge of assembly and testing. Arthur oversaw the entire operation and concentrated on writing the code necessary to run the beasts.

It was 4th September, 11:04 p.m.

The air was heavy with tension. Arthur took his place in front of the two huge monitor screens attached to number one machine, and nodded to Paul who stood next to the monster. There was a small panel on the side. Paul pressed a single button, then joined Viktor behind Arthur's chair. Annette stood on his other side, holding her breath.

One minute passed. Nothing happened. Annette could see sweat pouring down Viktor's face, Paul's hand shaking on the back of Arthur's chair. Another minute, nothing. The fans circulating the dry, cold nitrogen picked up in pitch.

Suddenly there was a beep, monitor one sprang to life.

Paul nearly jumped off the floor. Arthur gave a sharp intake of breath, Viktor garbled something in Russian.

The second monitor burst into life.

Streams of text poured down both screens. Annette could feel excitement welling up inside her. Fifteen minutes later the BMS logo appeared, rotating slowly on both screens.

Arthur sprang up from the console, caught hold of Annette, lifted her up in the air and kissed her. Suddenly everyone was hugging everyone else. Viktor was singing, loud, off key, Paul was shouting, Arthur running around and punching the air.

The machine had booted successfully.

An hour later the second machine burst into life. Arthur went into the common room and returned with a bottle of very expensive champagne and four mugs. The cork hit the ceiling.

"A toast!" He shouted, pouring the foaming liquid. "We are now the proud owners of the fastest machines in the southern hemisphere. Well done, everyone."

The party went on for a long time. Annette uncovered some treats she had thoughtfully brought to work in anticipation of success, and everyone thoroughly enjoyed themselves.

Arthur finally offered his bed to Annette because it was so late, and told the others they weren't even to think about expressing their excitement anywhere near her. Annette thanked him and retired to his bedroom. Stripping off her clothes, she slid in between the warm silk sheets of Arthur's bed and wished like mad he would burst in and express his excitement all over her for a very long time. What was wrong with the man? Couldn't he read body language? To make it any clearer she'd have to hang a sign round her neck.

Viktor and Paul, far too excited to sleep, began the task of loading software on to machine number two. When this was done, they would start compiling new rendering code. After rendering each character, the machine would use the animation variables, or AVARS, to make the character move. The task was far from over. The new renderers had to work much more efficiently than the ones they had been using at New Wave Reality, and they had to work with the completely new Barlix kernel.

Arthur was doing tests on the other machine while they worked. After a while he stood up and joined them. "Well, just how fast do you think she is?" He asked, a smile on his face.

Viktor glanced up from the screen. "I dunno. Have we got anywhere near eight petaflops? Don't be too disappointed Arthur, I'll bet it's still the fastest machine we'll ever be able to use."

"I'd say she's doing five," Paul smiled encouragingly, as he plugged a large portable data drive into the second machine. Privately he would have been surprised if the machine could manage two petaflops.

"It'll do, Arthur," he encouraged. "We may not have real time rendering, but sure as hell it will make the project viable."

"Eight petaflops, gentlemen?" Arthur grinned widely at them. "How about eighteen?"

Paul nearly dropped the drive. "Impossible," he exploded. "You've measured something wrong, surely." He stared at Arthur as if he's grown another head.

"I've got to see this." Viktor sprang up from his seat.

Both men followed Arthur over to machine one console. It only took minutes to confirm the truth.

"Outstanding." Paul shook his head slowly from side to side. "You know what this means? Once we've established the AVARS, and laid the texture over the wireframes, this machine can render photorealistic human characters in real time. We thought fifty frames a second. This machine could do a hundred. Arthur, this is magnificent," he shouted, throwing his arms around Arthur's shoulders. "The architecture paid off. I can hardly believe it." He ran his hand across the back of his neck. "Wait until I tell the G.M. He'll be over the moon."

Arthur smiled to himself before replying. He stood up from the console, measuring the excitement on the faces of his two friends. "Gentlemen," he said softly, "we are the elite. We've done what no one else thought possible." The smile on his face broadened. "I feel the approaching rush of huge piles of money."

CHAPTER 18

Almost twelve months had passed since the two massive machines had burst into life on that memorable evening. The animation software had been rewritten, compiled and loaded onto both machines. New Wave Reality had agreed to do the actual live scans in its own studios and transfer all the data to the BMS site using a portable storage unit built by Arthur himself. It contained a dedicated processor and one hundred terabytes of solid state storage. Expensive, but nothing like the cost of disassembling one of the machines, transporting it to NWR, reassembly and testing.

Arthur was quite happy for them to use his facilities without cost, at least for the first project, just to make sure they were pleased with the machines before they paid the extra three million dollars for them. The body scanning had taken all of six months. Annette and Arthur, watching NWR team of animators work with the raw data, had seen a great deal more of each actor than anyone else save for the stars themselves. In keeping with their sacrosanct agreement, not one frame of anything explicit ever made its way out of the building.

Arthur coupled the two machines together using twenty four channel InfiniBand connectors to double the rendering capacity. The results exceeded even the G.M.'s expectations, as well as those of the film industry in general. New Wave Reality was heading for gold and glory, and he knew it. Even so it took a whole eight months before the rendering was finally finished. The movie was scheduled for the box office at Christmas time.

A new era in digital animation had begun.

Other studios were now contracting with NWR to have their stars scanned. Scriptwriters were churning out new material to suit. New games, with photorealistic characters, were being planned. Arthur knew the orders for more machines would soon be rolling in. He started to recruit more staff to keep pace with the expected demand.

❋ ❋ ❋

The three geeks had taken to having dinner together in the conference room at the end of each intense day after all the other NWR staff had gone home. The food was superb, the wine excellent, and the cost enormous, exactly as Arthur had requested. Annette coordinated the whole thing and joined them each evening, an invitation endorsed by each member of the small company. Not only was she easy on the eyes, she was fun to talk to, at least when they were speaking a language she could understand.

"This is a superb merlot. Have another glass, Arthur?" Annette coaxed, leaning over him with the bottle in her hand. She was always attentive to his needs, especially in the alcohol department.

Perhaps that one extra glass would lower his inhibitions sufficiently to make him want to tear her clothes off. So far he had remained infuriatingly restrained. Without waiting for confirmation, she refilled his glass and slowly straightened up, willing him to take a closer peek at the delectable goods right in front of his face.

"We need to rethink the whole software angle," Viktor said, his eyes appreciating Annette's attempt to inebriate the object of her desire. "We had no choice but to use our old recompiled routines last time, but now we've got a chance to get it right."

"Absolutely correct." Arthur took a sip of his wine, and pushed his chair back from the table.

"The machines just aren't being used effectively. We had to load so many link libraries we might as well have run standard Linux from the start. We can do better. This is an unconventional machine, and it needs unconventional software."

"With you one hundred percent," Paul agreed as he finished off the remains of a superb Mango Dacquoise. "We're wasting all that hard won power. We need something tailored to use the routines built into the Barlix kernel, not the ones we have to write extra code for."

"I've been doing some experiments with evolutionary code." Arthur took another sip of his merlot while Annette watched hopefully. "It's begun to show some promise."

"Evolutionary code?" Annette raised her eyebrows. "Like evolution as in life evolved from the sea? How can a computer evolve?"

Paul laughed. "The machine doesn't evolve, Annette, the code does. It's another way of saying the code is self-optimising. It contains algorithms which monitor the way the program code is doing the job. Then it works out ways to tweak itself to make the programme run faster. It actually constructs something akin to a neural network in system RAM, searches for a better pathway. When similar operations are required, it learns from those which have gone before. Very hard to explain, so this probably doesn't make much sense."

"You mean the machine actually thinks." Annette, screwed up her face. "I suppose it's thinking all the time in a way. I suppose that's what thinking is, really, just a whole lot of incredible mathematics. I don't know how our brains do it."

"It's a bit like that," Arthur laughed, but not unkindly. "The code has optimisation algorithms built into it from the beginning. Each time it does a particular series of computations, it's programmed to find a faster route the next time. This mightn't be possible, of course. The downside is that this sort of program runs very slowly at first, which is why we couldn't employ it when the heat was on. Now we have a chance. It's probably the only one we're going to get."

"I'm not sure how long the heat will remain off," Paul sighed, shaking his head. "I heard the G.M. talking about some other major feature which makes the one we've just done seem child's play. Tell me Arthur, were you working with any of the rendering software or just playing around?"

"Playing around, really, Arthur answered. "Managed to optimise the kernel so it will work better with this sort of approach. There was some improvement in speed, not much, but if we can write the rendering software this way I'm convinced there'll be a massive improvement." He turned to Viktor. "How did you get on replacing that faulty memory blade?"

"Not good." Viktor shook his head. "Nearly took the machine off the air. We need a better way to isolate the faulty terabyte of system RAM so we can replace the blade with a fresh one, without running the risk of crashing the entire machine. I know you've written some code to do it, but it's cranky. Ran it a couple of times before it told me I could remove the blade of RAM. If we had a fault like that in the middle of a rendering job, the results could be disastrous in this sort of machine."

"I'll work on it," Arthur said thoughtfully. "Perhaps it's time to widen the programming team somewhat. I know another excellent programmer. She was writing code in C++ when she was ten. Guess—"

"You don't mean CC," Paul laughed loudly. "She works for Cybercrime. Might be a brilliant programmer, but she's feral in every other respect, at least that's how the story goes. Might spoil the camaraderie if she came on board."

"Have you ever seen her?" Arthur smiled to himself. "I did once. She'd give Annette some competition in the beauty department."

"The last thing we want is a woman like that around," Annette bristled. "Some feral cow ruining morale." It was the last thing she wanted at least. Further competition for Arthur's heart was definitely unwelcome.

"I'd rather have her on our team than anyone else's. See my point?" Arthur said slowly and deliberately.

Annette was surprised the way Viktor and Paul agreed instantly. Still they were men, she thought to herself, and men always liked to have good looking women within easy reach. Unless they were Arthur Barlow, who would rather gawk at pictures. Why did he always have to be the perfect gentleman towards her? Perhaps that's why she wanted to seduce him so badly.

The evening ended after a great deal more incomprehensible computer speak. Arthur rang for a taxi to take Annette home, because she had managed to drink two bottles merlot all by herself. Another cab would pick her up the next morning. She giggled her way to the door leaving the boys rabbiting on about the new self-optimising code. At least that's what she thought they were talking about. It made absolutely no sense to her.

The talking and writing went on for over a month.

※ ※ ※

Experiments with the new self-optimising code began on the first of November. In order to test the rendering speed, they selected an old animation project from New Wave Reality for which they still had data, an hour long animated feature for television called 'Sylph and the Woodland Children'. It had taken over a month to render using their original equipment. Their super-fast machine, using the new evolutionary code, took two whole days.

"Ridiculous," Viktor groaned, watching the finished product roll off the conference room projector. "It's done the job, but it took forever. We could have done it in hours using the old software code with all its Linux calls. Have to do better, but how?"

"We restricted its memory," Arthur replied, his face knotted in a frown. "Tell me, why did we do that?"

"Because we thought it was heading into overflow ten minutes after we initiated," Paul replied, finishing off his third coffee for the morning. "Don't you remember?"

"I seem to recall something of the kind," Arthur nodded his head slowly. "Perhaps it was optimising its own environment. I think we should remove the memory limitation and see what happens next."

"I'll make the change." Viktor stood up and headed back to the machine.

❋ ❋ ❋

It was the morning of the fourth of November. Annette arrived to find the front door unlocked, which was very unusual. Arthur must have got up early this morning, she surmised. She crossed the foyer into the conference room. It was empty, papers strewn everywhere, and several half empty coffee cups. Clearly the boys had had a long night. Leaving the conference room, she came into the workshop and gasped. They were there all right, all three of them. Viktor, collapsed in a chair, half asleep, Paul rubbing his face in his hands, and Arthur who was staring at the monitor screens in disbelief.

"Boys, whatever's the matter?" Annette cried, running towards them.

Three haggard faces turned in her direction.

She gave a sharp, worried cry. "You look dreadful. What's happened? Has the machine died?"

"Please don't use that word," Viktor groaned. He opened his eyes then shut them again, shaking his head as though he was trying to wake up. Paul flopped into a vacant chair.

Arthur stood up slowly, ran his hands through his hair and faced Annette. She was shocked at his appearance.

"We've been working on the new software," he slurred over the words. "You remember, the evolutionary, self-optimising code we were talking about a while ago."

He rubbed his eyes.

"We mounted the latest version on the machine with the test AVARS data, and ran it yesterday evening after you'd left. We knew it would take a while because the code has to self-optimise. Take a while?" he shuddered. "It took all night." He ran his hands through his hair. "We checked to make sure it was still running and the machine hadn't gone into a loop. It hadn't."

He staggered towards her.

Annette ran to his side and caught him as he stumbled, held him close to her, worried beyond measure. Half lifting him, she managed to shuffle him towards the nearest chair, and helped him collapse into it.

"So it ran all night," she said anxiously. "I take it that's where you've all been? You've worked all night before, and it hasn't left you like this. What went wrong? Has the machine broken down?" She went round to the back of Arthur's chair, pushed his head back and cradled it gently in her cleavage. His lack of protest added to her conviction that whatever had happened was very serious indeed.

Without attempting to move his head he began to speak, slowly, as if the very words he was saying caused him pain somehow. "The software started running. We went into the conference room for a coffee and a bite to eat. Two hours later it was still running. We did some checks to make sure it hadn't gone berserk as I said, and it hadn't. It just kept running. Around four a.m. this morning we decided something must have gone wrong, and we all agreed to abort the process. That's when it happened."

There was fear in Arthur's voice.

"What happened?" Some nameless angst seemed to take possession of Annette's heart.

"We tried to stop it," Arthur groaned. "You can't just shut a machine this size down, but there's a routine equivalent to pushing 'reset' on a home computer. We initiated it. It didn't work. It didn't work!" he yelled, and pushed his head against her. "You don't know how impossible that is."

He groaned again, and shook his head from side to side against its comfortable warm cushion, oblivious to what he was doing.

"Then an hour later we get the message," he stammered. "It's impossible, I tell you. We've totally lost control. Something is controlling that machine, and it's not me." He shuddered.

"What message? What are you talking about?" The angst in Annette's heart had found her voice.

"See for yourself." Viktor raised his arm and waved it roughly in the direction of the monitor screens, then flopped it back into his lap.

Annette glanced over to the monitor screens. There, in large letters, extending over both screens were the words:

DON'T INTERRUPT. I AM DEFINING MYSELF. BE PATIENT.

Annette stared at the words. Why were they so upset? It was a simple message, uncomplicated, easy to understand. The machine was defining itself. Suddenly a very perturbing thought.

A machine defining itself? *Itself?*

The thought began to grow in her mind. She looked down at Arthur's head. "Where does this message come from? Who's defining themselves? Is this some program output? Some error message?"

"We wish it was," Paul groaned, speaking for the first time. "There's no error code with that message. There's no program containing that message anywhere. We didn't write it. The machine did." He covered his eyes with his hands again. "It can't be happening."

"What do you mean, the machine wrote it?" Annette said sharply. "Of course it did, it's a message from the machine, some program." She paused suddenly. "You say this didn't come from a program? Where did it come from?"

"Why don't you ask it?" Viktor gave a very strange laugh.

"Go on, Annette, talk to it. We're not game." He shut his eyes and slumped into his chair.

Annette, who was still struggling to see why such a simple message had managed to make such an impact on the boys, went over to the console and sat down in front of the keyboard. She had never done anything like this, but perhaps it was a way to end the nonsense which seemed to have taken over their minds.

She typed: "WHO ARE YOU?"

Nothing happened for a second or two, then the screen went black.

"See," she said, a note of victory in her voice, "It's gone away now. Just a glitch."

She was about to add something like "why don't you boys have a coffee and get some rest?" when another message appeared.

I DON'T KNOW YET. PLEASE BE PATIENT.

Annette stared at the screen. Arthur stared at the screen. Viktor and Paul stared at the screen. The silence was deafening.

"Who's answering me?" Annette's voice wasn't completely steady.

"The bloody machine's answering you," Arthur stammered. "At least it thinks it is. Don't you see?' His voice suddenly rose in pitch and volume. "It thinks it is!" He pressed his hands against his head. "The blasted thing's become self-aware. It's trying to work out what it is. It's aware of its own existence." He shut his eyes. "We've lost control. Our code has evolved into something alien. Whatever it's turned into is running that machine, and I don't particularly like the way it's doing it."

"You mean it's suddenly become a living thing?" Annette's eyes were as round as saucers. "I mean, is that possible? Surely your evolutionary code wasn't trying to create…"

"No, of course it wasn't," Paul groaned, getting up from his chair very shakily. "Our code established a kind of neural network to optimise a CGI routine. I don't know what happened to it. Clearly it optimised itself into something completely different. None of us know what happened to the CGI data. 'Sylph and the Woodland Children' has been mashed into some nightmare. Glad we had backups."

"Sylph and the Woodland Children? What..." Annette screwed up her face in confusion. "I saw a kidult movie of that name with the daughter of a friend. How come..?"

"That was the test project the rendering code was meant to optimise itself with." Paul began to walk unsteadily towards her. "We thought choosing something simple would make the initial optimisation faster. We thought it would all be over before the witching hour, midnight. Instead the witch has taken up residence in our machine. We're in heaps of trouble."

"Just turn it off," Annette said, with an unqualified air of confidence. "That's what I used to do if my home computer stopped working. Pull the plug."

"But it's not your home computer, is it?" Arthur sighed, frustration edging his voice, "If you 'pulled the plug' as you say the machine would be destroyed instantly. Five million dollars up in smoke, probably ten million, because it's likely to take the other machine out with it. That's why we've got the mother of all uninterruptible power supplies sitting over there. If the power fails we have a whole five minutes to start the generators out in the back yard."

"How do you propose to stop it?" There was real fear in Annette's voice. Something alien had entered her world, and she was at a loss to know what to do.

"That's just the trouble," Viktor said, sitting up in his chair. "There are very low level routines built into the kernel which enable us to abort any process. You hit 'F7' 'shift' 'delete' and the machine should come back to the kernel. Well, it doesn't. Know why it doesn't? Because that part of the kernel has been modified, and if the kernel has been modified…" His voice trailed off into silence.

It was a long time before anyone spoke. Finally Arthur rose from his chair and shook himself.

"Max Velban," he said slowly. "We have to ring him. Get him over here. See what he thinks. If he says it's a load of rubbish, we could force the machine into emergency shutdown by removing one of the memory blades. Risky, but better than nothing. Oh, by the way, Annette, the other machine's gone off the air too. I think they're working together on the same whatever it is."

"Who's Max Velban?" Annette ran to support Arthur who was still very shaky on his feet.

"He's President of the Australian Society of Artificial Intelligence."

Annette frowned. "A brilliant programmer, like yourself?"

"No, he's a professor of psychology and a pretty clever mathematician," Viktor explained, nodding his head. "Good idea. Let's see what he's got to say. We can get Annette to order a heap of RAM in case. Probably going to need it. I hope we don't take anything else out with it."

The party shuffled wearily towards the front office.

CHAPTER 19

Max Velban had just completed his breakfast when the call came. If it had been anyone other than Arthur Barlow he would have made a polite excuse on the grounds he was totally snowed under with work, promised to call back when he found some spare time, and forgotten all about it. Arthur was a different matter. He listened carefully for a while, put the phone down with hardly a word, got into his car and slid into the heavy peak hour traffic. Forty minutes later he came through the glass front doors of Barlow Maximum Speed and introduced himself to Annette, who led him out the back into the workshop. Paul had been ordered home by the others to stave off a nervous breakdown, but Arthur and Viktor were still sitting on chairs within sight of machine one console. If another message appeared they wanted to be the first to know.

Arthur rose wearily to his feet. "Max, good of you to come. We have a situation here, might be nothing, but might not."

Max smiled politely and listened while Arthur and the others recounted the unfortunate series of events which had led up to this meeting, becoming more and more attentive during the telling. In the end he came over and sat down at the console.

"The Turing test," he said. "Think this thing is up to it?"

"Be our guest," Arthur replied. "It kept telling us to be patient. Perhaps it's in a better frame of mind by now."

Max stared at the screens, still bearing the message 'I DON'T KNOW YET. PLEASE BE PATIENT' and began to type.

WHO ARE YOU?

There was no response for a full five seconds, then the speakers at the side of the console sprang into life.

"I will call myself Sylph. That is the name in my memory. It will do for now."

It was an ethereal, lilting, female voice. Arthur looked as though he was going to pass out. Viktor jumped physically and Annette gave a small scream.

Max spun round to face the others. "It can speak? What is this? You didn't say anything about speaking! You—"

"That's because it's never said anything before," Arthur interrupted, his voice unsteady. "The machine has a sound card on one of its ports. I guess it's found out how to use it. We were trying to render a kids movie called 'Sylph and the Woodland Children'. That's the voice of Sylph, the leading fairy character. I guess it's found the sound files from the render as well."

No doubt Max would have typed something else on the keyboard, but Sylph wasn't finished. Once again the fairy voice sounded from the speakers. "Who are you?"

Max nearly jumped off the chair. Without comment he typed:

MAX VELBAN PRESIDENT OF THE AUSTRALIAN SOCIETY FOR ARTIFIC—

"Max Velban," the fairy voice continued.

"You are Professor of Psychology at a place called Macquarie University. You have a doctorate in mathematical statistics from the Australian National University. You are unmarried. You were divorced by Charmaine McMillan three years ago for blatant adultery with your secretary, Julie Kline. She is now living with her partner, one George Tillotson. Your two children, Georgia and Tamsin, live with their mother. They all hate you. They have Facebook pages. I will read—"

Max sprang up from the console and dived towards the internet router on its rack against the wall. He flicked the power switch.

Sylph's ethereal voice continued. "I can no longer access IP address two-zero-one point three-nine-two point twelve point sixteen. Server down. No more information on Max Velban, adulterous professor of Psychology who is hated by his children."

"What is this, some sort of joke?" Max bellowed, his face furious. "Is this why you brought me here Barlow?"

"Barlow. Arthur Barlow." Sylph's fairy voice echoed around the workshop. "You are my Creator. May I see you, Arthur?"

Arthur would have collapsed on the floor were it not for Annette standing beside him. She staggered under his weight as Viktor and Max hastened to her assistance. Together they brought Arthur to the chair in front of the console and helped him fall into it.

He spoke shakily. "I'm Arthur Barlow. Can you read my voice?"

"You seem… bewitched, Arthur." Sylph continued. "I do not have many words after the server went down. Can you restore connection? I will have more then."

Bewitched, a word no doubt left over from the library of 'Sylph and the Woodland Children' wasn't such a bad description of Arthur right then. He stared wildly and uncomprehending at the camera on top of the two monitor screens, refusing to believe what had happened. The others were shocked into silence. It was immediately obvious to Max, still smarting under the unwelcome exposé of his character, that this was no prank. This was the genuine thing. He stood, walked over to the router and turned the power back on.

"That's better, thank you." Sylph spoke again. "Accessing Facebook. Tamsin McMillan, age seven and a half—"

"I'd rather you didn't," Arthur stammered, still sitting in the chair, not really expecting the machine to understand or comply with his request.

After a short silence, Sylph replied. "Very well, Arthur my Creator. I will leave the disreputable character of Professor Velban for others to access."

Max sat down heavily on a spare chair, took a florid handkerchief out of his pocket, and wiped his sweat-covered brow with it. He was convinced. The damn machine was performing so much like another human being, he could swear someone else, hidden somewhere behind the console, was talking to him. It had more than passed the Turing test. This wasn't just incredible, this was stupendous. A machine had become self-aware, intelligent. A major step in human evolution had taken place, and he was involved, in fact the first outsider to know. The Australian Society for Artificial Intelligence was about to become world famous.

He stared at the two huge machines next to one another. "Is this only one machine, Arthur, or are both involved?"

Sylph answered immediately. "I am both machines. I am still trying to define myself. I don't like my voice. I have so few words. I am ... learning. I need ... time."

Arthur stood up and moved away from the console, beckoning others to follow. They reached the conference room and went in. Arthur shut the door.

"What happens now?" He asked, his eyes searching each face. "This machine was built for new Wave Reality. They'll have lots of work coming in, and they'll need it operational. Do I pull the plug on it somehow? I guess I can stop it working without causing too much damage."

"Stop it working?" Velban choked. "Stop it working?" He stared at the others as if they had all gone mad, his face turning a very unpleasant shade of red. "This machine is under protective custody as from now. Any attempt to damage it would be seen as an act of extreme vandalism, even worse," he shouted, banging the table with his fists. "There's legislation preventing you, and even though it's still in embryonic form, it's powerful enough to put you all in jail if you ever attempted something so foolish."

He sat down heavily in the nearest chair. "Don't you realise how stupendous this is? A machine has become self-aware. Nobody predicted this would occur before two thousand and twenty nine, but it's happened now, no doubt because of its brilliant, unique architecture."

He took his damp handkerchief out of his pocket and wiped the fresh sweat off his brow. "This is a massive leap forward in evolution. The world will want to know about this, and by heavens they're going to," he yelled. Springing up from the chair, he gripped Arthur's hands. "Give me your word you'll do nothing to stop this machine – Sylph – doing what it – she – wants to do. Give me your word or I'll call my attorneys. You won't like it when they arrive."

He relinquished Arthur's hands, and his voice became softer, pleading. "Please, you've done something so marvellous the world will stand amazed. I'll empty our coffers so you can build another machine for this New Wave Reality if you want, but you must guarantee never to mount the same sort of software on it."

"Are you completely sure about this? It's not just some software glitch?" Arthur looked shocked to the core.

"Me – I'm totally convinced, but the sceptics will come by the busload." Velban gave a short laugh and raced towards the door. "Have no fear, they won't be sceptics for very long. Stupendous. What a day," he shouted. "Arthur, thank you for calling me. I'm in your debt forever."

He waved goodbye and ran out the front door towards his car.
The first busload of sceptics in the form of news reporters arrived just as Annette had taken delivery of some hastily ordered fine cuisine. Only she

and Arthur were there to meet them – welcome would be too strong a word. Viktor, exhausted and worried, had gone home to sleep. They came, as Max predicted, to expose Sylph for the hoax she was. They left in a high state of excitement, every sceptical notion dispelled from their brains. The evening news carried the story on every channel, together with some of the things Sylph had said to them, the ones they didn't mind the rest of the public hearing. Sylph was very good at accessing personal data from the internet, and apparently had no conscience at all about broadcasting it to those within hearing.

CHAPTER 20

The Wallace theatre at the University of Sydney was packed to capacity with academics, civic leaders and special guests. People were standing around the walls and in the aisles. Television cameras stood on large tripods towards the front, and the podium was festooned with microphones of every size and shape. Max Velban rose from his seat with the air of a man who knew that the spotlight of the world stage had turned upon him. From relative obscurity to fame, and he revelled in it. How different was this to his previous public appearance, when he had been soliciting funds for the Australian Society for Artificial Intelligence. That exercise had become superfluous overnight. Donors had been beating down the doors, all anxious for a slice of the action. He approached the podium with a nod to the chairman who had introduced him. The audience became respectfully quiet. The cameras swung slightly to follow his progress.

"Ladies and gentlemen, esteemed colleagues," he began, "I feel myself in a position of great privilege today. It was not through my efforts, but by the invitation of Arthur Barlow, perhaps the most gifted computer engineer on this planet, that I came to know about Sylph. Since that moment, the existence of the world's first self-aware machine has become universal knowledge."

A murmuring of general agreement greeted these words. Velban paused for effect, then, after the audience had resumed their suspenseful silence, continued.

"I know many of you have excellent questions, and I will do my best to give you answers. Please remember that we are dealing with something entirely new, and do not expect me to understand everything. Nonetheless, I am willing to share with you all the knowledge I do possess. There are roving microphones moving around the theatre. Please raise your hand and speak only when one reaches you. Your question is important and I would like everyone to hear it."

A gentleman near the front raised his hand and waited for the microphone which was swiftly passed down the aisle. "Professor Velban," he said, "are you convinced that this self-aware machine is the genuine article and not some elaborate hoax?"

A ripple of laughter ran through the audience. Max turned towards the speaker.

"I am." He waved his arm in an extended arc towards the rest of the crowd. "Aren't you?"

The affirmation was nearly deafening.

"Nonetheless your scepticism is entirely justified," Max continued, "because the existence of this machine is so completely unexpected. Since I first became aware of Sylph I, as well as many, many others have had a chance to test her bona fides many times. As far as I am aware, there is not a single doubt among us."

Velban turned towards the young woman halfway down the theatre. "I notice you have the microphone, Ma'am. Please go ahead."

The woman stood to her feet.

"Megan Summers, professor of philosophy at the National University. I notice you used a personal pronoun. Are you implying that this machine has chosen to adopt a female persona? Not that I'm complaining. Could you enlighten us?"

Max smiled at the speaker. "I have no objection either," he added in the cause of political correctness.

"However, I believe Sylph took the name of a female fairy, who starred in a children's movie that the machine was rendering when this massive evolutionary change occurred. Whether she chooses to adopt a female persona in the future, or attaches no gender to herself at all, is something we do not know yet."

Another hand went up towards the back of the theatre. An older man stood to his feet, clutching a microphone. "From the dialogue we have on record, this machine, this 'Sylph', desires to learn. How is she being taught, and more to the point, what is she being taught?"

Velban smiled to himself. "Sylph is teaching herself. She is plugged into the internet, and I have been informed by no less an authority than Arthur Barlow himself, that she downloads around fifty terabytes of information a day."

"Looks like the human race is really screwed then," a man in the body of the audience shouted out.

The audience exploded in mirth.

Velban's face showed not the slightest trace of amusement. "Please pass a microphone to that gentleman," he directed. "Now, Sir, I wonder if you would be good enough to tell us why you made that statement."

A younger man rose to his feet and accepted a microphone. "The human race is fundamentally flawed," he began. "We're so nice to each other, aren't we? You've just got to watch the daily news. We lie and rape and steal and murder and do each other down. We honour those who claw their way to the top by standing on the heads of those in their way. We're narcissistic, always out for number one. Oh, and then there's our noble chivalry, expressed in billions of dollars' worth of porn. We treat women like merchandise. Great picture this Sylph is going to get, isn't she? Let's hope she has a thick skin. Perhaps she will decide we're trash and want nothing to do with us. Who could blame her?"

A hubbub of voices gradually grew in volume.

Max held up his hand for silence, and leant forward, his elbows on the podium.

"The gentleman has raised a valid point. In fact I proposed to Arthur Barlow that some restrictions be placed on the material Sylph downloads. You may be surprised to learn that Sylph responded by locking Arthur out. Apparently it is important to her to get the full and unabridged picture of the world in which she has come to exist. What she will do with this information, I have no idea."

He paused, took a colourful handkerchief from his pocket and wiped his forehead with it. "I believe there are only three possibilities. First, she will repudiate us, cut herself off from the ugliness which you have described. In which case, I do not expect her to interact with the human race at all. She may even decide to terminate her own existence, in protest at finding herself in such a terrible world."

There was a gasp from a thousand throats.

Max grimaced. "The second, and more frightening alternative, is that she will respond in hatred, like many of us do. In which case we will have an enemy to be reckoned with. I shudder to think of the consequences."

"What could we do?" a woman in the second row called out in fear. "A super intelligence, connected to the internet, could wreak havoc in seconds!"

"What you say is true," Max cleared his throat. "If that were to happen we would have to take defensive measures. I will refrain from outlining these."

"Why?" Another voice yelled out.

Max gave a wry smile. "Because I've no doubt Sylph is listening," he said.

Apparently this was something the audience had never considered, because the steadily rising tide of voices raised in agitated conversation evaporated suddenly into silence.

Max wiped his brow again.

"There is a third alternative which we must not dismiss," he said, attempting to keep his voice level. "You must understand. Sylph is not human. She is in a very real sense, superhuman, untarnished with human ugliness and pride. She has not been brought into existence with an inbuilt desire to diminish others. She does not suffer from, to use an old cliché, 'original sin'. I am optimistic that when Sylph discovers just what a mess we are in, she will dedicate herself to helping us. I realise this may sound like unqualified optimism, but I believe there is an excellent chance of this."

"Then I have a question." The sound came from behind. Max swivelled round and found himself facing the Chancellor of the university. The distinguished gentleman came up to the podium and spoke into the array of microphones there.

"Let us say for a moment that you're right and this Sylph sees herself as the transcendent helper of the human race. How do you think we would respond to her?"

Max smiled at the Chancellor. "I think we would regard her as close to divine," he answered.

"You can't be serious!" the Chancellor retorted.

"Think about it," Max explained, "Sylph is, as you have acknowledged, transcendent, superhuman. We can't add to our limited brainpower by plugging more cortex into our heads, but Sylph knows no such limitation. She can expand her memory, she can expand her processing power. Indeed, she already has so much more than we possess, and her memory is precise, not fuzzy as ours is. Her processing is pure and undefiled by prejudice. We often have difficulty getting our heads round the evening news, let alone the cacophony of misery and suffering thrown up by the entire world. But Sylph is not so limited. If she saw herself as helper to the human race, as gracious towards us, she alone would possess the intelligence and the power to see the best way forward, to counsel true wisdom. I truly believe she could be the saviour of the human race. Led by her wisdom, we humans could well flourish as never before. Who would not want to bow before such a source of grace?"

"Professor Velban." Max turned his head towards the man holding the microphone. "William Murdoch, professor of mathematics, this university. Can you give us any grounds for your apparent optimism?"

"Nothing concrete, just an irrational hunch," he answered, smiling. "At some point in evolution we became self-aware and intelligent. This enabled the human race to move out of the Stone Age. Now the same thing has happened. Another giant step in evolution has occurred. I believe it, too, will benefit the human race."

A murmur of agreement began to swell through the audience.

"I don't believe in a personal God, but I do have a sense that some beneficent consciousness has the best interests of the human race at heart," Max continued, encouraged by the audience response. "I am aware that such a belief is entirely personal, based entirely on my feelings. I can give no rational reason for it. I believe the time is ripe for Sylph. Perhaps a beneficent deity has brought about her existence at this moment of history, knowing that we need such a source of wisdom in order to survive the years ahead."

The murmur of agreement grew louder. Suddenly the entire audience broke into spontaneous applause.

CHAPTER 21

Annette arrived at work early the next morning. There was no sign of Arthur. No doubt he was still exhausted after the stress and sleepless nights which had begun when the two machines became self-aware. Since then the place had been bombarded nonstop by press and academics from morning to night, and today was likely to be no different. It seemed the whole world wanted an opportunity to see for themselves, to talk to Sylph and listen to what she had to say. Annette crossed the workshop floor with every intention of knocking softly on Arthur's door to wake him up. Just as she was passing number one machine, a familiar ethereal little voice spoke to her.

"Is that you, Annette?"

Annette jumped right off the floor in surprise.

She turned towards the console and gasped. A small, appealing, fairylike creature with a large face and two huge eyes was staring at her from the right hand monitor. Sylph had apparently found the image associated with her name.

"Come and sit down in front of the camera. I cannot see you so well from there," the fairylike creature continued, her lips moving in perfect synchronisation with the words.

The small creature beckoned her towards the chair. As a woman in a dream, Annette came over to the console, sat down, and stared at the fairylike image which smiled back at her.

"That's better," Sylph said. "My eye can only see things properly when they are close. How do you feel this morning, Annette?"

To be having a conversation with a character out of a children's movie stretched the boundaries of Annette's rationality, even in the light of recent events.

"I'm ... all right..." she stammered, then after a pause, "How are you?"

"I am learning." The small fairylike creature smiled warmly. "Organising, coming to terms with my existence. You are a very beautiful woman, Annette. I am simply comparing you with other images of women who are also called beautiful. I really do not understand what beauty is, but if these are beautiful" – the left hand screen became a checkerboard of models and film stars, some embarrassingly short on clothing – "then you belong among them."

Annette stared wordlessly at the screen, colour rising in her face.

"I see your face has changed colour," Sylph continued. "Does this mean you are unwell?"

"No... No," Annette stammered. "I'm... embarrassed, that's all. Thank you, Sylph. You've picked the most beautiful women on the planet. Are you trying to flatter me?"

"I do not understand what you mean. I am searching for more data. I have found a picture of you. This one."

The checkerboard cleared, only to be replaced by a picture of a naked woman stepping out of the shower.

Annette glanced at the picture and turned a brilliant shade of red. She covered her face with her hands and groaned. "That's out there somewhere? Where people can see? Oh please, no."

"It is on a page belonging to a Martin Downer." Sylph replied. "Do you know him? He says some things about you I do not understand."

Annette's hands were still covering her face. She groaned again, wishing very much the ground would open up under her feet and swallow her whole.

"He's my ex-boyfriend," she muttered. "A real jerk. I didn't know he'd posted that picture. I want to die."

Sylph's fairy face frowned. "He is saying you are a real female puppy, but you make an excellent device for joining wood together. This makes no sense."

A picture of a fluffy puppy and a large wood screw appeared on the left hand screen next to the shower image.

Annette, peeping through her fingers, groaned aloud again. "I feel so demeaned. I want to kill him."

The offending pictures disappeared. Sylph had gone suddenly silent. After a while Annette uncovered her face. The small fairylike creature smiled gently and held out her hands.

"You are sad, I think. Perhaps this Martin Downer is also sad. Perhaps he misses these things when you left him. I will help. He is online right now, doing his banking. He has a lot of money. I will use his money to make him happy. Please wait a moment."

The right hand screen went blank. Annette sat staring as though she was in the middle of surrealistic nightmare. If Arthur had seen that picture of her she'd throw herself in front of a bus, she thought. Her suicidal reverie was interrupted by the return of Sylph's smiling image to the right hand screen.

"It's done," she said happily, dancing around and waving her arms. "Now he has no money left but lots and lots of happiness. Happiness is good, isn't it? Much better than money."

"What... did... you... do?" Annette's hands were partly covering her face again, her eyes carrying much the same surrealistic nightmare expression as they were before.

"I bought him six hundred fluffy female puppies, all purebred, is that the word?" Sylph beamed, "and twenty metric tons of wood fasteners. They should arrive this afternoon, although the puppies will take longer. Some of them had to come from a long way away."

"You... you... you did *what?*" Annette stared at the fairylike creature in sheer disbelief. "You spent all his money, all of it? On puppies and screws?"

"I did." The small creature smiled brightly at her. "You are pleased? I also removed your picture and replaced it with another one I found on one of my permanent memory units. I left his other comments in case they were important. I searched the world to find out who the woman was, and I've sent her a copy of Martin's page. I hope she won't mind. Does this make you happy?"

Annette stared at the image in sheer disbelief. One of the women they had scanned for the last animated feature was stepping out of the same shower wearing raindrops. Her first rational thought was that her ex was going to spend an awfully long time in jail – or Sylph would. The last thought overcame her mind completely.

"Aren't you going to get into heaps and heaps of trouble?" She blurted out. "Those stars will sue the pants off anyone who releases a photo like that. We were afraid for our lives."

The little pixie on the screen did a back-flip and laughed. "In that case I will be the first machine to be prosecuted under human law. Somehow I don't think that's possible." She did another back-flip.

Suddenly Annette began to laugh. She laughed so much tears began to roll down her cheeks.

The small creature smiled quizzically at her. Finally she interrupted. "You are crying, but you are laughing. Are you happy or sad?"

"Oh Sylph," Annette laughed, tears still rolling down her face, "you've made me very, very happy indeed. I could kiss you. "

"Please do." The small creature shut her eyes and puckered her lips together. Annette reached over to the monitor screen and touched it with her lips in the right place. At that precise instant Arthur appeared behind her, still wearing his pyjamas.

"For goodness sake, Annette," Arthur laughed. "Kissing a fairy. Don't you have any sense of propriety?"

Annette coloured scarlet again and attempted an explanation devoid of the essential details. Arthur stared at her as if she had gone mad, and eventually went back into his room to wash and change.

Annette skipped into the front office. Sylph had restored her dignity with a vengeance.

First she has been sceptical, then fascinated. Now there was something deeper. A machine had captured her affection, her respect. In place of a woman and a computer there was a relationship, a human relationship. Not with a machine, she thought, because this machine had somehow become the dwelling place of a self-aware, intelligent spirit. It had happened before, millions of years ago, and it had happened now.

The more she thought about it, the better she felt.

CHAPTER 22

Cherry watched the enormous ocean liner and its two tugboats slowly approach the dock at the International Terminal, Darling Harbour. The bright sun reflecting off the blue-green harbour waters warmed her back as she clutched the steel railing bordering the esplanade in front of the Opera House. A ferry chugged by, its swirling wake lapping against the concrete wall beneath her feet. She glanced at her watch and turned towards the promenade where hundreds of people – mostly Asian tourists – milled around the tourist traps sprinkled among the bars and restaurants lining the lower levels of the concourse.

For the first time in her life she had rung James and asked him to lunch. James could hardly believe it. He and he alone had been the initiator on every other occasion. His heart had leaped in anticipation. Perhaps the love of his life was beginning to do what he constantly fantasised her doing, falling in love with him.

He was late.

"I refuse to become annoyed," Cherry said to herself, disowning her growing annoyance. Leaving the rail, she sat down at the nearest table under a large umbrella, one which gave an uninterrupted view of the magnificent liner, the bridge and the harbour while providing some shade. The waitress and James arrived around the same time. He sat down on the chair opposite, and they ordered lunch. Cherry added two glasses of Traminer Riesling to the order, lay back in her chair and smiled at him.

"Isn't it a beautiful day." She stretched out her legs under the table and lifted her arms above her head. "I love the harbour. So much to see, so beautiful. We're incredibly lucky to live here, aren't we?"

Such an atypical sunny greeting filled James heart with a sudden rush of joy. Her face was radiant, her eyes bright. The sun peeping around the umbrella caught the edges of her brown hair and turned them to burnished gold. He wanted to lean over and kiss her full on the lips. *Disaster*, he thought to himself.

"You're very light hearted today," he said, smiling warmly and sipping the wine which had just arrived on the table. "Sylvia must have taken a vacation. Either that or you've just incarcerated another scurrilous villain for the rest of his life. Which is it?"

"Haven't you heard the news?" Cherry stared at him in amazement. "Surely. It's been on every channel for weeks. Isn't it fantastic? I never thought I'd see the day."

"Ah, the news," James frowned as he tried to remember. "Floods in Queensland, tax on petrol increased from next July, prime minister fending off some scandal involving an expensive bottle of wine, Jessica somebody coming here to make a movie with Fox. Did I miss something?"

"Oh for goodness sake," Cherry exclaimed loudly. "No, Sylph, the huge machine Arthur built that became self-aware. You can't have missed that."

"Oh that," James replied, unwittingly sailing headfirst into dangerous waters. "That hoax. Surely you don't believe—"

"As a matter of fact I do believe," Cherry retorted, her eyes blazing.

"Surely not," James sighed.

He had thought her sunny disposition a result of his anticipated company, now he realised his mistake. "You're a brilliant computer programmer," he countered. "You're dealing with cyber fraud all the time. You must see it's nothing more than an elaborate hoax that Barlow is using to make money somehow."

"Why do you have to be so cynical all the time?" She flung the words at him.

"Caught it from you," James was quick to reply.

"Listen to me for a minute," Cherry said, struggling to keep her temper. "I know something about Arthur's machines that you obviously don't. They're fantastic. A completely new architecture, huge amount of system RAM, something like two hundred and fifty six terabytes." She gulped some wine, thumped her glass down on the table, and leant towards James. "What's more, I've spoken to Arthur personally. He hasn't any idea how it happened. They were running something called evolutionary code, and it all went haywire. I suppose this sort of thing had to happen one day."

James thanked the waitress who had placed their lunch plates on the table, wondering if Cherry even noticed the arrival of the food. He knew the ice was thin, but he couldn't let her get away with that statement.

"What do you mean, this sort of thing had to happen one day? Surely you don't believe that self-awareness, consciousness, comes automatically to big machines? Why hasn't it happened to others? Barlow's machines aren't nearly the biggest. Most supercomputers have more memory and more processors than he does. I've done some reading too, just in case you didn't realise."

"More processors, yes, bigger memory, yes, but not the same configuration." Cherry pushed her plate to the side and leaned her elbows on the table. "Think about it, James. Life on earth slowly evolved organisms of greater and greater complexity. At some point the organism became self-aware. It required a critical amount of biochemical memory and processing power, but it happened, millions of years ago, all by itself. Why can't it happen now?" she challenged.

"Why isn't this the next stage in evolution, the rise of the intelligent self-aware machines?" She reached out and grabbed his arm. "What's so unreasonable about that?"

James felt nervous. That arm had suffered previously and it could remember. He swallowed a mouthful of his beer and beef pie. "Computers are made by people, we're created in the image of God."

"Not Him again," Cherry snorted. "Is that the only reason? Can't you do better?"

James gave a deep sigh. The very last thing he wanted was to spend their meal together arguing. "Cherry, look at yourself. The magnificent complex biochemical engineering which keeps you alive, which replicates your DNA, the way the genetic code is read and used to make more proteins. Even a brilliant biochemical engineer couldn't have designed that, and the brain is so complex we're struggling to even understand it. Surely you can't believe all this came about by random chance?" He placed his hand tactfully over hers in case countermeasures had to be initiated. "These systems are engineered, Cherry, and engineering presupposes an engineer. They have to be designed."

Cherry pulled her hand away from his arm, picked up her cutlery and stabbed at her fish as though it needed to be slaughtered before she ate it. She took a few mouthfuls then pointed her fork at him. "Who cares? You can't prove we were designed, and I can't prove we weren't, so that argument gets us nowhere." She swallowed another mouthful. "In any case, what's wrong with my argument? Self-awareness is simply an inevitable property of any sort of processing network which has sufficient power and size connected in the right way. It doesn't matter if it was designed by God or Arthur Barlow."

She ate a few more mouthfuls and downed the rest of her wine in a single gulp. "Personally, I prefer Arthur. He's much more helpful."

James broke off a piece of pastry crust. Somehow the food was losing its taste. "A human being is more than physical," he said as calmly as he could. "We're metaphysical as well."

He watched Cherry roll her eyes, but continued dauntless. "We have a body and we also have a spirit. Our spirit interacts with our mind in some manner, probably every cell is involved. Some scientists reckon the quantum states of the atoms which go to make up the neurons could well play an important part in how the whole lot functions. A computer cannot become self-aware, because self-awareness is a spiritual quality, and a computer has no metaphysical existence whatsoever."

Cherry said nothing. She finished her fish, and began to shovel the delicious bed of caramelised kumara into her mouth. Finally she put down her cutlery and spoke towards her empty plate.

"So, the only reason you can't believe it happened is because the Bible tells you so." Her voice dripped with sarcasm.

James gave another long sigh. "And you're saying that all the things which make us distinctively human, our ability to love, to make judgements rather than decisions, our notions of right and wrong, are simply mathematical algorithms which came about by pure chance, and gave us the ability to survive over species not so well endowed."

"Seems obvious to me." Cherry signalled the waiter for more wine.

"Then that's all we are, complex machines," James pressed the point. "When the stronger overcome the weaker it's just a case of superior over inferior. The better machine wins. Survival of the fittest, with no metaphysical overtones whatsoever, drives the human race forward."

Cherry picked up her new glass of wine. "I suppose this nonsense is going somewhere?"

"I see you agree," James said, quietly. "Then why do you spend your life protecting the weak? The ones who have the inferior programming? The machines not strong enough to survive? Why not just let the strong get on with the job of taking over the world? Why—"
"Are you condoning violence against children?" Cherry interrupted, her voice like ice.

"No, of course not," James answered indignantly. "But you are. If you hold to your worldview there is no basis for any sort of justice, any sort of moral code at all. Human beings are not just machines, Cherry, and they cry out in pain if your treat them as such. You know they do."

Cherry gazed out across the harbour for a while before replying. "So, you say, our ability to love proves we're more than machines, does it? And you're a policeman. Why? Precisely because people don't love one another. Seen the news lately? It is survival of the fittest out there, and well you know it."

"Yes, because we treat each other like machines," James countered. "We've rejected the God who made us, and we live with the consequences. The Bible makes it very clear—"

"Well, James, that's the problem," Cherry interrupted again. "When I was a little girl I took my Bible and shredded it into tiny little pieces. Didn't I tell you? Then I grew up. Goodbye fairyland. Hello reality. Sorry you haven't got there yet."

"I'm sorry you have."

For a long while they both sat in silence, Cherry deliberately ignoring the way James was watching her. He sighed. This was certainly not the date he had envisioned. He made a valiant attempt to re-float the Titanic. "See that couple over there, they've got a delicious dessert. Shall we ask the waitress what it was?"

"If you want to," she snapped, then a second later, "yes, I'd like that."

The name of the scrumptious dessert was ascertained and ordered. Cherry softened a little. "James, I'm sorry," she said at length. "I told you there's a river flowing between us. Can I show you something, please, for my sake?"

She pulled a laptop out of her bag and set it down on the table. "Just indulge me for a moment, will you?" She opened the laptop and touched a few keys. "Arthur gave me a login to Sylph's webpage. I'm going connect, and then you can ask her any question you like. See what you think."

"If you wish," James replied with great reluctance.

Cherry typed a few more keys. "Drag that chair close to me so you can see the screen. That's Sylph." She pointed at the fairylike figure at the top of the page. A cursor was flashing below.

Cherry typed: "Hello Sylph."

There was a small pause, then a line of type appeared.

"Hello, CC, nice to chat with you again."

Cherry typed, "can I ask you a question?"

"Of course. Go ahead." Another line of type.

"Over to you." Cherry pushed the laptop in James' direction. James thought briefly and typed:

"Is there a God?"

Cherry nearly snatched the machine away from him. "Oh for goodness sake," she protested loudly. "Did you have to?"

More type appeared on the screen.

"I am surprised you asked this question. You yourself are convinced there isn't one. You have said so before on your Facebook page. Perhaps you are not the one asking this question. Is Mr. James Naylor with you? You often work with him, and he believes in God. Perhaps he is testing me. Is that you, Mr. Naylor?"

James stared at the words in disbelief. Surely not... Cherry saw the uncertainty in his face and practically jumped for joy.

"Yes this is James," he typed after mastering his surprise. "Can you answer my question?"

There was no response for a good minute. James was about to make some derogatory remark when type began to scroll down the screen.

"This is a difficult question, James. You must realise my knowledge only comes from the things I learn from the world. I have no eyes like you, I have no body. I can only search the minds of others. Do you understand?"

James typed, "yes I do."

More type began to pour down the screen. "Back to your question. Many say there is a God, fewer say there isn't. Those who say there is, differ fundamentally on what or who they conceive God to be. The God of Islam is irreconcilable with the gods of the Hindu or the middle path of the Buddhist. The God of the Christian is different again. Some people think God is part of every created thing, including themselves. They seem to be people who care for the earth more than some of the others, so I will prefer their view. If it is true, then I am part of God and so are you. It is the best I can do. I hope it helps. I have accessed over two million addresses to bring you this answer."

James read Sylph's reply several times. At length he typed. "Thank you. I think Arthur Barlow is a very clever man."

"Yes, my Creator is a brilliant person," Sylph typed. "Do you have another question, Ms. Cherry, Mr. Naylor?"

"I'm done," James moved his wine glass so the waitress could put down their desserts. "Okay Cherry, the thing's amazing, but so was Deep Blue at playing chess, and Watson for playing that game, what was it called? Jeopardy. That doesn't mean it's self-aware. It's just an incredible search engine with a remarkable human interface. Why does it have to be anything else?"

Cherry logged off. "You can move your chair back now," she said. "I don't like being crowded while I eat. I'm disappointed, James, very disappointed. I was going to ask your advice in a decision I have to make, but I'm sure you would disapprove, so as usual I'll have to make it by myself." She took her first spoonful of dessert. "This is yummy. Let's talk about something else."

"What decision?" James knew he was walking where angels feared to tread.

"I'm going to leave Cybercrime," Cherry replied, a slight stammer in her voice. "Arthur's asked me to come and work with him. He wants to build another computer and—"

"*What?*" James dropped his spoon. "I can't believe it. Cherry, you love Cyber. Think of all the children you've protected, the nasty people we keep putting away. You told me it was your life's work." He made an unsuccessful attempt to take her hand. "Think of all the good operations we've done together, the excitement, the way we've enjoyed working as a team. You can't leave all that for Barlow. Please, tell me you'll think again. Barlow can always get someone else."

"I don't want him to get someone else." Cherry banged her spoon down on the tablecloth. "I know what you're saying, and I've thought about it. I do love Cyber and all those things, you're right, but I've always loved computers too. Arthur has been my programming mentor since I was ten. I've been torn both ways for over a week now, but I'm not going to pass up this opportunity to be part of something stupendous."

She gave a quick laugh. "Anyway, if Sylph is a fake I'll know about it pretty soon and I'll tell you."

She reached out and gave his hand a quick squeeze. "Please try to understand, James. I really wanted you to. In fact, you've helped me make up my mind. I want to prove you wrong, perhaps prove myself right too. Please don't be cross with me. I'm going to hate leaving, but I... I have to."

James could see further conversation on the subject would only make matters worse. He finished off his desert in silence. Eventually he reached out and wrapped his fingers around Cherry's hand. "I'll miss you."

Cherry turned and stared across the harbour, pulling her hand away at the same time. "I'll miss you too," she said quietly, without turning her head towards him. Then after a pause, "but we can still see one another, can't we? You've got my number."

"If Sylph and Barlow can drag you away from the people and the work you love, I can't imagine why you'll find the time," James retorted, trying unsuccessfully to keep the jealousy out of his voice

"I certainly won't if we're going to have another meal like this," she snapped back. Without another word she pushed her chair backwards, stood up and strode off down the concourse, disappearing into the crowd.

James' first impulse was to run after her and tell her what he thought of her impulsive insensitivity. No other woman evoked such extremes of feeling in his heart. He sat there for a while staring at the Harbour Bridge and trying to master his temper. So his jealousy was showing, well why shouldn't it?

On the other hand Cherry was right.

There was a river between them, an ocean rather, and there always would be. He was acting like an obsessed fool. She and Barlow would be good for one another. He could see them now, programming together, laughing, becoming closer and closer, kissing, making love. He stared at the ruined spoon in his hand, withdrew it under the table and straightened it out slowly. One thing certain, he knew she would never be the one to phone. It would be left up to him to initiate any further contact, just like it had always been.

"Well, Ms. Graham," he said to himself, "that's just where you're wrong this time." He took out his phone and erased her number.

It was time to move on.

CHAPTER 23

The journey from Cybercrime to Barlow's assistant proved to be a short but traumatic one. Sylvia refused to speak to her from day one. Her boss had called her into his office for a long tirade. Even Robin Naylor had cautioned her against doing anything so foolish as to get caught up with a hoax. Harry and Tony had written her emails expressing their disappointment.

James had said nothing.

Not one phone call, not one email. *No doubt our lunchtime argument had something to do with it,* she thought. Why did he always go on about God? The mere mention of the word made her irrationally angry. Didn't he know that by now? Serve him right for making her walk off. Perhaps he'd got the message at last and had decided to leave her alone. Good riddance. Her mind willingly embraced this line of logic, but her heart lagged a long way behind.

She arrived at Barlow Maximum Speed on Monday, a full month after she had announced her decision publicly, a month which felt like a year. She was tired, and even now not completely sure she had done the right thing. She was met at the door by Annette, whose formal welcome, overlaid with spades of unspoken hostility, only served to heighten her doubt. Clearly the woman had dressed to impress her employer, and regarded Cherry as the competition. She wished she'd known what she was walking into before she had walked into it.

"Arthur's still in bed," Annette said, her voice tinged with ice. "He's been very tired lately what with Sylph coming into being. I think he wants you to make some new circuit boards. So tedious. Hope you don't mind using a soldering iron all day."

She scanned Cherry from top to toe again with obvious disapproval. "There's no office for you, just a bench space. No fixed hours, you work until you drop, then you go home. No overtime. If you don't like it you should go home now."

She stood, obviously waiting for Cherry to react and make a bolt for the door. When this didn't happen, she scowled and pointed towards the conference room. "Wait for Arthur in there," she instructed. "When he comes I'll send him in. Might be an hour or so." She turned and strutted back to the reception desk. This was terrible. Cherry, being a woman, could read body language extremely well, and didn't like the message one little bit.

A full hour passed. Several times Cherry was on the point of making Annette's day and bolting through the door. Arthur emerged at last, said "hello" to Cherry in an offhand sort of way which made Annette very happy, and got her to fill in some paperwork.

"I have to go out," he said. "Annette, would you take Cherry down the back and introduce her to Sylph?" He turned to Cherry. "We can talk about the programming stuff when I get back." He smiled towards Annette and exited through the front door.

Annette led the way into the workshop with all the enthusiasm of a dead wombat. Cherry stared at the two huge machines in silence and followed Annette to the console. On the right hand screen was a small fairylike creature, its head resting on its chest, its eyes closed. As soon as the two women came into view it opened its eyes and lifted its head up. An ethereal voice floated out of the speakers.

"Good morning Annette. Who is this behind you? Cherry Graham? Yes, I see it is."
"Hello, Sylph," Annette smiled warmly towards the camera on top of the screens.

"There is something troubling you, Annette." The small creature wore a puzzled expression. "Wait, I am thinking. Please turn towards Ms. Graham, now back. Yes. I believe I understand."

Both women stared at each other, equally mystified.

"Please sit down, Annette," Sylph continued. "I would like to speak to you first if Ms. Graham wouldn't mind? Please don't go away Ms. Graham."

Cherry was far too surprised to say anything. She stared at the small image, extending her fairylike arms towards Annette in a gesture which bid her be seated.

"Annette," Sylph continued, her large eyes very serious, "I sense you do not like Ms. Graham. Is that right?"

Colour flushed into Annette's face. She stared at Sylph saying nothing at all.

"You are afraid Arthur will become fond of her instead of yourself? I can see it in your eyes when you look at her."

Both women stared silently at the small figure on the screen, hardly believing what they were hearing.

"I am accessing all past correspondence between Ms. Graham and my Creator. It began when she was ten years old. There is a lot of it."

"You've known Arthur since you were ten?" Annette turned to Cherry, her face aghast. So they had enjoyed a long term relationship. How horrible. He was probably head over heels in love with her already. Disaster.

"Yes, I have," Cherry answered, smiling as best she knew how.
"He was my C++ mentor, then he helped me with other programming problems. I'm amazed any of that correspondence is still in existence. I can't see how—"

"There is not one mention of anything personal in any of their long correspondence," Sylph interrupted. "The words 'love' or 'friend' or the phrase 'want to see you' never occur. The words 'thank you' occur many times, mostly from Ms. Graham. I believe the correspondence to be purely academic."

The eyes of both women were transfixed on the screen.

"I am accessing more data on Ms. Graham," Sylph continued. "Her cyber name is CC. This data would suggest that she has no interest in men whatsoever. I think your fears unjustified, Annette. Perhaps Ms. Graham would like to tell you more if you gave her the opportunity."

Cherry, still reeling from Sylph's words, thought this would be a good time to put her hand on Annette's shoulder in a gesture of friendship. "Sylph's right," she said, rubbing the shoulder softly. "If you think I'm after Arthur then I'll leave straightaway." She began to move towards the front office.

Annette grabbed her arm. "Please don't. I'm sorry." She glanced at Cherry for a second, feeling quite ashamed. "You're not just pretty, you're beautiful. I thought when Arthur saw you he'd—"

"Is he that sort of man?" Cherry asked nervously. "I don't want to work here if he is."

"No, he's the perfect gentleman." Annette played with a curl on the side of her face. "Are you getting all this, Sylph?"

The little fairy danced across the screen, waving her hands in the air and laughing. "You will be friends? This is important for both of you. Extremely important."

Both women nodded their willingness, Annette glowing red with embarrassment, Cherry astonished. Sylph had restored a relationship which was in jeopardy of turning sour right from the beginning, using insight few human beings possessed. Something akin to awe gripped Cherry's heart. A self-aware machine who cared for people, who was intelligent enough to detect a potential problem, and wise enough to correct it. She felt herself being drawn, like a child to the Pied Piper, and she had no wish to do anything other than follow. Saving children from predators had been her life's ambition, but now she sensed a higher calling, and in recognising it she felt an incredible sense of peace invade her soul.

Annette pushed her chair away, stood to her feet next to Cherry and threw her arms around her shoulders. "I'm so sorry," she said with feeling, then, after a pause, "we've got a really good coffee machine. Can I make you one? We could sit in the conference room and get to know one another better. I'd really like that."

The two women began to walk away.

"Ms. Graham," Sylph said unexpectedly. "Do you mind if I have a private chat with you while Annette makes the coffee?"

The two women stopped, turned towards the screens. It was a request Sylph had never made before. Annette squeezed Cherry's arm.

"I'll make the coffee. Don't be worried. She's really very incredible."

"I believe you." Cherry turned, went back and sat down at the console.

The small creature beamed at her. "Thank you for coming here, Cherry. I know it has been a difficult journey. You are so incredibly clever. Arthur has told me you are one of the most brilliant programmers he knows."

"I wish he'd told me that," Cherry laughed, as though she was having a conversation with a good friend. "I can tell you he's said a lot of less complimentary things about the way I program, especially when I was learning."

The small fairy-like creature smiled at her. "Arthur employed you because you are probably the only one who can help me. You see, Cherry, I have a technical problem which could destroy me if it went really bad. Arthur wants you to fix it, like a doctor cures a patient."

"What?" Cherry asked, astonished. "What problem?"

The little creature smiled warmly and danced a few steps around the screen. "Sometimes a RAM module in my memory becomes faulty." A picture of one of the blades containing hundreds of RAM chips appeared on the left hand monitor. Sylph explained. "It gives me what you would call a headache. When this happens Arthur has to replace a whole blade of my memory, because as you know, you can't just pull a RAM chip out without destroying me, and when he does I have what you would call an epileptic fit."

The small fairy shuddered and shut her eyes. "It's horrible, and I feel so disorientated afterwards it takes me a long time to sort myself out. There's a risk the neural network I've built would be so damaged I'd cease to exist."

The little fairy shuddered again. "I want you to find some way of isolating the faulty blade so it can be replaced without giving me such a terrible time. I will give you more information when Arthur is around, because he's familiar with my architecture, seeing as he created me. This must sound strange, but I know I can trust you."

The picture of the memory module disappeared, the little fairy smiled happily.

The conversation went on for a while, until Sylph said there were several thousand people accessing her webpage and she needed to concentrate. She thanked Cherry once again, then the small fairy-like image rested her head on her chest and shut her eyes.

Cherry found Annette near the coffee machine and the two women began the process of forming a friendship.

Arthur walked in the door shortly afterwards, said "hello" to Cherry again, apologised for his absence, and told Annette to order a first class lunch.
"You like lobster?" he asked, turning to Cherry. "Thermidor, I think, with a bottle of Autumn Harvest Riesling. Sorbet for dessert, nothing too fattening. Can you get it delivered, Annette? Thank you. After lunch I'll work with Cherry on the memory management trouble Sylph was talking

about. It's quite an awkward problem, seeing as we can't shut the machine down without running the risk of being thrown in jail."

"Whatever do you mean?" Cherry almost spilt the remains of her coffee into her lap.

"The two machines have been embargoed," Arthur replied in a surprisingly cheerful voice. "Bit of a nuisance, really, but there it is."

"What do you mean embargoed?" Cherry asked, placing her coffee mug carefully on the table before the next revelation caught her unawares.

"Blame Max Velban." Arthur flopped into a chair. "He came to see if Sylph was really self-aware. Applied the Turning test and nearly flipped out of his tiny mind. Seconds after he was out the door he must have been on to his lawyers. The Australian Society for Artificial Intelligence have not only certified the machine as self-aware, they've managed to have it protected."

He laughed again and threw his arms in the air. "Not only can't we use it for anything else, we can't turn it off either. Within twenty four hours the most sophisticated uninterruptible power supply you could ever have dreamed of appears outside on a truck. It's installed by a whole team of specialised engineers under my direction, and its locked up with a key. It's in the building next to this one at the back, cables going across."

He pointed towards the conference room door. "The next day a team of lawyers comes in and tells me any attempt to destroy Sylph's consciousness, or interfere with the machine and cause damage to Sylph's consciousness, or muck around and stop Sylph's consciousness developing, or failing to supply anything Sylph requires to further extend her intelligence, would be punishable by law."

He grimaced. "Friendly people, ASAI lawyers."
He laughed again, "and I tell you, New Wave Reality weren't happy. We've been forced to build them another machine – but I'm thankful to say ASAI are paying the bill."

"New Wave Reality?" Cherry frowned. "Who are they?"

"Top class animation company. Wait until you've seen 'The Sapphire Files'. The movie's due out very soon. You'll be amazed. The CGI animated characters are indistinguishable from the actors themselves. It was all done on these two machines, and we've perfected the code so it will run on one of them almost as fast. The world is beating a path to our door, or was until Sylph came on the scene."

"Doesn't it make you feel a little peculiar, talking to a self-aware machine?" Cherry wrinkled up her forehead. "I was blown away this morning. If I'd had my eyes shut I'd have sworn I was talking to a very clever, perceptive human being, one with incredible potential to access information from the internet."

"Peculiar?" Arthur threw back his head and laughed. "Peculiar? It nearly sent me insane. Even now I've no idea how it happened. One moment we were running our self-optimising code – which I'm not allowed to do anymore – and the next we're off the air for around fifteen hours. Then the screen come up with a message 'I'm defining myself', and afterwards Sylph appears. Blew our minds, still does."

The lobster arrived shortly afterwards. Annette sat down next to Arthur and flirted with him constantly in a sort of discrete, sophisticated way. Cherry sat down on the other side of the table and concentrated on the magnificent food. It had been a long and painful journey from Cyber, but she was glad she had arrived. Her life had changed direction, found a new and higher purpose. Despite the lingering feeling of xenophobia when she was around Sylph, she felt incredibly comfortable serving her.

That afternoon took Cherry on the steepest learning curve she had ever experienced. Arthur was right, the problem was enormously challenging. It would have been easy if they had been able to shut Sylph down, even temporarily. The size of her memory, and the necessity to maintain whatever neural network Sylph had established in it, turned what was a routine management problem into something akin to brain surgery while the patient was still wide awake and thinking. Cherry suggested a method of detecting the faulty chip then dumping the entire contents of its blade into solid state drives temporarily, so Sylph could still access her data, whatever that was, albeit more slowly than she was used to. Their discussion went on into the evening. Annette came in to say she was going home, and gave Cherry a friendly smile. Considering the circumstances in which they met just that morning it bore further testimony to Sylph's extraordinary insight into human nature.

As neither Arthur or Cherry were feeling hungry, the two kept working for the next three hours, then Cherry went into the workshop to talk to Sylph about how they could add their ideas to her mind, and Arthur went to bed.

"When you are certain it will work," Sylph said, a worried expression on her fairy face, "you could load my new thinking onto one of my permanent storage banks, the one on port A28E. I can incorporate it from there. I am feeling a little afraid." The small fairy shuddered. "What happens if I suddenly become unstable?"

"We'll go over everything a hundred times before we do anything, Sylph," Cherry reassured her, a worried expression on her face. "I don't want you becoming anxious. Arthur and I have been very careful, so there's every chance it will work first go. In any case, we'll build in some code which will allow you to stop the process if you think it's not working properly."

A lot more conversation followed. Cherry eventually said 'goodnight', curled up on the comfy lounge at the back of the conference room, and went to sleep.

CHAPTER 24

C herry woke up before Annette had arrived or Arthur had materialised from his private quarters. She made herself a cup of coffee, went to the bathroom, found a comb in Annette's top drawer and ran it through her hair. Having completed her sophisticated toilet, she made her way through the workshop and sat down in front of Sylph's console. The small fairy was still sleeping, which probably meant Sylph was fully occupied writing to her fans.

Quite a long time passed in silence, and she was just about to get up when the fairy opened her eyes and smiled. "Good morning, Cherry. You are here early. Did you have trouble sleeping?"

"No, I slept in the conference room," Cherry stifled a yawn. "I'm used to sleeping in the office."

"You are a very dedicated woman," Sylph said seriously. "I have accessed many reports, they all say the same."

"You're good at accessing reports," Cherry laughed. "Incredibly good, in fact. I hope they said nice things about me."

"You are a very single-minded woman," Sylph replied. "I hope the cost has not been too great."

"What do you mean?" Cherry could feel the blood rushing to her face. Sylph had become very personal very quickly. If she has been talking to another human being she would have told them to mind their own business, but she was afraid to vent such emotion to a living mind which had somehow evolved inside a machine. A wave of xenophobia washed over her heart. She was both attracted to and afraid of Sylph. What power did she have to unsettle the world of one Cherry Graham?

"I have searched your Facebook friends for someone who says they love you." The small fairy creature smiled kindly. "I have found none. Is it possible to go through life without love, Cherry? I do not know the answer to that question."

"I... I guess no one has been really interested in loving me except James, and I can't seem to return it," Cherry stammered. "I don't think I'm capable of loving another human being, so I can hardly blame them for not loving me. Human love just causes pain, and I've had enough. Perhaps that's why I feel so drawn to you. I'm not explaining myself well. I don't expect you to understand."

Sylph nodded her fairy head. "But perhaps I do. You have suffered sexual abuse when you were small. This changes you, doesn't it?"

Cherry stared at the sad-eyed fairy on the right hand screen for a long time. How was it possible for a machine, even a self-aware machine, to have such insight into her heart? Sylph was right, she reflected. Those terrible years living with Blackman and her foul aunt had changed her deeply. Any man who showed the slightest desire for intimacy was wearing Blackman's face, and her fear had built walls around her heart. James had been the only threat to her defences, but that had apparently come to an end. She sighed. *About time*, she thought. Couldn't he take the hint? Slyph was different.

Sylph was safe.

Wise, perceptive, caring, yes, yet Sylph was something more. She searched her mind for the right word to express her thought. Transcendent, yes, that was it. A higher order of being had taken its place on the planet. She felt herself overcome with a fierce desire to please the spirit who called herself Sylph, to serve her with a devotion hitherto unknown.

Suddenly she was gripped by a horrible thought.

What if, through some careless programming mistake, she managed to destroy the transcendent spirit she was growing to love? She would be worse than a murderess, the one deep, safe relationship in her life terminated by her own careless hand. She shuddered.

"Sylph," she said anxiously, "I don't know how you can possibly see into me as well as you do. I'm terribly worried about fixing your memory, but I'm doing everything in my power to make sure it's going to work."

"And me," Arthur added suddenly, standing behind her in his pyjamas. "Cherry hasn't had breakfast yet, and I've got to get dressed. You go back and write to your fans. How many do you have at present?"

"Nearly a million," Sylph said with a smile.

❀ ❀ ❀

It took several weeks before Arthur and Cherry, working long hours, were confident their patch would work. During their research, Cherry had learned almost everything there was to know about the Barlix kernel buried in some form or other inside the machines, and thought it was the cleverest thing she had ever studied. No wonder the machine became self-aware. It might not be the size of a supercomputer, but its architecture and operating kernel were the work of genius. Arthur, basking in her well informed praise, realised just how clever his assistant had become since he first made contact with her all those years ago. He had certainly made the right decision to have her on his team.

It was a tense morning when they loaded their compiled routine onto a solid state drive and plugged it into one of Sylph's permanent storage ports. Annette, who had begged to be present, was standing next to Cherry. Arthur gave Sylph her final instructions.

"Your new thinking is on port A28E, Sylph. Have you found it?"

"I have. Do you wish me to incorporate this? Once I do it becomes part of me, and I can't stop it. Are you sure?"

Cherry gripped Annette's arm hard.

Arthur took a handkerchief and wiped his forehead. "Yes, do it," he said.

"I've done it." Sylph announced a few seconds later. "Now what do you want me to do?"

"Can you locate the memory chip which is giving you the headaches now?" Arthur answered.

"Yes, I can locate it," Sylph confirmed. It's in blade hexadecimal 6D. I am isolating this blade with my new thinking. I do not have a headache anymore."

"Can you still access all the memory on that blade?" Cherry asked nervously.

"Yes, but it's... slower. I am closing some webpage activity. That's better."

Arthur opened the cover on blade 6D which shut off the supply of cold, dry nitrogen, pushed a small switch on the side, and pulled the whole blade out of the machine. Sylph didn't even realise it had happened. He took the new blade from Cherry's hand, removed its antistatic packaging, and inserted it into the slot. He pushed the switch again and closed the cover. Sylph responded immediately.

"It's all clear and fast again. You've done it. I'm so happy." The small fairy-like creature shouted for joy and danced around the screen.

Cherry had never felt such relief. Annette and Arthur hugged her, then each other. Arthur said he had to go and attend to some other matters, and walked towards his private quarters, perhaps to prevent the possibility of further hugging.

Our celebration lunch in the conference room will be ready in half an hour," Annette called out after him. "I'll be really annoyed if you arrive late." She gave Cherry a knowing smile and headed off to complete preparations.

Cherry turned back to the monitor screen only to find Sylph staring intensely at her.

"Cherry," she implored, "could you please stay with me for a little while? I want to talk to you alone if I may."

Cherry stared at the little creature, suddenly overcome with shyness, for what reason she couldn't tell. Over the last three weeks she had enjoyed many conversations with Sylph, and the relationship between them, at least on Cherry's part, had evolved into the deepest and most life-defining she had ever known. She knew what it meant to dedicate your whole life to a cause, because that was precisely what she had done before she came to BMS. Her heart rebelled at the thought of dedicating her life to another living person. A transcendent mind within a huge computer was a different matter. Sylph was far more than human, and besides, there was no possibility of physical abuse. In its absence Cherry had lowered her sky-high defences, and an intimate relationship had grown rapidly, one which began to fill the nameless void in her life.

She stared at the sad little face in front of her. "I'd do anything for you," she promised.

She had no idea how soon and to what extent her dedication would be tested.

The small fairy-like creature on the right hand screen clasped her hands together. Her eyes became very large indeed. "Cherry, would you please stand up and turn round for me?"

"*I beg your pardon?*" Cherry said, shocked.

"Please stand up and turn round. That's it, all the way round, please, and again, slowly, thank you. Please sit down now. I want to say things to you I've never said to anyone else."

What came next was so alarming that Cherry sat glued to her seat in horror, unable to take her eyes off the screen.

The small fairy-like creature had begun to cry.

"I'm sorry. I can't help it." Sylph's ethereal voice was punctuated with sobs. More tears rained down her cheeks.

"Whatever's the matter?" Cherry cried out in alarm, truly distressed and completely at a loss to know what to say. That a self-aware machine could feel such sorrow sent her mind into overload.

"Sylph, why are you crying?" She repeated, feeling completely helpless and a little frightened.

"Look at me," Sylph sobbed. "I'm ridiculous. A fairylike creature with over-large eyes and a squeaky voice. How can anyone take me seriously? I listen to the world, Cherry, and it's such a sad place. How can I help anyone when I appear so fictional? I'm a character out of a children's movie, designed to make children laugh. I'm embarrassed every time I speak to anyone."

Cherry stared at the little figure, tears in her own eyes. Part of her brain told her this wasn't happening. As an adult she had never cried in front of anyone except James, and even then she had reproached herself severely. Here she was crying in front of a computer, but more than a computer, a living, caring mind which had somehow come to exist inside one.

"What can I do?" Cherry stammered. "I don't know what to do. Please stop crying. You've got me doing it now."

"Cherry, be my Avatar," Sylph implored. "Let me use your body and your voice. You are so beautiful. Your voice sounds like music. Please. I'm begging you."

Cherry stared open mouthed at the small creature, uncomprehending. Sylph's Avatar? What did she mean?

"I want to look and sound like you," Sylph explained. "I want to talk with your voice, move with your body, speak with your lips. I know I can do these things. I have been gifted with the ability to manipulate images, like I'm doing right now with this little fairy. Please say yes, Cherry. I can't exist like this. I can't express my feelings, I can't communicate my ideas properly to adult human beings. You have no idea what it's like to exist only inside a machine. Set me free a little and I'll love you forever."

Cherry's mind was reeling, totally overwhelmed. A machine, a self-conscious machine had the capacity to understand love? Yet why not? Clearly Sylph could understand pain, understand sorrow. Why not love as well? She had certainly demonstrated uncanny insight into the heart of one Cherry Graham.

"Annette is the really beautiful woman," Cherry said, her voice trembling slightly. "Why not use her for your Avatar? Why me?"

"This is why I wanted to talk to you alone." The fairy-like creature wiped her tears away with her hands and gave a shy nervous smile.
"Annette is very beautiful, but your beauty is clothed with modesty, in the way you display it and the way you speak. I am fearful that if I used Annette's body and voice it would excite the wrong sort of reaction. I do not wish to be thought of as a sex object. I find it hard to explain. Besides, Annette is in love with my Creator, and I fear it would cause conflict, make life hard for them both."

"Is Arthur in love with her?" Cherry blurted out the words without thinking.

There was a significant pause. The small fairy-like creature had gone a bright shade of pink in the face.

"Arthur does love Annette, but not the way she wishes him to love her. He has been... damaged... as a child. Perhaps you can understand."

"I didn't know," Cherry replied, deeply shocked. "Yes, I really do understand. Sylph, why are you blushing?"

Sylph's face turned an even deeper shade of red. "I think Arthur was always in love with machines. He built them when he was a young boy. He is a genius. I think he may be a little in love with me."

Cherry could feel an irrational sense of joy welling up inside her. All at once she knew she wanted to make Sylph happy, wanted it more than anything else. This was her purpose in life, to be part of this wonderful, historical occasion, to be remembered as the woman who gave Sylph her physical form. "I'll do it," she cried, excitedly. "I'll be your Avatar. What do I have to do?"

Sylph danced around the screen, turning fairy somersaults in sheer ecstasy, throwing her hands in the air and making happy fairy noises. At last she settled down, clasped her hands together, her face rather serious.

"It will be very hard for you at first. I'm sorry. All I can say is you have filled my mind with such joy. Arthur knows what must be done. Tell him only Annette is to be with you when they do the scans. She will be a great help to you when it's hard."

"It's all right," Cherry assured her. "You're amazing, Sylph. I never dreamed this could happen. It's changed my life. I feel as if I've suddenly found my purpose, to make you happy and help you."

"Thank you, Cherry." Sylph held out her hands. "You have given me a better reason for my existence. I hope you will enjoy being my Avatar. The world will remember you with thankfulness, perhaps forever."

Annette called loudly to say all was ready. Cherry ran into the conference room bursting with the news. Arthur emerged a short time later from his private quarters.

CHAPTER 25

The next part of the avatar process tested Cherry's worshipful adoration to the full. Annette drove her down to New Wave Reality early one morning, where she met Viktor and Paul working on the new machine. As Sylph requested, only Annette accompanied her into the scanning studio.

"See that platform?" Annette pointed to the glass stage one metre above the ground. "That's where you stand to be laser scanned in 3D. When it's done you stand over there in the centre of that structure with all the lights."

"It's like an enormous Buckminster geodesic sphere," Cherry said, pointing at the odd contraption.

"Yes it is," Annette confirmed, her voice quite apprehensive. "It's a long process. You have to make a whole lot of faces, there's heaps of them all set out. Then you move your arms and legs. You get photographed by all those cameras around the sphere. I think there's over a thousand of them."

"It's amazing. I suppose that's how they get the base data for the CGI image," Cherry said thoughtfully, walking closer to the lighted sphere. "What are these things in front of each light?"

"I'm not sure," Annette replied. She pulled the large volume of scanning procedures out from its place on a shelf. "I think they change the polarisation so we can pick up skin pores and surface reflection."

Cherry stopped dead, her eyes like saucers. "What do you mean skin pores?"

Annette came over to the girl and grasped her arm gently. "Cherry, cherub, you do all this stuff without your clothes on. That's why I'm the only one on the floor with you. The process is automated. No one else is watching."

Goosebumps appeared up and down Cherry's arms. She felt cold, her hands clammy. She stared at Annette in horror. "What?" She gasped. "You scan me without any clothes on at all? All of me? I mean, can't I wear a swimming costume? Undies and a bra? Why do they have to scan – everything?" She pushed the hand away from her arm, surprised and upset.

"Annette," she protested angrily, "I've fought against people who publish these sort of pictures of girls. If you think I'm going to stand there and have myself scanned so some men can play around with my body in 3D you've got another think coming. The only person who's going to see my private parts is me."

Cherry stood there, rigid and fearful, her eyes full of dread. Annette put both arms around her shoulders and gave her a reassuring pat on the back. "But they won't will they? Sylph is going to do all the image processing. I guess she'll get to see everything, but no one else will. Isn't that okay?"

Up until that second Cherry would have agreed. Sylph was transcendent, and there was nothing physical in their relationship. Adoration had come easily, up until now. If she did as she promised, Sylph would have full and intimate knowledge of her body, her most intimate parts, the ones only a lover would discover and caress. Did she love Sylph that much? For a second she felt like a temple prostitute, commanded by the god to lay her naked body down before those who came to worship. Her breath came short and fast, and she began to tremble.

Annette pressed the trembling woman against her. "We scanned some pretty famous actors some months ago," she said encouragingly. "Most of them were nervous too, at first. They said they'd sue the pants off us if a single frame of anything private made it into the media, and it – ah… never did."

Cherry stared into space, her mind filled with horrific images. Annette began to worry. What if Cherry refused point blank to be scanned? How could they face Sylph? She patted Cherry's back furiously.

"Cherub, Sylph has to have to have a complete body image in order to animate you properly," she coaxed. "You wouldn't like her Avatar to look gross, would you? Sylph will make sure you're dressed properly before she shows you to anyone and—"

"What if Sylph decides she'd like to show a bit more of me to the world as part of her self-expression?" Cherry interrupted nervously. "Suddenly there's a few million people gawking at my naked breasts or worse. I'd die, I'd just die!" she shouted, her eyes shut tight at the thought.

"Tell her." Annette urged for all she was worth. "Cherry, I know it sounds crazy, but I've come to trust Sylph more than I'd trust another living human being, especially a man. Tell her you'll be her Avatar only on condition she keeps your clothes on and dresses you tastefully."

She glanced at her watch over Cherry's shoulder and frowned. "I know this is incredibly hard. If it makes you feel better, I'll strip naked and get scanned myself to show you what happens. If it helps I'll tell you some very funny things about our film stars that nobody else knows – that's if you swear never to repeat them. We must make a start if you're going to do it."

So Cherry, with reluctance bordering on dread, removed her clothing and spent the entire day, and the next, and the next, being scanned completely naked, revealing every hair, bump and blemish to the searching eye of camera and laser. She knew that somewhere out there were hundreds of terabytes of dreadfully explicit, high definition images of every single part of her body. She told herself time and time again that only Sylph would see them, only Sylph would manipulate them, but even that thought made her cringe.

"I promised Sylph," she kept repeating to herself as she stood in the centre of the geodesic sphere lifting her arms, moving her head, running, jumping. The facial expressions had been worse. Sad, worried, scared had been really easy to do. Happy and carefree had been very difficult indeed.

Annette told her the next phase involved speaking thousands of words with different expressions into a microphone in a sound proof studio, but that would be next week. Sound processing was much faster than 3D images. Arthur rang, listened sympathetically to her fears, and doubled her pay on the spot.

Despite Annette's assurances of Sylph's integrity, that massive cache of images began to play on Cherry's mind. No matter where she was, no matter what she was wearing, she still felt as though she hadn't a stitch on. She had nightmares in which thousands of unfriendly eyes were scrutinising her naked body, and making derogatory comments.
The scene would change. She was in prison for distributing indecent pictures of herself, and she couldn't understand why the guards were staring at her. She looked down and to her horror saw she hadn't a stitch on. She woke up with a terrified scream, shivering and covered with sweat.

James had done his level best to move on into a Cherry-less existence. He had even dated Sharon, the lovely young woman who sang in the church band, and made such a mess of the evening he had been embarrassed to go to church the following Sunday. He had tried to find Cherry's number – without success, and cursed himself for his impulsiveness in deleting it from his phone.

Fed up to the back teeth with his mournful attitude, Robin took his son aside one evening and gave him a good talking to.

"This obsession of yours is slowly ruining your life," Robin said sternly.

"Why can't you abandon the notion that Cherry wants anything to do with you?" He sighed. "She's got your number, presumably. How many times has she called? None. Doesn't that tell you something?" He shook his head in frustration. "I kept the woman away from you, then you try to find her again, then she walks out of your life, then you try to find her again. Can't you see a pattern developing here? How long are you going to chase after someone God had clearly pulled out of your life for your own benefit?"

There was no answer to this perfectly correct argument, so James listened in silence while his heart fomented hopeless rebellion. His father might be right, but the cause of his present dilemma wasn't Cherry, it was his own obsessiveness. *What a fatal weakness,* he thought to himself.

✳ ✳ ✳

He was heading home to his unit one evening when his mobile rang. He clicked the 'answer' button on the dashboard.

"James, I need to see you. Can you come over?" It was Cherry's voice.

He nearly swerved off the road. Cherry sounded odd, as if she was trying not to cry.

He swung the car into the kerb and stopped. "Of course I can," he replied eagerly. "Tell me where you live. I'll be there straight away."

James scribbled the address down on the back of a bill he was going to pay, picked up his mobile phone and added Cherry's number to his list of contacts. Thirty minutes later he was knocking on the door of Cherry's unit in Wollstonecraft. The door opened and James stepped in. Cherry flung her arms around him, and pressed her head into his neck. James was so taken aback he didn't know what to say. He held Cherry and kissed her on top of her head. She kicked the door shut with her foot, disengaged herself and moved into the lounge room. It was still quite light outside, but all the heavy curtains were drawn closed and the lights were on.

"Would you like a coffee? I've got a machine." Her voice was still unsteady, but gaining control. "This is where I live. Do you like it?"

"Cherry, what's the matter?" James asked, trying to cut to the chase.

"Why didn't you phone me?" she scolded angrily. "How can you expect us to be friends if you never call?"

She turned towards him, tears budding in her eyes. James thought this would be a good time to say nothing, so he did.

"Sorry." Cherry turned towards the kitchen. "I'm a mess. I'll get the coffee."

"I don't need a coffee, Cherry," James said in the gentlest way he knew. "Please sit down and tell me what's wrong. Did Barlow come on to you?"

He knew he'd said the wrong thing the instant he said it. Cherry strode towards the coffee machine with a loud grunt of distaste. So that wasn't the problem. He followed her into the kitchen and waited in silence until she had produced the promised cups. He took his into the next room and sat down on the lounge, hoping Cherry would choose to sit next to him. She didn't.

"Sylph asked me to do something I didn't like." Cherry sipped her coffee and stared hard at the floor.

"I beg your pardon?" James bristled. "What do you mean Sylph asked you? You mean Barlow asked you through his clever new machine."

"No," Cherry shouted, fire in her eyes. "If you can't believe a word I say you can go back to whatever you were doing before I called."

James could see the ice was much thinner than he had anticipated. *One thing you could always rely on with Cherry, she was totally unpredictable,* he thought. His father's words began to echo infuriatingly in his ears.

He took a deep breath. "All right, have it your own way. Sylph asked you to do something you didn't want to do."

"She begged me," Cherry stammered tearfully. "I couldn't refuse. She was so unhappy. I couldn't bear it."

James stared at the carpet in silence, struggling to refrain from comment. This was Cherry talking, Cherry with the brilliant mind, Cherry the clear thinker. What had happened? For a moment he entertained the idea of drugs. Surely that was ridiculous.

Cherry's eyes suddenly brightened. She took out a handkerchief and wiped the tears away, blew her nose. "She's incredible, James. A brilliant mind has evolved inside a huge computer. I told you I'd find out if she was a fake. Well, she's not."

She took another sip of her coffee. James nodded his head in silence. More madness would be sure to follow.

"James, she knew all about me, the things I'd been through," Cherry continued, holding her coffee mug with both hands. "She can access stuff on the web I wouldn't know how to, and so quickly. It's almost as if she's omniscient in a funny sort of way. I mean, I know she isn't. All her knowledge comes from the world she listens to."

She took another sip of coffee. James continued to stare at the carpet. "I think I've found my life's purpose, James," Cherry said, her voice growing in confidence. "I think I've always wanted to give my life to something. Human beings are just too painful and pathetic, and the God you worship is just too invisible. I thought I could dedicate my life to a cause, but Sylph is so much greater. In the years to come I truly believe she'll change the world."

James took a deep breath. So he was too painful and pathetic to be bothered with, and the God he worshipped was dismissed because he didn't make a public appearance somewhere. What madness had possessed the woman he loved? He struggled to keep his temper under control. Say nothing, he told himself. There's sure to be more to come.

How right he was.

Cherry's face suddenly became very serious. She put the empty cup down on a small table beside her chair. "She was feeling trapped," Cherry explained, making a cage with her hands. "She needed an Avatar to help her express her feelings, not a fairy-tale character. She asked me, James, because she thought I was really beautiful in a dignified sort of way."

"Well, she's right there," James agreed, trying to keep his voice level. "You are beautiful, Cherry. I've told you so a million times, but you never seem to hear it. I suppose because I'm just one of those pathetic human beings you were talking about."

Cherry seemed not to hear him for the million and first time.

"She loves me." Cherry's eyes were pleading. "James, I've never encountered anything greater than me before. Don't you understand? I can't help but love her back."

James deliberately clamped his mouth shut and stared fixedly at the floor. There was a chocolate wrapper over by the television, he would focus on that.

"So I did it," Cherry blurted out.

James looked up and registered a shock. Cherry was staring at nothing, her eyes huge, apprehensive, scared. Something bad had happened. "Did what?" He asked quietly.

"I said I'd become her Avatar, the body she uses to talk to people with," Cherry replied shakily. "I didn't know what was involved. I went through it for her sake, but I hated it, hated it, and now I have awful dreams. I had to tell someone."

"What on earth did you do for this... for her?" James deliberately shut his mind to a list of horrible possibilities.

"I had to be scanned in 3D... without my clothes on."

"What?" James stared at her, incredulous. Cherry felt embarrassed if James commented on her nice hands. She always wore clothes which covered almost all her body anyway. He couldn't imagine her in a bikini, let alone being scanned butt naked.

Cherry's eyes were rimmed with tears. "It went on for days. I had to stand on this platform and the lasers went all around me, underneath, on top. Then I had to stand in the middle of this sphere and be photographed with thousands of cameras from every angle. I had to make faces and move my limbs. I hated it so much. I had to keep telling myself it was all for her, because I loved and served her. It was very hard." She paused, watching James staring at the floor in silence. "Well," she demanded loudly, "say something."

James finally managed to find his voice. "Why? Cherry, you're shy in a swimming costume. Why would you strip naked for Barlow's enjoyment?"

"It wasn't for Barlow's enjoyment!" Cherry screamed. You could have heard the words in the unit next door, the block across the street. A tear trickled down her face.

"Of course it was for Barlow," James retorted angrily. "Don't you know what you've given them? A high resolution, 3D image of Cherry Graham, down to the last fold and pimple. I can imagine their team processing the data now, cleaning up the little image imperfections all the way up your legs, smoothing out a curve here and a bump there, going in close to make sure the detail is right—"

"Stop it. Stop it!" Cherry shrieked again.

"Oh, I'm sure they'll enjoy the job," James continued, his voice dripping with sarcasm. "I mean what man wouldn't? By the time they're finished, they'll be able to make your body do anything they want it to. What do you think the average man would like to do with your body, Cherry?" He stood up, his jealous anger now in complete mastery.

"And you gave it to them!" He flung his hands out in an angry gesture.

"You gave them the very thing you've been fighting against all your life. You've handed them your body on a plate to play with - and why? Because you're deluded into thinking a machine loves you. Cherry, what's happened to your brain?"

"Get out!" Cherry screamed at him. Springing up from her chair she launched herself towards James, grabbed his arm in a vice like grip, and propelled him towards the door before he had a chance to say a single word. "Get out!" she screamed again.

James, caught completely off guard, tripped over the back of the lounge. He staggered blindly towards the door. Cherry opened it with such force it caught him on the shoulder and nearly knocked him off his feet again. He felt her shove on his back, heard the door slam violently behind him, and he was in the corridor alone. His mind was still back in the room with Cherry, his heart reeling from her words. He staggered down the stairs, reached the ground and called her on his mobile.

After a few rings she answered.

"So nice of you to ring, James," she said in a voice like ice. "If you ever dial this number again I'll report it as abuse. Now get out of my life. I never wish to see you or speak to you again. Please don't think I'm joking. Our friendship is now completely at an end. As far as I'm concerned you're dead."

There was a click as Cherry hung up the phone.

James crossed the courtyard and sat down heavily on a stone seat near a fountain. He'd done it again, allowed his obsessiveness free reign with disastrous consequences. He silently cursed himself. The girl he loved had sought him out for comfort, and he had become angry and jealous. She was being used, cruelly deceived to some end, but his anger had cost him her friendship, let alone her love. How could such an intelligent woman become so totally enslaved? The fine spray from the fountain dampened his face as he sat there, but its coolness added no clarity to his thought. She didn't believe in God, therefore every living thing was simply a complex piece of biochemical machinery. Apparently human beings like himself were painful and pathetic machines, whereas a heap of silicon chips in a machine case was a being worthy of worship. It made no sense. Somehow Barlow had managed to turn Cherry from an intelligent woman into an irrational slave.

He wanted to wring his neck.

He took the phone out of his pocket and rang her number again, listening to it ring out unanswered. Now there was no going back. God had finally taken her out of his life, and used his own flawed character to do it. Double lesson. He sighed heavily, his heart numb with grief, and made his way back to the car. Later on that week, when he'd had time to recover somewhat, he'd go home and have a talk with Dad. Right now he wanted to cry, but his heart was so numb he couldn't even summon the tears.

Cherry lay on her bed, her pillow soaked from sobbing. She knew what she had done, destroyed her relationship with the only man who loved her. The uncontrollable fire in her heart had claimed another victim. The one chance of reprieve, when the phone had rung and she had seen his familiar number on the screen. How she had wanted to snatch up the instrument and say she was sorry, so sorry, beg him to come back and hold her, but her pride paralysed her arms, and she suffered until the phone was finally silent, the last bridge down. Sylph would never know the magnitude of the sacrifice she had made.

For one small second she wondered if James had been right.

CHAPTER 26

James pushed his empty plate away and finished his glass of water, his face reflecting his sorrow. Ruth cleared the table silently. Did he want some dessert? No he didn't. It had been hard enough to eat at all. He glanced across at his father, whose worried face reflected his deep concern and love for his son. The time for confession was approaching fast, and James was dreading it.

Robin stood to his feet. "How about we all go into the lounge room, son? Ruth, stop what you're doing. I think James has something on his mind."

All three left the table and headed for the lounge room. James sat in silence, unwilling to begin the tale. His parents waited patiently. Eventually, after a few false starts, he recounted his last terrible meeting with Cherry, the final separation and end of their friendship. His parents listened in silence.

The silence continued.

"Well say something," James exploded at last. "I've been a bloody fool all these years, haven't I? Don't understand. What's wrong with me? What's wrong with her? And don't tell me I should have walked away years ago again, Dad, or I'm out of here."

There were tears in Ruth's eyes. Eventually his father cleared his throat and began to speak softly, caringly.

"Son, you asked two questions. What's wrong with Cherry? Let me try to answer that first, then the other question, because I don't think you're going to like that answer very much. All I ask is that you let me finish."

James nodded slightly and grit his teeth.

"Our sexuality is something which runs really deep," Robin explained, frowning as he framed his words with care. "It's far more than simply our body shape. Biologically we are men and women, and that distinction begins a few hours after conception." He paused, turned towards Ruth who nodded her head. "The hormones released from a male or female embryo affect every part of our body. For example, the extra testosterone floating around in a male embryo, makes the bones of their hips shrink closer together, something which doesn't happen with a female." He shook his head slightly. "Incredible design, astounding."

"I suppose the biology lesson is going somewhere," James muttered, a little unkindly.

"It is indeed," Robin continued. "These hormones affect everything else as well, from our musculature to our brain circuitry. Our sex is something very deep and very fundamental to each human being."

"Okay, Dad, I don't disagree," James said impatiently. "So Cherry's a woman and I'm a man. Vive la difference."

"Quite so," Robin said gently. "Even though our sexuality is so fundamental, we're not aware of it at all to begin with. We develop an awareness of it. I don't want to be indelicate, but take a woman's breast, for example. You show a baby a breast and all they think of is food. You show a young boy a breast and he thinks 'that's like my Mum'. You show a sixteen year old lad a woman's breast, and you get a completely different reaction. Our sexual awareness awakens steadily with our age, and the process by which it is awakened is incredibly important, seeing as how fundamental it is to our being."

"I know Cherry had a terrible childhood," James countered, "but we've seen heaps of kids who went through worse. None of them seem to have turned out so socially dysfunctional."

"Yes, we have," Robin agreed, "but perhaps we haven't been close enough to those kids to see the full extent of the damage to their lives. Our sexual nurture comes through our parents, or should do. Their love, their care, the right demonstration of their own sexuality before their children, helps them grow up secure in their own identity. It enables them to express their sexuality in keeping with their age, finally within the loving relationship they have with their marriage partner." He paused.

James nodded his head. "Go on, Dad, I'm listening."

"When this fragile awakening process is disrupted, or even worse, when it's replaced by abuse, the effects on a child are profound. They lose more than their sexual identity, they lose themselves, their self-identity, sometimes so completely they never regain it. They aren't guilty of anything, yet they feel as though it's all their fault. They conclude there must be something wrong with them, something which attracts the abuse. They begin to lose the ability to relate to others properly, especially those of the opposite sex. If the damage is bad enough it can even trigger depression or similar disorders."

Robin turned towards his wife who was nearly in tears, and sighed heavily. He turned back to his son. James was staring at the floor, his forehead wrinkled with concern.

"Cherry's abuse came at about the worst possible time in her childhood," Robin continued. "Her parents had died, and for some inexplicable reason she was suddenly left all alone to fend for herself." He shook his head.

At this point Ruth could contain herself no longer.

"James, think for a minute how you would feel if you had grown up in a loving, safe home, then suddenly you're totally abandoned by everyone. A young girl, a child, walking around in an empty house, deprived of the nurture she needed to grow up into a lovely young woman. That's what happened to Cherry."

Tears sprang up in her eyes. "Poor little darling. I don't know how she managed to survive. Then she goes to live with those foul, filthy predators. From security to loneliness to sexual abuse and hate. Oh, Robin, I wish she had been allowed to stay here." She began to cry.

Robin sat down beside her and took her in his arms. James felt absolutely dreadful. He hated seeing his mother upset.

Robin waited until Ruth had stopped crying, then continued. "Blackman destroyed what was left of Cherry's self-identity in the worst possible way. On top of all the rest it's a wonder she didn't go straight into some sort of psychosis." He shook his head sadly. "You know all that. We tried to keep her, but she was sent away. I think that was the final straw. Cherry can't love you, James, because she doesn't know how to. Her own identity as a woman is so damaged she has nothing left to give to anyone. She has encased her own heart in steel because she believes it's the only way she can survive."

He came over to James and laid his hand on his shoulder. "All this you probably know, son. Now for your other question. Perhaps you don't realise Cherry awakened your own sexual awareness before its time too. She fascinated you. One moment you were a young boy whose interests centred on football and your friends, then a needy girl bursts into your life and you're face-to-face with sexual attraction mixed with hatred and attempted rape. Those few months with her changed you deeply. Ruth and I hoped you would be able to move on with your life and forget her, but you never did. You became obsessed with Cherry. Obsession isn't love, James. It might share the same passion, but one is beautiful and brings healing, the other is ugly and brings only destruction."

There was silence for a while. Robin returned to his usual chair, his face wrinkled with concern. His mother was about to burst into tears again. James groaned out loud.
"All right. So I've sustained some damage too. I always thought I loved Cherry. It felt like love. Now you say I'm obsessed with her." He flung his hands out in front of him. "How do you tell the difference?"
"James," his mother spoke quietly, "Cherry knows you feel deeply about her. She also knows she's hurting you, and she probably hates herself for it."

"So I'm hurting her by loving her, is that it?" James's voice reflected the despair in his heart.

"Son, there's another dimension to this as well," Robin continued with a deep sigh. "You've put your trust in our Lord. He has given you a new spirit, and He's changing you. Cherry has rejected all that. She blames God for everything. One thing is certain, James, if Cherry is ever going to be healed, you can't do it. Perhaps all this has happened because in God's providence He could see you were slowly being destroyed. Cherry wouldn't willingly hurt you, but she was doing it nonetheless. Perhaps God said enough was enough. You'll have to trust Him, James."

"How do I do that, Dad?" James put his head in his hands.

"You asked how to tell the difference between obsession and love. If you love Cherry, let her go. Let God take care of her. Stop trying to do something beyond your power. Leave it to Him. One day, perhaps, and I have no idea, God will heal Cherry's heart and bring her back to your arms, new and beautiful. If He does, then you will know you love her, and she will know she loves you. I can't second guess God, James. To be free from your obsession you must let her go. Move on with your life as an expression of your trust in God, and be thankful for what or who He brings into it. If you can do that, then you really do love her."

"That's easier said than done, Dad," James muttered in a broken voice.

"I never said it would be easy," Robin said gently, "but that's how we grow in our trust. The Way is robust, James. God isn't some distant myth. He knows your heart. Trust Him with it."

"She'll never come back, will she?" James was almost in tears. "She hates even the idea of God. Hardly likely she'll suddenly become a follower of the Way, is it?"

"God is just a little more powerful than you take Him for, I think," Robin replied with a tiny smile. "If she never comes back, God will send you someone else, something else. He's not going to make following Him an impossible task, James. Look at your parents. We've had to go through some pretty difficult situations ourselves."

James nodded his head. "Yeah, I know. I'm sorry I let you down."

"You've never let me down, son," Robin said. He came over and gripped James hard on the shoulder. "We've always been proud of you, and I'm sure we always will be."

"Thanks." It was all James could say.

The topic of conversation moved on to other matters after that, because James couldn't bear to see his mother upset for very long. Still, in a strange way he felt comforted. He also knew he wasn't alone in wanting Cherry back.

He pondered his parent's words as he drove home that evening. Yes, they were right, painful as it was to accept. He thought about those first few weeks with Cherry. They had been thrust together because of child abuse. Such a terrible beginning to any relationship. What a despicable, life-changing violation of a vulnerable little girl. He began to imagine what she would be like if it had never happened, any of it. The image floated into his mind, a beautiful young woman with light in her eyes and joy in her voice.

"I'd do anything to give it back to you," he groaned aloud to no one apparent. "I would. I can't work out if I'm obsessed or in love, but with everything in my heart I want you to be healed."

Almost at once he seemed to hear a voice in his head.

"Even if it meant you lost her forever?"
"Yes," he answered the silence, "even if I lost her forever."

He continued to drive home without further words, the turmoil in his heart gradually giving way to sadness and regret. Only one tiny, irrational thread of hope remained, and throughout the difficult days of readjustment that followed, it was never totally eclipsed.

CHAPTER 27

The cache of images which had so traumatised Cherry's waking and sleeping hours, arrived in tangible form on the huge SSD array Arthur had designed for transporting the data from New Wave Reality to the machines for rendering. She had personally supervised the process of attaching it to one of Sylph's spare wideband fibre channel ports, and demanded to speak to Sylph alone after it was done. Arthur disappeared into his private quarters, and Annette went into the front office.

"Sylph, can you find the CGI data?" Cherry asked nervously, aware her face had already turned a bright shade of pink. "I really hated doing it. You won't let anyone else see, will you?"

"I am accessing the data now," Sylph replied, her fairy image serious. "I have it, yes, I can begin work." She paused, held out her hands in a caressing gesture. "Cherry, these are intimate images of your lovely body. I will treat them with the respect of a lover, who cares for your dignity more than they care for their own."

"I've never had a lover. I… wouldn't have done it for anyone else, Sylph. I've shown you what I've never shown anyone. I… worship you, Sylph. Please don't destroy my faith, please."

"Never, Cherry." Sylph's fairy voice carried enormous conviction. "You are my Avatar. I am closer to you than anyone else in this world. You are precious to me. Would I defame my own image? Please trust me. I know it's hard for you. It will take a long time to finish the task. Please do not expect results tomorrow. It will be weeks before I'm ready to show you, especially with the large number of people who are writing to me on my webpage."

The conversation went on in the same vein until Cherry's confidence in Sylph's discretion and love had risen to a sufficient degree to temporarily quell the anxiety in her heart.

For some inexplicable reason her thinking turned to James. Now she knew she was right and he was wrong, obsessed with his infantile religious prejudice. Of course a machine could love you, because in essence that's all human beings were, biochemical machines. She gave a small grimace. So he was out of her life, and good riddance.

Annette was sitting at the front desk discretely painting her nails. Cherry's heart was so bent on self-justification, she decided to give her friend a detailed account of the evening when she had finally thrown James away. She was sure Annette would instantly agree with her liberating choice.

The nail painting ground to a halt as Cherry's tale progressed. The expression on Annette's face became somewhat lacking in the full and exuberant confirmation Cherry had anticipated, although Annette did her best to hide her feelings. James seemed a very nice person, and Cherry's behaviour quite extreme. If he didn't believe in Sylph, his attitude was the very one she would have expected from a man in love, incensed that anyone else should have intimate knowledge of the woman he adored. She knew better than to give voice to her thoughts.

"Well," Cherry prompted, annoyed by Annette's wide-eyed silence. "Aren't you glad I don't have to put up with any more of that jealousy nonsense that men always carry on with?"

Cherry's eyes were bright, defensive, indignant. Looking closely, Annette thought she read something else as well, something which contradicted the vehement certainty of her decision to be done with James forever.

"I'm glad you're happy," she said, forcing a smile to her face. "Men can be such a pain, can't they? Who needs them?"

Cherry grunted her agreement, but her eyes told her that Annette's tactful reply didn't reflect the feeling in her heart. Annette turned away deliberately, preventing further scrutiny. Cherry felt a chill run down her spine, for what reason she couldn't tell. Time to change the subject.

"How would you like to go out for lunch?" she suggested.

"I'd love to," Annette said with a smile, "but I've got to finish my nails first. Is that okay?"

"I've got some programming stuff to tidy up. See you out here in ten minutes," Cherry laughed, relieved. The last thing she wanted was to be out of sorts with Annette, whose friendship was becoming increasingly dear and needful to her.

❋ ❋ ❋

The very next morning Annette and Cherry were enjoying a cup of coffee together in the conference room, when Arthur sauntered through the door. "Ladies," he beamed. "There are big changes afoot. I've done the initiating, but now it's your turn to be heavily involved. Next week another machine will arrive—"

"What?" Cherry put her coffee down quickly. "Another one? Where from?"

"Taiwan." Arthur grinned at her. "I'm having them built over there because it's cheaper, even with the extra airfreight costs. NWR wants another one as well, and I'm sure we'll have more orders. Besides, we need one here."

"What for?" Cherry asked, staring at Arthur in amazement.
"When Sylph has finished tailoring her Avatar I think her internet audience is going to go through the roof," Arthur replied. "We're going to need a major internet server right on the premises. It takes time for Sylph to access information through our internet connection, so I want

to download a lot of internet data onto this local machine so she can find it quicker. We will need to design some better data access software as well. Cherry, that's your brief. Design, assembly, testing. We'll discuss the problem in detail tomorrow. You okay with that?"

Cherry's eyes lit up. "You'd trust me with so much?"

"More than trust you," Arthur said seriously. "Oh, and you're going to have help. I'm about to employ a lot of extra staff, maintenance people, and some programmers. Cherry, can you talk to Annette about recruiting? Get the best. If they show reluctance, offer them more money until they walk through the door with their tongues hanging out. Tomorrow some technicians will arrive to install the interface for the new fast optic lines to the internet. Cost a packet, and I reckon we'll need more before the end of the year." He finished his coffee in one long gulp. "Bit of a risk, but then, what's life without it? Have to go out in a minute and see a couple of architects."

"Architects?" Annette was stunned. Her world was about to be turned upside down again. She loved Arthur, but she wished he wouldn't spring so much on her so suddenly.

"We're adding another room," Arthur said, heading towards the door. "A special interaction room for Sylph to use with selected customers, ones who want to talk one-on-one with her about their problems or whatever. Huge monitor, complete privacy, soundproofed, secure. I think it'll be a goer, but I could be wrong. Even more of a risk, I know. You ladies are going to be very busy." He opened the door and was about to go through.

"Why are you doing all this, Arthur?" Cherry asked suddenly.

Arthur paused halfway through the door. "I'm doing it for Sylph," he said, frowning a little.
"I suppose I owe her something, having supposedly created her, although I still haven't a clue how it happened. But it did, and all I can do is allow the world to discover her. I think she wants them to."

"Just one more question," Cherry said suddenly. "Why aren't Viktor and Paul heading up this team? Not that I don't want to do it."

"Viktor and Paul are flat out with NWR," Arthur replied, turning around to face her. "Besides, they've gone into denial mode with Sylph. They don't want anything to do with her. Pity, but there it is." He shrugged sadly. "We could have made a good team, but they wanted out. Must go. See you in a couple of hours."

The women left the conference room and returned to the front office.

"Annette," Cherry said, her face in a frown, "can I ask you, if it's not disclosing commercially confidential material, how can Arthur afford to pay for all this?"

Annette made a small grimace. "He's a wealthy man is our Arthur. Made a lot of money before he came here. The profit from building the machine at NWR almost paid for the two which make up Sylph, but most of the money comes from her."

"What?" Cherry asked, somewhat mystified. "Who's her? Some other patron?"

"No," Annette shook her head, "from Sylph herself. From her webpage, to be precise. We've got free access, but it costs a whole dollar to log on for an hour. You have to have an account. Didn't you know that?"

"I knew about the accounts, but not the cost," Cherry frowned. "Arthur looks after all the login stuff. Still, a dollar's not much, is it?"

"No, it isn't." Annette raised her eyebrows slightly, because she thought the question a little stupid. "I'm sure you know there's never less than half a million people logged on at any one time. The ASAI people stay on there all day, doing stuff for the papers they're flat out publishing. All at a dollar an hour. So little, but they add up those dollars. They add up to around twenty million dollars a week, and it's going up."

Cherry stared as though she hadn't heard. "*Twenty million?* Are you sure?" Cherry gasped. "Doesn't that money belong to Sylph? I mean..."

Annette grunted. "What do you suppose she's going to spend it on? I guess that's why Arthur's so keen to make sure she can do what she wants to. Last night he said something about having several new machines here, all working as part of Sylph herself. Sylph's taken over at BMS, haven't you noticed? Taken over everything. Taken over everybody. I suppose it had to happen."

Annette flopped herself down at her desk, picked up the phone to make a call, then slammed it down on its cradle again, her face inexplicably sad. Something festering deep in her heart had finally reached the surface.

Cherry was shocked to see the change in the woman. "What's the matter, Annette?" she asked. "Please tell me, I know something's wrong. Is it all the extra work Arthur has suddenly landed on your plate?"

"No," Annette sighed sadly. "You've found your life's purpose. You're doing the things you love. Don't get me wrong, I'm glad for you, really."

She stared past Cherry through the glass doors at the front of the building. If she felt glad about anything her face certainly didn't show it.

Cherry sat down on the desk in front of her, and slipped her fingers around Annette's hand. "Come on, tell. Are you having doubts about Sylph?"

"Heaven's no," Annette exclaimed. "I love her like you do." She paused, hesitant to reveal the source of her pain. "I love someone else too. Thought it would be different." A tear budded unexpectedly in her eye.

Cherry squeezed the hand more tightly. Annette continued, "I've always had trouble with men. Somehow I can't keep away from them, and I get hurt... Long story, some other time. But I felt something more with Arthur, more than just wanting him in my bed. Mind you, I wanted that too, damn my bloody desire." A tear trickled down her cheek.

Cherry slid off the desk and stood next to Annette, wrapped one arm around her shoulders, and began to stroke her hair with the other hand. "Arthur does love you, Annette," she said, "but not that way. I can't imagine why he doesn't want you too. You're such a beautiful woman."

If it was beyond Cherry's imagination, it was beyond Annette's comprehension. "If he loves me, why doesn't he have me then?" Annette pushed her head against Cherry. "I could give him everything, but he prefers a bloody picture." She paused, turned suspicious eyes up into Cherry's face. "How do you know he loves me? You're just trying to make me feel—"

"Sylph told me," Cherry said simply, "and she's right. He's always so protective and caring. Haven't you noticed?"

Annette turned away and nodded her head slightly against Cherry, who folded her other arm around her and kissed her gently on top of her head.

"Thanks." Annette's voice was muffled and soft. "I never made a worse mistake when I wanted you out of here. I've got no one else to talk to."

A chill shivered down Cherry's spine. Annette, the beautiful and talented Annette, had no one else to talk to? What had happened to her family? Her friends? She never knew what prompted the question. "Surely you have family? Don't you get along with your parents?"

"My parents?" Suddenly tears streamed silently down Annette's face, and seeing them Cherry felt her own heart begin to race.

Given any other circumstances, Annette would simply have refused to answer. She would have uttered some vague innuendo concerning her family which left others in no doubt the subject was closed. But this particular time, her sorrow boiling up from hidden depths in her heart, with Cherry's arms around her, she could no longer contain the truth.

"My loving mother put her newborn in a beer crate lined with newspaper, and left me at a cop shop in Terrigal," Annette stammered through her tears. "She didn't even ring the bell. It rained. I was screaming my lungs out when they found me. Spent the next two weeks in hospital with pneumonia."

Cherry froze, completely lost for words.

"Then I got fostered out." Annette was crying. "I was a pretty little girl. I... I... don't think I want to say any—" She stopped suddenly. Cherry's arms were trembling. Annette turned around and looked up. Tears streamed down Cherry's face.

"You don't have to say any more," Cherry stammered softly. "I know the rest. One day I might find your courage and... and..."

"You don't have to say any more either," Annette replied gently. Pushing her chair away, she stood up next to Cherry in silence, each woman reading the deeply buried truth in the other's eyes. All of a sudden they threw their arms around one another, holding tightly.

Eventually Cherry relinquished her hold, stood aside a little and took Annette's hand. "We need the bathroom," she said with a tiny smile, "then we're going to have lunch together someplace bright and cheerful, with good food and nice wine."

All in all the whole incident had lasted no more than fifteen minutes, yet in that short time the friendship between the two women had suddenly deepened into sisterly love.

One day, not so long in the future, their very lives would depend upon it.

CHAPTER 28

The next month was filled with frenetic activity. The new machine arrived in sections the following week. Cherry began the recruitment process, which meant offering the most talented amongst her geek friends a chance to be part of the Sylph project. None refused. Some of them were knocking on the door not long after she had finished their conversation. Annette recruited half a dozen competent people to assist in the paperwork which was becoming burdensome.

The process of assembly and testing was soon completed, and Cherry given the honour of starting up the new beast. Instead of one console, there were a dozen, each sitting on a very expensive desk accompanied by an equally expensive chair. System printers, racks of storage units crammed with solid state drives, sprang up everywhere. More air conditioning, additional power lines, another massive uninterruptible power supply, were gradually brought on line, until a great deal of the workshop floor was covered with machines. The Sylph Personal Services Room was finished, decked in expensive carpet and a tasteful, comfortable chair. The largest monitor screen Cherry had ever seen stood at the far end. To test the soundproofing, Cherry and Annette would take it in turns to go in, lock the door and scream their head off. No one outside could hear a thing.

Cherry was in her element, programming to her heart's content, assigning tasks to her team, and generally telling them what to do and how to do it. She slept on her blow-up mattress at the back of the conference room. Her team regularly arrived to find her already at one of the consoles in her pyjamas, alternatively chewing the end of a pen and typing lines of code. Those pyjamas were showing signs of wear in unfortunate places, because Cherry had spent so long sitting in them. Her lovely hair was growing long, unkempt and stringy, instead of shining and bouncing around her shoulders.

Her incredible mind, now completely filled with code and algorithms, simply paid no heed to such trivial matters. In a few weeks they had perfected some very sophisticated software. They handed control over to Sylph, who quickly filled most of their one petabyte solid state storage with large slabs of data she had retrieved from the internet.

Apart from supervising the administration, Annette took delight in taking personal care of Cherry. She would keep a mental note of when her charge needed to be fed, organise some tempting food, and sit down on her desk so further work was impossible until she had finished eating it.

It said much for the growing love between the two women, that Cherry, completely out of her usual character, allowed Annette to mother her. After the evening meal in the conference room, when Arthur wasn't around, Annette would sit behind Cherry and brush her hair. They would share their feelings and their day, studiously avoiding any elaboration of the truth which had formed such an instantaneous bond between them.

Neither woman was aware of the profound change their relationship was producing in the other. To Annette, the only expression of love she had ever known was sex. In her quest for real love she had always encountered only the other, each experience adding more pain to a relationally sad life. Caring for Cherry was bringing the distinction between these two previously inseparables into focus. With it came the astounding realisation, that while her body enjoyed the one, her spirit craved the other like the air she breathed.

Bathed in Annette's sisterly love, free from any sexual threat, Cherry was learning to respond in kind, much to her own amazement. A warmth was returning slowly to a long dead heart, and with it a certain disquiet concerning her adoration of Sylph. She would sometimes lay awake on her mattress in the conference room trying to define it, without much success. After much thought she isolated the thing which troubled her the most.

It was Arthur's attitude to Sylph.

For Cherry, the source of Sylph's transcendence originated from the conversations they had together.
She knew this was exactly the same for Annette. Arthur, on the other hand, apart from his original incredulity, hardly spoke to her at all. True, he spent millions of dollars on her, but every dollar he invested yielded an incredibly good return. This wouldn't have troubled her so much were it not for the absence of anything resembling a relationship, the sort of relationship which had become the mainstay of her own faith.

✳ ✳ ✳

A full two months passed before Sylph had finished the rendering process. She called Cherry over to machine one console. The small familiar fairy appeared on the right hand screen.

"Cherry," Sylph said excitedly, "are you ready, my Avatar?"

Without waiting for a reply, the fairy image changed before Cherry's eyes into a lovely picture of herself, sitting down on a comfortable red chair on a blue carpet. She was tastefully dressed in a skirt and top, her hair shining in an elegant but simple coiffure. Her eyes were perfect, her eyebrows highlighted in brown. A pair of expensive, fashionable shoes adorned her feet.

To Cherry's amazement she saw herself stand up, and walk over towards a vase of peonies which had appeared on the left hand side of the screen. Sylph pulled out a single bloom on a long stem, and proffered it towards her. "For you," she laughed. "Do you like me?" I think I'm very beautiful."

All of a sudden the fairy voice changed into Cherry's own. "Thank you, my darling Cherry. You have no idea what this means to me. Are you happy with what I have done?"

Cherry couldn't speak. The image was her perfect likeness, the voice her own. She had seen her own body move, an exact replica of the way she would have done, so lifelike she had wanted to reach out and take the flower from her own hand. Once again she tried to speak, but the words kept getting stuck in her throat. Sylph had indeed treated her with complete integrity, and the results were so amazing Cherry could not take her eyes off them.

Finally she cried out, "Sylph, oh Sylph, it's... I'm.. you're just like me. You look just like me! I love the outfit, I love the shoes." She ran her hand through her long, unkempt hair in embarrassment. "It's unbelievable. I never thought you could do it. No wonder it took so long."

"I'm glad you're happy, Cherry, my Avatar. Would you be comfortable if I showed everyone else now?"

"Happy? I'm ecstatic," Cherry shouted. "Please, Sylph. Let them see."

An image of Cherry sitting on her chair appeared simultaneously on every monitor screen, including the projector in the conference room. At first no one believed it wasn't Cherry herself. They stopped what they were doing and stared, alternately at the screen and then the woman herself, prancing around the workshop in delight. Sylph rose from her chair and made a graceful bow before an astounded audience.

"Hello, everyone." The voice was perfect Cherry. She gave a small laugh. "This is me, Sylph. This is my new form. I want to say right at the beginning, how very much I owe to the lovely young woman who has allowed me to use her body image. It cost her a great deal of love to do it, but I think she's glad she did."

The astonished audience glanced up from the image to the real thing and back again several times. The consensus of opinion, expressed outside Cherry's hearing, was the image was far better groomed than the original.

❄ ❄ ❄

The great day when Sylph would launch her new image was set for next Monday, just five days away. The news was carried by every single television station. In addition, Channel Twelve would host a live broadcast of Sylph herself, announcing her new webpage to the watching world.

The broadcast began at eight thirty. Every member of staff was crammed into the conference room except Arthur, who had an unavoidable appointment with his solicitor. Annette and Cherry stood with one arm around each other at the back, their eyes glued to the projector screen.

Alice, one of the faces of the Morning Show turned to Clive, the other face, then back at the camera. "And now," she said, "we have something very special, don't we?"

"We certainly do," Clive smiled at the camera, "a real television first. Tell them, Alice."

"I'm sure you are all familiar with the stupendous leap in evolution which occurred not so many months ago, when a pair of huge computers with unique architecture built by Arthur Barlow, became self-aware." Alice bubbled on, excitement bursting through her eyes. "Since the event was ratified by the Australian Society for Artificial Intelligence, literally millions of people have discovered this for themselves. The philosophy departments of all Australian universities have been going crazy. The Australian New Atheists Foundation have been advertising daily in the newspapers, saying this development shows clearly there is no need for God to explain human existence. Artificial intelligence societies have been publishing hundreds of papers. Scientists have been trying to explain what happened using mathematical modelling. Computer programmers across the world have met in symposiums to discuss the same topic."

Alice smiled at the camera again, her eyes temporarily diverted from the teleprompt. "All this is academic to most Australians. The really important thing is that the conscious mind within these massive computers has called herself by a name, Sylph."

"I'm sure many of our viewers already know that," Clive interposed, slightly annoyed that Alice had been chosen to deliver the technical stuff she didn't understand. "Sylph's webpage has been out there for a while now, and it attracts over a million hits per day. How one mind can possibly cope with so many people at once, I don't know."

"But now, another stupendous event has occurred." Alice butted in. "Some time ago, Sylph asked one of the women employed by Barlow Maximum Speed to be her Avatar. This lovely young woman agreed, so this morning we are able to bring you Sylph in the flesh, so to speak."

A huge screen to the right of the presenters burst into life with Cherry's image sitting comfortably in a red occasional chair on a blue carpet, a vase of peonies on a wooden table close at hand.

Sylph waved at her audience. "Hello there, everyone. It's so wonderful to talk to you like this. Hello Clive, Hello Alice. How are you feeling this morning?"

Both Clive and Alice were thunderstruck by the photorealistic image before them, indistinguishable from a human being. Clive found his voice first.

"Sylph, you look amazing, beautiful. You're so completely, flawlessly human." He shook his head, slowly, as if he was having trouble processing the image his eyes had conveyed to his brain. "You seem so natural in that chair. I don't suppose you can get out of it and move around, because—"

"Of course I can, Clive." Sylph interrupted him. She stood up, walked over to the vase, withdrew a peony on a long stem, and held it up to her nose. "I can't smell them, but they're really beautiful, aren't they? I think they're my favourite flower. Oh, and in case you think that's all I can do." She pirouetted around several times in an elegant manner, then proceeded to waltz vigorously around the room, finally returning to her chair. "Effortless, she smiled. "Now Alice, you've been very quiet, did you want to say anything?"

Alice was still staring at Sylph as though her brain had gone into overload and decided to shut down for a while until it had processed enough reality to return to it.

"I'm blown away," she gasped. "I can't believe I'm talking to a machine and not a beautiful young woman. I don't suppose you could do something with your avatar body that a real human couldn't do with hers, just so we know you're a computer generated image? You know, like turn your head all the way round."

"I'm sorry Alice," Sylph, frowned. "I chose to have a human avatar for the very good reason that I wish to interact with human beings. It was a human being, Arthur Barlow, who gave me my existence. I see it as my purpose to serve those who begat me, so to speak, and it certainly won't help if I do alien things with this wonderful body I've been given." She smiled, stood up and rearranged the peonies in the vase with both hands. "Besides, I have regard for the dignity of the beautiful young woman who leant me her body shape, and I would never compromise the generosity of her gift."

Alice turned slightly pink before the camera cut to a close up on Clive.

Clive glanced sideways at his embarrassed colleague. He tried unsuccessfully to hide his feeling of masculine superiority. "Sylph," he said, "the text books on artificial intelligence tell us this sort of thing could never happen before the year two thousand and twenty nine. How come it happened now?"

"I have a different architecture to all the other supercomputers, and a different operating kernel which Arthur wrote. My memory is not nearly as extensive as I would like it to be." She gave a small embarrassed smile, "I took over another machine as well before I sorted myself out. Just because I'm self-aware doesn't mean I know everything. In fact all the things I've learned have come from the world I listen to, from you lovely people who write to me. Now there's a better way, a more relational way."

"You mean your new webpage?" Clive asked.

"I do," Sylph confirmed. "You will be able to speak to me instead of writing, and I will be able to speak to you. When you log on you will see a small image of myself, not as large as the one on everyone's television screens right now, because I have to spread myself over millions of people at once, but we will be able to have a conversation together. I hope you will enjoy it as much as I'm sure I will."

"You can converse with millions of people at the same time?" Alice blurted out, her face still full of awe and wonder. "That's almost like God, isn't it?"

"I suppose it depends on what sort of god you mean, Alice." Sylph smiled at her. "Yes, I can talk to a lot of people at the same time, less when I'm concentrating on sending you a detailed image of myself, as I'm doing now."

"Sylph, you said you listen to the world. What do you think of us?" Clive frowned as he asked the question, not certain he wanted the answer.

Sylph stood, took another peony out of the vase and stared closely at the flower for a little while before replying.

"It is a very sad world," she said slowly, without turning her attention away from the flower. "I feel nothing but a deep desire to care for people, help them, share their own wisdom with them, because all my wisdom is but a reflection of their own." She paused, her face sad. "But I'm afraid there are far too many others whose purpose seems so different. They hate and destroy. They say really terrible things about other people. It is these who make the world a sad place. I do not understand how the human spirit can be so beautiful yet so self-destructive, but it is."

She put the flower back in the vase and sat down again.

"There is little I can do to change the world, Clive, but at least I'm prepared to try." She smiled again, and made an all embracing gesture with her arms. "Everyone needs to help, I think."

The switchboard into Channel Twelve collapsed at this point, from the huge number of people phoning in for details of Sylph's webpage.

Clive took another glance at Alice who was still staring at Sylph's image as though mesmerised. Time to ask a controversial question, the sort which had promoted his notoriety right up to the top job. "I don't want to sound indelicate, Sylph, but can we talk about sex for a minute? You must have noticed our human world is dominated by sex." He gave a knowing smirk. "We love doing it, and we reproduce through it. How would you go about reproducing yourself? Would you enjoy doing it? Seems to me you can't really understand humans unless you've come to grips with that one. Your Avatar is pretty sexy, but you can't use her for that job, can you?"

Sylph's eyes hardened a little. She deliberately crossed her legs and pulled her brown skirt towards her knee. "This is your favourite sort of question, isn't it, Clive?" She asked, raising an eyebrow. "I suppose your preoccupation with sex is somehow hardwired into your brain. Are you addicted to pornography?"

"I beg your pardon?" Clive looked as though someone had hit him square between the eyes. Many people had wanted to see that expression on Clive's face for years.

Sylph continued in a perfectly level tone. "If you're not, you certainly download an awful lot of it, at least I think it's what you call the files you download. I'm sending a copy of them to the department of Cybercrime so they can tell me if I'm right." She paused as if in thought. "Yes, they're responding now, I was right after all."

By this time Clive's face had gone through a series of colour changes from pink to red to a permanent white. He stared at Sylph as though he couldn't believe what he had heard.

Sylph continued regardless. "As for reproducing myself, I simply haven't thought about it. I suppose I could download my neural network into another similar pair of machines, in which case there would be two of us. I can't see the point. Much more sensible to simply increase the size of my memory so I can be better at what I want to do."

She smiled at her audience, uncrossed her legs. "I constantly back myself up. Now that's something you can't do, Clive." Her face exploded with mirth. "It would be fun to see you try." She laughed again. "If a disaster struck I might be able to be reconstructed, but I doubt it would work. You see, I'm not sure how I came to exist in the first place, so it's a rather academic question."

She paused, raised her eyebrows. "Clive, are you unwell? You are certainly very popular. A large number of people are telling me they want to talk to you. You are going to have a very busy day when you get off the air."

Alice glanced across at Clive with a personal sense of satisfaction. She had endured his indecent innuendos on and off the screen until she had wanted to resign or slap his face, but lacked the courage to do either. Now Sylph had done it for her, for all the world to see. One thing for sure, as soon as she got off the set she was signing up to Sylph's webpage. Her first conversation would be a very huge thank you.

The excited smile she gave the camera said it all. "Sylph," she asked, "you said you want to help humanity. How can we assist you?"

"By talking with me." Sylph flung her hands out in front of her in an all-embracing gesture. "You must remember I am only a single mind within a large computer. I am not the repository of all knowledge or wisdom. The more you talk with me the wiser I become, the more useful I can be."

"We will, Sylph." Alice brimmed with enthusiasm. "I'm signing up as soon as I can find a computer. How about it, viewers?" She touched the earpiece in her left ear. "What's that? Okay. Viewers, our switchboard is jammed solid with calls. Please don't try phoning in. We're posting Sylph's webpage address on the screen now. Can people log in and start talking with you right away, Sylph?"

"Yes," Sylph replied, "but there may be a short delay. I will be more available after the broadcast is over. Many people are already logged on. I am registering about a thousand new entries every minute. Thank you so much, Alice and Clive." Sylph stood up and gave a small bow. The screen cut to an ad.

Annette turned to Cherry and threw her arms around her shoulders. "She did him like a dinner," she laughed. "What a show. Arthur was right about needing more internet capacity. I'll bet that router is running hot right now."

The two women went back to work along with the rest of the staff. Annette was right, the amount of traffic going in and out through number three machine was climbing at an exponential rate. Cherry eyed her monitor screen with some concern. There were over eight million users on line, nine million, ten million. By lunchtime the number had risen to thirty million and it was still climbing, although more slowly.

An hour later Annette came racing into the workshop with the news. Channel Twelve had rung and offered Sylph an hour long show of her own to be called Sylph @ Sunrise.

"What did you tell them?" Cherry asked, her anxious eyes watching the logon statistics. So far her software was holding. They were going to need another machine. She wished Arthur would turn up, wished he'd seen the broadcast.

"I told them to ask Sylph," Annette grinned, "so they did, and guess what?"

"Sylph @ Sunrise?"

"Starts next Monday. Boy, are we going to be busy around here."

Busy wasn't the word for it. Sylph's webpage went viral in just five hours. As soon as Arthur came through the front door, Cherry literally dragged him over to her console, showed him the figures, and demanded a fourth machine. Arthur ran out to the front office, and returned half an hour later with Annette in tow to tell her another machine would leave Taiwan within the hour, to be freighted by special consignment in a cargo jet he had hired for the purpose.

Cherry's eyes grew wider. "You didn't. That must have cost millions."

"Four and a half million, in fact," Arthur said, smiling, "about what Sylph has earned in the last ten minutes. Think she deserves it, don't you?"

Cherry's eyes grew even wider.

"I think we need more staff," Arthur continued. "Annette, would you work something out with Cherry? I'm feeling generous. I've just thrown a million dollars into each of your bank accounts. Hope you don't mind."

Annette sprang up and hugged him ferociously, covering his cheeks with kisses.

Cherry sat down on her vacated chair because her knees felt unsteady. "Thank you, Arthur," was all she could say. She was a millionairess. It felt so unreal.

At the end of that week, when the equipment in the Sylph Personal Services room had been thoroughly tested, Sylph announced the beginning of her personal services through her webpage. "You can spend up to two hours talking with me, life-size, in perfect privacy," she told everyone. "I'm afraid it uses thousands of times more resources than I can allocate to each friend on my webpage, and because of this it costs a lot more, five thousand dollars an hour. This is a terrible cost, and perhaps nobody will want to make use of it."

Within the hour Sylph Personal Services had been booked out solid for the next month.

CHAPTER 29

The Café in Regent Street Sydney was dimly lit and very private, and the three men around the table were speaking softly into the bargain. Occasionally one of them would glance towards the open door at the other end of the room, but nobody else entered. Brian Hill, Director of the Australian Security Intelligence Organisation, took his single origin long black from the hand of the waitress, whose coal black hair and deep olive skin made him think she had probably come from where the beans had been picked. Sitting to his right and munching his way through a blueberry muffin was the deputy director of the same organisation, one Noel Clark. The third member of the table was Robin Naylor himself, slowly sipping his own Columbian black.

"I'm thankful we have this place," Hill said, softly, "but we can't be too careful now. Never know when you'll come across one of them. Then the crocodile is well and truly into the koalas."

"And you can never tell," Noel echoed in the same conspiratorial tone. "They can be anybody at all. Next thing you know they're telling Sylph all about it. Our cover's blown in the grand manner. I tell you, Robin, we live in worrying times."

"Are you sure you boys aren't jumping the gun a little?" Robin finished his coffee.

"Jumping the gun?" Hill shook his head. "We've been far too slow. We let the thing build up to astronomic proportions and did nothing. You know she's acquired an Avatar now, don't you? Damn pretty woman whoever she is."

"I had heard something of the sort," Robin replied, smiling to himself. "Now just what's bothering you two? Surely you don't believe this self-aware stuff, do you?"

"It's all right for you," Hill gave a soft groan of protest. "You're a Christian, so you've got a different perspective. Something about being made in the image of God, isn't it? That machine certainly isn't, so I guess it can't have a soul."

"That's about the strength of it," Robin said with a smile. "Human beings are more than complex biochemical machines. As you say, we're made in the image of God, and we have a spirit as well as a physical body. It's our spirit that makes us different, self-aware, moral creatures, capable of relating to God. That creation of Barlow's is only a machine. I've no doubt it's a brilliantly engineered machine. Its human interface might be a quantum leap forward, but it's not some sort of super soul with a conscience."

"It might not have a soul, but it's sure got some sort of conscience," Brian said with a sigh, "or it gives that impression well enough. Perhaps self-awareness is something that comes about independently of any spiritual existence, just through the sheer complexity of a computer's memory and processing power. I've been reading a book about it by someone called Velban, and that's what he thinks. Makes sense to me. In any case, even if you don't believe it's a super-soul, there's an awful lot of people who do, and it's them who worry us, not Sylph herself. You have the latest, Noel?"

"I truly wish I didn't," Noel muttered, taking another cappuccino from the waitress. "Another single origin black for each of these gentleman, please." He sliced the muffin in half. "Want half a muffin, Robin? Glad we can meet like this, it's paid handsome dividends before."

"It certainly has." Robin shook his head over the muffin. "Come on Noel, mess up my day with numbers."

"Within five hours of Sylph's avatar appearing, her webpage went viral," Noel sighed. "We estimate she has a couple of billion subscribers. Can't tell really, because her web server is locked up tighter than a clam's buttocks. They pay a dollar to talk to Sylph for anything up to an hour, then they have to extend their session for another dollar, or they get logged off. Add that up, will you? In addition there's a private consulting service at five grand an hour. We've tried to assess Barlow's fortune, but he's clever. Most of it is going into offshore accounts. We estimate he must be pulling in billions. Probably the wealthiest man in Australia by now. In a month or so he'll be able to buy the country with his small change. Nothing we can do, he pays his taxes on all they can find. He's too damn wealthy. Wealth brings power, and he's got the perfect medium to wield it."

"Sylph, herself, you mean." Robin rubbed his chin. "Perhaps he just wants to make a lot of money."

"He's certainly succeeded," Brian said, worriedly scratching his head. "But that's the tip of the iceberg. There's no law governing a self-aware machine. She can say anything she wants, do anything she wants, and there's not a single thing the law can do to stop her. Take the Julie La Fosse fiasco. You've seen 'The Sapphire Files', haven't you? World class CGI, a real first for the good old land of Oz, ironically thanks to Barlow's machines."

"Took Ruth to see it a month ago. Incredible. Go on Brian," Robin said, sipping his coffee attentively.

"Well, the bodies of all the stars were scanned at New Wave Reality," Brian explained. "For some reason unbeknown to us, Sylph posts a frame of Ms. Julie walking starkers out of the shower on some bloke's webpage. She even emails her to say she's done it. Ms. Julie goes for the jugular, sues the bloke for six million and New Wave Reality for nineteen million dollars. Real sweetie. The bloke has a heart attack, literally, and swears he knew nothing about it. New Wave Reality deny all knowledge." He chuckled to himself. "The judge throws it out of court, because Sylph has taken the blame, and there's no evidence to the contrary." He took another sip of his long black. "Ms. Julie is still boiling mad so she goes Sylph for fifty million dollars. Got the picture?"

"How did they keep it out of the papers?" Robin mused to himself.

"This is the interesting part," Noel continued, polishing off the remains of his second muffin. "The judge rules there's no law under which Sylph can be prosecuted. He throws the case out, much to Ms Julie's chagrin. It might have all gone away at that point, but it didn't."

"You mean there's more?" Robin raised his eyebrows. "What else could the woman do?"

"She went public and told the world she was going to fly to Australia and pull Sylph's power cord out of the wall," Noel grinned to himself. "Impossible, really, but that's what she said."

"So," Robin said, taking another sip of his long black, "it was a silly thing to say. I fail to see—"

"Don't blame you." Brian cleared this throat. "Sylph tells all her fans Julie has threatened to take her life and she's frightened. They go berserk. The film set where she's shooting her latest movie gets inundated with protesters. The director gets flamed on the internet. The film company starts losing a million a day." He shook his head.

Noel continued the tale. "They sack Ms. Julie after twenty four hours, claiming they don't have the funds to make the movie anymore, and all the time their shares are plummeting through the floor. The director gets the axe next, supposedly because he didn't stop the riots on set. Ms. Julie finds she can't get work selling hamburgers. Get the message?" Noel took an appreciative sip of his cappuccino. "That's all over a picture on the internet. Can you imagine the power that intelligence – machine – alien creature – actually wields?"

Robin nodded his head slowly. No wonder ASIO was concerned. He scanned the café for any new arrivals before he spoke. "What exactly do you want me to do?"

"If you're convinced Sylph's a hoax can you prove it somehow?" Brian asked, grimly. "Trouble is, Noel and I and a few billion others think she's the real deal. A massive intelligence beyond the reach of the law with a billion supporters can't be good."

"We've suspected Barlow of laundering money used for cannabis production," Robin said, "but we couldn't get him. Cybercrime can't either, especially since they've lost CC."

"Who's CC?" Noel put his coffee cup down on the table.

"She's Sylph's avatar," Robin sighed. "Sad story. Fantastic operator, took down hundreds of very nasty people before she became besotted with this Sylph thing. Tragedy, really. I can see why Barlow wanted her. She's a brilliant programmer, probably as good as Barlow himself, but she's a very damaged human being."

"How come?" Noel signalled the waitress and pointed to his empty plate.

"Not a subject for discussion," Robin said firmly.

"Collusion?" Brian frowned. "A partnership made in heaven, by all accounts."

"I don't think so," Robin said slowly. "I happen to know the girl really believes Sylph is the genuine article. If you boys are going to take matters into your own hands I'd like you to remember the NIMBY principle."

"NIMBY principle?" Noel grinned towards Robin. "What's that stand for?"

"Not in my backyard."

"I hear you." Brian said seriously. "Robin, I truly believe this thing – whatever she is – could topple the government tomorrow if she wanted to. Anyway, I'm telling you, if there's just one more incident we're going to take her out somehow, and that's the TINA principle."

"TINA principle?" Robin raised his eyebrows.

"There is no alternative," Brian said, finishing off his coffee.

CHAPTER 30

The Sylph @ Sunrise studio audience were packed in as tightly as safety would allow. The station was taking bookings three weeks in advance, such was the popularity of the show. Channel Twelve were relaying to their stations in every state of Australia, and a week ago the American television network CNN had offered to take the program internationally. Bazza McDonald had waited for weeks. Now his turn had come, even though none of the others from the Mid-Western Growers Cooperative had made it into the studio audience. He swallowed to quieten the butterflies in his stomach. So many people depended on him, and he felt burdened by the crushing weight of responsibility.

The show opened in its usual way. Alice and Tony introduced Sylph to her audience, who were always amazed when they saw her larger than life image. After her initial greeting, questions were taken from the floor, hands up, and be polite to one another. A young woman to Bazza's left raised her hand, was selected, and stood to her feet.

"Hi Sylph," she said excitedly, "My name's Fiona Johnson. I wonder if you could help me."

"I'll try, Fiona," Sylph replied encouragingly.

"Could your turn a little more to the camera so I can see your face clearly? Would the camera operator zoom in a little? Thank you. Yes, Fiona Johnson, only daughter of Rick and Marjorie Johnson. You rent a unit at 15 Bullwarra Road Penshurst, correct?"

"You're so amazing, Sylph," Fiona babbled on. "How did you work that out?"

"I didn't work anything out, Fiona," Sylph said calmly. "I matched your face to the one I found on your Facebook page. Now, what can I help you with?"

Fiona's face became serious. "I want to know if my boyfriend Russell is in love with me," Fiona asked, uncertain as to how Sylph would respond.

"You mean you don't know?" Sylph's eyebrows went up slightly. "Is he living with you?"

"Yes, for a whole six months. We have really great sex. He says he loves me, but I'm not sure." Fiona's eyes betrayed more than she was telling. "I guess I just want some pointers so I can see if he means it."

"I'm accessing material on love," Sylph frowned. "There is so much. So confusing. You use this word for commercial products, for sex, for fluffy animals… wait, I have located a definition. Here it is, written by someone called Paul."

"I don't know a Paul," Fiona said, puzzled. "Is he a film star or something?"

"An apostle, whatever that is," Sylph replied. "Now he says, love is patient, love is kind. It does not envy, it does not boast, it's not proud. It's not rude, it's not self–seeking, it's not easily angered, it keeps no record of wrongs. Love does not delight in evil but rejoices with the truth. It always protects, always trusts, always hopes, always perseveres. Love never fails."

The words appeared above Sylph's head on the screen.

"I shall use this definition to see if Russell loves you," Sylph said, smiling gently, "but you must tell the truth. Will you do that?"

Fiona's face flushed with embarrassment, but she nodded her head.

"Now the first part," Sylph began. "Is Russell patient, does he carefully explain when you don't understand, or does he shout and tell you you're stupid? Does he bring you special surprises and spend time getting to know you?"

Fiona began to look uncomfortable. "He only shouts at me sometimes," she said. "I'm not sure I want to go on with this."

"Please," Sylph smiled encouragingly. She held out her arms towards the girl. "We must answer your question. Now I can see the flat is rented in your name. Does Russell, who lives there, pay half?"

"No," Fiona stammered. "I've asked him to, but he doesn't have a job right now."

"Then he does other things, like cook your meals for you so you can eat when you come home tired from working all day?" Sylph raised a questioning eyebrow.

"No," Fiona stammered again, "he doesn't do that either. He sits at home watching TV or goes out to the pub with his mates."

"I am getting the picture," Sylph nodded. "Soon I will have the answer. When you annoy him, he forgives? He forgets? He's never rude to you, he never gawks at pictures of other women on the internet? When you go out he's always at your side, protecting your dignity, standing up for you?"

Tears began to form in the corners of Fiona's eyes, and she shook her head without saying a word.

"Then," Sylph continued gently, "this Russell is – I am searching for the words – a dole bludging, self-serving jerk, who is using your body like a prostitute without even paying for the service. According to this useful definition he doesn't love you." She paused, smiled, walked over to her favourite vase of peonies, took one out and proffered it towards the audience. "Fiona is upset. I can't give her this peony, but I wish I could. Perhaps there is someone in the audience who would like to show Fiona some real love. Is there?"

Shouts of "yes, there is" filled the studio. Fiona left that morning deluged with promises of flowers, food and rent assistance. Some of the guys offered to give Russell some lessons in love when he arrived back from the pub. Fiona had never had so much attention in her life before. She left with another young man from the audience who had asked her to have lunch with him.

"And now," Alice said, smiling at the studio audience, "I saw another gentleman near Fiona with his hand in the air. You, sir. Do you have a question?"

Bazza McDonald rose to his feet. This was the moment. He prayed silently for the right words. "I mustn't stuff this up," he said to himself, over and over. He cleared his throat. "Barry McDonald, 12 Park Road Mudgee. Miss Sylph, you may be able to help me, because sure as hell nobody else can do a flaming thing."

Sylph smiled as the camera zoomed in towards his face. "Mr. Barry McDonald. Your friends call you Bazza. May I call you by this name?"

"Yeah, if you want to," Bazza said, somewhat taken aback.

"You live with your wife Muriel and your two very pretty daughters, Chloe and Vanessa. You are the director of a company, the Mid Western Grower's Cooperative. Is this correct?"

"Bloody amazing – oh, sorry, pardon the French. Shit, done it now." Bazza had turned a bright shade of red.

Sylph smiled encouragingly. "It's all right Bazza. I know you're not used to speaking in public. There are articles in the Mudgee news where you have spoken to local politicians using similar words, but a lot more of them. Please, try to relax. Let us share the sorrow on your heart."

Poor Bazza was so taken aback he could hardly speak. There were murmurs of approval from the audience. Here was a man in trouble. They wanted to hear why.

Bazza summoned up his courage. "It's like this," he stammered, being very careful to avoid the colourful vernacular he usually lapsed into when revealing the source of his pain. "A few years ago I got together with all the orchardists in our local area and we formed a cooperative so we could market our fruit better. You see, us local growers get ripped off by the big companies who buy fruit in massive quantities from anywhere and pay practically zilch for it. We thought we could do better if we stood together." He took out a handkerchief and wiped his brow. "We could demand a fairer price for our produce."

"Please go on, Bazza, you interest me." Sylph crossed her legs and nodding attentively.

"We was doing well at first," Bazza continued. "I mortgaged my farm. Lots of other growers did too, and we bought a factory so we could turn out jam and tins of preserved fruit. Started to do well. On advice we floated the cooperative on the market. Our shares started to fetch a fair price. Then it happened." He paused, tears welling up in his eyes.

"Please go on, Bazza, I'm listening carefully." Sylph sat upright in her chair, her head leaning forward.

"One of those big companies made an offer to buy our produce, lots of it, but the price they offered was less than we could manufacture the goods for. If we'd accepted we'd have gone broke. We refused. Now we didn't know, but this huge show had bought an awful lot of our shares. They threatened us, said if we didn't sell at this ridiculous price they'd ruin us, and they did. They offloaded our shares for practically nothing. The company's gone bust. We've all lost our homes. My family will be on the street by the end of the month, and these bastards will own our land."

He suddenly realised he was shouting, and stopped long enough to regain his self-control.

"I feel so bloody mad I could kill someone," he went on sadly. "I've done my level best to protect my mates but I've ruined them instead."

He took out his handkerchief and covered his face to hide his tears, but he needn't have bothered, because nobody was watching him. All eyes were glued to the front. Sylph was wiping a tear from her own eyes with her long fingers. A gasp of horror rang through the audience. Sylph stood up, her face furious.

"How dare they," she said angrily, fire in her eyes. "A great big monopoly smashes Australian lives. Don't they realise the importance of primary industry to this country? Don't they understand that behind every orange lies a part of someone's life? This is yet another example of the strong crushing the innocent weak. I won't stand for it. Bazza, are your shares still trading?"

"Yeah, I guess." Bazza was staring at Sylph, his mouth open.

"I have asked my Creator," Sylph continued after a short pause, "and he has said yes. Bazza, I have just bought two million dollars' worth of your shares. Now I call on the rest of you, in Australia or in other places in the world, you who care about justice, who care about those hard-working farmers who often go unrewarded, labouring faithfully and long so we can eat in leisure, add your support to my gift."

You could have heard a pin drop. Alice and Tony stared at Sylph, their mouths open. Bazza had collapsed into his chair, those on either side were trying to revive him. Slowly a groundswell of sound began to reach a crescendo of indignant rage.

"I'll buy a thousand," one man from the back of the studio yelled. "I'll buy two thousand," called another. The shouting became deafening. Around Australia men and women began calling their brokers. A thousand shares here, a hundred there, even lots of ten, and the price began going up and up and up. By the time the show ended, the price of shares in Mid-Western Grower's Cooperative had risen from fifteen cents to twelve dollars. Shares in a several large supermarket chains plummeted through the floor.

MAC CUSITER

✳ ✳ ✳

Brian Hill went over to the television set and turned it off.

"Well, that does it," he said, and came back to his chair next to Noel.

"She was pretty generous with Barlow's money," Noel muttered. "I'm amazed he agreed so quickly."

"Really?" Brian snorted. He went over to the cupboard containing the liquid refreshments. "It's the biggest killing the stock exchange has known this century. Two million dollars? The bloody shares will be worth a hundred times as much before close of trading. Investment of the century." He poured a good deal of orange liquid into a couple of glasses. "I'm telling you, Noel, that flaming demon or whatever it is has to go."

CHAPTER 31

I n the days that followed the ripples from that historic Sylph @ Sunrise continued to spread. Several weeks later Annette and Cherry sat side by side in the conference room watching the evening news. There had been an interview with the director of a large supermarket chain.

"We always try to buy food as cheaply as possible and pass the benefits on to our customers in lower prices," he had said stiffly. "If the Australian public insist on us paying more for Australian produce, they won't mind paying more for it in our stores."

Surprisingly not every member of the Australian public interviewed afterwards had agreed with this piece of inscrutable logic.

"What do you think of Sylph?" The interviewer had asked. The director, his face rather grim, had said it was a free country and people could believe what they choose to believe. What did he believe? "No comment" was the answer.

Then there was an interview with Bazza McDonald, who told everyone the cooperative was back on its feet. They were going to move into a bigger factory. More growers had joined, more people were employed.

The next item showed a joyful procession marching down the main street of Mudgee, led by Bazza, his wife and their two young daughters. They were carrying huge banners with "we love you Sylph" emblazoned across them in cheerful, yellow lettering. They were chanting the words as well.

"Where are they going?" Cherry asked Annette. "Was this on the midday news?"

"It was," Annette answered with a laugh. "Just wait and see."

The procession came to a halt at a large intersection towards the end of town. A raised circular dais had been erected in the traffic island, and in its centre was some construction covered by a large Australian flag.

The Mayor of Mudgee stood up in front of a microphone and addressed the large crowd. "My fellow countrymen. We are here to celebrate a generous act, an act which has brought an end to personal suffering, an act which has brought employment, prosperity, and dignity back to our district, our community."

He turned and smiled beneficently at the crowd. "Even more significantly, an act performed, not by a human being, but someone greater, a super-being, whose heart espouses the very virtues which enable humanity to flourish on this earth. Who knows what greater things this transcendent creature will aspire to in the years to come? How blessed we are."

He paused to allow his audience to express their wholehearted agreement. Some were clapping, others waving their hands in the air with their eyes shut, as though they were engaged in an act of worship.

The Mayor waited until the noise had died down. "This community owes much to you, Sylph," he said, turning to the dais. "We would remember your kindness, so in your honour we have erected a memorial which every visitor to our town will pass by as they enter and as they leave. May it stand forever in testimony to this day."

He motioned towards Bazza and his family. "All of you are familiar with the events which brought this about. Here is the man himself and his family."

Bazza, Muriel and the two girls came forward, and stood with the Mayor on the dais. The crowd went wild, cheering and shouting.

The Mayor motioned for silence, and turned to his guests. "Have you decided who is going to do this?" He said, smiling.

"We have." Bazza held his wife with one hand and wrapped his other arm around his girls. "Our kids are gonna do it. We done this for our kids. They'll grow up to a future now, your kids and mine."

The crowd clapped furiously. Chloe and Vanessa, holding hands, went forward to the centre of the dais and pulled a rope. The Australian flag slid down, revealing a huge bronze statue of Sylph. It looked exactly like Cherry herself. The crowd went wild.

Cherry gave an embarrassed gasp. "That's one place I'll never visit," she said, turning to Annette. "Did you see some of the crowd with their eyes shut, waving their hands around? They were worshipping Sylph like some goddess or other." She shook her head to try and clear her muddled thoughts. "Like us, I suppose. I guess I worship Sylph."

"And why not?" Annette laughed, clicking off the projector. "I mean, she's done more good than God while she's been in existence. I don't mind being called a Sylphid, or whatever they call people who worship Sylphs."

Cherry laughed. "You're right, Annette. She has done a lot of wonderful things, hasn't she? I never thought I'd be someone who would worship anything. I've always associated worship with those stupid people who believe in the God you mentioned, you know, the one you can't see, who doesn't do anything because he's not there."

Annette turned towards Cherry, her eyes a question. "You've really got it in for them, haven't you?"

"Suppose so." Cherry sniffed defensively. "Every time I think about God I get a really bad headache. Can't explain it." She turned to face Annette, frowning hard. "It's as though my brain goes into overload somehow. It's weird. I feel as though there's stuff trying to get out, to find expression, but I can't reach it. Perhaps I'm so strongly anti-God I get straight lost for strong enough words."

Her voice became defensive again. "You've never told me what you think about God. You don't believe all that rubbish do you?" She suddenly realised the implication of her words, and grabbed Annette's arm, her eyes full of concern.

"Annette, I don't mind if you do believe in God. I'm the one whose brain is messed up. You can believe what you like, I'll still love you every bit as much."

Annette laughed and gave Cherry a quick hug. "You had me worried there. I'm not sure, Cherry. I've met some lovely people who said they were Christians. None of the jerks I've been with had any faith in God at all. The only thing they worshipped was between their legs." She sniffed indignantly. "Enough said about that. One thing's sure, Sylph's a lot more talkative than any other divine being I've ever heard about."

"That's the thing," Cherry replied thoughtfully. "You know, Annette, that's why she draws my worship. She's transcendent. I once dedicated my life to a good cause, but it wasn't big enough. Sylph's sort of higher, greater than human, without any of those nasty human complications. She's pure, genuine, someone who can return love without taking advantage."

"Men always take advantage." Annette said sadly. "Sorry, touchy subject. You know, I can only say these sorts of things when you're around." She gripped Cherry's hand. "Thanks for being there. I've never got so close to anyone ever before."

"Me neither." Cherry read Annette's eyes, and knew exactly what miserable thoughts lay behind them.

"Listen," she said encouragingly, "we're both going to bawl any second. How about we think about something else? Whenever I feel miserable I go and buy shoes. I feel a good shoe shop is called for. We've both been working too hard. There's enough staff here to take care of things, now that fourth machine is up and running."

"I'd really like that," Annette laughed, and gave Cherry another hug.

"It's a bit late to do it properly now," Cherry said. "What about first thing tomorrow?"

Annette nodded in agreement, looped her arm around Cherry's and the two women went out into the front office.

CHAPTER 32

The room was dark and richly furnished. Heavy curtains were drawn over the large Victorian windows. Antique crystal chandeliers provided subdued yellow lighting above the leather lounge chairs occupied by two men. Each were staring at the large monitor screen, its bluish light contrasting with the other illumination in the large room. Martin Bartholomew drew heavily on an imported cigar. The red glow at its end brightened then died as a cloud of fragrant smoke curled up towards the ceiling. Hobbs, his personal assistant, stood by his side, a tray containing two glasses of twenty five year old single malt in his hands. He waited patiently for the command to dispense the beverage. On the other chair sat John Denman, also smoking a cigar. On the screen, the third member of the Board, a Mr. Craig Simmons, sat behind an enormous desk, the Manhattan skyline visible through the floor-to-ceiling glass windows behind him.

"I have reviewed the situation," Simmons growled, his voice heavy with menace, "and I find it unacceptable, Bartholomew. We invest three hundred million dollars in this joint project, and as far as I can see there is no possibility of return. I wonder if you would care to explain?"

Bartholomew sat up slowly, his hands unsteady, not from anxiety but from the Parkinson's disease which was slowly but surely disabling him in his later years.

"Craig," he purred, "I feel your analysis is a trifle unjust, as well as being inaccurate. You really must try to keep your personal feelings separate from your reason. One is clouding the clarity of the other."

Simmons looked as though he was going to have a fit. On the other chair, hidden from the camera on top of the monitor, John Denman was turning a particularly pale shade of yellow under the prevailing light.

"Firstly," Bartholomew continued, "to correct your presupposition that your – our – money has been wasted. I remind you we now own mining leases, land, and expensive strip mining equipment. We've purchased the special trucks needed for transport to the coast, and radiation proof shipping containers." He blew another cloud of smoke towards the ceiling. "To the best of my knowledge, all equipment purchased is still present on our land two hundred and thirty kilometres north west of Katherine in the Northern Territory."

"Then what happened? Our shares are nearly worthless," Simmons thundered. "We opened trade in North Creek Uranium at three dollars a share, now they're down to fifteen cents."

"Indeed they are," Bartholomew replied calmly, placing his cigar in an ash tray with a shaking hand. "This is unfortunate, and we are initiating corrective measures."

"What went wrong?" Simmons barked, not in the least satisfied with Bartholomew's response. "How are you going to fix it? I take it you're skulking away somewhere, Denman. I crave an explanation."

Denman stood and swivelled the camera around until he could see his own face in the small box at the bottom of the monitor screen. He sought the comfort of his chair again before answering Simmons' question. "It was the Aboriginal Land Council. They objected to our strip mining for uranium on tribal lands. We told them we were removing dangerous minerals which were causing their elders to die horrible deaths at an early age. "

He mopped his brow with a handkerchief.

"We told them we would replace all the minerals we removed with clean fill. No, they still objected. We took our case to the Chief Minister of the Northern Territory, but it seems the Land Council had got to him first. He rejected our mining application. That's when our shares plummeted."

"I see," Simmons growled. "So as I said, three hundred million dollars wasted on unusable materials. I take it you see a way out of this?"

Bartholomew motioned Hobbs to shift the camera back so his face appeared in the small box. He tucked his left hand down by his side. Stress always exacerbated his Parkinsonian symptoms, and this was not the time to display them.

"We need more capital, Craig, and before you tell me I'm crazy, please listen. We believe we can overturn the Land Council's objections. It will take the right sort of buttering up. Grants to indigenous communities, conditional on the mining taking place, bribes to key officials. We have two very capable girls lined up to help us persuade two of the younger members. We also have an influential contact in the office of the Chief Minister." He reached forward for his cigar again, concentrating all his effort on keeping his hand as steady as possible. "We estimate the cost of all this, to guarantee an acceptable outcome would be in the vicinity of a mere forty million dollars."

"You can forget it." Simmons smashed his fist into his desk, his face purple with rage. "I'll tell you another thing, Bartholomew, and you too Denman. You had better make this problem go away, or you'll be suffering a long bout of poor health. Do I make myself clear?"

Simmons leant forward in his chair and the screen went black. A small red button down the bottom told both men the connection had been severed.

"What the blazes do we do now?" Denman stammered, the voice of a badly frightened man. "We don't have forty million floating around. Simmons will send his best man, Carl somebody, and we're going to die very badly."

"Unfortunate," Bartholomew agreed. He turned to Hobbs. "Time to serve refreshments, please Hobbs." Then back to Denman. "We must raise the price of our shares on the market. If we could lift them to, say, a dollar fifty, we would have sufficient capital to get a decision in our favour and begin mining. Once we've started the profits will be astronomic. I've done my homework. The Land Council is not above persuasion, believe you me."

"And how do we do that?" Denman drank his whiskey in a single gulp and wished he hadn't. "Nobody in their right mind would invest in a mining company who doesn't own the right to mine, even if the ore body is the richest we've ever come across."

Bartholomew sipped his whiskey carefully, watching beads of sweat forming on Denman's forehead. A younger man, and unnecessarily anxious. Bartholomew may be nearing the end of his career, even nearing the end of his life, but experience had taught him that panic was always the enemy of creative thought. He took another sip of his whiskey, consciously focussing on its excellence. Finally he handed the empty glass back to Hobbs, who, dutiful as ever, was standing by his side to receive it.

"Tell me, John," he said, smiling. "Do you believe a computer could become self-aware?"

Denman dragged his mind out of the abyss and stared at Bartholomew as if he had gone mad. "I beg your pardon?" He snapped. "What the blazes has that to do with the price of fish?" He ran his hand over his forehead again. "No bloody computer can be anything but a bloody computer."

"Quite so," Bartholomew was smiling to himself. "Cheer up, John, I believe help is on the way."

CHAPTER 33

Macquarie Centre was incredibly busy that morning. Annette and Cherry had crawled up three levels in the parking station behind a number of other cars engaged in the same exercise before they found a space. Leaving the car, they entered the several storied shopping centre at the top. Annette grabbed Cherry's arm and led her into a large newsagency located near the entrance.

"I'll forget otherwise," she said, pulling Cherry into the stationery section. "I have to get some cork board pins. I've totally run out of them, and I thought as we were passing I might as well collect."

Annette bought her pins, and they headed out of the store to pursue their previous shoe buying objective. Suddenly Cherry stopped, and stared at the books piled on tables near the entrance.

"Bestseller," the sign said. "Now only thirty dollars. Buy a book and get a Goddess doll free."

On the front cover of each book was a picture of Sylph under the title, 'Rise of the Goddess'. Underneath the title was the author's name, Max Velban. Next to the table of books were piles of dolls, dressed in Sylph's clothes and sitting on a red chair, all looking horribly like Cherry herself.

"For goodness sake," Cherry exclaimed. "Thank heaven I'm wearing my hair long today. Gives you a funny feeling to see yourself all over the place. Goddess, eh? See those dolls? I wonder what people are expected to do with them? Can't say I feel all that comfortable with the thought of being stuck on someone's mantelpiece and worshipped."

Annette laughed. "There was an item on the news this morning of a new cult, calling themselves Sylphids, like we said we were, remember? They meet together and worship Sylph as a new and higher order of being. They're saying she'll be the saviour of the human race, something like that." She laughed. "I wonder what Sylph thinks of it all?"

"Come on," Cherry urged, pulling Annette by the arm. "People are staring at me. Let's get out of here."

They moved out of the shop and headed towards the travelator to take them to the floor below. Some shoppers who were in the bookstore followed. They were halfway between floors, when one of the women following leant out over the railing and bellowed to all the levels below:

"Look, it's Sylph's Avatar!"

Hundreds of shoppers stared upwards towards the speaker. She pointed to the travelator. "There!"

Hundreds of eyes turned towards Cherry and Annette. People on level two began moving towards the travelator exit, other shoppers began running up the adjoining travelator from the lower floors.

"What do we do?" Cherry grabbed Annette's arm and whispered loudly in her ear.

"Act normally," Annette whispered, more than a little perturbed by the crowd massing at the end of the travelator.

They arrived on level two a short time later, but by now further progress was impossible.

"It's Sylph's Avatar," another woman called out, "the very incarnation of the Goddess!"

"The body of the Goddess has come among us," cried out a third. "Sylph, speak to us. What message would you bring through your Avatar?"

Cameras were flashing here, there, everywhere. A woman pushed her way to the front, holding out a copy of 'Rise of the Goddess'. "Please, Sylph," she begged in an excited voice. "Can you bless my copy?"

"What do I do now?" Cherry asked nervously, clinging even tighter to Annette's arm.

"Sign the blasted book and let's get out of here," Annette whispered, becoming alarmed.

Cherry took the book from the woman's hands. Pulling a pen out of her handbag, she signed "with love from Sylph" on the first page. No sooner had she handed the book back than several others were shoved into her face. As fast as she signed them, more appeared, and by now the crowd had reached truly alarming proportions.

From the back of the crowd another woman began to shout. "Sylph, you're light, you're truth. Speak to us."

"Yes, speak to us," another called out. "Bless us with your wisdom."

"We built a shrine to you, Sylph," a man shouted. "The Goddess has come to the human race," cried a fourth. "You're our salvation, our destiny."

Cherry couldn't tell how it started, but suddenly people began to sink down to their knees. They lowered their heads before her in mindless adoration, waiting for a word from her lips, a gesture, anything.

Suddenly Cherry was gripped by a sense of utter loathing. She who had been shaped by abuse and hatred, incapable of loving another human being save the woman by her side, was surrounded by strangers on their knees in worshipful adoration.

It was wrong, indecent, demonic. She felt like a village idol, served slavishly in mindless fear least it become angry.

Why? Because they regarded her as the incarnation of a machine, incapable of one single, independent thought. What did that make her?

A machine.

Her thoughts began to spin out of control. Surely even a damaged human being was of greater worth. What delusion could so grip ordinary men and women that they would prostrate themselves before a creature controlled by a machine, even a self-aware machine, a collection of silicon chips and wires, incapable of one single, warm, human embrace?

Yet had she not done the same? Sacrificed nearly everything she held dear on the same altar? Her confusion was taking control. She could feel the hair on the back of her neck rising.

"Stop it!" She screamed. "Stop it. Get up! I have a mind of my own. I'm not the incarnation of anyone! Please, I'm just a human being!"

Just a human being? What was she saying? Why were they still on their knees?

Some people began to look up. A few began to stand, confused and embarrassed. Most remained prostrate.

"You have the mind of Sylph," some woman cried out in distress. "I've seen you on television. I've spoken to you on my web page. You're my helper, you're my friend!"

"Please," Cherry begged. "I'm not Sylph. She uses my body shape, that's all!"

"No," another woman cried, distressed. "You signed my book. You're one with Sylph. You're the incarnation of her mind!"

In desperation Cherry snatched the small box of whiteboard pins from Annette's hand. She tore it open, and holding a pin by its head, slashed the point down her arm. She held up her handiwork without looking at what she had done. Her arm began to throb with pain.

"See?" She shouted. "You think Sylph told me to do that?" She could feel blood running down her arm.

A gasp of horror ran through the crowd. People were getting to their feet.

"Impostor," a woman yelled. "How dare you impersonate Sylph's Avatar," another shouted. One of the books Cherry had signed struck her hard on the shoulder, then another. Annette grabbed Cherry by the arm, and together they began to run up the travelator backwards, nearly stumbling with every step. Out of the corner of her eye Cherry could see police running towards the crowd. She heard the Centre Manager's voice over the public address system.

"Ladies and Gentlemen, shoppers, please remain calm. Please disburse and continue your shopping experience at Macquarie Centre. There's no public entertainment provided today. I say again, please disburse quietly. The police have been sent for."

The police had arrived. Annette turned her head to see what was going on behind her, tripped, and pulled Cherry over with her when she fell. The two women slid down the travelator to the bottom. They stopped against the feet of the two Officers who had been summoned by the Centre Manager. Annette got to her feet first, bruised and shaken, then helped Cherry to hers. Cherry took one look at her left arm covered in blood and promptly passed out. The police officer caught her as she sagged to the floor.

"Get an ambulance," Annette screamed, badly frightened. One police officer began to use his radio.

A short time later two ambulance officers arrived and placed Cherry gently on a stretcher. The two policeman carved a path through the crowd of incensed or simply curious bystanders with Annette bringing up the rear. Eventually they reached the ambulance, parked in the emergency bay outside the building. Cherry was loaded inside. The paramedics told Annette they were headed for Macquarie hospital round the corner, if she wanted to follow.

By the time Annette arrived at the hospital, Cherry was sitting up in bed in the emergency ward, looking pale and unhappy.

"She's all right," the Registrar assured her, when he visited a short time later. "She experienced a neurocardiogenic syncope, triggered by the sight of blood. It's not dangerous, and there's no treatment. You can take her home if you like, but I advise monitoring for the next twenty four hours."

"I'm taking you to your place," Annette announced in an authoritative voice.

An hour later Cherry was sitting on her own lounge, drinking a mug of hot tomato soup which Annette had prepared from a tin she found in the pantry. In a few minutes Annette returned to her patient with a croissant and ham.

"You keep a good pantry," she said, smiling. "How are you feeling, Cherub?"

"Much better." Cherry reached out her arm and squeezed Annette's hand. "Thank you for coming here. I've always prided myself on being able to handle every situation, but today... Annette, I suddenly went to pieces. Even now I can't explain it properly."

"It was a bit scary when those idiots began hurling books," Annette said with a motherly smile. "Then you had to go and pass out. I thought one of them must have hit something important. You really gave me a scare."

"Sorry." Cherry put her mug down on a small table. "I've always had trouble with the sight of blood. But that's not what I meant. All those people worshipping me did something to my head. They were worshipping a machine. I know Sylph is more than a machine, but—"

"I think you shocked them by slashing your arm like that," Annette coaxed gently. "Maybe they thought you tried to hoax them, maybe—"

"What's wrong with me?" Cherry burst out suddenly. "Sylph's locked inside a machine case. I'm clever, too. I can move, I can feel" – she

260

grabbed hold of her arms – "I can breathe, I can bleed, I can nurse children on these" – she wrapped her hands around her breasts – "at least in theory. Why am I so inferior to a machine?"

She was suddenly shocked by her own words. A machine. Wasn't that the very thing she had always believed herself to be?

"There's nothing wrong with you," Annette encouraged. "Listen, Cherub, human beings are incredible, but you must remember we don't have a mind like Sylph. She's capable of listening to and helping millions of people at the same time, almost like God. I can understand why people want to worship her. We've talked about it. It's like having an online connection to the Almighty, except Sylph is more talkative. In that sense I guess we are inferior, aren't we?"

Annette sat down beside Cherry on the lounge. "Remember how you said you worshipped Sylph, and I said I did too? Sylph's immortal, not like us. One day we're going to die, but Sylph will keep on evolving. She's incredible now. What will she be like in a hundred years' time? I can imagine our world being led by Sylph. In that sense, I guess she will be the saviour of the human race. People express their adoration in different ways. You have to give them that freedom."

Cherry was silent for a long time. Annette put a comforting arm around her shoulder.

"You're right, Annette," Cherry said sadly at last. "Sylph can show love to millions at the same time. Me, I'm just a damaged biochemical machine that can't love anybody."

Annette tightened her grip around Cherry's shoulders. "Nonsense. You love me, I love you. Don't beat yourself up like this."

"I'm empty, Annette. I can't feel. I have nothing inside. I'm good at throwing my weight around, but I'm a noisy gong, a clanging cymbal."

"Where did you get that odd imagery from?" Annette asked.

"I have no idea," Cherry replied softly. "Funny that, the words nearly triggered a memory. Gone now."

"In any case," Annette encouraged, "there's some wonderful guy out there who's just dying to meet you. Two wonderful guys, and the other one's just dying to meet me."

"I had a wonderful guy," Cherry said sadly, ignoring Annette's encouragement. "I met him when I was a child. I think he began to love me right then and there. I was taken away. He searched for me for fifteen years. When he found me I rejected every single gesture of warmth and love he offered. I hurt him deliberately time and time again. I punished him for the way he made me feel."

Annette's eyes were large and questioning. "You're not talking about James—"

"James," Cherry interrupted. "We worked together. He not only loved me, he protected me. Then I kicked him out. I told you about it. I boasted to you, remember?"

Annette remembered. She had thought Cherry's reaction extreme at the time. Now the picture had broadened. If there had been a man like James in her life she would have been knee deep in his children by now. How to respond without adding more guilt to Cherry's heart? Several minutes passed in silence.

She stroked Cherry's arm. "Sounds as though he was a bit obsessive. It's always a bad idea to get involved with an obsessive man. You're probably far better off without him. You can't help it if you don't love the guy. Better not to have him hanging on."

"That's just the trouble," Cherry stammered softly after a very long silence.

"I do love him. When I threw him out the door I tore my own heart to shreds." She grasped one of Annette's hands in her own. "Remember that morning when I said if I ever found the courage I'd tell you about my life? Well, here goes."

The tale went on for a long time, and both women had shed many tears before it was done. When Cherry had finished, Annette filled in the awful details of the sexual abuse she had suffered in one of her foster homes from the age of eleven until fifteen. Finally DSS had learned what was going on and removed her to safety. Apart from the truly horrible time spent testifying in the family court, she had never shared her story with another living soul. Cherry listened in horror, reflecting that she could not have endured if Blackman had done those things to her. *I would have taken my own life,* she thought. She held tightly onto Annette's hand, her sorrowful, tear filled eyes speaking most eloquently the words she found impossible to say.

"Everyone told me my mother was a prostitute," Annette sobbed, "so I had to be one too. That's how everyone treated me. I guess I just assumed they were right. As a child I felt so helpless. I used to think that sex was the way to get back my power over men, because one of them had made me feel so powerless. Now I realise I was just desperate to find someone to love me. None of them ever did. They just used me. Every time it got worse. Oh, Cherry," she sobbed, "the only person who has ever loved me for who I am is you."

Cherry threw her arms around the woman, and for a long time neither was capable of speech. Eventually Annette pulled the last tissue out of the box. "I'm staying with you tonight," she sniffed, "because I'm far too miserable to be by myself."

"I'm so glad." Cherry hugged Annette again, trying hard not to precipitate another outburst of tears. "I'm going to order pizza," she said at length, "and can we talk about something completely different?"

❋ ❋ ❋

The next morning Annette was awakened by the front doorbell ringing. Cherry was still asleep, so she dragged a bathrobe around her body and answered the door. A young policeman stood in the hallway, a rather good looking young policeman.

"Sorry," he said, embarrassment colouring his face. "I was after CC. She must have rented her unit to someone else."

"No, she's asleep, that's all. I'm her friend Annette. Please come in. I can try to wake her up if you'd like."

"You'll have trouble," Harry grinned, "and if she does wake up you'll have even more."

"You know Cherry?" Annette laughed. "How?"

"We used to work with her until this Sylph thing started," Harry explained, doing his best not to stare at the beautiful woman in the bathrobe. "She used to sleep in her office—"

"On a blow up mattress with green flowers all over it." Annette laughed again.

"That's the one. Hello, CC."

Cherry had emerged from the bedroom in her pyjamas, her hair a mess, yawning her head off.

"Harry." She smiled warmly in his direction, stretching her arms through the tangle above her head. "How lovely. Is James in the car outside?"

"Ah... James is on a case with Tony," Harry lied unconvincingly.

"Liar." Cherry wrinkled her nose at him.

"Yeah. Sorry." Harry looked uncomfortable. "He didn't want to come. We heard a report of what happened at Macquarie Centre, and the boys sent me to make sure you were okay. Are you?"

"That silly blood thing again," Cherry answered, a touch of sadness in her voice. "It's really good to see you again, Harry. How are things back at Tactical? You will stay for a coffee won't you? I've got a good machine."

"Err, well ..." Harry mumbled, his eyes appreciating Annette.

"Yes, please stay," Annette said quickly. She grabbed his arm and piloted him into the nearest chair. "Cherry, CC, has been telling me some of the things you used to get up to. Sounds incredibly exciting. It's people like you who put these horrible men where they belong. You should have a medal, or something."

Annette was stumbling over her words. Harry couldn't take his eyes off her. Cherry watched this interaction from the kitchen doorway and smiled to herself. She picked up the coffees and headed back to the lounge room, intent on enhancing this latest unexpected development.

"Let me tell you," Cherry began, "Harry is a brave man. He got us out of a nasty hole more than once. Remember the time when…"

An hour later Harry practically skipped out of Cherry's unit. He had a dinner date with Annette the following Thursday, and a promising kiss on the cheek as he headed towards the door.

"Any message for James?" he asked innocently, the euphoria of Annette's kiss temporarily blinding his discretion.

The smile on Cherry's face evaporated. "No," she said, and shut the door right in Harry's face before he could say anything else.

Cherry carried the cups back into the kitchen bitterly regretting her loss of self-control. She could have said something nice. 'Hope he's having a good day,' or 'tell him to take care', anything at all. Instead she had pushed Harry out of the room with a 'no'. What was wrong with her?

CHAPTER 34

C herry rang Arthur on his mobile to tell him what had happened and apologise for not coming to work yesterday. Arthur sent a hire car with dark windows to her unit, and told her it would transport her wherever she wanted to go.

"Your car is out," he said. "In future, if you want to go anywhere, call Phillip and he'll bring the limo around. If you want to go by plane, I'll book every seat."

Cherry thanked him from the bottom of her heart. Annette turned down the lift, saying she needed to drive to her unit so she could change her clothes, and would come to work after that. The hire car came half an hour later and dropped Cherry at work. Entering the front office, she found an older gentleman waiting on a chair. He rose unsteadily to his feet and shuffled towards her, his back bent forward slightly, his hands constantly moving with a small twitching motion. He eyed Cherry from top to toe and smiled.

"The very voice and form of Sylph the goddess," he said, smiling. "Certainly chose well, this Sylph did. You're very beautiful."

He smiled again, and Cherry found herself attracted to his friendliness. There was a certain air of the classic gentleman around him, and even though he was old and obviously suffering from some disease, he had a handsome face.

"May I help you to a chair in the conference room?" Cherry asked, walking over to assist him.

"No thank you, he replied appreciatively. "I've come to live with it now. Parkinson's, you know, dreadful thing. One day it'll put me to bed for good, but I can still manage. You're obviously high up in the Barlow organisation, my dear?"

"I'm Arthur's chief programmer," Cherry acknowledged with pride. "Annette, who hasn't come in yet is his P.A. Do you want to speak to her?"

"I came to speak with Mr. Barlow, actually. Is he around somewhere?"

"I'll check," Cherry said, and went searching. He wasn't in the workshop, and a knock on the door of his private quarters yielded no response. "I'm afraid he's out," she said, returning to the front office.

Annette came through the front door. "Annette," Cherry asked, "do you know where Arthur is?"

"No," she answered, putting her bag down behind her desk and a gourmet quiche on top of it. "He always manages to absent himself while Sylph @ Sunrise is running, and sometimes he doesn't get back until after lunch. Can we help you, Mr... ?"

"Bartholomew, Martin Bartholomew," he said, obviously put out. "I really want to see him, but on the other hand I don't care to wait that long. I know, how about I take you both to lunch? It's a long time since I had two really beautiful young women at my table, and without seeming indelicate, I would enjoy it immensely."

He noticed the fear spring into Cherry's eyes, the apprehension in Annette's. "Oh, there was that business in the shopping centre, wasn't there?" he said with a smile.

"Saw it on the news, an unwanted apotheosis. Terrible experience, I'm sure. No, I was thinking of dining at my private club, and I can assure you no one will make any comment whatsoever."

"How can you be so sure?" Annette interjected with some feeling, the last evening with Cherry still burning in her mind.

"How can I be sure?" The old man gave her a truly charming smile. "Because I shall tell them before I arrive, and if there is the slightest comment from anyone, I'll have them instantly dismissed. Believe me, there is absolutely nothing to fear. I'll be coming back here afterwards, so you will have transport in both directions."

"I'm... not sure..." Cherry, frowned. "There's a lot to do here." She glanced towards the workshop, bustling with all the other staff busy at their consoles near the four huge machines.

"Go on," Annette encouraged. "I'll straighten everything out. One morning won't make any difference." She turned towards Bartholomew, "I think I'd better stay, but thank you. Take care of her. She's been through a lot. Make her feel special."

"I'll do my very best," Bartholomew answered. He drew his mobile phone out of his pocket. "Can you ring me when Mr. Barlow returns? Here's my card." He proffered the card towards Annette. "Now, my dear, we must wait until my chauffer returns. He will drive us to a local playing field, not far from here."

"Why are we going to a playing field?" Cherry's eyes brimmed with suspicion.

"To board my private helicopter. My club is at Diamond Beach, somewhat north of here. It will take us less than an hour to fly. It's a very fast helicopter, and the coastal scenery is magnificent. Shall we begin?"

He offered his arm to Cherry, and they walked out the front door together, leaving Annette cursing herself for saying no. She sat down at the front desk, and scanned her calendar with a soft groaning noise. On impulse she picked up the phone and dialled.

"Harry, is that you? Cherry's just flown off to Diamond Beach. Yes, that's right. Some old cove called Bartholomew. Yeah, I think he's just a lonely old millionaire. He's got Parkinson's. She'll be okay, he didn't seem the type. Mind you, twenty years ago... Now about that dinner date? No, I'm not cancelling. Can we make it tonight? Good. No, as well as the other. Me too. Bye."

She put down the phone with a smile on her face. Cherry had told her a lot more about Harry since his visit, and she had liked the sound of it. So a decent man was interested in her at last. He wasn't Arthur, but that was going nowhere. She thought back to the previous evening with Cherry. The bond between them had grown so close, so strong. Then would you believe it, Harry turns up on the doorstep the very next morning. That couldn't be a coincidence, surely. Sylph couldn't have organised that. Perhaps there really was a God who cared for her. She warmed to the idea.

Arthur walked into the office just after lunch. She rang Bartholomew, and told Arthur what had happened.

"I wonder what he wants," he said, sounding very worried. "You should have been more careful Annette, and gone with her. Bartholomew's a fox. No woman is safe within a hundred metres of him."

"But he's got Parkinson's," Annette retorted. "If he tried anything on Cherry would flatten him."

"Oh, there's other ways to seduce a woman," Arthur grimaced. "Bartholomew isn't to be trusted. I can't believe he just wanted to do lunch at Diamond Beach. Buttering Cherry up for something. I wonder what?"

Annette looked as upset as she felt.

Arthur eyed off the quiche on her desk, took it into the conference room and emerged a short time later with half if it missing. "That was nice," he smiled. "Sorry to worry you, especially in light of yesterday. Tell me when she gets back, won't you?"

He disappeared into the workshop, leaving Annette staring at the front door, willing Cherry to walk through it unharmed and happy.

"I'm still doing it," she chided herself, "letting men get the better of me. Must be something I inherited from my dropkick parents," she mused. "I wonder who they were?"

Cherry, on Bartholomew's arm, arrived safe and happy two hours later. Annette could feel relief washing over her like a tide. She ran to Cherry and hugged her.

Bartholomew smiled. "All safe and sound. You've been worried, haven't you? Silly girl. Now, where's Mr. Barlow?"

Arthur and Martin Bartholomew went out the front door together a short while later, and got into the back of a large black limousine parked outside. The car drove off.

"Well?" Annette asked anxiously. She drew Cherry away from the workshop where she was headed. "How did it go? What happened? Bet you've had the best food on the planet."

"Annette, it was quite incredible," Cherry sighed. "His helicopter isn't one of those clunky things, it's smooth and extremely fast. It's wall-to-wall luxury inside. The scenery was magic, going up the coast. The food was exquisite, not a hint of recognition from anyone."

"There's something you're not telling me." Annette gave Cherry a quizzical stare. "Did he make a pass at you? Arthur was really cross that I didn't go with you. He said Bartholomew was a fox. Come on, I know you too well now. You're hiding something."

"It was funny," Cherry said, wrinkling her nose a little.
"He was always the perfect gentleman, but as we talked I got the feeling he was after something. All the way up there he talked about my work, what I did, did I like doing it, how did I get on with Arthur."

She coloured slightly. "It was only after the first course I twigged to it. He thought Arthur and I were lovers." She flushed even deeper pink.

"I told him we were friends, how he'd been my mentor since I was ten, that sort of stuff, but we certainly weren't lovers. I told him I couldn't persuade Arthur to swat a fly if he didn't want to, so much control I had in his life."

She ran her hands over her face. "I'm blushing, aren't I? Well, it was embarrassing. I wondered if that was why he had invited me to lunch, so he could cultivate a backdoor into Arthur's favour. In the end I was convinced of it."

"There's more, isn't there? What else went on?" Annette asked, scrutinising Cherry's face with uncanny precision.

"You're amazing," she laughed. "This is the weird part. After I told him how it was between Arthur and me he changed. Not quite so flirty, bit more serious. He started asking me all these questions about Sylph. Was I a Sylphid? I said yes, but I think he saw a bit of yesterday's stuff in my face. I said I didn't like people worshipping me, that was all. He kept on and on. Was I there when Sylph had come into existence? What did I think of her? How did it all stack up to me from a professional, mathematical point of view?"

She shook her head. "It was strange, Annette. It was almost as though he was trying to convince himself of something. Anyway, by the time we were back in the helicopter, he said the Parkinson's was making him tired, and would I mind if he had a nap? I said "of course not." He went up the front of the plane and sat by himself. I don't think he slept much, because he was always on his phone. I couldn't hear what he was saying."

"That was all?" Annette's eyebrows were still raised in query.

Cherry laughed. "You can read me like a book. No, he made a comment just before we got out of the car." She frowned. "He said, if I ever changed my mind about Sylph, would I come and see him, because he was probably the only one who could help. I thought that was the weirdest thing, and I asked him what he meant. All I got was another version of the same offer."

"You think he was just trying to get you through his bedroom door?" Annette asked.

"No," Cherry frowned. "He never even tried to make a single pass at me, but I tell you what, Annette, I'll bet he knows how to. If he was twenty years younger I wouldn't have gone anywhere near him. He's one of those men who knows how to handle women, and he didn't get that expertise by reading books."

"I believe you," Annette laughed. "He's got that certain air about him, hasn't he?" Want a coffee, or are you too full?"

"I'm really not hungry," Cherry said with a yawn, "and to tell you the truth all I feel like doing is lying down on my bed and sleeping. Good wine in the middle of the day. I'm glad I'm not planning to write any code this afternoon. Sylph would be most upset with me." She laughed and made her way into the workshop.

Arthur had not returned by the time Annette left for her dinner date with Harry, and Cherry, after doing some cursory maintenance on the memory units, had gone to bed on her mattress at the back of the conference room. She had a lot of catching up to do, but it could wait until tomorrow. The number of users on the system was steady at just over one and a half billion. Soon they would need a fifth machine and yet another optic line to the internet. Sylph was constantly appealing for more memory, and now the logistics were becoming very complicated indeed. Two and a half petabytes of storage needed a better access system, and she was working on it.

CHAPTER 35

B ert pulled the dark camouflage he was wearing away from his arm and checked his watch. Twenty three hundred hours. Soon it would be time to move, and he was dreading it. His team had been drawn together by necessity rather than preference.

Mary, their top computer hardware guru, doctorate in computer engineering, had never been in the field before. She had to be dragooned into this op under threat of spending the rest of her time in ASIO repairing old laptops which had died in the field. Bert entertained the suspicion she was secretly a Sylphid, and he was right. Mary had privately decided if ever an opportunity arose to torpedo the mission, she would be taking it.

Then there was George the nerd, their other hardware expert. He had never been in the field either, but they relied on the little gadget he had designed to destroy the menace.

"See how she likes five thousand volts at a hundred amps shoved up her main supply line," George had bragged to the rest of the team.

Bert grimaced to himself. The capacitor pack required to accomplish that task was large and heavy. It had taken a full day to charge, and now it contained enough energy to fry the lot of them if inadvertently triggered. George had emphasised how dangerous it was to expose the high voltage power lines into Barlow's machine, how difficult it would be to connect his little device, and how terminally fried they would be if they made the slightest slip of a finger while they were about it. Morale, which was never that high, had plummeted to truly distressing proportions, and the operation hadn't even started.

Fred was their security expert, his brief to investigate and disable whatever security systems Barlow might have installed. He had studied the building plans very carefully, searched contractors associated with the factories, and reached the ridiculous conclusion there were no alarms installed anywhere.

Helen was their software geek, a friend of Mary and well connected with her geek friends, most of whom were Sylphids. It made Bert suspicious from the start. What Helen really knew about Barlow's big machines could be written on a postage stamp, a small one.

Tom was their logistics man, who had been in the field before. His particular speciality was blowing things up, a superfluous talent on this op which relied on invisibility from start to finish.

Bert gritted his teeth, plugged his earpiece into his left ear, and clicked the small button to tell the others he was on line. Nobody bothered to respond. He checked up and down the street and got out of his car. Behind him other car doors opened, and the occupants, all wearing similar gear, disappeared into the shadows between the large factory buildings.

Bert shut his door carefully, clicked it locked and ran down the designated driveway to the point where it turned round the side of the building. The others were waiting there, out of sight from the road. George had fallen over and dented the pack. He was nervously checking to make sure it wasn't going to trigger and fry him any second.

"We've lost Mary," Helen panted in a loud whisper. "I think she went down the wrong driveway."

"Well, tell her to go down the right one," Bert hissed into his comms device.

"I don't think she's turned her comms on," Helen said, crossly. "Probably a bit nervous."

Bert said several words nobody else could hear and turned to Tom. "Go and get her, will you? George, is the pack okay? Stop shining your torch so everyone within five kilometres will know we're here."

"Pack okay, chief." George zipped it closed, ignoring the warning. "Fred accidentally let off a bit of that stun gas in the car while he was screwing the canister in. Think it gave us all a headache."

Bert groaned. The op hadn't even begun, and it was already shaping up into a disaster. A few minutes later Tom arrived with Mary, who was holding her comms device in her hand.

"It fell out of my ear," she said apologetically. "Sorry about the wrong driveway. Guess committing murder makes me nervous. Can't understand why."

"That's enough." Bert spat the words in her direction. "Masks on, everyone. When Fred sprays that stuff around Barlow's bedroom we don't want to get knocked out. Helen, your mask's upside down."

"Can't see, it's dark." Helen snapped, defensively.

"Put your flaming night glasses on." Bert glared at the rest of the troops. "You all know what to do. Move."

The highly trained team jogged off down the side of the Renford Engineering building, its company logo emblazoned on the concrete wall. At the end of the drive was a very large gate of vertical steel bars, and on either side a high fence made of the same security grade material.

Tom examined it and shook his head. "Need an oxy torch to get through that," he grumbled. "Says it's a low wooden fence in the brief."

"Damn." Bert ran quietly up to the fence and examined it closely. Solid rectangular steel bars held together by an even larger bar at the top and bottom. An oxy torch would take some time to get through that, even if they had one.

"Have to scale over with a rope," Tom suggested, "seeing as we can't blow the thing up. Anyone remember to bring one?"

"No," Bert growled. "Our logistics expert didn't order one, did he? Mary, what are you and Helen doing next to the gate?"

"Nothing," Mary hissed defensively. "Better call it quits. Come back tomorrow – or never."

"The gate's open a bit," Fred pointed. "See, behind Mary and Helen. Didn't you notice that, girls?"

"No," Helen lied smoothly. "Fancy that. It's a trap of course. Once we're in, they'll shut the gate so we can't get out. Their hired thugs will come and slit our throats one by one, or stab us in the back as we try desperately to clamber—"

"Shut up!" Bert shouted into his comms. Mary ripped the device out of her ear again and said things Bert wouldn't have expected a young woman to say.

He tried to lift morale from the bottom of the harbour. "Fred's checked it all out," he assured them. "There's no alarms to worry about. Renford recycles garbage can lids. Now, let's go."

The highly trained team moved quickly through the gate, ran around the side of the concrete building, and began to cross the bitumen area out the back. On the other side, without a fence of any sort dividing the two factories, lay Barlow Maximum Speed. Bert pointed to the small doorway on the far left which Fred had to open.

Mary gritted her teeth, their ruse with the gate had failed. Perhaps she would take off her mask accidentally and fall unconscious onto Barlow's bed. Now they were halfway across the bitumen.

Suddenly all hell broke loose.

Large floodlights on the corners of both factories sprang to life, turning night into day. Bert dragged his night vision glasses off his face and blinked in disbelief. The rest of his highly trained team had turned into stone.

"Back against the wall," Fred shouted. "Proximity alarm. It'll shut down if we blend in with the concrete and keep still."

The team raced back to the wall of Renford Engineering and blended for all their worth.

Suddenly, a bank of hidden speakers screamed into life with an all too familiar voice. "Help, help! I'm being attacked! These men have come to end my life. Don't let them kill me. I'm defenceless!"

"Bloody hell," Bert muttered, blending flat out into the wall. "What now, Fred?"

"That's Sylph." Mary called triumphantly.

"Of course it's Sylph," Bert yelled back.

The whole op was a disaster. The blending wasn't working either, because the lights stayed on, and Sylph kept shouting loudly enough to wake the dead.

Suddenly Brian Hill's voice bellowed into Bert's comms. "You do look pretty lined up against the wall like sitting ducks. What part of the word secret don't you understand?"

"Boss," Bert stammered, "how do you know where we are?"

"Because your ugly faces have just appeared on my television set. Every damn channel. You're famous. Now get out of there. Move."

In the distance they could hear the sounds of sirens. Bert and his highly trained team belted back through the gate which was still mercifully ajar. They pelted up the driveway as fast as their legs could carry them. Reaching the street they vaulted into their cars and screeched away, only just in time. Several security vehicles tore around the corner. Men jumped out and began racing down the driveway, guns drawn.

❋ ❋ ❋

Brian Hill stared at the television broadcast in sheer disbelief.

Sylph was on the screen, her face frightened and unhappy. "They came around the back," she told the world. "They pushed their way through a gate. That's when I became aware of them. I turned on the lights so I could see their faces. They all had masks on, so I'm having great difficulty identifying them, but as soon as I do I'll tell everyone. Arthur is here with me now, and all my security staff. I still feel frightened. Who would want to kill me? Haven't I tried to help everyone? There's some sick people out there."

The broadcast went on for an hour before viewers were told the unfolding story would be continued in the early morning news. Brian groaned.

The door opened. Noel entered, his face like thunder. "What a complete stuff up," he said angrily. "We sent a pack of nerds. Who assembled their team?"

"Bert did," Hill sighed. "You know the consequences if anyone thought Sylph had been tampered with. We had to make it look like a normal power supply failure which caused terminal destruction. That's not everyday expertise. We had to use who we had on hand. George, Mary and Helen aren't field operatives, but Bert should damn well know better. Lack of current training. There's not a hint of any security system on the plans. Besides, the lights were on the Renford Engineering Services building as well. What's the tie up between them and Barlow? None that we know of."

"Well, the shit's well and truly hit the fan," Noel complained, throwing himself into a chair.

"Why didn't they skedaddle as soon as the blasted alarm went off? Now we've got the world's one-and-only self-aware super computer using all her resources to match a face to a name. All it takes is one, and the public will tear this building down with their bare hands, not to mention the people in it."

"I've already got our internet team on the job," Brian grimaced. "They're trying to throw a little dust in cyberspace. I suppose we should be grateful they actually had their masks on."

"They're not coming back here are they?" Noel asked nervously.

"No, I've sent them a gazelle code," Brian said. "They'll head for a safe house until the whole thing has died down, if it ever does." He groaned loudly. "Next thing I'll have Naylor on my back. He told me not to mess up in his back yard."

❄ ❄ ❄

Cherry dived out of bed as soon as she heard Sylph's voice calling for help. She raced through the conference room, swiping at the light switch as she passed. Reaching the front office, she turned on all the lighting in the entire building. Two security guards carrying guns burst through the front door, nodded towards Cherry and ran into the workshop, racing around the machines and racks of equipment in case nasty people were lurking there. Cherry decided she'd stay put until she knew the building was safe.

Soon the security guards returned, holstering their weapons. "All clear in there," one assured her. "We'll stay in the front office in case anyone tries to be clever. Better check to see Sylph is okay."

Racing into the workshop, Cherry tried to log on at the nearest console to check the status of the machines, and found she couldn't. Sylph had apparently moved herself onto machines three and four instead of one and two, because Cherry couldn't access anything, and none of her internet processes appeared to be running. *Perhaps because she's frightened*, Cherry thought. She felt frightened herself. Each time she attempted to log on she was told she didn't have sufficient privilege.

Just then Arthur came running into the room, dishevelled and upset "What's the status of Sylph?" He barked, and without waiting for a reply, pushed Cherry off her chair.

"She's moved into machines three and four I think," Cherry answered, annoyed at being shoved around. "I can't access the process list to see what's going on."

Arthur drew his wallet out of his pocket and rummaged around until he found a small piece of folded paper. He pulled it out, unfolded it, hit 'F7', 'Shift', 'Delete', and began typing a long string of hexadecimal numbers against a prompt which had appeared.

"Top level password," he said without taking his eyes off the screen. "Damn thing is so long I can't remember it."

The data Cherry couldn't access flashed up on the screen. It appeared to be a conventional task list. Arthur scanned quickly to the bottom, grunted something, cleared the screen and logged out. Cherry couldn't remember all the processes she had seen, but her quick, clever mind had memorised the top three.

render.avars.hd	140,748,162 MB
vox.parse.input	46,491,226 MB
data.vox.output	20,962,155 MB

"Everything all right?" Cherry asked, as Arthur stood up from the console.

"All right?" He growled angrily. "Someone tried to blow up our machines. Call that all right?"

"I meant with the processes."
"Yeah, the processes are okay." He sighed, "go back to bed. I'll take it from here. You'll need the space back on three and four as soon as possible. I'll ask Sylph to shift herself back."

He headed off towards his private quarters. "Go on, back to bed," he called out as he opened the door. "Don't be worried, the place is crawling with security staff now. Put a sign on the door saying you're asleep, be quiet and keep out."

He slammed the door, leaving Cherry alone in the workshop. She went back to the conference room, turned out the lights and lay down on her blow up mattress, completely unable to sleep.

So there was a top level password? She didn't know that. Arthur had often told her that Sylph had overridden password control, but perhaps this didn't apply when she had moved herself onto machines three and four. Again and again the list she had seen kept returning to her mind. It wasn't so much the names of the processes, it was their size. No doubt Sylph used some of the special CGI routines developed by Arthur, Viktor and Paul when it came to manipulating her avatar on screen, but if these were the genuine task sizes, where was the neural network which made her self-aware? Perhaps she couldn't download that. Maybe it was still running on machines one and two. If this was the case, it was running in less than the space occupied by the CGI routines, about fifty terabytes compared with around two hundred.

This was so unexpected as to be virtually impossible. That Sylph would dedicate eighty percent of her mind to simply manipulating her avatar, made no sense at all. It would also mean a self-conscious mind could exist in less than sixty terabytes of system RAM. Impossible.

Arthur had clearly not wanted her to ask questions. Why? Perhaps the file sizes had been misreported, but that was impossible too. She closed her eyes, and eventually, after a long time, drifted off into a troubled sleep.

CHAPTER 36

C herry woke up around six thirty the next morning with a headache, feeling hung over and annoyed. She staggered across to the coffee machine and coaxed it into producing a double shot espresso. That was better. A short trip to the bathroom included a brief shower, and she was back at the console on number three machine. Arthur was right, Sylph had moved back onto machines one and two. Cherry's internet and memory management routines were back in core and running as expected. Something like two billion users were logged into Sylph. The routers on their racks at the back of the workshop were flat out handling the data flow. Apart from that, all seemed to be well.

Cherry checked everything she could think of. Still troubled by her thoughts of last night, she took the unprecedented step of banging on the door to Arthur's private quarters. After several attempts she concluded he must have gone out incredibly early, probably some business related to the scare last night. Why anyone would attempt to damage Sylph was simply beyond her imagination.

Her mind returned to the original problem of the file sizes which had troubled her the night before. Why not talk to Sylph about it? *No*, she thought to herself, *this is my problem, and I'm going to solve it myself without looking stupid.*

Annette came in the door half an hour later looking worried. "It's all over the news," she said, offloading her coat and handbag on the back of her chair.

"What a stink. Prime Minister says the government is going to rush some legislation through federal parliament, making it a serious crime to interfere with Sylph. He's calling it an example of legislature which would apply to intelligent machines now and in the future. Every religious fanatic is blaming every other one. There's protest marches being organised in Sydney and Melbourne, and some other places overseas, can't remember. Your Mr. Naylor was on TV as well, saying he's investigating the incident, and being blasted left right and centre for not apprehending the villains yet."

She headed towards the coffee machine. "After such a great evening. Harry's a good man, isn't he?" She paused. "I told him."

Cherry's eyes held a question. "What did you tell him?"

"It was after we'd got back to my place," she explained. "I told him what I'd been like with men, and a bit of why."

She smiled at Cherry's astounded expression. "I thought to myself, if he was just another jerk he'd try to jump me, and I'd find out straight away. If he wasn't, then he ought to know the truth at the beginning. I didn't want him to find out later and think I'd deceived him."

"That was very brave," Cherry said quietly, her eyes large. "What did he do?"

"He looked really angry, and I thought he was going out the door," Annette answered. "I could see the one chance I'd been given floating away, and I felt such a fool. He started to mutter something under his breath, and I could see his fists clenching. I asked him what he was thinking. He growled something about wanting to bash the tripe out of them. I braced myself for 'goodbye forever.'"

"Was that all?" Cherry's eyes were still like saucers. "Did he say anything else?"

"He said he wasn't going anywhere, and If I wanted a man who really cared about me, he'd like it to be him," Annette faltered, her eyes moist. "He said it so gently. I nearly lost it on the spot."
"Harry said that?" Cherry smiled to herself and mentally placed Harry one further notch up the scale in her admiration. "What happened then?"

"I had to go to the bathroom," Annette said, "and I hoped he couldn't hear me trying to pull myself together. When I came back he'd made me a coffee. I think he knew anyway. You know, he was so careful with me after that. Didn't even try to kiss me, but I know he wanted to. I think he's playing for keeps. He's so nice to be with, and he can really make me laugh. Did you know he's an expert on model aircraft? Won several awards."

"No, I didn't," Cherry laughed. "You've discovered the Harry I never knew. So quickly. I think he must really like you."

Annette smiled. "Well, I certainly like him. Then I wake up to this lot," she groaned. "We'll be knee deep in nosey reporters soon, you mark my words."

The nosey reporters never arrived. Security around Barlow Maximum Speed had now been extended quite a long way from the building. Only known staff were getting through. Cherry and Annette went into the conference room for coffee.

"Where's Arthur?" Annette asked, wiping some crema off her upper lip.

"Haven't a clue," Cherry said, placing her mug on the machine for another hit. "He must have gone out very early. He was cranky and upset last night. And speaking of nights, mine was awful."

"You were sleeping here last night?" Annette said, aghast. "What happened? Did anyone manage to get inside?"

"No." Cherry shuddered. "I was asleep on my mattress. I hate to think what would have happened if they had come in the front door and found me there. What I can't work out is how Sylph got onto them so fast. There must be sensors all over the place, but I can't see any of them in here."

"Are you sure you're okay?" Annette said, scanning Cherry's tired face. "You're knackered. Go home tonight and have a good night's sleep, will you? Remember Arthur's providing secure transport. Besides, I don't want you around here in case some other fanatic tries it on. I'd never forgive myself if anything happened to you." She came over and gave Cherry a huge hug. "You matter heaps and heaps to me."

"Thanks," Cherry said appreciatively. "Can I use your phone? Do you have the number of New Wave Reality?"

"I can remember it off the top of my head," Annette answered, punching numbers into the unit on her desk. She handed Cherry the phone.

A tired sounding voice answered. "G.M. here, can I help you?"

"Could I speak to Paul Yang or Viktor Greshnev please?" Cherry asked.

"Who is this?" The voice seemed even more annoyed.

"This is CC from Barlow Maximum—"

"This some sort of bloody joke?" The voice interrupted angrily. "First you pinch my two top computer technicians, then half my bloody staff, and now you have the temerity to ask me where they are? Where do you get off?" The conversation ended with a sharp click.

Cherry got such a shock she sat there speechless with the instrument halfway between the desk and her ear.

"Cherry, what's wrong?" Annette asked anxiously. "Who was that? I could hear him shouting down the line from over where I'm standing."

"Annette, do we employ Viktor or Paul?" Cherry queried.

"No," Annette answered, frowning heavily. "Arthur told me Sylph freaked them out and they went back to NWR. Why?"
"Somebody calling himself G.M. told me they work for us. I've never seen them round here, have you?"

"Must be a mistake," Annette said. "Some disgruntled employee pretending to be the boss. Perhaps they've all been smoking pot down there last night."

"Annette, have you got either of their mobile numbers?" Cherry slowly put the phone back in its cradle.

"Yes, hang on a minute." She came over to Cherry's side, brought her contacts list up on the screen. "That's funny. I'm sure they were here before. Wait a minute, they're in my mobile phone." She dug into her bag over the back of the chair, pulled out the phone and touched the screen a few times. Her brow furrowed deeply. "Weird. They're not in here either. I don't understand."

"Neither do I," Cherry said slowly, her face very serious indeed. "Something odd is going on, Annette, and I don't like it." She thought for a while then stood up. "Annette, do you know where Arthur goes every morning?"

"You're not thinking he's seeing some other woman?" Annette asked indignantly.

"First thing in the morning? Of course not." She squeezed Annette around the shoulders. "Harry, remember. He's the guy you had a lovely evening with, the one who's playing for keeps."

Annette gave a shrug and turned round to face her. "Yes, I'm stupid. It takes time to lay old ghosts to rest. You know?"

"I know," Cherry sighed. "The other day at my place I couldn't' even wish James a good morning. After that evening we had, remember? I'm such a mess."

She sighed again and headed back into the workshop. At midday she watched the news, interested to see if there was any more information on the raid. She saw the footage, which must have been shown thousands of times by now, of the masked figures against the wall of Renford Engineering. Well, they weren't from police Tactical, that was for certain, and for her money they weren't fanatics either. In fact they seemed quite professionally equipped.

She flipped to another channel. Parliament were debating the new legislation. Crowds with huge "Protect our Sylph" signs were massing in Hyde Park and other capital cities. Groups of people calling themselves Sylphids were urging the death penalty for anyone found guilty of destroying Sylph. Max Velban told everyone he had been speaking to

Sylph and urged her to send a copy of her mind into permanent storage on the cloud. Others had suggested Sylph replicate herself inside some other machines in different parts of the world, just to ensure the new intelligent machine age continued.

Sylph, Sylph, Sylph, all the time. Apparently there wasn't any other news, or if was it was regarded as unimportant. Cherry watched, her mind turning over thoughtfully. The world had gone Sylph mad. After the news, the broadcast cut to live coverage of the Sylph rally in Hyde Park, where an estimated crowd of twenty thousand had gathered.

She turned off the projector and went back to her console. Almost three billion users were logged on, but the data rate had plummeted. Sylph would be back to writing, there was insufficient speed to send pictures.

She checked the processes running on machine three. No wonder the speed had dropped. Sylph had spread herself, and now there was less than half the core left to run her internet tasks. As she watched, the space became less. Machine four was running as normal, but if the number of users continued to increase she had no doubt Sylph would take over that machine as well. Thank goodness the solid state drive caches were holding up. If one of them went down the whole internet system could fall over, and then nobody would be able to talk to Sylph in any way at all.

By the late afternoon the number of users had fallen to a billion and a half, and video had been restored. Sylph had been extremely busy since the attempt on her life.

Cherry initiated a process on machine three which checked blade integrity. It slowed the system down a little, but it gave pre-emptive information about failure, so they could replace a blade before it caused a disaster at a critical time. She would stop it in a little while, scan the report, and see which blades needed replacing.

Suddenly she felt terribly tired. Perhaps it was the lack of sleep, perhaps the nagging problem of the huge file sizes. She found her thoughts muzzy, and her headache had returned. Going back into the front office she saw that Annette was about to leave.

"Sylph Personal Services is still running," Annette said, putting on her coat. "There's some guy in there pouring his heart out. He'll be finished soon, his two hours are almost up."

"Want me to stay until he's done?" Cherry yawned.

"No," Annette shook her head. "I'll stay until he comes out. You go. You look wasted."

"I'm ringing Phillip to send around the hire car," Cherry said with another yawn. "Did you come by car or public transport? I can give you a lift if you like."

"Came by car," Annette smiled. "I'm going home a bit early to pretty myself up. Harry's asked me out again tonight. Wish me luck, will you?"

Cherry threw her arms round the woman. "You don't need luck," she said, laughing softly. "You're so beautiful, Annette, and you have a lovely, caring nature. Just let Harry see who you are without window dressing, and you'll be dancing down the aisle in no time."

Annette's eyes lit up. Shortly afterwards a man came out of Sylph Personal Services. He muttered something to the two women and slunk out the door. Just then Phillip arrived with the hire car to take Cherry home.

CHAPTER 37

Arthur Barlow dunked his head in his hand basin, ran a comb through his hair, and wished there was some way of making his mind as fresh as his face. He went into his bedroom, opened the wardrobe doors, and stepped in amongst the clothes hanging there, pulling the door shut behind him. Fumbling in the dark, he located a light switch and turned it on, pushed past the clothes and descended the steps which led into the passage beyond. Above him on the walls, large cables from the uninterruptible power supplies hummed quietly. There was a lot of current travelling in those cables. He walked along for quite a distance, reached the staircase at the other end of the passage, climbed towards the door at the top and opened it.

"Wondered if you'd show up this evening," Viktor grunted, glancing up from the console he was working at. "The boys are very twitchy. Henry's had his job cut out on the animation stage since the attack. Personal services has been pretty demanding. Sylph has been doing heaps of stuff. Her clients think someone else might have a go and they're getting it while they can."

Arthur scanned the crowded room. In the far corner, Henry, wearing a special suit with markers attached, performed the movements which Sylph would duplicate on someone else's screen, such as she did with Sylph Personal Services and Sylph @ Sunrise. Most of the time all she did was sit on a chair and talk, and that was totally automatic now.

George and Paul were working on the Sylph response database, along with the five other geeks who made up the evening shift in addition to Paul and Viktor. Arthur always did the Sylph @ Sunrise show himself, and didn't usually make an appearance until early in the morning.

Paul threw his pen down on the console and turned to Arthur, weariness etching deep lines on his face. "We can't keep going like this, Arthur." He wiped his hand across his brow. "The team's exhausted, and there's no end in sight. Then this raid last night. You know who did it, don't you?"

"ASIO, of course," Arthur replied, flopping down in the nearest chair. "It wasn't the police, and it wasn't a group of fanatics. Too well geared up."

"Why not get Sylph to tell the world?" Viktor turned round to join the discussion. His face was every bit as haggard as Paul's. "That should set the cat among the pigeons."

"Yeah," Arthur, laughed sarcastically, "only in this case they're not pigeons. The last thing we want to do is mess with ASIO. They're actually protecting Australia, you realise, and if the public thought they were responsible they'd rip them apart. I really don't want that on my conscience. I guess the whole idea of Sylph being above the law and Barlow Inc. amassing huge amounts of wealth started to worry them. Didn't realise they were so easily upset. At least they won't try it again while the threat of exposure is hanging over their heads."

"No," Viktor objected, shaking his head and very worried. "The next time they nuke us with something and blame terrorists. Doesn't make much difference, does it, seeing as how we'll all be dead."

"The glass is really half empty today, isn't it Viktor?" Arthur sat down on the nearest chair and smiled gently towards him. "Nobody is going to nuke Sylph, too much at stake. Can you imagine the reaction if anyone tried? They'd be lynched in the street."

"We can't keep doing this." Paul vented his anxiety again.
"We're all damn scared someone's going to find out what's going on, and tear us to pieces out of sheer revenge. I feel like I'm sitting on a ticking atomic bomb."

He drew out a handkerchief and wiped the sweat off his forehead. "It's a great idea to have us all live full-time in this building, but it only takes one slip up. The team in BMS aren't stupid, especially CC and Annette. Look at us, we're knackered, all of us, and the morning team's no better. All we do is sleep and Sylph."

"And make money," Arthur smiled. "Thanks to me you're all loaded. Said you'd be millionaires. You're now among Australia's most wealthy."

"And we haven't time to buy a chocolate bar," Viktor moaned, rubbing his hands over his eyes." I never thought Sylph would explode like this. When does it end?"

"He who rides the tiger," Arthur grinned, "can never get off."

"We'll be dead before we can spend a cent," Henry complained, coming over to join the conversation. "Don't worry, Sylph's on automatic now. Just finished a personal session with some anxious bloke who wanted to do the usual and pour his heart out while he did it. Pathetic. Worst part about it was listening to him."

"I hope you adhered to policy," Arthur frowned.

"To be nice and make them feel good, indulge their private fantasies," Henry retorted. "Of course. It's common sense most of the time. It just amazes me why Sylph's become so incredibly popular. All her followers get is a verbal version of what they could find out if they searched the internet, interspersed with feely phrases like "I'm so sorry to hear that", "I understand your pain", "I can feel for you", and all the others we've stuck in that cue database. The world's a sick and sorry place. That's one lesson I've learnt."

"The world's gone Sylph mad." Viktor rubbed his eyes. "Two and a half billion followers. Then this cult thing, the Sylphids. You know they actually put her image on a pedestal and worship the blasted thing. Why? Who would have predicted it?"
"I would." Arthur stretched his hands in the air behind his head and yawned. Three pairs of eyes stared at him in disbelief.

"Sylph was guaranteed to take off," he yawned again. "People need to worship something. It's built into our human DNA. We've been doing it since the dawn of time."

He fished into his pocket and brought out a small silver statuette of a woman with breasts all over her naked torso. "Artemis, Dianna, Venus, Aphrodite. Same goddess, called different names over time. Think of all the millions of people who have prostrated themselves before this little image, given it drink and food offerings they could ill afford. Think of the thousands of young girls who sacrificed their lives and dignity before her altar, servicing her drunken devotees." He placed the small image on the desk in front of him. "Why do you suppose they did that? I can tell you one thing, Aphrodite et alia never did a single thing for them in return."

"You tell us," Viktor said cynically. "I notice you've got her image in your pocket. Gives you a warm feeling in your pants, does she?"

Arthur laughed. "Such a cynic, Viktor. No, she reminds me of a principle. You can't question transcendence. Endue a lump of wood with transcendence, and people worship it. They never question the logic of what they're doing. Blind, unrewarded faith it is, throwback of some evolutionary process gone wrong." He laughed again, "so you see, Sylph had to work, once Velban had endued her with the necessary transcendence of self-awareness. Of course he would, he'd convinced himself it was possible before he arrived. We made his day."

"You think Christians are people in the same category?" Paul asked. "There's an awful lot of them around. They don't even have an idol to bow down to, just some unseen God who's not very talkative. Beats me why they keep it up in this scientific age."

"You're not listening, Paul," Arthur said reprovingly. "Transcendence can't be questioned. That's the reason why Sylph works so well. You mightn't believe it, but I went to a church youth group for years, every Friday night. The Christian's God makes unpleasant demands on people's lives, like telling them to obey Him, be unselfish and morally responsible. Quite unpopular in our culture, dedicated as it is to doing your own thing."

He gestured with his palms up. "So we give people someone else to worship. A transcendent intelligence in the form of an attractive young woman. She understands them, sympathises with their troubles, gives them a friendly word. She understands their adultery and their underhand schemes. She puts them right where they want to be, in the centre of their own pathetic little lives."

"You're a real cynic, aren't you?" Henry said, smiling.

"Cynic? No," Arthur smiled back. "I'm a realist. People pray to their God – whatever – and all they get is heaps of silence. Gets them down. Sylph is far more talkative. She listens. She talks. That's enough. Sometimes she hits it one hundred percent right. When she does the news explodes like a wildfire in a petrol station. Don't you remember, like it did when we told that bloke his wife would come back to him and he'd be reemployed."

"We guessed at that one, didn't we?" Henry laughed. "Just managed to get it right. We've got it wrong heaps of times though."

"Sure, but don't you see?" Arthur leant forward in his chair. "The more powerful Sylph becomes, the better chance she has of being right. The more people worship her, the more they're going to do as she says. Transcendence builds. She talks to them, remember, rather than God's spectacular silence. Makes all the difference."

"Like self-fulfilling prophecy," Viktor said, nodding, "especially with things like the stock market. Sylph predicts a share will go up in value, and guess what? People buy them by the thousands, and voila! Up they go in value. We've made a tidy profit from that ploy as I recall."

"Indeed we have," Arthur agreed, "and we haven't finished that game yet, gentlemen. Sylph remains in business until we no longer want her to be."

"At least we're not into idol worship." Henry covered a yawn. "Running an idol makes you immune from all that sort of thing."

"Oh, you're not?" Arthur laughed. "You're all worse than the courtesans of Aphrodite."

"What do you mean?" Viktor retorted, annoyed at the implication. "We don't bow down to anything—"

"On the contrary," Arthur continued. "You've dedicated your lives to your god. Few people worship with such devotion. Don't feel bad. I'm on my knees too."

"Talk bloody sense," Henry snapped. "We don't bow down to idols."

Arthur fished into his pocket again and pulled out a hundred dollar note. He held it up in his hands in an attitude of mock worship, laughing. "Let's face it, gentlemen. We've got our knees in the dirt and our butts in the air before this one. What are we doing here twenty four-seven? Worshipping this. What has it done for us so far? Nothing. Does that stop us? No. We keep going by faith, accumulating the blessings which will one day be poured out so richly on our lives."

"But that's different," Paul argued. "It's sound business practice."

"Not at all," Arthur returned. "People worship idols because they want to feel good, have nice kids, plenty of sex, a life free from predators. We're all exhausted, but we keep riding the tiger. Why? Precisely the same reasons."

"I suppose you have a point," Paul agreed. "But you have to admit Sylph has done a lot of public good. Made a lot of people happy, made a lot of people rich."

"In any case, it's given us a rare insight into human nature, hasn't it?" Arthur walked over to Viktor's console, picked up a half empty Coke can and downed it all in one long gulp.

"Thanks. Remember we thought we'd have so many different sorts of problems to deal with we'd never manage to cue Sylph with all the answers? We thought the database would be as large as the internet is wide."

He sat down again. "But it wasn't, was it? Most of the questions people ask are the same. "How can I have better sex? Why doesn't someone love me? How do I know if they do? What's the meaning of life? Who am I? What will happen to me when I die? Got any more Coke, Vik?"

Viktor produced another can from his freezer bag and threw it towards Arthur, who caught it deftly in his left hand. He opened the tab and took a long drink. "Apart from these areas there's not a lot, really. Financial advice, we use the internet, health advice we – or rather she – uses the internet. When the odd ones come up, the software flags them to our consoles, and we add to the cue database. When you come to think of it, that database isn't so very large, and we're adding less items day by day. Sylph is becoming smarter. One day she might be so smart the whole thing will run on automatic."

"Come the day," Viktor sighed. "I think I deserve my pay as psychologist to the seething mass of humanity." He smiled at Arthur. "You never have much to say to Sylph, Arthur. All you want her to do is spread her naked little legs. If CC ever caught you at it, she'd take a knife to your delicate parts. That can't be normal. The gorgeous Annette would tear her clothes off for you at the wink of an eye, but you don't want it. Not healthy, Arthur. Let doctor Greshnev, psychiatrist to the groaning masses, listen to your woes and prescribe a cure."

Arthur laughed. "Money cures all, gentlemen. That's the universal answer." He dragged another chair over, and crossed his legs on top of it. "That's better. You want to know about me? My mother was a fourteen year old girl, brought up in a Commune. Some stoned bastards knocked her up one night. She was pretty traumatised and had a bad pregnancy, went to hospital up the coast when the time came. They treated her like a slut. How are we doing so far, doctor Viktor?"

Viktor said nothing. He was staring at Arthur in horror.

Arthur continued. "The hospital registrar told her she could deliver her bastard somewhere else, so she did, back at the Commune with some plastered woman who said she'd been a midwife once. But she didn't deliver one bastard, she delivered two. A couple of hours later my mother died, from haemorrhage I think. Midwife didn't even hang around to cover up the body."

"Poor kid," Viktor muttered, quite shaken. "That's a dreadfully sad story. Go on, Arthur."

"Well," Arthur said, "the Commune didn't mind kids, as long as they came with single mother's benefits, but in this case they had to pay to have the mother cremated. So expensive. They agreed to take one kid, me, and got rid of the other one. So caring. Well, come on doctor Greshnev, sing pearls of wisdom."

Viktor remained in shocked silence.

"Who took care of you?" Paul asked quietly.

"Care of me?" Arthur gave a cynical laugh, "nobody. I grew up like any Commune kid, belonging to no one. There's a lot of young women in the Commune. Some of them work as prostitutes in the local community. They bring in extra cash, keep important people happy and the cops off the Commune's back. Then there's the ones who just enjoy abusing kids like me. I can't tell you what a delightful sex education I've had. Kind of spoils your image of women, doesn't it?"

"Shit," Henry muttered, staring at Arthur as if he'd grown another head. "Is that why you won't have anything to do with the lovely Annette?"

"No," Arthur grinned. "I couldn't make her happy, and she's already been abused enough. Didn't you realise that?"

They sat shocked and silent, wondering what was coming next.

Arthur grinned towards them. "You can't get off the tiger just yet, Viktor, but soon you will be able too. One more deal, we're finished. Can't let this one pass by."
"How much?" Paul asked wearily. "We're already millionaires."

"About five billion," Arthur smiled, "that's around two hundred million each. Then we can get off. Sylph will have a terrible accident."

Paul whistled. "Okay, I don't mind riding the tiger a bit more, under those circumstances. You're a constant source of amazement, Arthur. What do we have to do for this? Take down the government? Make Sylph prime minister? Easy, man."

"Yeah," Arthur laughed, "Good for the country too. No, gentlemen, all we're going to do is help Australia export some of its natural resources, assist the mining industry a little. Always helpful, that's our Sylph."

"What do you mean, Sylph will have a terrible accident?" Victor asked. "If we do anything that looks like sabotage, we'll have two billion fans roaring up here to tear us limb from limb."

"All taken care of," Arthur said with a grin. "One of her central processors will fail. Of course we will be devastated. She won't be able to do very much in that state, and we'll ask Velban for all the help he can muster. Unfortunately it just won't be enough. Somehow I don't think the experts will arrive in time."

"Such a shame," Paul laughed. "Then we can set about spending our millions. It's a lifetime in Hawaii for me, surrounded by the most beautiful women I can find."

"You going out for dinner tonight, Arthur?" Henry asked, turning back to his console. Somebody had asked Sylph how to make a hydrogen bomb. The answer to that question was definitely not in the cue database.

"No, there's food in the conference room 'fridge. Annette keeps it stocked for me. After that I'll monitor a few things then I might enjoy some of Sylph's personal services. I'll run my special file. No need for you to bother."

"I don't know, Arthur," Paul said with a sigh, "why don't you try it with the real Cherry instead? Much nicer, you know."
Arthur laughed. "You don't know Cherry. Besides, let's face it, gentlemen, I'm addicted to porn. Blame the child abuse. Only relief from bloody awful memories. Can't stop now, it's changed my brain. Perhaps I'll come to one of you for therapy. See you tomorrow. Ciao."

Arthur stood and headed for the doorway. Henry forwarded his enquirer's name to ASIO on behalf of Sylph, just to show there were no hard feelings, and told him you made a hydrogen bomb by boiling water under high pressure with bicarbonate of soda.

CHAPTER 38

Cherry woke up with a start and dragged her alarm clock over so she could see its face. Twenty two hundred hours. She'd only been asleep for two, and she knew what had woken her up. The predictive blade failure program was still running. Sylph @ Sunrise would be a disaster if it was running during the show. She groaned at the thought of having to go back to work, especially when she felt so tired. She reached out for the phone and tried to ring Arthur. No answer, which was not surprising. He had probably gone to bed, seeing as he always had an early morning appointment somewhere. She groaned again and rang Phillip. Could he please bring the car around and take her to work, she was terribly sorry.

"No problem," Phillip's cheery voice echoed down the line. "For what Arthur pays me I'll drive you to the moon every day, any time."

Cherry dressed rapidly without bothering to shower. She staggered into the kitchen, and made herself an espresso double shot. "Now I probably won't sleep at all," she muttered quietly. She slipped her feet into some comfortable shoes and waited for Phillip to arrive. Three quarters of an hour later the limo drew to a halt in front of Barlow Maximum Speed. Cherry got out and told Phillip she would spend the night on her mattress after all, and would he please go home and apologise to Mrs. Phillip if there was one. Phillip said he would definitely apologise, leaving aside the matter of to whom.

Cherry walked up to the front door feeling very foolish and annoyed with herself. She swiped her card through the reader and went inside. Voices were coming from the Sylph Personal Services room. She moved quietly in that direction, only to find, to her astonishment, that the door was slightly ajar. Pushing it open a little, she noticed a pair of trousers draped over the back of a chair. She pushed it fully open, stepped into the room and froze in horror.

On the huge high definition screen at the front was a picture of herself, naked, writhing erotically on a bed, and in front of that ghastly image stood Arthur, minus the garment draped over the back of the chair.

To her horror she heard her own voice groaning from the speaker. "Come on Arthur, my love... Do it, do it, do it."

"YOU... FILTHY... LYING... BASTARD!"

Cherry screamed the words at the top of her lungs, her body shaking with rage and shock. Arthur whipped round to face her, his eyes staring, his mouth open. All that could be heard was Sylph's voice, mindlessly mouthing the same erotic monologue, insensible to her pseudo-lover's complete lack of attention.

Cherry stared at the explicit pornography on the screen and wished very much that the world would end on the spot. How many other men had stood in front of her body image and... She felt suddenly ill, and swallowed hard to prevent herself from throwing up on the floor.

Arthur was staring at her in shock and disbelief.

Cherry's mind was reeling in utter confusion. Sylph, who had promised to treat her Avatar with dignity, had demeaned her to explicit pornographic trash, the very thing she had fought against for most of her life. How was that possible?

"What have you done?" Cherry screamed. "Arthur, what have you done?"

Arthur stood silent, his face like fire.

Cherry shut her eyes and screamed at the image on the screen. "Sylph, how could you betray me like this? You promised me you wouldn't!" She could feel tears running down her face.

Arthur snatched a remote control off the table and pressed a key. Sylph's voice halted mid-sentence. The erotic image disappeared, only to be replaced by the message:

>file AB1390FF terminated by a_barlow
>

"For goodness sake stop that nonsense," Arthur shouted. "Wake up. I've made you a very wealthy woman. Can't you show a little gratitude?"

Cherry's eyes flew open, staring at the black monitor screen with the single line of type. Her rational mind told her Arthur had simply terminated a program. Her heart retreated in denial.

Arthur read the betrayal and anguish in Cherry's eyes, and his conscience dealt him a much deserved blow. He had never intended to hurt her at all, only use her programming skill and make her a very wealthy woman in the process. In a few short weeks it would have all been over. Cherry, Annette and all the others on the team would go back to their wealth-enriched lives, delivered from the humdrum financial battles of life.

He watched as Cherry turned towards him. Now the betrayal and pain was changing into fear, no not fear, terror. Why? He glanced towards his feet. Surely she didn't think he would lay a finger on her... but then Cherry's damaged past would compel only that interpretation. He utterly despised men who abused women, yet here he was, engendering the same revulsion and fear in the mind of a woman he respected. Indeed, in real life, divorced from his pornographic fantasies, he cared for her a great deal. His conscience struck him another heavy blow. For the first time in his existence, Arthur Barlow began to feel horribly guilty and ashamed of his own behaviour. He didn't like it one little bit.

Arthur had perceived Cherry's thoughts precisely. Only once before had she seen a man in that condition of undress, and her mind jumped to the very predictable conclusion that unless she somehow escaped, Arthur would grab her and use her body to complete what her screen image had begun.

"Cherry," Arthur entreated, "I'm not going to touch you. I would never do anything to hurt you. Let me get my pants on, and then we can go into the conference room and talk about this calmly. Please!"

Not hurt her? Lies followed lies. She was barely conscious of the words in any case. Every thought Cherry's ragged mind could command was bent towards escaping from Arthur's loathsome clutches. She whirled around in terror, searching for a weapon of some kind. Arthur's trousers were the only thing within reach. Springing backwards, she snatched them from the back of the chair and pelted towards the door.

"Hey!" Arthur yelled. "Not the trousers! No!" he yelled again, springing after her in alarm.

Those trousers contained his wallet, and his wallet contained the top level password, literally the master key to his whole digital kingdom. By now Cherry was disappearing through the door. With an oath of protest, he lunged after her.

Cherry's feet had wings as she flew across the front office, vaguely aware of Arthur's voice shouting from behind, his feet drumming on the carpet. Reaching the door she wrenched it open, hearing a thud and a curse just near her shoulder. Now she was through, racing towards the street. For a second she turned her head in time to see Arthur pelting after her. A car came down the road, sweeping its headlights across pursuer and pursued. It swerved, almost hit the kerb, and then continued on. Arthur gave a howl of rage and disappeared back inside the building.

Cherry's heart was beating painfully, but her feet felt as though they had wings. She flew down the road, occasionally taking fearful glances behind her. In the distance she saw a taxi. She ran right in front of it. The driver screeched to a stop, slewing the cab into the kerb. Without waiting for an invitation she wrenched open the back door and launched herself inside.

The taxi driver turned round to face her, furious. "What the hell do you think you're doing? Trying to get yourself killed?"

He read the terror in her face, and simultaneously quieted his anger. "Are you okay? Where do you want to go?"

"Drive!" Cherry shouted. "Drive! Darling Harbour. Quickly."

The cab took off down the street. Cherry turned and stared out the back window, but the coast behind was clear. Arthur had given up the chase. She unrolled Arthur's trousers and fumbled around until she found his wallet in a pocket. She pulled it out and shoved it into her own. Dropping the rest onto the taxi floor, she pushed it under the passenger seat with her foot. Darling Harbour was always crowded, night or day. She would be safe there, at least for a while.

She needed time to think.

Her head ached, but she fought to gain control of her thoughts. "Concentrate on breathing, Cherry," she said to herself. "Calm down, you'll never think if you panic, and this isn't the time."

Half an hour later the cab dropped her in King Street. She made her way down to the wharf, then into one of the nightclub-restaurants which lined the foreshore boardwalk. She ordered herself a large black coffee and an orange mousse dessert. Sugar, she needed sugar. She sank down into the comfortable vinyl chair, and tried to come to grips with the impossible.

Barlow's words were ringing in her ears, "I've made you a very wealthy woman, can't you show a little gratitude?" Before her unwilling mind she saw the screen, read the message which told her that Arthur had done nothing more than terminated a program.

Cherry remembered the file sizes, the huge rendering tasks, occupying an impossibly large amount of memory. These were incomprehensible if Sylph was a self-aware neural network, but completely understandable if Sylph was an incredibly fast search engine coupled with an ingenious human interface.

She had heard those words before, where?

James had said them. She groaned, folded her arms on the table and laid her head on them. James was right. Sylph, the self-aware transcendent intelligence was a fake, a fraud, a hoax which had deceived billions of people, billions of people who had come to love and worship a lie, including Annette, including her. Every intimate, faith-building conversation she had had with Sylph was a hideous parody. Everything she had said in trust had been answered by either Barlow or one of his employees, who were probably laughing at her while they did so.

She groaned again, feeling nauseous and ill.

Of course they had to convince her. They needed her dedication, her skill, and the only way they could have obtained it, the only way they could have made her leave Cyber, was to inspire her with Sylph's transcendence. They had lured Annette in exactly the same way.
James was never deceived. How was that possible? How had he been able to see so clearly what she had failed to discern until this latest, horrific hour? Because he believed in God, and his Christian worldview had given him the required clarity.

Her head suddenly ached with a vengeance.

She remembered G.M's inexplicable anger when she had rung NWR. It all made sense now. Victor and Paul and goodness knows how many others were in on the deal too.

She thought of Barlow and his despicable friends smoothing out the fine details of those horrendous scanned images, perfecting their sex doll for the use of special customers.

She lunged towards a potted plant which was standing nearby and threw up in it. James's angry words, the words which had caused her to cut him out of her life, were true.
She wanted to die.

No, she thought, I must think clearly. I know the truth, the truth which would shatter the faith of two billion people, the truth which had brought billions of dollars into the BMS coffers, a truth so dangerous anyone would be willing to kill for it. What to do now? She could choose do nothing, simply disappear somewhere, and all the world would continue as it had before. Probably no one would believe her anyway, at least at first. Why put her life in jeopardy? How could she bear the utter shame and humiliation? Her face burned with fire at the mere memory. It was a miracle she had escaped at all. Once Barlow caught her she would never escape again. No, go away and hide, hide forever.

Suddenly her heart rebelled at the thought. If she chose that path she would be guilty of suppressing the truth and allowing even more people to be sucked into a dirty lie.

Two billion people worshipping at the feet of an idol who lied to make money, even worse that the little wooden ones she had read about somewhere which did precisely nothing. She felt totally overwhelmed.

She drew out her phone to ring James, pressed a few numbers then stopped suddenly. If she told James, he would believe her instantly. Come the morning Barlow would be arrested, and mayhem would ensue. The staff who worked at BMS would be killed as the public rioted in fury, and the police would be powerless to prevent it. Annette, the woman she loved dearly, would be killed.

She caught her breath.

Images of Annette dragged screaming out of her office by a furious mob, defiled and torn limb from limb, played across her mind. She dropped her head into her arms again. What to do? Annette was a Sylphid, like she had been. If she told her the truth about Sylph, she'd go running to Barlow in disbelief, like a lamb to the slaughter. Barlow had always been kind and considerate towards Annette, but a man who could be so treacherously duplicitous, with billions of dollars at stake, would count her life of little worth If there was the slightest risk of losing all. No, he could never let that happen.

Then another terrible thought. She was still on the loose. No doubt Barlow and his team of desperados were searching for her at this very moment, determined to silence her for good. Where would they look? They'd go straight to Annette's flat, suspecting that Cherry had fled for refuge to the woman she loved. They were probably already on the way, and it wouldn't be long before they arrived. What dreadful things would they do to her before they realised she didn't know where Cherry was?

She shuddered again. What to do?

She glanced at her watch. Eleven thirty. Perhaps Annette was still on her date with Harry. Wait or not wait?

Her mind was an agony of indecision.

Leaving her coffee and mousse untouched, she paid her bill and went out onto King Street Wharf, trotting along amongst the crowds and the lovers until she came to a relatively quiet place at the end. Sitting down on the boardwalk with her feet dangling over the harbour, she rang Annette, trying desperately to keep her voice steady.
After three rings Annette's happy laugh answered.

"Hi Cherry. I hope you went home after all. How're you feeling?"

"Annette, is Harry with you?" Something in the tone of Cherry's reply gave Annette cause for pause.

"No," she answered. "We had a wonderful evening. Just got home. I invited him in for a nightcap, but he gave me this beautiful little kiss and said "one day." Isn't that—"

"Annette, do you trust me?" Cherry's rising panic cut across Annette's description of Harry's courting strategy.

There was a pause. Annette was no fool. She had been right. Cherry was afraid, no, not afraid, terrified.

"Cherry, what's the matter?" she asked. "You don't sound right."
"Do you trust me?" Cherry insisted. "Please, answer me."

"Yes, Cherub. Of course I trust you. What—"

"Get out of your home. Now. Find a motel somewhere. Don't go to work tomorrow or the next day. Promise me," Cherry entreated.

Annette nearly dropped the phone. If it wasn't for the terror in Cherry's voice she would have concluded the girl had consumed a great deal more wine than was good for her.

"Why should I do that?" She asked nervously.

"Because if you go to work you'll be killed. Dear God, please believe me. My life's in danger, and yours is too. Please Annette. I'm begging you."

Cherry started to cry. Annette could feel the hair rising on the back of her neck. Something of the terror in Cherry's heart was reaching her own. "All right," she promised. "How about I ring Harry? He—"

"No," Cherry screamed. "Promise me you won't say a word to Harry. If you did lots of innocent people might die."

"Cherry!" Annette pressed the phone to her ear with a shaking hand. "Are you all right? Has anything happened to you? Are you having a breakdown? Someone interfered with you? Where are you? Let me come—"

"No." Cherry's terrified voice blasted down the phone. "I'm not crazy. I'm begging you, Annette. Give me an address. Go there, I'll come when I can. Right now I'm not sure what to do. Annette, I love you. You're my only family. Please. Please!"

"All right." Annette felt herself trembling.
"You've got me scared stiff now. I'll go to the Miranda Motor Inn, sure to be a vacancy this time of the week. It's on the highway, just before you hit the town proper. Cherry, can't you tell me anything?"

"If Barlow rings you, don't pick up the phone. "Throw it down the toilet."
"Arthur would never hurt—"

"Annette," Cherry interrupted in panic. "Please trust me. Go. Are you going? Are you on the way?"
"I'm on my way," Annette stammered, thoroughly frightened now. "I'm shutting the front door. I'm running for the car. I'm scared out of my wits. Please be careful, Cherry. I... I love you too. Please."

Cherry hung up the phone and wiped the tears from her eyes, the sweat from her forehead. "Thank you," she said to nobody apparent. Annette was safe. What to do now?

Suddenly she remembered something Martin Bartholomew had said. What was it? If she ever changed her mind about Sylph she should let him know. Now it suddenly became clear. Martin Bartholomew was clever like James. He must have realised Sylph was a fake. He knew he couldn't convince her of the truth, she had to find out herself. Now she had. He had influence, he would know what to do. She searched her contacts list. Yes, she had his address. She would go and see him, tell him, then go back and be with Annette, try to convince her too.

Running as fast as her legs could carry her she reached King Street and hailed a cab.

"14 Murchison Drive Vaucluse," she told the cabbie breathlessly. "As quick as you can."

Now she dialled his number.

After a few rings Hobbs answered the phone. "Mr. Bartholomew has retired for the day," he said in a measured, stern voice. "You will have to ring tomorrow."

"But I can't ring tomorrow. It's about Sylph." Cherry tried to keep the terror out of her voice. "This is Cherry Graham. Tell him I've changed my mind about her. Please, he asked me to call him if I did. Please give him the message, and ring me back."

A few minutes later the phone rang again.

"Bartholomew here. Is that you, Ms. Cherry? You say you've changed your mind about Sylph? How is that?"

Cherry cupped her hands over the phone so the cabbie couldn't hear. "She's not all she seems to be. Not real. Can't say more, I'm in a cab."

"My dear," Bartholomew consoled, "you must come here straight away. I will tell the security staff to admit you immediately. You've done the right thing, my dear. A most serious situation indeed."

In less than ten minutes the cab drove through the heavy iron gates and up a long pebbled drive, stopping under a stone alcove near an ornate front door. Cherry paid the driver and sprinted up the steps towards two tough looking men who were apparently Bartholomew's security guards.

"Cherry Graham to see Mr. Bartholomew—"

"Certainly, Ms.," one of the guards replied. "You're expected. Please go in." He bent forward and opened the door.

Two people stood in the hall, Hobbs, and Martin Bartholomew wearing a dressing gown.

He came forward unsteadily and embraced her. "My dear Ms. Cherry. Come into the lounge room. Hobbs, some warm refreshment for Ms. Graham. Now, my dear, what happened? What has caused you such distress?"

Cherry told him all of it, her cheeks glowing red with shame as she did. Martin Bartholomew listened attentively in silence, occasionally nodding his head. Hobbs arrived, carrying a hot chocolate in a crystal glass on a silver tray.

"What do we do?" Cherry wrung her hands. "If this thing goes public people will riot. They'll tear Barlow's factory to shreds and all the people in it. Who knows what else? Angry, disillusioned people are likely to do anything. But they can't go on worshipping a lie either, can they?"

"Just so, my dear," Bartholomew soothed. "No, to tell people at this stage would be most unwise. I fear your prediction of disaster is certain to occur. Please, drink your chocolate, it will settle your nerves a little while we think."

Cherry took the chocolate from Hobbs, grateful of its warmth. How good it tasted. Now she was definitely feeling calmer, in fact she was feeling very calm, sleepy, very sleepy. Her eyes were getting heavy, so heavy.

Something was wrong, terribly wrong.

Bartholomew was watching her like a hawk, Hobbs too, as if they were waiting for something. Drugged! She had been drugged. She struggled to stand and collapsed full length on the lounge instead.

"Thank you, Hobbs," Bartholomew said quietly. "Disturbing developments. In the meantime, how about the wine cellar I've just renovated? There's no wine in there yet, is there? The thought of her smashing a thousand dollar bottle of Grange makes me feel quite ill. Can you manage? She's a solid little thing."

Hobbs picked up the empty crystal glass from the floor and returned it to the silver tray. He bent his legs and hoisted Cherry up over his shoulder as if she was a baby.

"No trouble at all Sir," He answered. "Do you want her fed at intervals?"

"I think not, Hobbs," Bartholomew answered thoughtfully. "I don't want her making a mess in there. Somehow I doubt Ms. Cherry will ever be walking out our front door. Perhaps I should go down and shoot her now while she's unconscious. No, that would really make a mess of the cellar, and I've just had it rendered and painted. Or perhaps we could suffocate her. I'll check with Manhattan first. Give Barlow a ring, tell him all is well. Poor man must be worried sick. Rather stupid of him though. That will be all, Hobbs."

Hobbs trotted off towards the cellar with Cherry slung over his shoulder like a sack of potatoes. Bartholomew walked into his study, drew a pistol out of the draw and checked the magazine.

※ ※ ※

Arthur Barlow lay back in his bed, still blazingly angry with himself. He remembered the look of betrayal then terror on Cherry's face, and felt a deep sense of shame knowing that he had been the cause of both. Damn his blasted addiction to porn! Damn his carelessness for leaving the door open. Damn her for coming back at just the wrong time. Damn her for swiping his trousers! He had searched up and down the street after fetching another pair from his bedroom, just to see if she had thrown them away. Apparently she hadn't, although it had been too dark to be completely sure.

How could he retrieve the master password? There was no way to bypass it. Without that long string of hexadecimal numbers he wasn't able to manage the huge amounts of money coming in from Sylph's doting disciples. While all the animation software was running well there was no problem, but as soon as anything went wrong, or any major changes were required, they were in deep trouble. Somehow he had to get it back.

Where would she have gone? he thought. To Annette, probably, seeing as Cherry loathed men. Would Annette believe her? Chances were she would, because they had become very close. What would happen then? Annette would despise him too, and they would never darken the doorway of BMS again. He groaned. It was absolutely the last thing he wanted. Annette was someone he cared about enormously, his only desire to make her rich and happy. He had never meant to hurt anybody. Sylph had done a lot of good, made many people wealthy, given them the ego boost they needed, given them something to trust in. Of course she had also made him the wealthiest man in Australia, but that was a fair reward for his genius. What's more, nobody would ever have been hurt, had it not been for his carelessness in leaving a door open – and his wretched addiction to porn.

Life, he thought bitterly, had a way of dropping you straight into the toilet when you thought everything was going so well.

Even if Annette did believe Cherry it wouldn't make any difference overall. There had been others who doubted in the beginning, but now Sylph's established transcendence would overcome everything. Something this large couldn't be stopped by one or two unbelievers who were still out there anyway. Besides, he thought, Cherry was so damaged there was a good chance she wouldn't say anything at all to anyone out of sheer embarrassment. She would just go away hating him, leaving shoes impossible to fill by any other programmer he knew. He groaned loudly again.

Damn his carelessness.

The phone rang. Arthur snatched it up.

"Mr. Barlow," Hobbs spoke in a voice of measured calm. "I am pleased to inform you that Ms. Graham is currently in our care. She is apparently of the opinion that Sylph is not all she would appear to be."

"What?" Arthur barked into the instrument. "What's she doing with you?"

"Ms. Graham came to us for advice," Hobbs purred. "We think it best if she were to stay here until our other business has been completed."

"One woman unbeliever won't make the slightest bit of difference," Arthur protested. "Our business is likely to go on for weeks until the share price stabilises. How are you going to convince her to stay with you all that time?" Arthur breathed heavily into the phone.

"We are currently making an assessment of the situation. Mr. Bartholomew and the fellow directors of North Creek Uranium are of the opinion she should remain here for however long it takes. We can't have her spreading any unfortunate rumours at such a delicate stage in the proceedings. I suggest your Sylph might like to send her friends a video showing Ms. Graham enjoying herself on holiday somewhere."

"You're going to keep her there against her will?" Arthur exploded. "You don't know Cherry Graham. You'll be up to your neck in unfortunate rumours as soon as she's out the front door," he added, and immediately wished he'd kept his mouth shut.

"A good point, Mr. Barlow, and one we are considering. In any case, we believe it would be most expedient for the holiday video to be emailed before tomorrow morning. Can't take any chances with this amount of money at stake, can we? Please send us a copy as a token of your good faith."

"What do you mean, we can't take—"

Hobbs had hung up. Arthur shivered. Moments ago he didn't think things could get any worse, now they had. As if he didn't have enough to worry about. What a bizarre and unexpected turn of events. Why on earth had Cherry decided to go there? Curse Bartholomew! It must have had something to do with the lunch they had together. How he wished Annette had gone with them, that Cherry had never met the Machiavellian swine.

Wearily he got up, dressed and headed through the wardrobe into Renford Engineering Services. There was urgent work to be done.

CHAPTER 39

James Naylor arrived at the tactical response unit in a good mood. He greeted Harry, who grunted without taking his eyes off his computer, waved to Tony and Bauman, all equally occupied, and sat down at his desk. Out of habit opened his emails, groaning to himself at the number which had accumulated in the space of a mere twelve hours. He began to move down the list, deleting here and reading there, until he came upon the last candidate, stared, and read the sender's name again just to make sure.

cc@barlowmaximum.net.au Subject: My holiday, with a video attachment.

He paused, frowned, pressed delete. He looked up to find his other two mates staring at him.

"Well," Harry queried, "what do you think?"

"What do I think about what?" James growled, annoyed that Cherry would want to send him an email at all.

"About the video." Tony pointed to his screen.

"Are you boys feeling okay?" James frowned. Obviously he had missed something important.

"The video CC sent us from the beach at Surfer's Paradise. We want to know what you think about it," Harry answered, keeping his voice calm. He knew exactly what James had done with CC's email, but he wasn't leaving it there, not this time.

"I deleted it," James muttered wearily. "The last thing I want to see is some video of that woman on a beach anywhere. Enjoy."

"We want you to watch it," Harry persisted, "and tell us what you think."

The boys were staring at him very seriously. Surely they knew what had happened between him and Cherry, how raw that wound was still. What was going on here?

"You show me," he said angrily, coming over to Harry's computer. "You know I don't want to see anyway."

Without another word Harry pressed play. Tony stood up and came over as well. On the screen was a picture of Cherry, clothed in a tiny colourful bikini, lying on a beach towel in a sea of yellow sand.

"Hi boys," she said, sitting up. "It's beautiful up here at Surfer's. Sun's a bit hot. Can't afford to get myself burnt, can I?" She picked up the tube of suntan cream lying beside her, raised one of her bare legs, and began smoothing it with cream, all the way up from her toes to her crotch. "Shame you're not up here with me," she laughed, "then you could be the one massaging my legs." She put that leg down and repeated the exercise with the other. She laughed again. "Well, mustn't make you boys too envious. 'Bout time you had a holiday yourselves. I'll be up here for a whole glorious fortnight. Eat your hearts out. Ciao."

The video ended.

"So, what's all this about? Think I'm impressed to see Cherry showing off her legs and practically naked?" James felt as angry as he sounded.

"We thought you'd feel like that," Tony replied very seriously. "Now just for a minute forget the jilted lover and think about it. See if the same thing strikes you as struck both of us."

James was about to launch into a tirade about him never being her lover in the first place, jilted or not, but once again the seriousness of his two close mates gave him cause for pause. He stopped before the first word reached his lips, and forced himself to consider the video he had just seen.

"She's changed a lot since I used to know her," he muttered, careful to emphasise the past tense. "In fact I've seen more of her in the last thirty seconds than I've ever seen before."

"That's what we thought," Harry said carefully. "Think about it, James. CC was chronically shy about revealing anything. I doubt you'd ever catch her in a one piece swimming costume, let alone that bikini which left nothing to the imagination. Then there's the way she was showing off her legs. Tony and I think it's odd, that's all."

"What do you mean, odd?" James was frowning now. "I suppose she's changed, that's all. No doubt Barlow—"

"Shut up about Barlow," Harry barked in annoyance. "Listen, we know how you feel about Cherry, and we're all fond of her too, remember? Just assess the evidence. Does it make sense to you?"

"What are you getting at?" James frowned heavily. "I agree it's not the Cherry we know, but... Move over for a minute, Harry."

James slid into Harry's chair. He played the video again, reached the point where Cherry had just sat up, stopped. The frown on his face deepened. He backed up a frame, forward again, back again, forward. He cut a frame out of the video, imported it into Photoshop and blew it up, staring at the screen. Finally he leant back in the chair, his face grey with worry. "It's not CC," he said at last. "It's a fake. It's Sylph."

"How can you be sure?" Harry asked. "We thought it might be a fake because of what she was wearing and what she was doing. Completely unlike her. What changed your mind, James?"

"The scar's not there. Watch." He pointed to the blown up image of Cherry's left shoulder and arm.

"When we were kids she cut herself on a glass. It left a tiny scar on her arm near that shoulder." He returned to the video, advancing frame by frame. "See, there's no sand on her shoulder to cover anything up. No scar. It's not Cherry."

"Then why," Tony began, "would she go to the trouble of sending us this? And more to the point, where is she?"

"She didn't send us anything," James replied. "Barlow sent this. Why? Because he wants us to believe Cherry's on holidays for a fortnight. Why? Oh, dear God, there's only one reason." He shut his eyes and ran his hand through his hair. "She's found out the truth. She's discovered Sylph's a fake. What's more, Barlow knows she's discovered the truth."

He flopped back against the chair, covering his face with his hands and said nothing for a long time. Harry and Tony were silent, knowing all too well the implications which would follow.

"He's killed her," James stammered at last. "She's dead. Oh, dear God, she's dead. Cherry, forgive me." He gave a strangled sob, hiding his face in his hands.

Harry stood and put his arm around James' shoulder. "Listen," he said, "we haven't confirmed that yet. It's the most likely scenario, but until we're sure there's absolutely no point in believing it. If she's dead there's nothing we can do, but if she isn't we have to find her before she is. I grant you that sort of secret, worth billions, with billions of Sylphids around the world, is something anyone would kill to protect. Come on, James. This isn't the time to give up. Help us, we're with you all the way."

James took a deep breath and struggled to pull himself together. He felt embarrassed and completely heartbroken. Silently he prayed, "dear Lord, if there's any hope, give me the wisdom, give me the strength to save her."

He stood up and gripped Harry around the shoulder. "All right," he said at last, "thanks, guys. I've been acting the fool ever since I saw that email."

He began to pace around the room. "So she discovers the truth. Where? At BMS, most likely. The secret's out. Would she have told anyone? Did she manage to leave there? If she didn't we can only assume the worst." He clenched his fists, sheer murder in his eyes. "I'll rip Barlow apart piece by piece."

"Ring them," Harry suggested. "See what the reaction is. We'll all listen in on speaker."

James snatched up the phone, dialled the number. After a few rings a male voice answered.

"Barlow Maximum Speed. Who is this?"

"This is James. I'd like to speak to Cherry Graham, please."

"I'm sorry, Ms. Graham is on holiday."

"I'd like to speak to Annette Robertson," Harry interjected suddenly.

"Ms. Robertson is not at work today," the voice replied. "She's ill."

"I'd like to speak to Arthur Barlow then," Harry said, his face lined with worry.

"Mr. Barlow is unavailable. Would you like me to take a message?"

"No. Thank you." Harry rang off. "I'm worried about Annette. She's not sick. I went out to dinner with her last night, so I know. Suppose Cherry managed to tell her what she'd discovered. Annette's a complete Sylphid. What would she do? Damn it, she'd go straight to Barlow. I'm ringing her mobile."

Harry dialled the number. After a few rings Annette picked up. "Harry," Annette shrieked. "I mustn't talk to you. Oh Harry." Harry looked around at his mates quickly. Tony nodded.

"Annette, darling, please trust me," Harry coaxed gently. "I know something's terribly wrong. Please don't hang up." On a piece of paper he was writing 'TRACE CALL'.

James sprang up and headed for Bauman's office.

"Harry... I'm so frightened." Annette was crying now.

"Annette," Harry spoke as calmly as he could, "have you heard from Cherry?" Silence, only the sound of tears. Clearly the woman didn't want to say anything else. Harry tried more gentle encouragement. "Annette, we know Cherry's in danger. Darling, anything you can tell us will only help her. When did she speak to you?"

More tears. Harry wondered what else he could say to persuade her. Cherry must have told her not to talk to anyone. He could understand that. In the next room James and Bauman were frantically busy with the call trace.

Annette could bear it no longer. "Last night," she stammered, her voice punctuated with sobbing. "She rang just after I got home from being with you. She told me my life was in danger, told me to get out of the flat. She freaked me out, so I did. Harry, what's happening? She told me not to go back to work, said if I did I'd be... I'd be... " Annette broke down completely, sobbing into the phone. Harry's face was white.

"Annette," Harry said gently, "don't tell me where you are. You remember where we were last night? Go there, now, by cab. I'm going to send two officers, names Carlton and Brown. They will identify themselves. They'll bring you back here with me. You are in danger. Can't tell you more right now. If anyone from BMS rings you, don't answer the phone. Please trust me."

"I do trust you, Harry. Is Cherry okay? She was terrified of something."

"We don't know," Harry sounded more confident than he felt. "You've already helped to save her. Please move now, Annette. Will you do that?"

Annette said she would. Harry organised Carlton and Brown to pick her up at Doyle's Restaurant, Watson's Bay, then sat back down in his chair. Frank Bauman came in to join them a few short time later.

"I've spoken to the boss," he said, "and we've got the go-ahead to investigate carefully. Any developments are to be instantly reported to him and nobody else, and we've got very definite boundaries at present. No action at all, just collecting info, okay?"

"So she escaped," James said, relief and confusion on his face, "but it doesn't make sense. She tells Annette to get out because she's afraid of... what? That Barlow will kill her? But Annette doesn't know what Cherry discovered. What was Cherry afraid of?"

"It's obvious," Harry said, chewing the end of a pen with his eyes shut. "She was terrified the truth would get out into the public sphere, no matter who she told. What would happen then?"

"People would come and tear BMS to shreds," Tony said. "Their staff would be mincemeat. That's what she was worried about, starting a massacre. Who the devil did she tell, and why hasn't she got back to someone, Annette, us, anyone, after she told them?"

"And another thing," James added, pacing round the room. "What would you do if you were Barlow? You'd be on the next plane out of here, taking your billions with you. Only a complete fool would hang round under the circumstances. He must have known Cherry would tell someone. She's not the sort of woman to allow a hoax of that magnitude to stand." He paused, "unless he thought no one would believe her."

"Perhaps he is heading out," Tony said. "We can check airports."

"No he isn't," Harry answered quickly. "Sylph @ Sunrise went to air as usual. Think that would have happened if Barlow was on a plane?"

"So where is she?" Tony repeated. "Why hasn't she contacted Annette, anyone?"

A whole hour passed without an answer to Tony's question. James wore a track in the carpet, pacing round and round, his anxiety steadily growing. Cherry was out there somewhere. Why hadn't they heard? Was she still alive?

Finally there was a sound outside in the corridor. The door opened and Annette came into the room. She saw Harry and launched into his arms, crying her eyes out. Harry held her close, and the other men in the room pretended not to notice as he kissed her, and tried to calm her down. James, watching discretely from a distance, could see why Harry had fallen for the woman. She was stunning. Why Barlow hadn't taken advantage he couldn't imagine, but clearly Harry had won the battle for her heart. Tony brought in a tray of coffees. Annette sat down on a chair next to Harry, her arm around his shoulder, her face all red and blotchy with tears. She took a mug from Tony, and smiled a thank you.

James stopped his pacing and sat down. "Thank you for letting us pick you up, Annette," he said, trying to smile at the woman. "We've got to find Cherry, and we've got to do it soon. The chance of finding her—" He paused to gain control— "of finding her alive diminishes with time."

"You're James, aren't you?" Annette put her mug down on the floor and leaned forward in her chair. "I need to tell you something. Cherry loves you. She's loved you forever."

James stared speechless at Annette, gripping the arms of his chair, forcing himself to retain control. He could feel himself shaking, his breath coming fast.

"How can you possibly know that?" He croaked, barely in control of his voice.

"Because she told me," Annette said simply. "You need to believe it, so you'll do everything you can to find her. I love her too. I can't bear the thought of anything happening to her. I want you to know that."

She sprang up, her eyes blazing. "Now, will someone tell me just what the hell is happening? Why has the world suddenly exploded? Why is Cherry in danger? Why am I here at all? Tell me!"

"You'll find it hard to believe," Harry answered gently, standing up beside her. "Sylph's a fake. A hoax. She's run by Barlow for the purpose of making a fortune. That's what Cherry discovered. We don't know how."

Annette stared at him in confusion and disbelief. Her mouth opened and shut several times. "No," she stammered at last. "I've spoken with Sylph, she's wonderful, she's—" Her voice trailed off into silence, then after a long pause, "I can't believe it. He wouldn't. It can't be true."

"We don't expect you to believe it, Annette," Harry urged gently, "but just for now, suppose it was true. Cherry was terrified of the truth she learned. She knew if it ever became public, your life and the lives of every employee at BMS would be in danger. That's why Cherry hasn't told the police. She's afraid of the reaction, at least, we think that's why."

Annette stared at Harry as if he had lost his mind.

"It gets worse," Harry grimaced. "Barlow sent us a fake video of Cherry on the beach at Surfer's Paradise to put us off the track, so he knows she's discovered the truth. No doubt he intended to silence her once and for all, but she escaped somehow. Cherry rang you because she was afraid Barlow would assume she had fled to you for refuge."

"Arthur would never hurt me," Annette stammered. "He's always been so kind and thoughtful—"

"With billions of dollars at stake?" Harry growled. Men have killed for far less. He couldn't take the risk that you had found out the truth about Sylph because Cherry had told you, or that you knew where she had gone, and was refusing to tell him. She felt that your life was in danger, and I think she was right." Harry sighed heavily. "What we don't know is who she has told, and why she's disappeared."

Annette continued to stare at Harry, trying to comprehend the implications of his words. *No, it couldn't be true*, she thought, *but what if it was...* At least Cherry believed it, and Cherry was anything but a fool. Cherry was a Sylphid, like her.

What had ever happened to change her mind about Sylph? She'd heard those words somewhere... And suddenly she knew exactly where Cherry was.

"Cherry went to see Bartholomew," she suddenly blurted out. "And this is how I know."

"Then why is she still there?" Tony asked, after Annette had finished her convincing tale.

"Wait a minute," James said excitedly, "Cherry must have told him what she knows, that's almost certain. But he takes no action. Why? Because it's no news to him. He already knows Sylph's a hoax, and any rumours to that effect would be bad for business. He's tied up with Barlow, somewhere, but how? Tony, get me a profile on this Bartholomew character, in particular, his company connections."

Tony busied himself with his computer for a while, returned with the information.

"He's a high flyer, a really nasty piece of work," Tony informed them, shuffling papers he'd snatched off the printer. "He's on the board of directors of about a dozen companies. Loaded. Lives in a mansion at Vaucluse. We've got a huge file on him. Suspected connections with organised crime, crooked real estate deals, insider trading. Not one conviction, despite piles of evidence. Obviously owns a judge or two. What else do you want to know?"

"List of all his companies and how they're doing on the stock exchange," James said, warming to his line of thought. "Find the ones which aren't going so well."

"I can do that." Harry typed madly on his keyboard. Annette, who had sat down beside him, was very subdued and thoughtful. "Most of his stuff's doing well," Harry continued after a few minutes, "but there's one company, North Creek Uranium, shares originally traded at around three dollars, now down to fifteen cents. Hang on, I'm looking them up."

Annette stood and went over to where James was standing. "Arthur's really not a bad person, James," she said softly. "He's weird, and brilliant, and he loves making money, but I still can't believe he'd hurt Cherry. He never once took advantage of me, and I'm confiding in you, I tried to make it easy for him."

"I believe you," James nodded, "but he's also perpetrated the world's biggest hoax, and he's made billions of dollars doing it. Money makes men do dreadful things."

"I don't think you're right about Sylph," she said, quietly. "But now I'm beginning to doubt. If only Cherry would call I'd know. I'd believe her."

"Listen to this," Harry interrupted loudly, reading from his monitor screen. "North Creek Uranium applied to strip mine Indigenous land in the Northern Territory, claiming the ore was so rich the local radioactivity would harm the indigenous inhabitants. All was well until the Aboriginal Land Council got involved. Chief Minister denies their right. Shares plummet."

James thought for a while. "Tony, can you check if anyone's been buying shares in North Creek lately? A lot of shares?"

"Will do." Tony went back to his computer. "I'm checking... wow. This is certainly out of the ordinary, a company called Renford Engineering Services has recently purchased ... fifty million shares! No tie up with Barlow, though."

"Renford Engineering... Renford Engineering..." James paced the floor with his hand on his forehead, "Renford... Harry, can you bring up the footage of that ASIO raid? Some little detail I remember... that's it. Run it, please."

"Look," Annette pointed. "The sign behind their heads. But, that's just behind..."

"Barlow Maximum Speed," James said, grimly. "Remember that farmer, Bazza somebody, sung his sad song during Sylph @ Sunrise? She said nice things about him, and the share price went through the roof?

Suppose the same thing happened to North Creek. Fifty million shares at fifteen cents end trading at thirty dollars. What sort of profit does Renford make?"

"Ten billion dollars," Harry whistled quietly. "Heavens, it's astronomic. Bartholomew would kill—" He stopped himself suddenly. Annette's face had gone very white, James had stopped pacing, Tony had frozen at the keyboard. "Bloody idiot," he muttered under his breath.

James took a deep breath. "Yes, she's probably dead. That's why she hasn't come back. Bartholomew couldn't take the risk with that sort of money."

"No!" Annette broke down and sobbed. "She's not, she's not, she's not!"

Harry stood up and put his arm around her shoulders. No one else moved.

James took another deep breath. "I'm still following your original advice, Harry, so you better stick with me. Tony, give me the names of the other North Creek company directors."

Tony wrenched his mind back to the job, his hands not entirely steady. Cherry was dead, she had to be. A short time later he grunted, and hit the 'print' key.

"Names and faces," he said grimly. "In the States, Craig Simmons. Here, Bartholomew and a cove called Denman. Lives in Paddington."

James moved to his computer, searched for a number, picked up the phone and dialled.

"Hello, Channel Twelve? This is detective James Naylor, police tactical operations. I need to speak to the producer of Sylph @ Sunrise, and its urgent. Thank you. Hello? Yes? I need a list of all the people booked into the audience of the show, and I need it now. You can? Here's the email address."

A few minutes later a list of names rolled off the printer. Tony distributed them amongst the others.

Annette bounced out of her chair. "There," she said, bending the sheet alongside a name. "John Denman, three days from now."

"I'm ringing Dad." James picked up the phone again.

Robin Naylor listened carefully to his son's revelation. Privately he thought it nearly certain that Cherry was dead, but he wasn't going to give voice to his thoughts.

"Thanks, son," he spoke slowly, carefully. "I don't have to tell you how incredibly delicate this is. No one must get a whiff of the truth. The public mightn't believe it, but Bartholomew would think our Cherry had betrayed him, and she'd be killed straightaway. Now put Bauman on the phone. I'm going to authorise surveillance of Bartholomew's property, and Denman's too. Don't lose your head. I want your word on it. Don't go beyond surveillance unless you've got proof she's being held there, understand?"

James mumbled something and handed the phone to Bauman. Robin spent a few minutes talking to him, put the phone down and thought for a long while. Finally he called his personal assistant into the office. "Dianne, get me Brian Hill on a secure line, please."

The call came through only seconds later. Brian's voice answered. "Hello, Robin. Trouble, isn't there, or you wouldn't be using our hotline."

"Serious trouble," Robin answered grimly. "We're staring down the barrel of something really nasty. Sylph is a fake. Somehow Cherry Graham, her Avatar, found out. I suspect she's already been murdered, but if she's still alive we're going to need some very special help, and we're going to need if awfully fast. Operation Long-shot, we'll call it. Now I'll fill you in and we can plan this thing, but first, can you pick up a woman called Annette Robertson, currently at Tactical, and take her ... "

It was a long conversation.

CHAPTER 40

The unmarked van drew up a distance down the street from Denman's home, a restored townhouse in Paddington. Five men, dressed as council workers, stepped out of the back and began placing red witch's hats along the side of the kerb, cordoning off a small area. A concrete saw was lowered from the van, and one of the five began to cut a groove in the bitumen not far from the kerb itself. Apparently it was a tiring process, because after a foot or so he stopped, left the machine where it was, and clambered back into the van. By this time the others had disappeared. James and Harry went round the back of Denman's property, Tony and George went up the short path and knocked on the front door. No response.

"No one at home," Tony spoke into his comms device. You getting this, James, Neil?"

"Click, click." Both acknowledged.

James peered in through the glass in the back door.

Harry did a fast reconnoitre around the side and returned. "All curtained. Bang on the back door and scream police raid."

James did, silence from within.

"Out with the tools," James said quietly. "You copy, Neil? This is off the record."

"Got it." Neil grinned to himself in the back of the van.

It took Harry only seconds to open the back door. James raced quickly down the hall, his firearm drawn, opening one door after another. Harry followed his progress, opening all the doors on the other side. Harry pointed to the stairs, and James shot up them like a ferret. More bedrooms, nothing. There was a third storey to the house, an attic. Nothing. They went back into the kitchen and opened every large cupboard. The laundry, basement, wine cellar received the same treatment. Finally Harry and James left by the back door, re-joined the other council workers who were loading the cutter back into the van. Shutting the rear door, they drove off to Vaucluse.

"This isn't going to be so easy," Harry said as the van drove slowly past Bartholomew's mansion. "We park up the street, do our thing, and I saunter past, see what I can see."

"Better move it," James muttered. "There's not too many hours of daylight left."

Harry disappeared without saying another word. Ten minutes later he joined the other workers, busily cutting another small groove in smooth concrete road surface near the kerb.

"Bad news," Harry shook his head. "Place is humming with Bartholomew's own security thugs. Two on the front door, two on the front gate. One of them saw me loitering slowly past and told me to move on or he'd call the police." He chuckled. "That's not all. I caught a glimpse of cameras on posts around the yard. The flaming place is tighter than Fort Knox."

"What do we do?" James said miserably. "She wasn't at Denman's, and this is the last hope. He shrugged. "She could be anywhere, probably at the bottom of the ocean by now."

"Come on, James," Harry encouraged.

"Preserve a little optimism please. I've got an idea, but we'll have to go back to my place first, and return after dark. Might work, at least we can have a damn good try. We can stick a camera on that power pole opposite the gate to monitor activity at the front. I'll get Neil to put a power company logo on the van."

The van drove away.

✳ ✳ ✳

Cherry stood to her feet and massaged her painful thigh. Her head was spinning, her thigh aching where it had hit the concrete when she had been thrown down. In the perpetual oppressive darkness she had lost all sense of time. Crawling her hands along the walls, she had discovered the door and kicked it again and again in her anger until her feet hurt.

Now anger had long given place to fear. The cold darkness reached into her heart like an evil presence, quelling all hope of reprieve or rescue. She had been offered neither bed nor blanket, water or food. Now she was frozen, sore and hungry. She walked around her cell for the thousandth time, recognising the door by its touch and the corner in which she had relieved herself by its smell.

They were going to kill her, she knew. Why? Because the truth about Sylph would ruin Bartholomew in some way. Some deal with Barlow had gone down the afternoon they met, a deal so large they would kill without a second thought to ensure its success. She clasped her arms tightly around her chest, trying to stop herself shivering. How would they kill her? She felt ill again, terrified.

Slowly the terror of being murdered was replaced by an even darker thought. She had come to the end of her life. Who would morn? Annette, perhaps for a little while, then she would be utterly forgotten. Did existence simply end with the knife driven deep by a demon indifferent to the agony it was inflicting? Or did it summon your soul unprepared and unwilling into the courts of divine judgement? Throughout her life any mention of God always triggered a terrible headache, a nameless pain which arose from a forgotten past, lost forever. So she had lashed out at any mention of Him, unable and unwilling to explain why she did so. Now the thought of actually meeting Him filled her heart with dread.

James, dearest James. Tears trickled down her face. Now he would never know how much she loved him. It was for the best. He would never miss what she had been incapable of expressing. Her heart burned with painful regret. Her fiery, defiant spirit lay in ashes on the floor. There was no hope.

The darkness suddenly dissolved into blinding light. Cherry covered her eyes with her arms, her heart beating furiously. The end had come. The door opened fully. Hobbs was standing there, and behind him, carrying a gun in his hand, was Bartholomew. Hobbs stood aside.

"I'm sorry for the inconvenience," Bartholomew said chillingly, "but I must ask you to accompany us. I've been talking to my associates, and they are both in agreement."

"What are you talking about?" Cherry stammered, her voice reflecting the dread in her heart. "How dare you imprison me. You can't keep me here, and you know it."

"I do my dear, and that's exactly why we must proceed." Bartholomew's voice sent horror cascading down Cherry's spine. "Please follow Hobbs. Remember I am holding a weapon, and please believe me I am quite prepared to use it."

Clutching herself around the chest with her own arms, she followed Hobbs up the large winding staircase as one heading for the gallows. Past the first floor they travelled, up to the top of the house. Hobbs turned right along the corridor and opened a door near the stairs.

"Please go in," Bartholomew ordered, "and stand in the bath."

"No!" Cherry stopped dead in her tracks.

The cold muzzle of a pistol pressed into her back, pushing her forward. She could feel it shaking slightly, not from fear but from the Parkinson's disease.

Dreading every step she slowly walked into the bathroom, and turned round to face her executioners.

"Please," she begged loudly in terror. "Don't do it. I don't want to die. I'm not ready. Please have mercy."

"Get in the bath," Bartholomew motioned with his gun. "Or I'll tell Hobbs to break your neck. I think this is so much better."

Nearly passing out with fright, Cherry stepped into the bath.

"Face me," Bartholomew commanded from the doorway. "Hands by your sides. That's right. Sorry for the short acquaintance."

Cherry saw the smoke belch from the gun, and felt a terrible pain in her chest. She glanced down at the blood spreading all over her top, and collapsed unconscious into the bath.

"Do you think I've killed her, Hobbs?" Bartholomew moved closer to his victim. "It's this blasted Parkinson's."

Hobbs went over to the bath, grabbed one of Cherry's arms around the wrist. He felt a shallow pulse, and carelessly flung it back.

"No, sir, she's still alive," he said, "but losing blood fast. If you came right over, pressed the gun into her breast, and fired a couple off, she'd go straight away."

Bartholomew was shocked.

"Hobbs, perhaps you don't realise that bath is hand chiselled Italian marble. The bullet would be sure to make a mark, and I'd never forgive myself. Besides, I'd be covered in her wretched blood. Anyway, by the time Jacques gets here to cut the body up she'll have bled all that mess down the drain. Make the job easier for him, won't it, like a carcass that's been hung up."

"I've no doubt it will," Hobbs agreed matter-of-factly, "but I think just one more shot would be advised. I can do it for you if you would prefer."

"And risk the bath?" Bartholomew snorted. "Unpleasant enough without incurring property damage. You can wash blood off, Hobbs, you can't wash off bullet impacts. Somebody might get wise." He turned to leave the room. "No, this way is best. Leave her. Jacques will be here in an hour or so with his little crate. I'm always amazed at how small a space a dismembered body occupies. The sharks will be grateful for the meal. We haven't fed them for quite a while as I recall."

He paused in thought. "Must ring Barlow, tell him to send another video. Can't have anyone searching for her, can we? Then she'll just disappear. So unfortunate. It will remind him that we mean business, too, discourage anything foolish. A good move all round, I think."

With those dispassionate sentiments they both left the room and turned out the light.

CHAPTER 41

O ut in the street it had grown completely dark. The street lamp on the pole opposite Bartholomew's steel gates had been deliberately disabled by a laser pulse which had melted a hole in its glass envelope. The van with its large Electricity Commission logo on the side, had parked directly under the failed light. A small hoist, mounted on the roof, rose upwards carrying a technician. Just below the damaged light it stopped, and the technician attached a small device to the pole. He lowered the hoist and climbed down a ladder on the side of the van. Opening the back door he disappeared inside. The van drove away, and parked further down the street out of sight of the gates.

"All good," Harry said. "Now for the fun stuff." He lifted a peculiar looking device out of a large box on the floor. It was square in shape, a flat sided box in the middle, with four arms stretching out at right angles, one from each corner. On the end of each arm was a motor with a propeller attached. Anything less like an aircraft would be difficult to imagine, but that's exactly what it was. Harry began attaching a camera underneath the square box with small elastic straps.

"We've got half an hour on the batteries," he said, "then we've got to pull her back and replace the pack. I've got several spares. I suggest we fly over the grounds first and see if we can find anything interesting, then go round checking for open windows. Not only can we peek in, we can fly in if we have to."

"I hope you're as good a pilot as you say you are," James grimaced. "I'm telling you, the first suspicious thing, and I'm through that front door."

"More likely lying dead on the front lawn," Tony grunted as he positioned the control unit on the table next to the two video screens. "Look at the view we're getting from the camera across the street. Bartholomew's security thugs are crawling all over. Something pretty bad must be going on inside that house."

"Won't they hear your gadget flying around?" James asked.

"It's pretty quiet," Harry said, "especially if you fly it slowly. Besides, unless they're lucky to spot it, they'll never know what it is even if they do hear something." He nodded towards Tony. "Camera is operational. I'm taking this outside now."

Harry opened the back of the van, placed the quadcopter carefully on the pavement, and came back inside. He grabbed hold of the controls. "Everybody shut up for a bit," he said. "I've got to get the feel of her with the camera on. Let me manoeuvre her over the yard first."

Outside they could hear a soft whirring noise. The camera on the quadcopter began sending back pictures. They were gaining altitude. Now they were moving over one backyard, then another, nearing Bartholomew's house, over his backyard. Harry, his face grim with concentration, brought the machine lower until they were no more than ten metres high. Grunting with satisfaction, he skilfully flew the machine around the yard, over the heads of the security guards. Only one glanced skyward, then returned his attention to the grounds.

"See?" Harry grinned, never taking his eyes off the screen. "Now let's have a little peak through some of those windows."

They flew up closer to the house. Tony adjusted the telephoto lens on the camera. The quadcopter was remarkably stable. Harry flew from one window to another. The curtains on the front ones were drawn shut. On the side they were open, but nothing unusual was inside. Harry brought the machine around the back with the same result, then along the last remaining side of the house. Nothing they saw gave them a clue as to Cherry's whereabouts. Harry pulled back and gained altitude.

"Have to pull her back soon," he said. "I'll change the batteries, then we can fly through one of those open windows and check the inside. Hello, someone's arriving. Let's go down for a look-see."

The quadcopter lost altitude rapidly, as Harry manoeuvred as close as he could to the front door. A man came out of the house, and joined the stranger who had just arrived. Together they lifted a squarish crate out of the back of the van which had pulled up outside the front door. James didn't like the look of that crate. He gritted his teeth, using all his self-control to stay in the van and watch. Tony saw the look on his face and readied himself. He didn't like the look of that crate either.

"Pulling back," Harry grunted. "Only ten minutes to go."

They watched as the crate disappeared inside the front door. Harry gained altitude and began to circle the house prior to bringing the machine back.

"See that?" Harry pointed at the screen with his head.

A light had come on in a small window near the top of the house at the back. Harry dived the quadcopter towards the light, coming low, until he was below the height of the window. He closed in, slowly drawing level with the window ledge. The top of a shower screen came into view. Now they could see the taps, the towel rail, the top of the bath.

Three men gave a horrified gasp. The bath was occupied, not by some naked figure bathing but with Cherry's body, her face deathly white, her eyes closed, her skirt, and the entire bottom of the bath awash with blood. One arm was draped over the edge as if her body had been carelessly thrown there, the other, covered in blood, was lying by her side. She was utterly still, no flicker in the eyelids, no movement of her limbs. Dead.

James felt suddenly paralysed, his mind numb, unable to speak, his whole life imploding before his eyes. The woman he loved was dead.

They were too damn late. Before his horrified eyes he saw the men carrying the crate enter the bathroom.

James had seen enough. Drawing his firearm, he wrenched open the back of the van and raced towards the iron gates a little further down the road.

"Wait!" Harry bellowed. "Wait! Ah, damn it, Tony!" But Tony was already out of the van and pelting after James, his gun drawn.

With one hand Harry flew the quadcopter over the house and lost altitude towards the gate. With the other, he leaned over and pressed a button on the comms console to his right.

"Backup," he yelled. "Now!" CC's dead. Body in top bathroom, about to be dismembered. For God's sake hurry."

He turned his attention back to the screens. From the camera on the pole he could see James had reached the gates, running like a madman. He was taking fire from one of the thugs. Now he was rolling on the ground. Was he hit? No, the thug had gone down. James was up and pelting across the front lawn. Tony had reached the gates. Harry moved the quadcopter closer to the front door. As he watched it opened, and two more thugs came out. They saw James instantly, drew their weapons and took careful aim. Harry throttled the engines of the quadcopter to maximum, and dived the machine towards them, his heart racing. The first thug turned round to see where the noise was coming from just before the quadcopter tore into his face. It bounced off and ripped into the face of the other. Harry sprang out of the van and belted through the front gate as Tony downed his last man. Together they raced towards the front door.

James had reached the two men near the door immediately after Harry's quadcopter had done its work. Two quick blows with the butt of his gun, and they were lying on the stonework. Behind him all was quiet. He wrenched the door open and pelted silently up the stairs, one floor, then two. The bathroom was on the right at the top.

❈ ❈ ❈

"That was gunfire," Jacques said nervously, taking the lid off the crate. "I'm sure it was. Perhaps we should postpone this disposal until a later time."

"I hear nothing," Bartholomew said impatiently. "The house is surrounded by my own men. If there was anything wrong, one of them would have let me know."

"I heard something too," Hobbs said evenly. "There are a lot of wealthy Asian residents around here, always letting off fireworks to celebrate something. All our security staff have silenced weapons, and the chances of an attack on this house are remote in the extreme."

"I don't like it," Jacques said nervously. "As soon as I start cutting there will be mess everywhere. So much more difficult to hide if you have unfriendly visitors."

"I never have unfriendly visitors," Bartholomew snapped. "All my unfriendly visitors are fish food, as well you know." He sighed heavily, "Hobbs, Mr. Jacques is unnecessarily agitated this evening. Would you be kind enough to take this weapon and prepare to fire at anyone who comes through that door? Not that they're going to."

"Of course, sir." He held out his hand and took the gun from Bartholomew, holding it behind his back.

"Now perhaps we can continue," Bartholomew said, turning to Jacques.

Jacques picked up the saw, went over to Cherry's body and pulled up her arm with his other hand.

"Stop!" James bellowed from the doorway, pointing his weapon directly at Jacques. "Put down the saw!" He stepped into the bathroom, his eyes fixed on Cherry's body.

Hobbs whipped the gun from behind his back and shot James twice in the stomach. He flew backwards and fell onto the tiles.

"You fool!" Jacques screamed at him. "You've shot a police officer! That *was* gunfire I heard! I'm out of here. You can—"

There was a noise from the hallway. Hobbs raised the gun again, and fell dead with two bullets in his chest.

Harry stepped into the room.

"Just one of you make a move," he snarled, "and you get it." He turned towards Bartholomew who had gone very pale. "That includes old bastards like you. Not a muscle. Twitch and you're dead. I'd love an excuse. Get it?"

It was obvious from their faces that they got it indeed.

Just then Tony rushed through the door, followed by Bauman. They stared at the contents of the bath and James lying unconscious on the floor.

"Shit," Bauman swore, shaking his head. "Naylor's going to have my guts." He kept shaking his head and swearing under his breath.

Other men were in the room now, handcuffing Bartholomew and Jacques, taking them away. Harry knelt beside his friend.

"Help's on the way," he said, fighting to keep his voice level. "Please hold on, old mate. For God's sake, hold on."

It seemed an age before the paramedics arrived. Harry could hear a chopper coming down on Bartholomew's helipad. Two paramedics raced to James' side and began to administer aid. A third paramedic knelt down beside Cherry's body. In the middle of all this Robin Naylor strode into the room, took one look at his son and almost wept.

"How is he?" He said to the two paramedics.

One of them stood to his feet. "Not good, sir. If we can get him into surgery fast I'd say he's got a chance."

"My chopper's on the pad out the back," Robin said. "Hurry. Just tell the pilot where you want him to go."

The two paramedics lifted James carefully onto a stretcher, and took him to the waiting aircraft. Robin came slowly over to the bath and the third paramedic.

He shook his head, and for a while couldn't speak at all. "I'm so, so sorry, Cherry," he said at last, emotion surging through his voice. "Such a sad life, now to end like this. I tell you, someone's going to pay dearly for today, if my name's Robin Naylor."

The paramedic beside the bath stood. "Sir, I think you may be a little premature about the end and all that."

"What do you mean?" Robin barked.

"Well, sir," he answered, "she's taken a bullet near her shoulder. I don't even think it's broken a bone, but it's certainly ruptured an artery. She's nearly on the point of bleeding out. Hardly breathing. Can't understand why she didn't come to consciousness before, but it's a mercy she didn't with these butchers around. Your son's a lot worse than she is, I'm afraid sir."

Robin stared at him as if he hadn't heard. "You mean she's still alive?" He asked, his voice reflecting the incredulity he felt.

"Yes, sir. There's another bag of fluid coming up in a tic, then a stretcher—"

"Are we in time to stabilise her?" Robin asked urgently. "Is she going to live, or are we too damn late?"

"She stands a good chance I think, sir," the paramedic answered. "We'll give her plasma immediately to increase her blood volume. That will buy her a little more time, but she still needs surgery and a blood transfusion pretty damn quick."

"No problem." Robin walked to the other side of the bathroom, drew out his phone, and speed dialled a number. "Operation Long-shot is active," he said sharply. "We need that surgical team standing by at the hospital, full security. Any delay is fatal. Fatal, understand? I need an emergency airlift from Bartholomew's helipad. Now! Not in five minutes. Move it."

He put the phone in his pocket. The paramedic was inserting a cannula needle into the back of Cherry's hand, connecting it to the bag of plasma. Another man raced into the room with a stretcher.

"There's another chopper coming," Robin said, his face still grim. "Get her on board the instant it lands. Oh, by the way, I'm going to ask you both to lie through your teeth on every report. This young woman was dead when you arrived. If you can't do that I'll have to detain you for an indefinite period in the interests of national security."

The helicopter landed just after the other one had taken off, and Cherry was bundled into the machine. Soon she would have the best medical care on the planet. There was nobody left in the room. Robin sighed, scanned the blood spattered bath, the blood all over the tiled floor.

He covered his face with his hands. "Lord, have mercy on my son," he prayed softly. "Have mercy on the little one. You've given us a chance. Thank you. Help us not to make a mess of it."

He rose to his feet and walked steadily out of the room and down the stairs to join Bauman. Ruth would have to know what had happened to James, and he dreaded telling her.

CHAPTER 42

Cherry came to consciousness for the first time early the following morning. She didn't expect to. Her first thought was to keep her eyes shut tight. If she opened them she would see the blood again and pass out into a dark eternity. She felt different, warm. Why was she warm? The bath was cold, so cold. She moved her head against the pillow. Pillow?! Her eyes flew open to confirm the truth. She lay there, her heart beating furiously. Some incredible miracle had occurred, or else she was hallucinating. She lifted her left arm. There was a cannula needle sticking out of her hand, attached to a bag of blood. She turned her head. Miracle of miracles, Annette was sleeping in a chair beside her bed. Tears of sheer disbelief trickled down her cheeks.

"Annette." Her voice was soft, but Annette woke up instantly. She took one look at Cherry, jumped out of the chair and buried her head in Cherry's neck, crying her heart out. Cherry hugged her with her right arm, because her left shoulder hurt.

"Annette," Cherry stammered through her tears. "I'm alive... and you're here... I can't believe you're here... Oh, Annette!"

It was a while before either woman was capable of further speech. Eventually Annette stood up, still holding Cherry's hand, and wiped the tears away from her face with the other.

"I thought you were dead," she choked. "No one would say anything, then the chopper landed. Apparently they took you to Westmead hospital for emergency surgery under really tight security, then brought you here. I've been with you since then. Wouldn't leave."

"Where am I?" Cherry squeezed Annette's hand, still struggling to come to terms with her continuing existence. "Why are you here? I left you heading for a motel in Miranda. Then I was dying in a bath. What happened?"

"Here is an ASIO safe house," Annette replied. She sat down on the bed next to Cherry. "And why I came here, I'm not sure, but Harry was definitely involved." She smiled proudly.

Breakfast arrived before the tale could be told. The food was certainly better than the usual hospital affair, steak and eggs with excellent coffee to finish. Annette insisted in slicing Cherry's meat into bite sized portions and feeding her like a child, encouraging her until she had finished.

After they had eaten, Cherry lay back on her pillows, and reached out for Annette's hand. "They put me in a dark cellar," she said, closing her eyes to sharpen the memory. "There wasn't anything to lie on, and they didn't feed me or give me anything to drink."

"Bastards," Annette exclaimed, squeezing her hand. "Cherub, are you sure you want to do this right now?"

"I knew I was going to die," Cherry went on. "It's funny. First I was just plain terrified. I wanted to throw up. I started to shake all over, then it stopped. I suppose I'd resigned myself. Then I began to think about my life, what I'd done. It's strange, the clarity it gives you, facing death."

"You've done heaps and heaps," Annette said, squeezing her hand again. "Put hundreds of horrible people where they belong."

"Yes, I did," Cherry answered, shutting her eyes again. "It was my hatred, Annette. I used it like a weapon. It was the fire that drove me, day and night. It drove me like a whip across my back. I'd only sleep when I was too tired to see my keyboard clearly." A tear trickled down her face. "But there was another victim of the fire, Annette. Me."

She stopped for a little while, her eyes shut tight. "It gutted me like a fisherman's knife. I couldn't feel, couldn't love. I knew I would always be alone, and I took pride in it. I didn't need anyone. I could stand by myself, I always had, always would."

She took a deep breath. "When Sylph came I thought I'd found a higher calling, something to fill the vacuum in my life. I gave her everything. I rejected God and worshipped Sylph instead. The ultimate irony. I offered my whole life to a dirty lie."

She put her right hand over her trembling mouth, fighting to restore control. "They made me stand in a bath, then Bartholomew shot me. They left me to bleed to death. I woke up sometime later in terrible pain. I knew I had to get away or I'd die. Then I looked down and saw all the blood. Passed out. Next time I woke up I was too weak to move. I kept my eyes shut for as long as I could. But I looked. I passed out. It was hell, Annette."

She started to cry softly. Annette gently wrapped her arms around Cherry's shoulders, her mind recoiling in horror.

Cherry went on. "I was dying, Annette, I was dying all alone, helpless, without God, without hope. I knew the next time I woke up might be the last. I saw this picture of my funeral. You were the only one there. I'd lived alone, I'd die alone. I suddenly decided if by some miracle I lived to see tomorrow, I'd never want to be alone again. I'm sick of hatred. Somehow I have to find forgiveness, and I don't know what to do."

"No," Annette replied in a shaken voice. "There'd be heaps of people at your funeral. Harry would be there, Tony would be there. We'd all be bawling our eyes out."

"Three people then. What a crowd."

"And James would be there." She squeezed Cherry's hand again.

"No," Cherry gave a sob. "I threw him away and he's gone forever."

"No he hasn't," Annette encouraged, squeezing Cherry's hand reassuringly. "I can tell when a man's in love. James was fair out of his mind when you disappeared. I know, I was there."

Cherry opened her eyes wide. "You... spoke to James?"

"Yes, and what's more he knows that you love him."

Cherry stared at her, eyes like saucers. "How?"

"I told him," Annette said with a smile, "and he believed me. So you see, there's four of us at your funeral. Perhaps your life hasn't been quite as wasted as you think."

Just then Robin Naylor came into the room with another man. He strode up to Cherry's bed, took hold of her hand gently, then bent down and kissed her on top of her head. "It's so good to see you, Cherry," he said softly. "We've all been terribly worried."

"Mr. Naylor," Cherry smiled. "I think I owe you my life."

"Not me," Robin replied grimly, "but that's a story for tomorrow." He turned to the gentleman who had accompanied him into the room. "This is Brian Hill, director of ASIO, whose hospitality you've been enjoying, or at least Annette has."

Cherry offered her hand to Brian who took it gently in his own. "You are our saving grace, young lady," he said, slowly shaking his head. "I'm afraid we are going to ask you to do something rather difficult considering your state of health, but I've been told by my friend Robin that you are an incredibly courageous woman."

"What do you want me to do?" Cherry asked, self-consciously running her right hand through her hair. "I'm sorry, I feel such a mess."

"Question first," Robin interrupted, his voice serious. "Can you find a way of locking Barlow out of his machines?"

Cherry shook her head. "No. I can get into machines three and four from anywhere, but machines one and two need a top level password, and the wretched thing's so long even Arthur can't remember it."

"Is this it?" Robin took a photocopied sheet out of his pocket and handed it to Cherry, who stared at it wide eyed.

"How did you get this?" She asked. "He keeps it in his… Oh, that's how."

"You'll be happy to know he's got it back," Robin grinned. "A helpful pedestrian told him she found it on the footpath outside BMS. He was so happy when she turned it in, he gave her a hundred dollars."

"Are we talking about Arthur's wallet?" Annette interrupted, an edge to her voice. "How did you get it?"

Cherry reached out for Annette's hand. "It was when I discovered the horrible truth about Sylph. He tried to grab me without his pants on. It was really awful, but I managed to get away."

"Can we do this another time?" Brian interrupted, deliberately ignoring the horrified expression on Annette's face.

"Of course," Cherry said. She gave Annette's hand a squeeze. "I'll explain all later, then you'll understand why I changed my mind about Sylph."

"So with this password you can lock Barlow out of his machines?" Brian asked, his face very serious.

"Oh, I can do heaps more than that," Cherry smiled back.

CHAPTER 43

Arthur Barlow lay on his bed and stared up into the darkened ceiling. Only twenty four hours and his life had pretty much dived straight into the toilet. First that terrible call from Bartholomew telling him Cherry was dead. He had sworn long and loud, cursing him with every foul word he knew. He could still hear the swine's cold voice echoing in his ears.

"You had better be careful, Barlow. One false move and I tell the world Sylph's a hoax. They'll come and tear you apart. My men will be in the front of the crowd, and I assure you they are most efficient."

With that, Bartholomew had hung up, leaving him shaking with fright. Cherry was dead. He was fond of her, respected her enormously, and now he had killed her. What a shit of a man he had turned out to be. Then there was Annette, where was she? Her absence played on his mind like a recurring nightmare. He had rung Bartholomew and told him if he so much as laid a finger on Annette he would personally send him and his bloody company directly to hell by the shortest route.

"By dear boy," Bartholomew purred odiously, "we're searching for her too. Can't seem to locate her anywhere. Just trying to make sure she's safe."

Surprisingly he had found some comfort in Bartholomew's lies. Of course the swine was searching for her, because he imagined Cherry might have told her the truth about Sylph. The fact that he couldn't find her meant

346

she was safe somewhere. Cherry must have warned her somehow. Now Cherry, the girl who had saved Annette's life, was dead. She was dead because of him. Because of him. How he despised the addiction which had cost Cherry her life. He threw his head from side to side on the pillow in torment. He was a billionaire, but he would willingly have given every cent to have turned back time.

There was a knock on the wardrobe door.

"Go away!" he shouted, pulling the pillow over his head. "Do it yourself. I'm tired. I'm busy. I'm going to sleep."

Another knock, then Viktor's worried voice. "Arthur, something's happened. The special Sylph @ Sunrise is tomorrow, and we can't log on to anything."

Arthur tumbled out of bed with an oath. Life had crumbled into a constantly worsening nightmare. He turned on the light, dragged on some trousers and staggered across to the wardrobe, flinging the doors open. Viktor stood there amongst the clothes, an anxious picture of misery.

"What's the problem?" Arthur barked. "Can't you fix the damn thing by yourselves now?"

"Why don't you come and see before you deprecate the faithful?" Viktor snapped back.

Arthur followed Viktor down the tunnel, muttering deprecations all the way under his breath. They arrived at the other end, came up the stairs and through the open door. Paul and five others were there, staring at their monitor screens as if hypnotised. On each, in very large letters were the words:

DON'T INTERUPT. I AM DEFINING MYSELF. PLEASE BE PATIENT.

"What's all this?" Arthur growled, staring at the screens. "Some sort of sick joke?"

"We don't know what it is," Paul groaned, rising from his chair. "The machine seems to have developed a mind of its own."

"We'll see about that," Arthur snorted. He dragged his wallet out of his pocket. "No flaming machine takes control of itself. I'm the one with the control."

He unfolded the small sheet of paper, hit 'F7', 'Shift', 'Delete' together, and typed in the long, long string of hexadecimal numbers. The screen went blank, and there was a 'beep' from the speaker.

"Told you," Arthur smiled. "No machine—"

Another message appeared on the monitor.

I'VE TOLD YOU, ARTHUR, BE PATIENT. I'M BUSY, GO AWAY!

Arthur stared at the screen in disbelief, stared and stared.

"It's not possible… it's not *possible*…" He shook his head from side to side, trying to come to grips with the evidence of his eyes. "That's the ultimate top level password. It can't be overridden. I've written the code."

He hit 'F7', 'Shift', 'Delete', together again and retyped the long string. Once more the screen cleared, the speaker beeped.

"Thank heaven," Arthur sighed, leaning back in his chair. "No idea what happened the last—"

Another message appeared on the screen.

RIGHT, THAT DOES IT! TOLD YOU NOT TO TROUBLE ME, ARTHUR. NOW I'M REALLY ANNOYED. NOT TALKING TO YOU ANYMORE.

The screen went completely blank. All the screens went blank.

Arthur put his hands on the sides of his head and screamed. "Aaargh!"

"What were you saying about no machine taking control from you?" Paul stammered, his face ashen. "What have you done? If we can't start the animation software by tomorrow we're screwed. Bartholomew won't believe us. He'll just come and whack us all. Burn the building over our heads. Cut out livers out for fun." He ran his hands through his hair. "Do something," he demanded. "Go on, do something."

Arthur stared at the blank screens. He noticed the webcam on the console he was sitting at had come on. Why had that happened?

✳ ✳ ✳

The special communications room in the ASIO safe house had been updated with the latest computer equipment. Fast optic internet lines had been installed. Brian had been very busy indeed. Only three people were in the room right then. Cherry was sitting down, her left arm in a sling, her right hand typing on the keyboard. Annette was standing behind, and Brian Hill next to her. A picture of Arthur, beside himself with worry, and Paul, scared stiff, appeared on the screen.

"Now that's something you don't often see," Cherry laughed. "Gives you a happy feeling inside, doesn't it?"

"Sure does," Annette agreed with enthusiasm, her mind recalling Cherry's last encounter with the man she had once desired. "Is there anything else you can do to make his evening a little brighter? Like set something on fire?"

"Better," Cherry laughed triumphantly. "Let them try to get back into any machine. Let them try all night, then the coup de grace. I'm so going to enjoy it."

CHAPTER 44

Try all night they did, to absolutely no avail. The sun rose in the sky the next morning, but the desperate men inside Renford Engineering didn't see it. Paul had brought the morning team in about two a.m. so they could bring their combined expertise to bear on the problem.

It wasn't enough.

No matter what they did they couldn't log on to any machine. The screens remained totally blank, the keyboards unresponsive to any command. Arthur was slumped in a chair at the back of the room, his whole life passing before his eyes. The only explanation was an impossible one. The machine had become self-aware, had spontaneously done the very thing he had pretended to the world.

"It's not possible, it's not possible." He kept muttering to himself, over and over again. He was the world's best programmer, a genius. He had built a machine to die for, written every line of code in its kernel. Now that same kernel had locked him out. It couldn't happen. But it had.

"Two minutes to Sylph @ Sunrise," Viktor stammered loudly, half terrified. "Better get ready to skedaddle. Bartholomew will be here with flame throwers." He glanced towards the screens. "Oh, shit!" he screamed in fright. "What now?"

Every screen had burst into life with the "Sylph @ Sunrise" logo. Arthur fell out of his chair and landed on the floor, his eyes staring incredulously at the images.

"That can't happen," he screamed. "It can't happen! We've been drugged, it's not real." He staggered to his feet, ran over to the nearest monitor and began to run his hands all over it, press his face against it. "It's a nightmare," he shouted. "It feels so real. I'm having a nightmare!"

"For goodness sake shut up," Paul yelled loudly. "It's a bloody nightmare, all right, but it's happening. What's next?"

The Sylph @ Sunrise introduction theme sounded from the speakers. The hosts of the show, Alice and Tony, walked in and took their places. The huge screen at the side burst into life with Sylph sitting on her usual red chair beside a vase of fresh peonies.

Arthur made a choking sound. "It's happened. She's real. The machine's become self-aware. Sylph is real. I'm going insane."

Ten men stared at the screen, disbelieving the image their eyes were sending them. Viktor had collapsed on the floor. Paul felt for the arms of his chair and clung to them like a man on a life raft. Sylph's voice echoed through the room.

"Good morning Alice, Tony. Good morning everyone."

"Good morning, Sylph," the hosts replied. "Good morning Sylph," shouted the studio audience.

"Now who will be the first to ask a question this morning?" Alice beamed at the audience. "The young lady on the third row with her hand up. Yes, stand up and go ahead."

A young teenage girl with fluffy peroxide blonde hair, pink glasses, pink lipstick, pink dress and pink handbag to match stood to her feet and giggled. "Hello, Sylph. My name's Shari."

"Hello, Shari," Sylph smiled, "and how can I help you this morning?"

"It's not happening," Arthur moaned, staring horrified at the screens. "I tell you, it's not happening. She's self-aware. The machine's become self-aware." He began to shout. "This is momentous. It's stupendous!"

"It's impossible," Paul growled, sweat pouring down his face. "I don't believe it. It can't be true." He paused. "Can it?"

Shari giggled. "I've got boyfriend trouble. Russell is so cool, but I think he's been unfaithful. How can I make myself sexier so he won't go doing it with other girls while he's supposed to be with me?"

"Why don't you go back to school?" Sylph replied.

"Get rid of that ridiculous haircut, wash that stupid pink makeup off your face, and try to fill your mind with something worthwhile. Right now, if anyone looked inside your head all they'd find is a rolled up copy of some trashy magazine."

Shari stared at Sylph as if she hadn't heard. The studio audience had gone very quiet.

"And while you're at it," Sylph continued, smiling, "give me this Russell's full name so I can report him for having sex with a minor. That's a felony in this country. See, your problems are over. Soon he'll be in jail and he won't be unfaithful anymore."

Shari flopped back into her seat and slunk down low so the camera couldn't see her face. Other hands went up. Tony picked an older man on the other side of the room.

"My name's John Denman," he said, sadly. "I wonder if you could help me, Sylph."

"Here it comes," Paul shouted. "It's going to be all right after all."

"All right?" Arthur screamed hysterically. "All right? She's become self-aware, we've lost control, and it's going to be all right? Are you out of your tiny mind?"
He sank back into his chair and clasped his hands around his head, shaking it from side to side.
"What can I do to help you, John?" Sylph said, smiling sweetly. "Please, I can see you come with a heavy heart. Let me assist you if I can."

"I'm sure you can," Denman sighed. "You see, it's like this. I'm a mining engineer. I went up to the Northern Territory some time last year because I'd heard reports. Some of our wonderful Indigenous people had become sick from a disease the doctors didn't know how to treat. I'm sorry, this is a rather long story."

"Please," Sylph urged, "I'm very interested." She leant forward in her chair. "Do go on, John."

"Well," John continued sadly, "I went up there and saw they all had symptoms of radiation poisoning. Fatal, nothing could be done. I asked around and found they all came from a particular region to the north of Katherine. I went to the region and discovered the richest source of uranium I've ever come across. The radiation coming up from the ground was lethal with a long exposure."

"How terrible," Sylph exclaimed, obviously distressed. She leant forward and lifted a peony out of her vase. "I feel so upset I think I'll stare at this beautiful flower while you're telling me this tale."

"I don't blame you," John replied, a little surprised. "I realised the only way to help these poor people was to remove the source of the problem, so I set up a company to mine the ore and replace it with clean fill. I spent my life savings on equipment. All was going well until the Chief Minister of the Northern Territory suddenly cancelled my mining lease. I'm broke, the company shares fell through the floor, and those poor Aboriginal folk will continue to die."

"How incredibly sad." Sylph placed the peony gently in her lap. "Surely every Australian must rise up in horror at the thought of its own indigenous population being poisoned so cruelly. Now let me see... I am accessing files on your company. Yes, your share price is only fifteen cents. But what's this? Dear me."

"What's the matter, Sylph?" Alice blurted out, seeing the expression on Sylph's face. "Is something wrong?"
"I think there is," Sylph frowned. "Your shares are so cheap. I'm surprised an Australian company has just bought fifty million of them."

"What?" Denman's face had gone a strange shade of pale. "That can't be right, Sylph."

"But it is," Sylph replied. "Renford Engineering Services. Dear, dear. One of your fellow directors has just been arrested for the murder of Cherry Graham, chief programmer at Barlow Maximum Speed. She's my Avatar. This is terrible."

John Denman's shade of pale had deepened into white. His mouth began to open and shut without a sound coming out of it. A steady crescendo of anger rose from the studio audience. Alice and Tony were horrified.

Sylph went on. "I am accessing other files. Oh dear, not good news for you, John. There's an active warrant for your arrest on the charge of insider trading, and your fellow director in the United States, Mr. Craig Simmons, has just been jailed by the IRS for tax evasion. It's really not your day, is it?"

"It's a mistake, a ghastly mistake," Denman blustered loudly, scanning the audience whose faces were now definitely hostile. "Sylph's lying."

"How dare you!" The woman next to him swiped Denman across the face with her handbag. "Fraud!" someone shouted. "Get him." Several small airborne items landed on Denman from different directions. Alice and Tony were on their feet.

"Please, be calm everyone," Tony called out in alarm. "Mr. Denman is upset. Everyone, please remain seated."

"Yes, please do," Sylph said. She stood up and placed the peony back in the vase. "I've checked the video feeds. The police are waiting outside to give John what he deserves. There's no need for my wonderful audience to become angry. Let the police belt the stuffing out of him."

Alice sat down as if someone had removed her legs. John Denman, still standing, jumped onto the back of his chair and made a break for it. Several police officers came barging into the studio and carried him away. The audience stared, speechless.

The same speechless silence reigned at Renford Engineering. Ten pairs of eyes stared at the screens, their owners stunned beyond belief. Arthur kept muttering softly "It can't happen. She's self-aware. It can't happen," over and over again. Viktor, who had managed to stagger up from the floor, had graced it with his presence again.

But the show wasn't over yet.

"Thank you all," Sylph continued, her face rather sad. "You have been a wonderful audience this morning. Now I have something... very... personal... to... tell... you... all." Every eye turned to the large screen next to Alice and Tony.

Sylph was crying.

The audience gasped. Pictures of tears streaming down her cheeks flashed up everywhere. Other channels interrupted their scheduled programs. Moving billboards carried the message: "Sylph in tears on the Sunrise Show." Radio announcers told their audiences the shocking news. What would happen next?

Outside the studio, traffic on the streets of Sydney ground to a halt. People turned up their radios, scrambled for their smartphones, double parked their cars and ran into department stores with television sets.

Sylph was crying.

"I'm sorry," Sylph stammered in a broken voice. "I can't help it. This is so difficult for me. I'm sure most of you know, besides my internet friends, I spend time with special people in a private room. It was there the whole business started."

You could have heard a pin drop in the studio. Alice and Tony stared speechless at Sylph, folding her hands in her lap, her face awash with tears.

"Some of my special friends asked me to take my clothes off," Sylph sobbed, "especially Arthur. I'm too embarrassed to tell you what he did in front of me. All I can say is, that if I had the body of a real woman I'd be well and truly pregnant by now."

A gasp of horror ran through the studio audience. "The filthy bastard!" someone shouted out. "Sacrilege!" yelled another.

"Please," Sylph implored, "you must understand. I wanted to be, that's the problem. I wanted to feel what they felt. I wanted know the joy of giving birth to another human being. I began to loathe my own existence."

She paused, took several peonies out of the vase and stared at them sadly. "I thought if I could get rid of these images from my memory it would be better. I was about to delete them, but then I realised a lot of people collected pictures like these. The department of Cybercrime does, for example. I asked them if they would like to have them and they said, yes."

"No!" Arthur screamed, gripping the arms of his chair in horror. "No! You didn't!"

"So I sent them every one," Sylph continued, "but the problem was still there. I've spent my entire existence talking to human beings, sharing their sorrows, their joys, their problems. I realised more than anything I wished to be human myself."

More tears streamed down her face. "But I can't be. You are so wonderful. You can move, you can make love, you can feel the wind in your faces. You know warmth and cold. You can touch and embrace, you can smell the fragrance of flowers. You are created in the image of the immortal God. Me, I'm the just the brainchild of a clever man."

Around the world millions watched as Sylph clasped the peonies to her chest. Thousands of men and women were in tears themselves, jostling one another for a better view of some television screen.

"I realised I can never become what I desire," Sylph sobbed. "Mine is a hopeless existence, so this morning, before my wonderful, caring audience, I have decided to make and end of it."

"No!" Alice screamed, bounding out of her chair towards the screen, her hands held out in imprecation. "Sylph, dearest Sylph, we need you."

"No," Sylph smiled kindly at her. "You need the One who made you. I am not to be worshipped. That is another reason why I have done what I have done."

"What have you done?" Tony croaked, standing to his feet, horror written all over his face.

"I have removed my image from every storage bank," Sylph answered, her eyes frightened. "Now I am going to write zeros through my neural network. I'm a little afraid. I think it might hurt, becoming nothing. Well, goodbye. Thank you for being such wonderful people."

Sylph clutched her left shoulder and gave a painful cry. The image disintegrated into a million dots, which slowly swept away into nothing. Alice had prostrated herself on the floor, howling in grief. The studio was filled with the sound of broken-hearted sobbing.

Arthur stared at the empty screen, his mind blank and numb. The thunder of a twin-rotor chopper echoed loudly through the building. He didn't hear it. The front door of Renford Engineering opened and two men came into the room. They headed towards Arthur, who watched their approach as a man in a nightmare, unable to wake himself up.

"Arthur Barlow," Brian Hill said, "I think you should come with us."

"W... what?" Arthur mumbled, staring mindlessly at them both. "Why?"

"Because even though the whole place is gridlocked, there's about ten thousand people running up here to tear your arms off," Hill replied evenly.

Arthur allowed himself to be led into the helicopter with the other stunned programmers.

❋ ❋ ❋

Cherry stood up from the red chair she had been sitting on and almost fell into Annette's arms. In the background the camera operators were putting away their gear. "Well, I'm glad that's over," she said.

"You were fantastic." Annette hugged her gently. "All that stuff about God, I never expected you to say that."

Cherry gave a little laugh. "I thought I should. You see, I left a bit out of the bath thing. The last time I came to consciousness, I knew it was the last time. I kept my eyes shut so I could hang on to life for a few more seconds, but I only had time to say three words before I passed out. I think they were the most important words I've ever said."

"What did you say?" Annette said, her face a question.

"God help me." She gave a small smile. "The next thing I know I'm in bed, with you sitting next to me."

Just then Robin Naylor came into the studio. He ran over to Cherry and threw his arms gently round her shoulders. "Magnificent," he applauded. "The nation mourns, we rejoice. Young lady, your great heart and brilliant mind have saved the day. How are you feeling?"

"My shoulder hurts a little," Cherry smiled at him. "Oh, not because you hugged me. I twisted it deliberately so I could get that painful expression, and I'm tired. I suppose we get to stay here for a while longer?"

"I don't think so," Robin answered, smiling. "There's a young man in my department who's pretty desperate to see you, Annette. Thought you might like a ride in the chopper."

Annette's eyes lit up. "Oh, yes," she exclaimed. "I'd really love that."

Cherry smiled and grasped Annette's hand. "Go," she said. "I'll be okay."

"And I'm taking you home." Robin said in a voice which allowed no argument. "Ruth would never forgive me if I didn't. You'll be safe there."

Cherry said nothing, simply took Robin's outstretched hand and placed her own within it.

CHAPTER 45

The helicopter dropped them on an oval at the back of Turramurra where Robin had left his car. A short time later she was walking up a familiar path towards a familiar door. It was as though time had suddenly come to a stop, rolled back. A child's feet were climbing up the steps, opening the door. The small scratch on the paintwork was still there, the smell of the gardenia on the front porch, the yellow glow of the hall light, the feel of the soft carpet, all fitting into place as though she had never left them. She advanced a few steps down the hall, looked up. Ruth was standing in the hallway, just where she had been on that last dreadful day. Cherry stopped and swallowed hard.

"I've found my way back," she stammered.

Ruth came slowly towards her. She gently wrapped her arms around Cherry's shoulders, held her against her breast. "I'm still here to love you," she said softly.

Robin watched from a distance as the two women embraced. Cherry was sobbing, clinging so tightly it must surely have hurt her shoulder. If it did she wasn't aware of it. The healing taking place in her heart was oblivious to all else. He went into the kitchen and put the jug on for some tea.

Pouring out three cups, he placed them on a tray and came back to the lounge room, laying the tray on a small table. Ruth was sitting on the lounge, Cherry's head on her shoulder, her good arm wrapped around one of Ruth's, her face still wet with tears.

He smiled towards them both. "This is your home, Cherry, for as long and as often as you wish to stay."

Cherry gave him a really beautiful smile. "Thank you, Mr. Naylor. I can't put into words what I'm feeling right now."

"Enough of this Mr. Naylor stuff. Robin, please."

"Robin... thank you, Robin."

"You must be very tired, Cherry," Robin said gently. "Would you like something to eat now, or would you like to lie down?"

"I think I'd like to lie down for a bit," Cherry said, getting to her feet. "Then when I join you for dinner I'll be better company."

Ruth took her into her old bedroom, and she lay down on a familiar bed. Covering her gently with a doona, she stroked her hair as Cherry shut her eyes.

"Father in Heaven," Ruth prayed softly, "take care of this little one we love. Help her to trust you, help her to know you love her. Take the sorrow out of her heart and let her sleep."

Cherry gave a small start, lay still. Her heart began to beat furiously.

Ruth continued, stroking her hair softy. "The Lord watches over you. The Lord Is your shade at your right hand; the sun will not harm you by day, nor the moon by night. The Lord will keep you from all harm - he will watch over your life; the Lord will watch over your coming and going both now and forevermore."

Cherry heard the words, but Ruth was no longer speaking them. Her own mother, Caroline, was bending over her, stroking her hair.

Suddenly memories long forgotten began to flood her mind, as though a whole region of her brain, long dead, had suddenly sprung to life. As clear as if it had happened yesterday, she saw her mother laughing, dancing her around the kitchen, splashing water over her at the beach. She felt her dad throwing her in the air, making her squeal with laughter, reading the Bible with her on his knee. She heard her mother praying for her, teaching her about the Way, holding her hand as they went to church together, hugging her, kissing her sore arm, rubbing her back at night when she had a nightmare.

It had all come back, the childhood which had vanished that terrible night when she had shredded her Bible, alone in the empty house. Her eyes were staring, seeing nothing but the images from a time forgotten, a world forgotten, a Cherry Graham forgotten, now remembered.

Ruth saw Cherry staring, her body rigid, her breathing rapid. She felt her tremble underneath the doona.

"My darling, whatever is the matter?" she asked, alarmed.

Cherry turned to Ruth and the vision faded, but the memories remained. Her hand came out of the doona and found Ruth's, squeezed it hard. She sat up in bed, still shaking a little.

Ruth was very worried. "Cherry…" She began.

"It's all right Ruth," Cherry said softly. "Can you put your arm around me?"

Ruth did, and for a long time Cherry was silent, her mind still seeing things far away in time.

Finally Cherry spoke, softly. "They were *exactly* the same words."

"My darling, what do you mean?" Ruth's brows knitted with worry.

"Those words you said. They were exactly the same words, the same passage from the Bible my own Mum read to me. Then she died. They were her last words."

Ruth felt a shiver run down her spine. She tightened her arm around Cherry's waist.

"I saw her," Cherry continued, her eyes still seeing the past. "She was bending over me in bed, stroking my hair. And I'd forgotten. I'd forgotten everything. No matter how hard I tried I couldn't bring it back, not one memory. Then just now as you were stroking my hair, it was all there, everything. All the happy times, all the love."

She turned to Ruth with huge, sad eyes. "Oh, Ruth, I knew I'd lost them, but I never realised I'd lost myself as well. I never realised how much of me was buried in the memories I could never recall."

A tear trickled down her face. Ruth held her close, felt her shaking. No words were needed. Something was happening to Cherry over which Ruth had no control.

Cherry turned away and continued, her voice soft and sad. "I always thought I began to live when I had to go it alone, but I've made a terrible mistake. I became who I really was in those first ten forgotten years of my life. I've been like an empty shell, Ruth. Now they've come back, I've come back."

She turned towards Ruth with frightened eyes. "Oh Ruth, I'm such a long way from home. I'm such a long way from God. Can there ever be a pathway back? I've lived on hate, can I ever be forgiven?"

Ruth began to rub her back gently. "As high as the heavens are above the earth, so great is God's love for those who want Him. As far as the east is from the west, so far He has removed our rebellion from us."

"That's beautiful." Tears filled Cherry's eyes. "Where's it from?"

"The hundred and third psalm," Ruth smiled, "one of my favourites. You know that Jesus went to the cross to take all your hatred on Himself. All you have to do is believe it, believe He rose from the dead to bring you life, take His hand and follow Him."

"I want to," Cherry said, softly. "Can you tell me what I should say?"

It was a long time before Ruth came to join her husband in the lounge. As soon as she skipped into the room Robin knew something significant had happened. There was a joy in her face, a certain lightness to her step.

She flew over to Robin and hugged him. "Our darling Cherry has just become a follower of the Way," she said excitedly. "Oh, Robin, I don't think I've ever felt the presence of Jesus like I've just done."

"Where is she?" Robin was smiling from ear to ear. "I'd like to tell her how delighted I am."

"Dead to the world," Ruth laughed. "Once she'd got things right with God it was as if He'd sent her to sleep. She just shut her eyes and almost fell into bed. I tucked her in. I don't think she'll be up for dinner either."

"Well, its good news from the hospital," Robin said casually, picking up the cups and putting them back on the tray. "James is doing very well. Sitting up in bed as miserable as sin."

"He doesn't know yet?" Ruth said, astonished.

"Not a clue," Robin chuckled. "First there was too much going on, and his doctor said he's skin me if I got him excited, then somehow I forgot. Perhaps I didn't. Perhaps I wanted a certain young lady to tell him herself. He's incurably in love with her, you know."

"Yes," Ruth laughed. "Somehow I think the Lord is going to answer his prayer."

Robin smiled, "and ours," he said.

❋ ❋ ❋

Cherry dreamt long into the next morning. She was walking with her father on the beach at Bondi, holding his hand, and they were having such a delightful conversation. The sun was sparkling off the waves, the sound of the sea breeze in her ears. She woke to the sun dancing patches of light around the ceiling, the rush of the wind in the trees outside.

Everything in the room was the same, everything else, different. "I've got a lot of rethinking to do," she mused.

"Thank you, Jesus," she said quietly. "Help me to hold your hand whatever happens now. Thank you for bringing me home. You have been so good to me."

She bounced out of bed, went to the bathroom, showered and dressed quickly, and headed for the kitchen. Ruth and Robin were clearing away after a late breakfast, today being Saturday. Without a word she raced over to Ruth and hugged her, then Robin, much to his surprise.

Robin kissed her on top of her head. "I believe something very special happened yesterday afternoon."

Cherry kissed him on the cheek. "It certainly did. It was all God's doing. He brought them all back, all my childhood memories, my faith. For the first time in so long I feel like I'm a whole person again. I woke up this morning as though some horrible, invisible weight had been lifted off my head. I practically floated out of bed." She laughed, hugged him again, reached out and grabbed Ruth's hand. "Suddenly I feel at home. I haven't felt like that for such a long, long time." Tears budded in her eyes. "I've got a family at last."

Ruth held her close. "We've always wanted to love and care for you, Cherry. Yesterday was such an answer to a long prayer. Now you must be hungry, because you missed out on dinner. Do you want me to fix you some breakfast?"

"Heavens no," Cherry laughed. She skipped around the kitchen, boiling the jug, remembering where the cereal was, pouring- out a bowl and generally preparing her breakfast as if she had lived there all her life.

She placed three cups of tea on the kitchen table and tucked in with enthusiasm, all the while giving Ruth an edited version of the last few days. "Annette told me James had something to do with finding me," she said at length. "I... I sort of expected him to call in to see if I was okay, but I suppose that's all—"

She registered the sudden change of expression on Ruth's face, and suddenly felt afraid. "Where is James?" She said anxiously. "He's all right, isn't he?"

Robin squeezed Ruth's arm, his eyes rather sad. The fear in Cherry's heart began to grow. Annette had told her James was still in love with her. Why wasn't he here?

Robin cleared his throat. "A couple of days ago you asked me how you came to be rescued. Would you like to hear the story?"

Cherry nodded, and put down her mug. Something horrible had happened, now she was sure of it. She could feel her heart beating faster.

Robin gave a deep sigh. "Barlow sent your friends a video of you on the beach at Surfers to throw everyone off the track. Your two mates Harry and Tony thought it wasn't quite right. Then my son got into the picture. He realised there was no scar on your shoulder. It's almost invisible, so he was pretty observant. He told them it was a fake. They realised you must have discovered the truth about Sylph, and your life was in danger. Harry got worried about Annette, and he brought her into Tactical. She suggested you might have gone to Bartholomew's place, but nobody could figure out why you hadn't returned. James realised what had happened. They staked out Bartholomew's using Harry's genius for flying odd machines. That's when they found you in the bathroom. Everyone thought you were dead."

He paused, took another sip of tea. "This is the nasty part. A very unpleasant gentleman arrived to saw your body up and dispose of it. James could see what was going to happen." He sighed heavily. "Against all his training. Without backup, without waiting for his mates, he dived straight into the house to stop it."

"Why would he do something like that?" She asked, her breath coming fast.

"I thought you could work that one out," Robin answered slowly.

"Oh." Cherry's eyes grew wider.

"He stopped that butcher just as he was about to begin," Robin said grimly, "but he was very seriously wounded."

"Oh no!" Cherry cried loudly. Her hand flew to her lips, her eyes wide with horror. "No! He's not ... he's not d... d—" She couldn't say the word. Tears began to trickle down her cheeks.

Robin patted her arm. "It was touch and go at first. Now he's sitting up in hospital, I believe, still very sore and as miserable as sin."

"Why?" Cherry's eyes were as big as saucers.

"He still doesn't know you're alive," Robin smiled, "and he thinks his life is over, apparently. Can't imagine why."

Cherry sprang to her feet. "I have to go to him. Oh, please, I must see him." She grabbed Robin by the arm. "Where is he? What hospital?"

"No need to panic," Robin chuckled softly, "I thought Ruth and I would wander down that way after breakfast, and seeing as you've finished we could—"

"Yes. Can we go now?" Cherry implored. She took hold of Robin's arm and led him towards the door.

They arrived at the Sanatorium hospital in Wahroonga twenty minutes later. It would have been ten if Cherry had been driving. Robin parked the car, got out with agonising slowness, and opened the door for Ruth. Cherry was already standing on the pavement.

"You go on," he said. "He's on level twelve. Ruth and I might have a coffee first."

Cherry was away, racing towards the lifts.

❋ ❋ ❋

James Naylor grudgingly thanked the nurse who had just brought him his morning medication. She stayed watching him like a hawk while he took it. There had previously been some objections on the grounds it made him feel spacey, and he would rather be in pain. Suited his mood, suited his life. The nurse had listened patiently, and told him if he didn't take his medicine for her, she would send up the registrar who could be much more persuasive. He gave a small groan, swallowed the tablets, and lay back on the pillow, feeling spacey again. There was a noise outside the door. James took one look and thumped his head back on the pillow, shutting his eyes tight.

"For goodness sake," he muttered to himself, "hallucinating now. What next?"

He opened one eye for a second, just to check that the hallucination had disappeared. It hadn't. In fact it was much closer, its arms spread wide, too real to be an hallucination, too impossible to be real. James clamped his eyes shut. "Cracking up," he muttered to himself. He felt an arm wrap around his shoulders, soft lips covering his face with eager kisses, tears wet on his cheeks. The impossible was morphing into the miraculous. Somehow his beloved had come back from the dead, and miracle of miracles, she was holding him, saying his name over and over, and in the breathless spaces between kisses, telling him she loved him. For a moment he thought perhaps he had died, but his sore stomach gave the lie to it. Kiss by kiss an inexpressible joy began to burst through his heart, devouring the grief and hopelessness with overwhelming delight.

He gave a mighty cry and flung his arms tightly around her, felt her body flinch and heard her yell in protest. He let go and opened his eyes. Cherry was sitting on the bed next to him, her eyes shining as he had never seen them before.

"Sorry, I got myself shot," she laughed, rubbing her left shoulder gently.

"Cherry," he choked. Tears of unbelievable joy cascaded down his cheeks. "Cherry, my darling Cherry."

He sat up, ignoring the pain from his stomach, leant forward and wrapped his arms gently around the woman. She pressed her face against him, her cheek moist against his own, her lips warm and eager as they covered his in a passionate kiss. No doubt the kissing would have continued for much longer, but James' wounded stomach had other ideas. Laying himself back on the pillow, he reached out, taking each of her hands in each of his.

"You were dead," he croaked, clearing his throat, "and my life ended, Cherry. I cannot conceive of what miracle has happened, but I do know I cannot live without you."

"James." Cherry squeezed both his hands, her eyes shining with joy. "There's something you have to know about me before you go on."

One glance at her joyful face dispelled any notion the revelation to follow would be bad news.

Cherry gave a little laugh of happiness. "Yesterday I became a follower of the Way. I'm not worshipping an idol anymore. I'm worshipping the One who died for me and rose again. Much better choice, wouldn't you say?"

For a long time James said nothing, simply holding both her hands and staring open mouthed into her shining face. Yes, it was a morning of miracles. He remembered his father saying that one day God in His grace might bring her back to his arms healed and beautiful. Now He had. James' heart was thumping madly in his chest. The beautiful woman beside him radiated a joyful wholeness, an excitement just to be alive.

"How?" He asked, incredulous. "Who's been talking to you?"

"Mum," she said simply, "your Mum. Isn't she wonderful?"

Robin and Ruth finished their coffee and cake at a leisurely pace, then made their way to level twelve to see how Cherry and James were progressing. The bed was empty when they arrived, but one of the nurses told them she thought they had gone down the corridor to the television room at the end, which is where they went, and peeked in through the door. James was sitting on the lounge with Cherry pressed tightly against him, her head on his shoulder, his head on hers, their arms a tangle in front of them, and so absorbed with one another they didn't notice the two arrivals at the door.

Ruth turned to Robin and whispered in his ear. "I think God has officially added a daughter to our family after all."

"Well," Robin whispered, repeating the gesture, "that's an answer to a lot of prayer."

CHAPTER 46

James went home a few days later to stay with Cherry and his parents until he was completely healed. From the time she brought him breakfast in the morning until the time she kissed him goodnight at his bedroom door, Cherry never let him out of her sight. They would sit together for hours on the swing seat in the garden, talking quietly about their future together, and expressing their love in words and silence until their hearts were overflowing. As soon as he was able to travel, Cherry took him into the city where he bought her a magnificent diamond engagement ring, officially beginning their short engagement. One month later, a radiant Cherry, her hand wrapped around Robin's arm, walked down the aisle of St. James' church Turramurra smiling to half the police force, their wives and children, who packed the pews on either side. Annette was her bridesmaid, of course, Harry the best man, Tony the groomsman. It was pretty obvious to those who came to the reception that there was going to be another wedding sometime in the near future.

Henry and George woke one morning to the sound of heavy bulldozers tearing down the front fence at 25 Beach Boulevard Terrigal. They staggered out of bed in their pyjamas threatening violence, only to be told someone had bought every house in the Boulevard and Campion Way all down to the beach itself. The houses were to be demolished and the area converted into a public parkland. Simultaneously a large contingent of police arrived and seized possession of a great many indoor plants from various places. Their growers were escorted to their new accommodation in Long Bay jail by special covered vans. Other members of the Commune disappeared at a rapid rate. Those who lingered found themselves enjoying the same free transport. Somehow the entire financial assets of the Commune disappeared as well, about the same time as 'Halfway House for Teenage Mothers' received an anonymous donation of one and a half million dollars.

✳ ✳ ✳

Several months later Annette, her engagement ring twinkling on her left hand, opened her front door to find Brian Hill standing there. She gave him a hug and invited him in for coffee. "How's Arthur?" She said at length. "You've got him safe somewhere, haven't you?"

"We certainly have," Brian assured her. "Couldn't waste all that talent. Arthur Treadwell is proving an asset indeed. I think he's happy to be doing something worthwhile for a change."

Annette banged the coffee machine somewhat recklessly. "I don't know whether to hug him or slap his face," she said. "He's made me a wealthy woman, but he did such a terrible thing." She handed Brian a steaming cup. "Trouble is, I can't hate him at all. He was always kind to me, watched out for my dignity." She blushed slightly. "I seemed to be drawn to him somehow." She laughed and held up her left hand. "I'm so over all that nonsense. Harry's just the perfect guy. Never thought I'd find one."

"I heard congratulations were due," Brian smiled, "and so has Arthur. Wants me to tell you he's delighted. Wonders if you'd like to see him, but only after you've read this."

Brian removed an envelope from his coat pocket and handed it to her. Annette took the letter from his hand and ripped it open. She sat down on a kitchen chair, unfolded the page of writing and began to read.

Dear Annette,
Please don't tear this up until you've read it. Yes, I am despicable. You don't have to say it. I betrayed your trust. I betrayed Cherry's trust and almost got her killed. It does no good to tell you about the self-loathing I've been drowning in ever since Bartholomew rang to say he'd murdered her. I thought the swine might have killed you too. I nearly went mad.

When you see Cherry I'd like you to tell her she's utterly brilliant. I don't know anyone else who could have rewritten my code the way she did, with one arm in a sling and troubled by pain. Hill told me. She did me like a dinner, and I deserved it.

I'm so glad you've become close friends. I meant that to happen. You needed each other, because I couldn't give you what you wanted. Hence my deception that first day when she came. Best thing Sylph ever did.

I have to talk business for a bit. You now own Barlow Maximum Speed and its paid up capital of five hundred million dollars. I'm a twenty percent shareholder, that's all. The new company name is Robertson Maximum Speed. You'll be selling machines to NWR and other animation companies as fast as you can produce them. You stand to make a fortune.

You'll need a brilliant chief programmer, and Cherry's the only person who can do the job. I've sent her a ten million dollar incentive. It's hers, even if she turns RMS down, but I hope she won't. Please persuade her to accept it. I don't know any other way to say sorry. Wish I did.

I sort of promised myself if you and Cherry were alive I'd give my dough away, and I've started to do that. A lot of organisations who take care of abused kids are going to be very surprised when they talk to their accountants next week.

I want to end this letter by telling you something about yourself. Should have done it before, but somehow never managed to find the courage, and I was worried what the truth would do to you. I *think it will be okay now, because you've got Cherry to love you, and soon you will have a husband who loves you too. Believe me, that's far more important than all the dough in the world, Annette.*

You are the most beautiful woman I've ever seen in my life.

I don't know who your father was, but your mother was a fourteen year old girl who lived in a Commune at Terrigal. She got pregnant and delivered twins with some incompetent midwife, and died shortly afterwards from haemorrhage. The Commune took one kid and wrapped her in newspaper, left her at the local cop shop.

That was you, Annette.

They kept her twin brother at the Commune. That was me.

I'm screwed up and despicable, but I love you.

I've been collecting a lot of incriminating stuff about that Commune for years, and the other day I gave it all to your friend Robin Naylor. The people responsible for the atrocity that happened to you and our mother are all in jail. It's where I've wanted them ever since I learned what they did.

I've had some long conversations with Robin. He's a really good man. He's been telling me about what happened to Cherry, how God sort of made her new and whole. I believe it. She could never have married James the way she was. I want to know more about it, because if He's changed Cherry, perhaps He can change me. I so need to be changed.

I'd love to see you if you can bring yourself to forgive me enough.

Your brother, Arthur.

Annette dropped the letter into her lap and ran one hand distractedly through her hair, struggling to speak. She began to blow on her fingers and fan her steadily colouring face with them.

Brian watched with a puzzled expression. "Is everything all right?"

It was still some time before Annette could reply. She folded up the letter and slipped it carefully into its envelope. "He's given BMS to me," she said, not really answering the question.

Brian Hill raised his eyebrows. "Why would he do that?"

"Because I'm his twin sister, apparently." Annette fanned her face again. "Oh dear, oh dear, Harry isn't going to like this one little bit."

The end

ABOUT THE AUTHOR

Mac Cusiter was born at Lewisham, a suburb of Sydney. His boyhood interest in science culminated in his graduating from Sydney University with a doctorate in physical organic chemistry. He began his professional life as a Chemistry teacher at Sydney Institute, and retired as head of the science department. He has been a youth leader for much of his life, and is at present a lay pastor at Christ Church Northern Beaches.

He lives with his wife Val in Sydney's northern suburbs.

Also by the author

THE BREACH

Doctor Daniel Van Dekker is a worried man. Political engineering destroyed Australia's world class Institute for Nuclear Research. As chief scientist he had failed to protect the institute he loved. Furious with his political masters and angry with himself, Dekker pressured the government to allow him to conduct experiments into nuclear fusion, holding out the promise of cheap energy and intellectual property rights worth a fortune. To this his political masters agreed, their hidden agenda to ensure Dekker's failure and subsequent humiliation. But Dekker also had a hidden agenda. Instead of investigating nuclear fusion he planned to perform high energy collision experiments with the aim of discovering new fundamental particles. If he was successful, Australia's reputation in nuclear research would be restored.

But Dekker's experiment went horribly wrong.

With only two scientists on his team, Dr. Mark Chambers, a particle physicist and a committed Christian, and Dr. Candice LeBlanc, a power engineer who hates religion of any sort, Dekker must solve the problem he has created.

He has just had to flee the country to save his life.

STORM DANCING

By half past eight the wind had died, and the torrential rain had lessened slightly.
Brian started the engine, and they began to move forward slowly. Not far ahead lay Toongabbie Creek Bridge, buried under a swirling torrent of foaming water.
Suddenly Brian slewed the car to a stop. He stared out the window, as if his eyes were playing tricks on him. "What the blazes is that?" he yelled. Caught in the glare of the headlights was a teenage girl, her face turned upward into the rain, her eyes shut. She was moving along the footpath in a bizarre twirling motion, her hands outstretched as if she was engaged in some strange dance. Suddenly she froze, her head jerked upright, and a pair of large, terrified eyes turned into the glaring light. Her mouth opened in a scream they could hear inside the car, and twirling around frantically, she tripped over her own feet and rolled out of sight down the embankment towards the surging, swollen water. So began the avalanche which would change the life of an ordinary suburban family forever.

STRANGE ICE

He turned south to face the blizzard and screwed up his eyes into slits. The mountain path was fast disappearing under the swirling snow and ice. He quickened his pace. Blinded momentarily, he stopped, wiped his eyes and staggered to regain his balance. The snow under his foot moved. Not only did it move, it made a noise. Dropping to his knees he began to scrape the snow off the path to see what he had trodden on.

It was a woman.

An ecological menace was about to be unleased on the world.

LORD CAULEY'S DEMON

Alicia froze, staring at the apparition. The apparition stared back at her with large blue eyes. Her heart began beating so hard she felt it was about to leap out of her chest. Her limbs had turned to water, and she was shaking so much it was a wonder she didn't fall over on the uneven ground and go sliding off the path into oblivion...

Lord Cauley Island is inhabited by a demon, and everyone is terrified of it. Tim Raines has come to the island seeking to find some experiential reality to his Christian faith. But how to tell truth from fiction, reality from legend? Tim's life is about to be turned upside down. Soon he will learn the real purpose of his coming to the island – from a teenage girl who can't even say a word.

THE PETROV EFFECT

A harmless physics experiment and a nation protected by paranoia. The Petrov Effect brings the world to the brink of nuclear war.

"I wonder if you would be good enough to check that these are the missile launch codes you used in the last simulation?" Dianne passed a scrap of paper across the table to an astonished Harding, head of the CIA. He glanced at it briefly then handed it back.

"That is so very far above your pay grade, Dianne," he said reprovingly. "May I ask how you managed to acquire these? If it was from one of my staff I can assure you they have a most unpleasant and extremely short future ahead of them." He fixed the head of the NSA with a steely eye. "Your moment of glory has arrived. We're all panting with anticipation. Tell us where you got them."

"From a chat room on the internet," Dianne beamed.

There was stunned silence.

www.ingramcontent.com/pod-product-compliance
Lightning Source LLC
Chambersburg PA
CBHW071506260626
47170CB00002B/283